SEEKING
SANCTUARY

SEEKING SANCTUARY

FRANCES FYFIELD

ALFRED A. KNOPF CANADA

PUBLISHED BY ALFRED A. KNOPF CANADA

National Library of Canada Cataloguing in Publication

Fyfield, Frances
Seeking sanctuary / Frances Fyfield.

ISBN 0-676-97614-X

I. Title.

PR6056.Y47S43 2003   823'.914   C2003-901755-9

First Edition

www.randomhouse.ca

Typeset in Plantin Light by M Rules
Printed and bound in Canada

2   4   6   8   9   7   5   3   1

For Donna Leon

PROLOGUE

(Documents in the possession of K. McQ., E. Smith and one other, viz, one draft will and one final version, for dispersal as and when necessary.)

Document 1

DRAFT WILL

Dear Smith, I'm returning the draft will, with explanatory notes. I wish to <u>die</u> very soon, so get on with it, I can't stand it any more. If I die and someone comes for me, I'd rather it was Satan than God.

THIS IS THE LAST WILL AND TESTAMENT of me, Theodore Calvert. *(With <u>bugger</u> all to show for myself except a house, a friend and an obscene amount of money. Everything else is lost.)*

    1. I hereby revoke all other wills and testamentary dispositions made by me, prior to the date of this, my last will. *(Fifteen, at the last count.)*

    2. I appoint E. Smith, solicitor, to be the executor and trustee of this my will, with power to appoint an additional executor and trustees if he thinks fit.

    3. I wish to be cremated. *(I mean, <u>burned</u> to a crisp after death, without prayers of any kind, and my ashes thrown in the face of the nearest priest to show my contempt.)*

    4. The said E. Smith, or any executor or trustee whosoever he shall appoint, engaged in a legal capacity, shall be paid all usual professional charges for work or business done in proving my will or in the execution of or in connection with the trust thereof, including work or business of a professional nature which a trustee could do personally. *(Blah, blah, <u>blah</u>.)*

5. I leave the following specific bequests:

To Kay McQuaid, the sum of £20,000 per annum, as long as she is resident in my house. *(Is that enough? She never did me a bad turn, did she? Or did she? Only person I trust, anyway.)*

6. SUBJECT TO AND AFTER PAYMENT of my just debts, funeral and testamentary expenses, I GIVE, DEVISE AND BEQUEATH all my real and personal estate whatsoever and wheresoever not otherwise disposed of by this my will, inclusive of anything I might stand to inherit, unto my trustees upon trust to sell, call in and convert the same into money, with power to postpone the sale, calling and conversion thereof as long as they shall in their absolute discretion think fit. *(Blah, blah, blah.)* My trustees shall hold the net proceeds of sale, calling and conversion upon trust for a period of two years after my death, paying any existing standing orders specified in the addendum to this my will, in the meantime. *(Blah.)*

7. I GIVE, DEVISE AND BEQUEATH the proceeds of the said trust fund to my two daughters, to be shared between them equally ON CONDITION THAT for the aforesaid period of two years, they remain free of SIN. *(No, I do not mean they should obey the ten commandments and all that crap of the catechism of their mother's ghastly church. I mean real SIN. I want them to blaspheme, dance on graves, do sloth, gluttony and wildness, but you said I couldn't make it a condition. Conditions have to be negative. I wish them to be rude and rebellious and even disgusting. I don't believe in SIN, but I want them to know what the avoidance of it involves. I wish them ANYTHING but their mother's destructive piety.)*

For the purposes of this my will, SIN is hereby defined as INCEST, CRUELTY and TREACHERY. The commission of the sin will be self-evident. *(Your advice to limit it. This is*

4

not a random selection. I can't think of anything worse than the categories I've described, except murder, and all these involve murder of the soul. These are the sins of which I was accused, always in the name of God, by my wife, and the only ones I have never committed. (Gettit?)

8. IN THE EVENT of either of my daughters being discovered to have been in the commission of any of the aforesaid variations of SIN, the bequest to them fails and the residue of my estate shall pass to Jack McQuaid, absolutely. (Why? You idiot, why? Because it might, just might, redeem him, and if not, it may as well go to the devil as anywhere else.)

Signed by the said THEODORE CALVERT as his last will in the presence of us both present at the same time who in his presence and in the presence of each other have hereunto subscribed our names as witnesses.

(Don't ask why, Smith. I am going away into that dark night and shall be gone for a long time. Grief kills me. Just do as I ask, for Godsakes. I don't mean for GOD'S SAKE. NOTHING is for God's sake. I HATE GOD, I hate God ... I hate that Christ and all his shoddy saints. I hate the level to which my daughters are reduced. I hate the God of my wife, a perverted, obsessive Christian who raised my children steeped in holiness, cocooned and stole them from me, taught them to hate me, and I hate the Church, which moulded her madness and fear of the devil. And taught me, thereby, what hell is like. It is losing the recognition of your own flesh and blood and having them revile you. It is the knowledge of hatred and impotence and heartbreak, being useless and watching your children wasting their lives. It is being eaten alive with love and regret. Hell is HERE.

Send this back quickly. I want to die.

5

Document 2

FINAL VERSION

𝕿𝖍𝖎𝖘 𝖎𝖘 𝖙𝖍𝖊 𝕷𝖆𝖘𝖙 𝖂𝖎𝖑𝖑 𝖆𝖓𝖉 𝕿𝖊𝖘𝖙𝖆𝖒𝖊𝖓𝖙 of me, Theodore Calvert.

1. I hereby revoke all other wills and testamentary dispositions made by me.

2. I hereby appoint E. Smith, solicitor, to be the executor and trustee of this my will, with power to appoint an additional executor and trustee if he thinks fit.

3. I wish to be cremated.

4. The said E. Smith, or any executor or trustee whosoever he shall appoint, engaged in a legal capacity, shall be paid all usual professional charges for work or business done in proving my will or in the execution of or in connection with the trust thereof, including work or business of a professional nature which a trustee could do personally.

5. I leave the following specific bequest: To Kay McQuaid, the sum of £20,000 and the residency of my house for two years.

6. SUBJECT TO AND AFTER PAYMENT of my just debts, funeral and testamentary expenses, I GIVE, DEVISE AND BEQUEATH all my real and personal estate whatsoever and wheresoever not otherwise disposed of by this my will, inclusive of anything I might stand to inherit, unto my trustees upon trust to sell, call in and convert the same into money, with power to postpone the sale, calling in and conversion thereof as long as they shall in their absolute discretion think fit. My trustees shall hold the net proceeds of sale, calling in and conversion upon trust for a period of two years after my death, paying any existing standing orders during the meantime.

7. I GIVE, DEVISE AND BEQUEATH the proceeds of the

said trust fund to my two daughters to be shared between them, equally, ON CONDITION THAT for the aforesaid period of two years, they shall both remain free of SIN. For the purpose of this my will, SIN is hereby defined as INCEST, CRUELTY AND TREACHERY. The commission of the sin will be self-evident.

8. IN THE EVENT of either of my daughters being discovered to have been in the commission of any of the aforesaid variations of SIN, the bequest to them shall fail and the residue of my estate shall pass to Jack McQuaid, on sufficient proof of his identity, absolutely.

Signed by the said THEODORE CALVERT as his last will, in the presence of us both present at the same time, who in his presence and in the presence of each other have hereunto subscribed our names as witnesses.

WITNESSES:

CHAPTER ONE

Honour the Lord your God

The convent chapel was as warm as a hospital ward. The climate inside was humid with a series of scents, wilting flowers, disinfectant, damp overcoats, starch from the bright, white chasuble of the Bishop, the odour of sanctity from his hat and the overpowering, choking smell of incense. The receiving of the Eucharist followed a sermon lacking either real conviction or sincerity. Anna Calvert watched the row of nuns waiting to receive the Sacrament before resuming their places on the opposite side of the aisle from where she sat, and blew her nose.

The oldest of the Sisters had died; granted she had died at an age and condition that made death appropriate, a release from discomfort bravely borne and the final stage on a long, narrow pathway to heaven, but it still marked the final breath of a good heart. They were celebrating the death of a woman whose achievements and profound influence the Bishop chose not to mention, and Anna wondered why. It was an occasion for praise, but he seemed to have difficulty in remembering names and elected instead to deliver a homily on the state of the Catholic Church, peppered with dire messages along the lines of how we must all, even the deceased, atone for our sins.

Anna blew her nose again and eased the damp collar of her blouse from the back of her neck to relieve her own sense of puzzlement. Why was it so airless? The window behind the altar curved gracefully towards the ceiling in as perfect a peak as the Bishop's hat, shaped to reach out to heaven, and the trees, visible through the glass, making it seem as if they were in a forest of birches. She looked sideways towards her younger sister, Therese, who sat on the other side of the aisle next to the other nuns, looking ridiculously young in their elderly company. Therese, who was also looking towards her with equal anxiety, twiddled her fingers in a minute, secret signal of reassurance and rolled her eyes. Anna ducked her head to hide a smile of relief. Maybe there were some advantages in such a dry, impersonal service that inhibited tears.

What did the Bishop mean by *sins*? Sister Jude had been able to define malice, because she was fond of definitions, and she may have made mistakes, but *sin* was something quite unknown to her, unless humour and irreverence counted, which, judging from the style and content of this miserable, artificial ritual, they did. Good taste and emotion were also notable for their absence. Sister Jude was the aunt of Anna's late mother, but also a tutor, friend and inspiration, mentor and sufficiently grand, substitute grand-mother. She had been a teacher in the real world: she had been a piece of wonder. She had provided stability and wisdom to this small community of Sisters. And, although she might have quar-relled frequently with her great-niece, the only inconsiderate thing she had done was to die when she was still needed, like everyone else had done. Overwhelmed by loss, Anna reminded herself that the act of dying had not been wilful, to use one of Jude's words. It had merely been a question of everything else but the mind wear-ing out.

The old Sisters stood in a row, heads bowed, hands clasped in the attitude of servants, looking like a set of tearless statues. It was a drab occasion, Anna thought with a spurt of despair; dry and drab. No weeping or wailing, the only gnashing of teeth her own. Formulaic, taped music, dull prayers intoned dully, no sense of occasion or grief. Service number 52, as bland and impersonal as breakfast cereal, peculiarly loveless and as such, an aid to self-control.

The heat exaggerated the scent of the lilies she had provided, left overnight in the chapel along with the body in the coffin and now almost dead, while tiny Sister Jude, her most consistent if critical friend, despite a difference of fifty years, began to putrefy. There had been no substance in those bones and no sin, either. The drone of prayer failed to do justice either to the dead or to the unspoilable dimensions of the chapel. For the sake of the living, Anna swallowed the thistle of tears.

They crowded out from the soft light inside and spilled, politely, through the building and out into the road at the front, single file through the narrow door. Therese joined her. She tucked a stray strand of Anna's hair behind her ear and Anna did the same for her, before they linked elbows tightly as they walked to the funeral cars. The rough material of Therese's long-sleeved tunic felt warm against Anna's skin. She squeezed her arm gratefully and felt the pressure returned. The cemetery was miles away. They sat in one of three sumptuous vehicles, which looked suitable for the carriage of a visiting pope, and watched the rain form into glistening drops against the windows. Admiring glances were cast at the two blonde girls, so indisputably sisters, sitting calmly with their fingers interlaced, intensely proud of one another. They united to put at ease the two ex-pupils and a relative of the deceased from the unknown side of the family they had never met, all conscientious Catholics complimenting the service and applauding the presence of the Bishop.

The route out to the suburbs and beyond was long and ugly, a last tedious journey in search of the appropriate cemetery for the exclusive use of those of the faith.

'She might have preferred a field,' Anna murmured to Therese.

'She'd have loved this upholstery,' Therese said, both of them suppressing a sudden desire to giggle, which seemed to go with the occasion. The funeral cortège passed the wire fencing surrounding an industrial complex and then the cars wound uphill to the cemetery with its view of the wire fences beneath and the grey sky beyond. Anna did not want her to be buried here. It seemed the final indignity to be interred among everlasting flowers on graves to the mumble of prayers by rote in that condescending idiom, which had begun to enrage her.

The words at the graveside were as neutral as those indoors and there was a rule that governed funerals, dictating that it should always rain and that all persons present should behave with a shifty stiffness as if under suspicion themselves. They gathered round the hole in the ground as the coffin was lowered and water sprinkled upon it from a plastic bottle by the deputy substituted for the Bishop, who had already gone on to another appointment. He intoned the prayers in the manner of one practising fast elocution by reading the telephone directory, and Anna had the urge to fling her piece of earth over the crowd instead of letting it drop on the casket where the other pieces of earth landed with small, thumping sounds as if they were pelting the dead. Shoulder to shoulder with Therese, anger and indignation began to fill her head like a mushroom cloud, until she thought she would explode with it. Therese leant against her.

Then the contemporaries of Sister Jude, four of the very oldest Sisters, Matilda, Agnes, Joseph and Margaret, with gowns and veils flapping in the wet breeze, suddenly stepped forward in unison. With one accord, led by Margaret, they began to sing.

Salve, Regina, mater misericordia,
Vita, dulcedo, et spes nostra salve,
Ad te clamamus, exules filii hevae.

12

Hail, Holy Queen, mother of mercy, hail our life, our sweetness and our hope . . . Thin, reedy, elderly voices of peculiar, wistful beauty. They huddled together, feet planted uncertainly in the muddy earth excavated from the grave, the plainchant wavering, the notes as clear as the chiming of bells, the sound of it spontaneous and pure. Lumpen women, singing to the greater glory of God, with lungs and hearts and soul. *O clemens, O pia, O dulcis Virgo Maria* . . .

For a moment, Anna knew them.

They both wept, she and Therese, in each other's arms, with their feet rooted into damp grass, weeping as if it would never end. Weeping in loss and bewilderment, while Anna also wept with sheer frustration, because from beyond her grave, Sister Jude had done it again. Set the Hound of Heaven upon her *again*: she could hear the beast baying and Jude's light recitation of her favourite poem, echoing behind the singing. *I fled Him, down the nights and down the days; I fled Him down the arches of the years; I hid from Him* . . . The sound died on the air. The noise of distant traffic intruded, subduing the slighter sounds of flourished handkerchiefs, shuffling feet and grief.

'You remember that poem she liked so much?' Anna mumbled to Therese. 'Say you do.'

'Course I do,' Therese said, into her ear. 'Yes, I do.'

From those strong feet that followed, followed after . . .
They beat – and a Voice beat
More instant than the feet –
'All things betrayest thee, who betrayest Me.'

Therese's hand on her shoulder moved to stroke the back of her neck, reluctant to let her go.

'Just keep saying it, Anna. Say it again and again. It's a good one. Will you be all right?'

13

'Yes. We have to be, don't we?'

'We should be used to it by now. Us dear little orphans. Poor little us.'

Anna smiled slightly at that, dashed at the tears on her face with a fist, leaving a red mark on her cheek. The mocking of any suggestion of self-pity was a running joke between them.

'Hey, sis, less of the *little*. I suppose you're going back with the old crows?'

'I must. Sister Joseph is beside herself . . . you understand?'

'Course I do. Don't worry.'

'You won't come in for lunch?'

'You know I won't. Take care, love.'

Anna did understand. Therese was her real sister, but the Sisters were her family now, as they had been for over a year, and all the same the priorities hurt like a blister. So much that she found she was murmuring that wretched poem with imperfect memory as the car to which she was directed filled and the occupants shrank away from her. A pretty *little* girl who muttered words to herself and manufactured an inane grin.

'Sorry,' she gabbled with manic cheerfulness. 'I was trying to remember her favourite poem. About God chasing a soul all over the world . . . She made me learn it off by heart. Do you know it? And isn't the Bishop a SILLY OLD FART?'

A parishioner patted her hand, in pretended understanding. After all, the dear deceased had never distinguished in life between the mad and the sane, and it was better to follow that good example than be shocked. The sun broke through and the group of four eased themselves into platitudes as they drove back, with Anna hunched in the corner, disturbingly silent. She slipped out of the car without farewells as it came to a halt beside the narrow door, ran to the end of the road and disappeared, knowing with a flush of humiliation how they would see her now. A strange, spoiled child, they said. How old was she? Twenty-two, apparently, looking fifteen. Such a small girl. A little touched in the head, maybe.

She went left and left again, on to the main road. Left again, past the walls of the convent, which looked like any other walls, up the road on the left and into the block of flats where she lived. The more direct route into the convent would have been through the back door into their garden, which she passed on the way, but nobody ever used that. The door was embedded into the wall and almost obscured with ivy. Once inside her apartment block in the next-door building, she ran up the five flights to her own, took off her tidy clothes, put on T-shirt and shorts and went up to the roof.

The route to the roof was via a retractable stepladder from her attic living room, out through a dormer window not intended as an exit, on to a flat surface flanked by a parapet that went two thirds of the way round. Anna had told Sister Jude that this was the true kingdom of heaven. A small walkway surrounding a raised roof, housing a ventilation shaft and other furniture such as an open tank covered with wire. Heaven, if anywhere, was above the height of the trees, with sufficient space to lie in the lead-lined gunwales and catch the sun.

From the back, with her elbows propped on the parapet, she could see the convent garden. Straight into it, or as straight as it could be in the late reaches of summer, before the foliage began to go. It was ironic that in wintertime, when the human movement in this garden was minimal, she had the greatest chance to spy, whereas in summer, when there was far more to watch, she was forced to see it in tantalising glimpses down through the trees. There were the smaller trees at this end, wavering things, beastly sycamores, the weed of trees, but loved by birds. The ivy covered the inside walls; there were numerous shrubs and over-flowing berberis and blackcurrant bushes. Still, she could see the paths in the wilderness, and Edmund, the gardener, sitting on a bench by his shed in the clearing at the end, getting his breath. Edmund was always getting his breath. Through the trees, she could see how his belly flowed to his thighs and the empty barrow by his side was in danger of capsizing. A youth came and joined him, lifted him gently by the arm and took him into the shade.

Anna frowned, forgetting the grief for a full minute. The sight of this youth made her heart skip a beat. She had seen him before, several times, but she did not know who he was and she needed to know who everyone was because it was part of her mission to look after Therese and make sure she was safe. He had yellow hair before the trees obscured him and he had become, insidiously, part of the landscape. They should get a tree surgeon to those trees – there were too many scyamores, they starved the ground upon which they grew – but not even Sister Barbara would hire a tree surgeon to perform on the day of a funeral, because those days became a Sabbath and anyway, all surgeons cost money. Breeze stirred the trees, which were shabby in late summer; the same breeze stirred Anna's long hair. Restlessly, she prowled round the small domain of the roof space, holding on to the parapet with one hand. It was chest height; she could not have fallen over, but she always held it as she moved.

On the south side of the roof space, she could look down into the road, which was a fine contrast with the peace of the over-grown garden. It was a single carriageway road with a small row of shops, café, the Oppo Bar, the delicatessen, florist and upmarket grocery with newspapers, luxury shops, to complement the residents with money in a pleasant part of London. Plenty to watch from up here, from the emptying Oppo Bar at night, to the greengrocer unloading in the morning, with the satisfaction of bad-tempered traffic jams around parked cars at rush hour. It was early afternoon quiet. Anna returned to the garden side, sat with her back to the parapet wall with a view of nothing but her own feet. Out of the breeze, the heat warmed her; she kicked off her shoes and cried a little more.

It was as well Therese had not come straight out into the garden, but then she never did. Her flesh and blood sister, not her sister in Jesus bloody Christ, but the dear one who had once been called by another name and was now called Therese. If she had seen her, she might have shouted down at her, *Are you really all right? Are you sure?* and only been heard as a distant shout enough to give away the game and reveal the very act of watching. Therese, we are too young to be bereaved, like this. We have no one left. What did we do to deserve it? Where are you, *sister* Therese? Doing God's will in the kitchen? Oh, you stupid, beautiful drudge.

The convent drawing room was heavy with the scent of flowers removed from the chapel. Father Goodwin held his teacup awkwardly and reflected briefly on the fact that in all the years he had been coming here, he had never yet managed to explain to them how he preferred instant coffee in a mug and a seat by a kitchen table, to the faded glories and polish smell of this receiving room. Rooms like this were peculiar to convents; he never encountered them anywhere else. A room saved for best, like an old-fashioned parlour and referred to as such, used only on high days and holidays, cleaned within an inch of its life in the meantime and furnished with a couple of solid sideboards, circa 1930, too heavy to shift, too ugly to be saleable. At least, he noted with approval, there was the underlying smell of tobacco and the pile of plastic stacking chairs in the corner, which indicated it had once been used far more than it was currently, before Barbara arrived as a relatively recent Sister Superior. It had justified its spacious existence with meetings of Alcoholics Anonymous once a week, The Mothers' Guild and other charities, which Barbara had decided simply did not pay. He thought he might prefer the company of the Alcoholics to that of Sister Barbara and then he reminded himself of his Christian conscience. She was a good woman and if she was also insensitive, that was forgivable. She was trying to preserve the unpreservable and the vulnerable, and there was a certain virtue in it. She was also a woman of genuine conscience, a listener, capable of changing her mind. Sometimes she was limited by lack of imagination. What else could he expect? He drained the teacup with loud appreciation and thought first of what a hypocrite that made him and then, wistfully, of what he was missing on television. Arsenal v Tottenham. The Races. That was what he had planned for the afternoon before he caught the train.

'It was a good send-off, Father. The family were very pleased. I wished you'd have been there.'

'So do I. But you wanted the Bishop and I had another dying soul. Dermot Murray, did you ever know him?'

He did not say that he had been glad of the intervention of duty. Sister Jude had been an obdurate friend and her demise made him sick to the heart. Barbara did not know Dermot Murray and she did not care. She crossed herself quickly.

'A very good send-off. Even with her loss, little Therese excelled herself with the lunch, they ate it all. I don't know how she manages with that foul-mouthed girl alongside. Who must be a trial to her. She's so conscientious, so *mature*, for twenty-one.' She leaned forward, confidentially. 'And do you know what, Father? The contributions were tremendous. We're actually in profit. The Undertaker always does me a good deal. We might branch out into doing funerals, professionally, even weddings, perhaps. We're committed to Sunday Mass, of course. The chapel, as the Bishop says, is a resource. Should I have taken the money from the relatives? Still, they should be grateful we've kept Sister Jude for all these years.'

He did not suggest that such gratitude was inappropriate.

Jude's pension had kept her; a good pension after forty years teaching, pocketed by the Order in return for hospice care. She was not a charity case. She had been an investment. This was not a diplomatic suggestion, simply one that crossed his mind. He had been fond of Sister Jude, an intellectual of the most pragmatic kind, a lover of gossip and laughter and the keeper of secrets. Through her, he understood this institution better than he might have done if his only source of information was the Principal, whom he faced across the teacups. The strain of the day and the week before was beginning to tell on her. Barbara was in charge of a dying institution, but it did not make her immune to the personal force of death. Everyone had loved Jude, although some, like Barbara, had also been afraid of her.

'Father, I can't stand it. I wonder if God put me upon earth to tolerate a set of mostly elderly eccentrics gathered under the same roof, for a terrible number of different reasons. As well as bad language from the staff.'

'Yes, he did.'

'And do I have to tolerate the council tax and that greasy estate agent writing to me every day, telling me how much the place is worth?'

'Yes, you do.'

'And do I have to put up with the Bishop's bursar phoning on a weekly basis, suggesting the place must be commercially viable, pull its weight, or otherwise it goes on the market and the Sisters out to grass?'

'Yes, you do.'

'And do I have to live in a building that is falling apart in all directions because we can't pay anyone to get anything mended? And do I have to live with that wilderness of garden and the old goat of a gardener who's fit for nothing any more?'

'Yes.' His breath became shorter and he was dreaming of football. Dreaming of another kind of *YES*, the roar from the

19

terraces on his television screen, which would leave him punching the air, incoherent with pleasure.

'And do I, and the rest of us, have to put up with that vicious little minx coming in and out as she pleases, simply because her sister Therese is one of us and she herself lives so near? Do I have to do it, now her aunty's dead? The minx, the silly—'

'*YES!*' he shouted. 'YES! Especially, YES.'

She was stunned into silence, put down her own teacup with extreme caution and quietness before she remembered to close her mouth. 'Why?'

He paused. 'Because she is shunned by heaven and poised for hell. You, we, cannot take responsibility for pushing her in either direction. You *must* let her in. Whenever she wants.'

There was a fly buzzing at the window, unlamented. He longed to swat it at the same time as feeling grateful for the distraction of the noise. The game would be half over by now, even allowing for histrionics and injuries. Sister Barbara adjusted the folds of her skirt, disturbed, unconvinced, disappointed with everything, even the fly. He remembered diplomacy.

'Anna could be very useful to you. And besides, they stand to inherit a great deal of money,' he added, hating himself.

'Who told you that?' she asked sharply.

'Sister Jude did. Of course, she was a great friend to the whole family, before the girls were . . . ill. And before their mother, poor soul, lost her reason.' He was choosing his words carefully.

'Oh Lord, I knew Isabel Calvert, too,' she said, decisively. 'We were at the same school for a while. She was very devout, even then, poor woman. A lesson to us all. Marries a rich man that much older and what does she get? A swine who abandons her with two sick children. It just shows you the dangers of not marrying a Catholic. Did Jude also tell you he'd abused the girls?' She leaned forward confidentially. '*Sexually*, I mean.'

'She did tell me that suggestion had been made,' he said

delicately. The fly continued its futile racket. 'I understand it to have been her opinion that the abusive parent, if either, was the mother.'

'Absolute nonsense,' Barbara stated. 'Everyone knows the woman was a saint.'

They glared at one another. Christopher Goodwin knew he could not win an argument based on hearsay. He shrugged and smiled, prepared himself to move. Once he got home, he could take off the dog collar. Although he felt as naked without it as Barbara probably would without her uniform, there were days when it was an affliction. Someone must have opened a window to let in the fly: he wished they did it more often.

'Well,' he said, rising, 'the Calvert family brought you the only young novice the order has attracted in years. There must be something in that. Novices are as rare as hens' teeth, are they not?'

She nodded in reluctant agreement. 'Surely. Therese is a blessing. It's Anna who's the curse.'

'These things are sent to try us,' he murmured, hating the cliché. 'And even a curse can be useful.'

He patted her shoulder in the manner of a senior uncle, although she was older than he, marvelling as he did so at the fact that she, the most decisive and competent of women, was always slightly deferential to men. They all were, with the exception of the late Jude, and he was never sure if it was ingrained, or if it was mocking, or if it was the result of a constant need for the foil of masculine opinion. A man could get away with murder in a convent. They were vulnerable to their own deference.

'The boy Edmund has been bringing with him to help is an exceptional worker,' Barbara said, rising and changing the subject while moving to the door in one fluid movement. 'Would he take over on Edmund's wages, do you think?'

'You can't sack Edmund, Sister, you simply can't.'

'I'm *sick* of putting up with lazy second best for the sake of charity, but I suppose you're right. A pity: the boy's a good Catholic.'

Knowing this was the ultimate character reference, Father Goodwin held his peace.

'We'll talk about it at the meeting tomorrow, shall we? Anna said she would come and take the notes. You know how good she is at that, as well as with the suggestions, computer literate, too. She's a breath of air, Sister.'

'Yes, I suppose so.'

They parted beyond the door, she to answer the phone, which shrilled in the near distance of her office, he to make his way to the front door. He was fond of this particular corridor, although always preferring it on the way out to the way in. The floor was flagged with black and white stone, diamond shaped, and the walls were panelled with warm wood, reminiscent of the graciously clumsy house it had been and where the relics of the former beauty now remained solely in the corridor, the refectory and the chapel. It had been bequeathed to the Order in the last century by a holy spinster, who had run her family house as a primary school for the poor of the area. The nuns were to continue her good work and reside in her house for ever. But the school was long closed; the place was a home for those in the Order either in transit or too old for further use, while outside its walls, the poor of the parish were thin on the ground.

Sister Agnes was waiting in her seat by the door, where she sat for most of the day in her small cubby hole, occupying a hard seat, reading in the poor light from the leaded panes of the window next to her head and never looking at ease, even when she was asleep. Why, for Lord's sake, did she not have a better chair? He looked at her fondly as she struggled to her feet and opened the door he could easily have opened for himself. She was dimpled and pink-cheeked and plump and breathless, with the smile of an

22

angel. He always wanted to hug her and plant a big smacking kiss on her papery cheek, and he never did.

So, he argued to himself as he walked quickly down the street in the evening sun, feeling as he always did after interviews with Barbara as if he had been let out of school, the place does have a purpose after all. It is to keep women like Agnes, who could no longer live in any other way, safe and free from harm, locked inside a goldmine. It crossed his mind to visit Anna Calvert, but God help him, he was charged with so much to tell her, he did not have the strength and he did not want to ring her doorbell praying she would be out at work. Besides, she would be back inside the chapel later, saying her own version of prayers; she would not be able to resist that. The child haunted the chapel. God would help her. Father Christopher Goodwin changed his mind about going home at all, and went for the train. The Lord was also served by partaking of the pleasures of friendship and any man had to pace himself, even a priest.

Such a *deceitful* door, Anna thought, a door that gives no indication of what lies behind it. It was flush with the wall and the pavement, with a spiteful lintel above it, so that rain dripped directly on to the head of a waiting visitor on rainy days. The fabric of the door was wooden and cracked with something churchlike about its unvarnished, faded contours and the discreet mullioned window, about the size of a tile, set at eye level. The bell was on the side, high in the wall, so that she had to reach to ring it. A normal height person would not have to stand so close to the door to demand entry in this way, but Anna did. She was so small she could shop in the children's department: it was as if her height had failed to grow into the maturity of her figure. She reached for the bell, almost pressing herself to the wood, and then stood back, quickly. The door had a way of taking a person by surprise. Agnes lurked behind it, hardly ever bothering to look through the window, the worst, most indiscriminate doorkeeper they could have chosen, but there was no choice because this was her self-appointed task and she was not to be separated from it. The bell rang; she answered it. If she operated by anything, it was smell rather than sight. She would let in the devil, even without sheep's clothing, and when she saw it was Anna, turned away in disappointment, holding the door open politely nevertheless. Anna was hardly a novelty and not even a sinner, although in Agnes's eyes, sin was the privilege of men.

'I'm sorry for your loss, Anna. Did you want Therese?' she asked in her quavering voice. 'It's six o'clock, you know. She may be resting before supper.'

'No. Thank you.'

'The 'thank you' sounded hollow. Anna strode down the black and white corridor, which always, somehow, pleased her. The tiles were worn to a dull sheen in the centre, the black sharper at the edges near the panelled walls. The geometric pattern invited a game of hopscotch, the way she had played when she came here first as a reluctant child visitor, only slightly fascinated by the prospect of visiting someone described as an aunt, but very old, dressed in a bonnet and looking like a bat. Sulky, dragged by her mother to see her mother's Aunt Jude. Therese trailing behind and hiding resentment with better success than her elder sibling because she was instantly charmed by the place and she was, in any event, instinctively charming herself. Anna had remained churlish until she was told, yes, she could hopscotch on those black and white tiles and go into the garden and shout if she liked. A little noise would do the place good, Jude said, which puzzled her in retrospect since there had been a small Montessori school for fifteen girls held in a single classroom to the side of the corridor in those days. A long time ago. Sixteen years.

The chapel looked spare without a coffin and the profusion of

24

flowers, a large enough room to seat fifty with ease and in the current state of emptiness smaller, cooler, sweeter than ever. There was a traditional altar against the back wall, and a long, narrow table in front for the preparation of Communion. Dominating the whole, elegant room, the crucifix hung centre stage across the tall window, which arched to the ceiling, letting in a strong, colourless light that beat against the Cross, so that it cast a shadow from the window to the door and the figure of the crucifix was blurred and featureless. Anna crossed herself with the automatic gesture of one who had learned how at the same time she had learned speech, nodding at the figure.

'OK, Jesus? Is your dad in tonight?'

The silence was profound. She crossed her arms. Behind the face of the Son, there was always that of the Father. Preferably, a round-faced paterfamilias, like an old Italian restauranteur.

'Oh, stop messing about. You heard me.'

The birch trees in full leaf flicked against the curved window. The small windows, set high on each side of it, shone like jewels. There was a draught from one of those, opened with a pole to clear the incense and mercifully forgotten. Christ drooped on his cross. Anna nodded, satisfied by the sounds of the trees.

'OK, you're in tonight. Where the hell were you this morning, Lord?'

The crucifix did not answer. She sat, cross-legged, in the centre of the aisle. There was a low rail separating her from the area of the altar, not intended as a barrier between officiating priest and congregation, but a simple necessity for those who could only kneel with a little support. Some of the nuns insisted upon kneeling to take Communion; those in tune with modern traditions stood. Easier for the priest if they knelt, especially if the priest was like Father Goodwin, permanently stooped although nimble enough when he raced down the road away from the place. Still, he beat the shit out of that Bishop.

25

'You definitely weren't here this morning, Lord. The whole thing was perfectly, bloody godless.'

The silence was incomplete. She could hear the tall birch trees breathing through the high window behind the altar. It was the window that lent the place distinction, curving the full height of the high wall in the shape of an upturned boat, with the leaded panes in the shape of elongated diamonds, smoky glass, slightly blue with no other colours, giving the place a bright but subdued glow, even when the sun hit hardest. Framed in pale oak, the window seemed as if it was leaning in towards her, as if she was sitting in the shelter of the boat; it embraced. The crucifix was made of the same pale wood as the surround of the window. She could see it more clearly from the aisle as she sat in the shadow of it. The figure lounging uncomfortably upon it, with well-muscled arms, elongated torso and, to Anna's mind, greasy, outmoded hair in an unbecoming shade of brown, looked as if he might have been in an Armani suit, or at least, if lain flat, slightly contorted on a deckchair. The face had the look of a hangover, a slack mouth, and half-closed eyes. Refined puzzlement was the most prominent impression and for a murdered man in a cumbersome loincloth, he was remarkably clean and free of blood, far more an effete Italian than a chunky carpenter.

When Anna spoke to God, or as like as not, hectored him, she spoke to the God who had inspired the window, rather than this depiction of his son *in extremis*, but her eyes still strayed to the vague face of the crucifix.

'You know what?' she said. 'You can't make up your mind if you want them to be sorry for you or fancy you.'

She was jeering without shouting. Even in the worst throes of anger, contempt and frustration, she could not shout in the chapel. In the street, she could yell, she could raise two fingers and bawl at strangers, but in here she could not shout although she often longed to do so. In here, a shout would become little more

26

than a whisper. There was still the lingering smell of the incense, an aftertaste from the earlier service despite the open window.

'I cannot understand,' Anna said, 'why, if you really live in this place, with all this light, you let them coop you up without air. Then let them fill the place with smells. You've no control, Lord, you really haven't.'

She removed herself from the middle of the aisle and sat on one of the chairs. They had rush-covered seats, which tickled the back of her knees. The neglect of human comfort infuriated her. Even God did not demand it.

'I have come, dear Lord, to announce my *evil* intentions. Do you hear me?'

The sun was passing over the window. Once, she had believed that the shafts of sunlight that shone from behind clouds signalled the presence of angels and it was the angels who finally blew away the clouds. Sometime later in the history of her imagination, the shafts of sunshine became a kind of heavenly semaphore between saints.

'Dear Lord, I am going out to intoxicate myself and possibly fornicate. In other words, get off my face and maybe find a shag.'

The wind made a soothing noise in the birches. Again as a child, she had thought that the sound of the wind in the trees was the sound of God, breathing. Because God, she had been told, made everything and she could not imagine a silent Creator. A God who had made the world would surely signal the fact by making as much row as possible. All natural sounds belonged to God; only the sounds of cars and aeroplanes and machinery belonged to man.

'Did you hear me?'

Get drunk and have a shag? Which commandment did that offend?

'All right, then. I could strangle Agnes on the way. That would make it worse, wouldn't it?'

Yes.

Anna spread her hands in despair.

'Damn you, how can you do this to us? Oh, I don't mean me in particular, but them. Why are you letting this place go to hell and why have you trapped her in it? You're the one who seduces virgins like my bloody sister, and you aren't even good-looking. You *bastard*! You *fucking fraud*!'

This time her voice did reach shouting pitch. Almost. As she regretted it, mumbling an apology, she heard the sound of the door behind her. Anna did not move, sat waiting for the footsteps to come towards her, light steps in soft shoes. Therese always wore soft shoes. A figure, taller than her own, sat beside her. Out of the corner of her downturned eyes, Anna could see that she held an old missal, which she placed quietly on the seat to her right. Therese always carried something.

'Anna, stop it.'

Anna breathed deeply and let her hands uncurl in her lap. 'Stop what, little sister? I was only praying.'

'Yes, I heard you. You're sad and it always makes you cross. You weren't praying, you were denouncing. Why should Jesus listen to you if you call him a bastard?'

'But that's what he was. Exactly. A bastard, born on the run.'

'Even less reason to abuse him.'

Therese was angry, Anna could tell. She was satisfied. Her gentle, soft-voiced sister vibrated with a fury which would be as it always was, short-lived, ready at the faintest hint to turn itself into forgiveness, understanding or supplication, not necessarily in that order, but with an inevitable, infuriating progress. Even angry, she was full of grace, sitting with her back as straight as a pole, knees together, heels raised off the floor, feet arched like a delicate dancer about to practise.

'Grace is a virtue, virtue is a grace . . .' Anna chanted.

'And Grace is a naughty girl who would not wash her face,'

Therese finished. 'But then, there is always amazing grace, how sweet the sound.'

There was an awkward silence for a full minute apart from the murmuring of the trees outside and Therese's soft breathing. Then she touched Anna's bare arm. Anna flinched, until Therese's hand wrapped itself around hers and stayed there.

'Oh, Anna, love, why do you do it? Why do you beat yourself up?'

'And how do you manage to recover so quickly, you cold-hearted niece?'

'Because I had to prepare the food. That was the best I could give. Jude loved food, you know that.'

'God's drudge, that's what you are.'

'So you say, but it's my choice.'

'It's a waste of your life. Cooking food for old women. A con trick, a waste of life.'

'And yours, I suppose, is that much better?'

'I'm free.'

'If you say so.'

There was a contrast in the colour of their skin. Therese's slender forearm emerged from the same plain blue blouse she always wore indoors, an arm as white as milk while Anna's was berry brown. Therese's lack of pigment seemed to her to be a sign of captivity: prisoners looked like that. The anger surfaced again; she struggled to control it.

'I wonder if it was always going to turn out this way. Pre-ordained, if you excuse the expression.'

'God's will? I really don't know. All I know is that I am usually perfectly happy and I would dearly wish the same for you.'

'Oh, shuttit. Do you know what you sound like?'

Therese continued to hold her hand firmly. 'Listen, lovey, you can question me as much as you want, but you mustn't worry the others. You can't suggest to women of their age that their lives, lived in faith, are nothing but a sham. It isn't fair. It achieves nothing but pain.'

'What did I say? I merely suggested to bloody Barbara that without the shackles of the Sisterhood, Sister Jude might have been something special. A force in the real world.'

'She *was* a force, you idiot. And without the shackles, she might have been nothing at all. Lost without trace. And so might I.'

'You'd always have me. You always have. I'd hold you up.'

'You aren't enough. No human being is.'

There was a wariness in her voice that suggested a conversation often repeated, if not in the same words, at least with similar themes. Therese lifted the missal from the seat beside her and placed it in Anna's lap.

'The relatives went to her room, to choose whatever they wanted. I got there first.'

'Jude had nothing to leave.'

'She had books and tapes. I took her old missal, for you.'

Anna touched it. It was very old, bursting with holy pictures and notes, held together with an elastic band. It repelled her, slightly. She did not want it and yet knew it was hers.

'Do you want me to go away?' she asked humbly. 'Am I just a nuisance?'

'No, of course not. We would all miss you. You should only go when you're ready.'

'Not without you.'

Therese sighed. 'And you tell me *you're* free.'

She detached her hand, gently but finally, pulled Anna's hair and brushed past her bare knees in the calf-length skirt which looked, like her blouse, a well-worn piece of second-hand clothing and smelled, faintly, of the kitchen. She genuflected to the altar, made the sign of the cross and left in her soft shoes. There was a slight draught as the door closed quietly. The room was darker without her. Anna felt thwarted, drummed her feet on the floor.

Small feet. The noise was swallowed in the space, but still comforting.

'So you see, Lord,' Anna addressed the trees and the darkening sky of the huge window, 'you see how she trusts me? She leaves me here, knowing I won't wreck the place. Well, don't bank on it. You've wrecked more lives than you've ever saved. Anyway, they can do that all by themselves. You *BASTARD!*'

In the darkening light of the room, the vibrant colours of the Stations of the Cross shone from the walls. The supercilious agony on the face of the crucified Christ remained immobile, along with the pristine white folds of his modest loincloth. She wanted to cut the wire that held the crucifix to the ceiling, watch it fall and break into pieces. She wanted the walls to come tumbling down, like Jericho: she sat still, gripping the seat of the chair and willing it to happen.

Then there was the pistol shot.

One of the large panes of glass in the main window shattered. The glass imploded into the air: a shower of glistening hail caught the light as it cascaded to the floor in silvery fragments, tinkling and colliding, rolling away in a lethal dust until the silence resumed. Anna scrambled from the seat, grabbed the missal and ran for the door. There she stood and looked back. Half of the broken pane remained in the frame, with sharp, jagged edges. The sound of the trees was louder. *Nigh, nigh, draws the chase, With unperturbed pace, Deliberate speed, majestic instancy . . .*

She ran down the black and white corridor and out of the building. Agnes's chair was empty; no one heard. Anna went on running.

In another garden, the jackdaw fell to earth. Kay McQuaid picked up a housebrick to finish it off. Full of fleas.

Got you, by God, you bastard.

31

Chapter Two

Thou shalt not make to thyself any graven image

The magpie had fallen to earth in a shower of debris. It was no longer the jet black of springtime. Edmund saw the matt dullness of the feathers and the curled feet as he picked it up carefully in a cloth, feeling the warmth of it through the flannel, holding it gingerly in case it should horrify him with a sudden movement, the throb of a heartbeat or the opening of a single eye, but it was dead enough; would have been dead as it fell, dead when the branches of the tree through which it descended caught at its wings and delayed the fall, until it landed in a flurry of feathers and pale green leaves. Edmund wept. Carrying the burden respectfully, arms extended so that it should not be close to his own body, he stumbled from the birch trees along the path towards the bottom of the garden, tears blurring his unsteady progress. Tears and shame. The path was uneven crazy paving. At the end, by the statue, he stumbled. The dead bird fell out of his hands as he collapsed in the attitude of a penitent, falling against the knees of Sister Matilda, who sat calmly on the stone bench, which in turn rested against the ankles of the statue of Michael the Archangel, leader of the angels of God, predominant in the fight against Lucifer. She was telling the rosary from the beads hung at her waist – *Hail Mary, full of Grace, The Lord is with thee, Blessed art thou among women . . .* – beneath the statue of the saintly hero, half-covered in green moss. It had been a damp summer. Edmund's stumbling fall was cushioned by the folds of Matilda's habit, bunched round her knees.

'There, there,' she murmured. 'He'll not have tears before bedtime, you know. Sit down, Edmund, dear.'

Edmund rose, groaning and weeping, sat on the stone bench beside her, muttering the latter half of the prayer he had heard her begin, the sound of it a balm to his spirit. *Holy Mary, Mother of God, Pray for us sinners, Now and at the hour of our death. Holy Mary . . .* It sounded like mumbled swearing. The dead magpie was at his feet. Averting his eyes, he pushed it further away with his foot and looked towards it briefly as he dropped the white cloth, intending to cover the body. The beak of the bird protruded, sleek and dead. Edmund's shoulders heaved with sobs.

'What have I done? What have I done?'

He leaned forward and buried his head in his hands in palms that smelt of death. If he looked, he would see the bird already crawling with maggots, or that was what his eyes would imagine. Matilda placed her ample hand on the broad of his back and rubbed gently. Then she leant forward and hugged him, her arms round his shoulders and her bosom pressed into his spine. He could feel the warmth of her, but it could not yet calm him.

'I heard the blackbird this morning,' he sobbed. 'It was *singing*, singing like it did in April. As if there was a dawn for it. As if it was the end of the world. A blackbird! Singing in September!'

She waited for him. Ever since she had forsaken the chapel for the garden, hours in his company had informed her of the power of the blackbird's song, how its voice rose and fell, the fount of all music in the dawn choruses of the year. How the jubilant song of it celebrated broods of babies, nests and warmth, and how the nurturing of their life in this garden, alongside his other friends, had been the crowning glory of all the years of Edmund's tenure. Some of it she could hear; some of it she could not with her inconsistent deafness. There was an ongoing family of great tits which fed from his hand, but the blackbirds were the triumph. There were families and visitors, foragers and predators. She withdrew from the hugging of him and resumed a slow, rhythmical rubbing of his back.

'But they don't *sing*, this time of year, do they? I mean, they *call*, but they don't sing. Do they? They've finished singing, you told me.'

'Blackie *sang*, I tell you. He sang the way he sings with a brood in the nest. He *sang*. And then the magpie drove him away.'

Again, she waited, rubbing his back with the one hand, caressing the feet of St Michael with the other. St Michael should have smooth feet, covered in skin-deep gold leaf, warm to the touch. These feet were pock-marked with moss and decay, rough and cold to the touch. Leaning forward, she saw the dead magpie. It was bigger than it looked when it strutted on a branch, smaller than it seemed on the wing. Ugly brute, the noisy bully of the garden, entirely without charm to her mind.

'So, I said . . . I said . . . I said I wished he were dead,' Edmund sobbed. 'Because he's a tyrant. He drives the others away and he eats their young. Most of the year here and I thought he would go. God knows, I've tried to make him uncomfortable. But when the blackbird sang and he drove it away, Oh Lord, I hated him. But kill him? God forgive me.'

'St Michael would forgive you,' she said. 'He would have throttled the horrid thing at birth.'

She turned and looked up at the statue. The feet of the Archangel Michael rested comfortably on a fat stone serpent, which he had clearly overpowered with the spear embedded in the form of it, his hands still holding the shaft, his face upturned to the sky. St Michael occupied the right-hand side of God in heaven. He had led the good angels in the battle against the devil and *he* knew that ultimately, enemies must be killed. Edmund was not like that. To Edmund, the life of a bird was sacrosanct, even a vulture. The sobbing resumed.

'But I only said I *wished* it were dead. I watched it fly and *wished* it. If it had stayed, making that noise, driving the others away before the weather turns cold, they won't come back and nest. I wanted it to go. I didn't mean to kill it.'

Matilda marvelled at the power of prayer, and did not feel a shadow of Edmund's guilt. He had spoken with such vitriol on the subject of the magpie from February right through to July and with greater passion when the other birds, the blackbirds and the great tits, had been brooding in their well-established nests and he had spent a fortune on cheese and nuts to augment the food supply, feeding the magpie too, to keep it quiet. Then it had left. The return had been a bitter blow. She had prayed for the demise of the bully of the garden, and her wish had been granted. The downside of the wish was turning Edmund into a murderer. She wondered how he thought he had killed it. With a catapult, like David did Goliath? Hardly. She smiled and shook her head.

There was no doubt about the ownership of this garden and to whom it was dedicated. It had become to be designed, cultivated and entirely orchestrated as a reserve for birds. Matilda was always puzzled that no one else in the convent appeared to notice this. It was a secret she shared with Edmund and St Michael and would have loved to share with Sister Joseph, if Joseph were not so transfixed with misery and so irritated by Matilda's intermittent deafness. Everyone else simply accepted the garden as being increasingly impenetrable, blaming Edmund's infirmities and in the case of Barbara, her own indifference to anything that happened beyond the inner walls.

The uncontrolled ivy that covered the back wall unchecked was encouraged to proliferate because certain birds liked it for nesting. The low branches of the newer sycamores were perfect perches for fledglings, who would be in danger if they slept on the ground. The ivy hid Edmund's nesting boxes beloved of the great tit, and the virginia creeper camouflaged the holes in the wall, which he had enlarged in the hope of attracting home the house sparrows and the robin redbreast family, which had sojourned, quarrelsomely, two years before. The blackcurrants were solely for blackbirds. The oversized, ugly garden shed, which was supposed to house Edmund's gardening tools, was bare of anything much except fork, spade, hammer, nails, knives and twine, plus his seat and a sack of grain. Matilda did not know what he had done to deter the London pigeons, but it would never have been poison. She suspected it had been the effective use of a water pistol.

Edmund kept the area nearest the convent building at the back of the chapel neatish and tidyish, with a single flowerbed. Down this end, he let the shrubs encroach, encouraged two small, gloomy holly trees, which were good for winter berries and supporting mistletoe. The overweening cotoneaster, which crept across the path around the bend from St Michael, had an orange fruit the birds adored. Edmund was a gardener who could not prune.

Matilda withdrew her hand from his back, suddenly disturbed. She held on to her rosary, tightly. The warm wooden beads were a constant comfort. She had learned to slip it in her pocket when she came down this end of the garden, in case the clicking sound of it should alarm the birds.

'Edmund, dear, how did the poor brute die? It didn't just fall from the sky because you wanted it dead, did it?'

Or because I prayed to St Michael for exactly such an event, she thought, and her mind wandered. Really, Edmund was as intractable as her dear Sister Joseph: they would neither of them accept affection and forgiveness, as if they could never believe they deserved it. Dear St Michael, so much more accessible than God. Such a nice young man. She had created a whole personality for him, as well as a wardrobe. St Michael was a deferential, charming lieutenant with perfect manners and he was the only one, standing on the right side of God, who could tell God jokes. She relied upon that now, to hide a distinct feeling of misgiving. She leant further towards Edmund to hear his reply, although her deafness was confined to distant sounds and she was grateful for the cocoon it made. Matilda wanted nothing more than human voices and birdsong to intrude upon her consciousness, and only the sounds of her favourite people and favourite feathered friends, at that. There were voices she liked and those from which she shrank. She liked Edmund's burr: she liked little Sister Therese's youthful voice; she liked the shriller, more definable voice of that wicked sister of hers, the one who was probably named after St Ann, the mother of Mary, as boring a saint as any. Much better to be named after an angel, like Michael.

'How did it die?'

'I don't know,' Edmund mumbled. 'I wanted it to.'

'So did I, but *how*?'

'He fell out of the sky. The chapel window broke.'

'Oh, dear.'

She knew in an instant. The boy had done it. She thought she had heard him, but perhaps she was wrong. That glorious, blond-haired boy, who had slunk around Edmund for the last two weeks with the solicitousness of a doting grandson. She had seen him, sliding past earlier as she sat there, where she so often sat, treating her as if she was dumb and blind as well as partially deaf. An old woman held no interest for a boy, and when he did speak, she did not like his voice.

'*You* didn't kill it,' she protested. 'He did. The boy. The one who's got you by the balls. He did. He's got an air rifle. I saw it.'

'No. Francis would never do that.'

'He just did.'

'No, he's gone home, hours ago. He never did. He loves the birds, does Francis.'

She closed her eyes and considered Lucifer the Serpent, who was once, in her imagination, a quite magnificent brunette youth with a pushy torso, slim hips and great big forgive-me eyes. Francis bore a passing resemblance to that Lucifer. It was an impression she could not quite shake off, despite wanting to like him if only for his name. St Francis was the patron saint of birds, and a boy with his name must be good, surely part of the reason Edmund adored him, even granting the fact that Edmund was an old, celibate homosexual, by no means beyond the demons of desire that Francis had awoken. He had no idea that Matilda knew what he had scarcely guessed himself. The crying had stopped.

'Francis would never do such a thing,' he said firmly. 'Even if he thought it was what I wanted. Either it was done through prayer, or someone else did it. And now I'd better bury that bird.'

She nodded, and slapped his back, heartily. If that was going to be the version of events, so be it. She was not going to add her two pennyworth or tell tales.

'When you've done that,' she said, 'do you think you could give St Michael a wash? Get rid of the moss on his feet?' And the bird shit, left by the magpie, which had been the final insult.

Edmund leant his dusty hand on her knee to lever himself upright. 'Good idea.'

By the time he had gone, it was almost dark. Matilda had the fleeting thought that perhaps the young fledgling magpie sons reared in this garden might come back on some vengeful mission to look for their brother, but she dismissed the thought. The birds slept early and for now it was peaceful silence. As she moved up the path towards the beech trees and the clear ground, she paused to wave. She always knew when someone was watching.

Yes, it had been a sin to pray for the death of a living thing. Perhaps it was also a sin to ignore God in favour of saints. She never could pray, except to an image. And she wished that Sister Joseph, whom she loved and had loved for years, would accept her own virtues and forget the rest.

Seventy miles away, Kay McQuaid flung the dead jackdaw on to the compost heap at the bottom of the garden, wiped her hands on her trousers and walked back to the patio. It was a short, unencumbered walk across a close-cropped lawn with a circular flowerbed in the centre, containing purple dahlias and not much else. There were neat shrubs around the edges of the walls, flower-pots on the patio, which was the same size as the lawn and the most important feature of the garden. A modest sized garden, encroached upon and thoroughly tamed by a conservatory and a patio and the ruthless application of insecticide. Low maintenance was the key. Too much shade was provided at certain times of day by the low tree that flourished next door. It was the best a tree could do so near the sea, but if it had not been preserved by the family next door, Kay would have been over there with an axe long since. Anything that diminished the sporadic sunshine of an English summer was forbidden. The bloody jackdaw had come from that bloody tree.

The sound of the sea at the front of the house was a soothing background murmur, punctuated with the shrill cry of a seagull.

'Cheers,' she said to her companion, raising the glass she had left on the table.

'If it had been a pheasant,' he said, referring to the dead bird, 'you could cook it.'

She shook her head. 'You might. I doubt if I'll cook anything ever again. Have the peanuts.'

'You could grow vegetables instead of lawn. Eat them fresh.'

She yawned. 'Oh yeah? I got too much tension already, this time of year. I put the sunbed out, lie down, cloud comes over. I get up, take it in. Then I take it out again, then I take it in, and then I go and look at brochures for where else to go. I haven't got any time to cook, God help me. Anyway, thanks for coming all this way. It's always good to see you.'

'It's an easy journey. A break for me. You know I love coming here. How did the bird die?'

'It came in the window, dirty beast, looking for my rings. I threw a plate at it, managed a hit. Not enough to kill it, mind. It was poorly to start with. Something it ate. Might have had a heart attack. They feed the wretched things next door. Then they come and shit on the patio.'

Father Goodwin looked around the neat area. There was a water feature consisting of a stone pond, guarded by a gnome with a fishing rod and bright red and green garments. The patio floor was grey brick, designed, he thought in his ignorance of such things, for the embellishment of a few minimalist pots with monochrome evergreens, the sort he had seen in magazines. He read the style sections, mainly for the food, if there was time after the sports pages. Easy to tell what Kay had added. Orange and yellow geraniums, pink daisies and all of the seven dwarves. He eyed the one sitting to the side of the water feature, which he otherwise liked for the soothing sound of it.

'Now, Father, what's the matter? You wouldn't be here if there was anything good on the telly. No, there never is tonight, is there? And stop looking at Droopy like that. He won't hurt you. He's a helluva lot friendlier than those horrible things you had in the presbytery. I always did hate that one of the Sacred Heart, the one in the glass case. The one of Himself with the heart on

41

the front of his robe? Pickled Jesus, I used to call it. Well, we Catholics grew up with those things. Perhaps that's why I like the gnomes. I must miss that kind of furniture. Are you sure you don't want a drink? Yes, you do. Help yourself.'

He went indoors, past the Pogenpohl kitchen with the air of clean disuse, through to the lounge beyond, as different from the nuns' parlour as anything he could imagine, making him pause to wonder what it might have looked like before Kay's relatively recent tenure as the sole occupant had stamped her definitive mark on it. Plain and functional, he guessed, without the addition of throws in vibrant colours, a huge TV-video console and a drinks cart, in the form of a wheelbarrow drawn by a toy donkey, full of highly coloured bottles of everything ranging from Tequila to Southern Comfort, through Slivovic to Martini, gifts and mementos from foreign travels, largely undrunk. There was banana liqueur from the Canaries, Metaxa brandy from Greece and something suspect from Turkey. Father Goodwin seized upon a bottle of Jameson's, noting that only the bottle of Tanqueray Gin bore the sign of fingerprints. That was Kay's tipple, treated with care. The shininess of the display was admirable. You can give a cleaning lady new tastes, he thought, but you can't stop her cleaning.

In the fireplace, there was a large gold statue of Buddha with a well-polished stomach, which she may have put there simply to annoy him. He found a glass in the kitchen and sloshed a liberal dose of Irish whiskey for himself. Kay, sitting on her sunbed, nursed her long gin and tonic with the still melting ice and a cocktail stirrer with an umbrella on the top.

She was as brown as well-tanned leather. You didn't need a hot summer to get brown, she had told him: you simply needed time to sit in the sun whenever it came out. Especially if you'd done a bit of Tenerife in the spring. Brown skin suited her alarming choice of clothes. She was small and round and early forties, several years younger than himself, her face as sweetly wrinkled as a walnut shell, with dark brown eyes at odds with springy, bleached hair, turned even lighter by the occasional bursts of sun. He had adored her, in his understated way, ever since she had crashed into the presbytery, a skinny girl, cursing to high heaven at the time, along the lines of how she didn't want preaching, she wanted a bloody job. Kay had got her bloody job: no one else wanted it even then, on those wages. After two weeks of reasonable cooking and cleaning, she produced the hitherto unmentioned illegitimate son. He watched her now, surreptitiously. Not much changed.

'Are we all caught up with the news?' she asked, brightly.

She had lasted five years in the presbytery before finding the plum job with the Calverts, with plentiful, colourful rows in the meantime. Food had been thrown, he forgot why. Holy water under the bridge, she said, later. But the plum job with the Calverts had turned into the job from hell until they divorced, and Kay ended up as housekeeper to Mr Calvert, in his separate house, by the sea. This very house, which bore some resemblance to the way it was when he had been alive in it.

Kay and Christopher Goodwin had always stayed friends, usually by short letters, for which he thanked every saint in the universe. He drank his whiskey and thought, God was good, and this was a compensation enough for the guilt of evading his duty and missing the match.

There were several compensations for missing the match. Mrs Katherine McQuaid, being drunk enough with the sun and the gin to speak freely, was a bonus for a wretched day. He put a touch more gin in her glass. Yes, the news of the old parish had been thoroughly covered, right up to the last funeral. She always wanted to know every detail of the Calvert girls.

'Oh, give us a good shot, will you ever, Christopher? Then I'll be able to pray to God for better weather and someone to supply me with drugs.'

'You want for nothing, Kay. You've landed on your feet. Not even your son bothers you.'

'No, he's to make his own way and not sponge off me. But what do you mean, I've landed on my feet? None of this is permanent, although God knows, I've earned it. This is Cinderella stuff. The pumpkin'll be arriving any minute. So don't you be telling me to get off my arse and do good works.'

'Would I? Didn't he leave you enough for ever?'

'Theodore? No, he bloody did not. I can live in this house for now, but his lawyer can repossess it whenever he wants. Enough money to last a year more with a few holidays thrown in. He wasn't *giving* me anything permanent. He just wanted me to go on housekeeping and he made it worth my while.'

'Isn't that rather cruel?'

'He could be cruel, for sure, but what's so cruel about it? A taste of the good life's better than no taste at all.'

'Isn't that what he gave his wife, too?'

'Now, you look here, *Christopher*, don't you join in maligning the dead. The trouble with you is that you're a fool for women. You're so soft on them, you always believe they're right.'

He knew this was unjust, but she was at least partially accurate. He was soft on women because he simply liked them best.

'I'm not maligning him, Kay. But doesn't a man's choice of wife reflect upon himself? You said he wasn't happy with the girl he had here. Can't have been all their fault.'

She adjusted herself on the sunbed, prepared to be angry, without quite having the energy. It was getting cold out here, but not cold enough to justify going into the conservatory. She tucked the folds of her capacious purple robe round her ankles. He wasn't sure what you would call a garment like that.

'Look, he left his wife because she wouldn't let him near his own children. You don't stay with a woman who gives you the evil eye and treats you as if you were the devil. The only other

44

girlfriend was that one he caught on the rebound, greedy little cow. You never could tell if she was feeling his prick or his wallet or both at the same time.'

He laughed, the moment for argument over, which he regretted, slightly.

'And he was very good to Jack.'

'Yes, he was too, but I'm not going to talk about Jack.'

Kay's virtues included her passion for argument, which allowed him to indulge himself. There was nowhere else he could have an argument and no one he could argue with: he was the peacemaker, the listener, and that was his role. But with Kay, he could manufacture a quarrel just for the hell of it: they could have a shouting match and then forget all about it, no offence taken. The fact that he disagreed with her on most subjects helped, as did the way she flaunted her heresies, and she wanted pastoral care like she wanted a hole in the head. What a relief. Even the torture once provided by her physical presence was a dim, almost comfortable memory, but despite all the ease of this friendship, there were questions he never dared ask. Such as exactly what relationship Kay had had with the rich employer who had elevated her status to that of housekeeper, rather than cleaner, and endowed her so eccentrically. Nor had he ever asked her who was the father of her son. That would have been impertinent.

'Remind me of how fairy godfather Calvert made his money?'

Kay winked at him. 'Nothing fairy about him, Christopher. He made it wanking, sorry, banking.'

She only ever called him Christopher when she was two gins down. Christopher was such a pansyish name, and besides, that particular saint, as she never failed to remind him, had been knocked off the saintly calendar thirty years ago. Christopher, for whom a million medals had been forged, was no longer a proper saint for universal intercession. It seemed like the story of Father Goodwin's life.

'I like the golden Buddha,' he said from the increasing comfort of his chair.

'Oh, that?' she said, waving a brown hand with crimson nails. 'Thought I might become a Buddhist. They're ever so friendly.'

She struggled upright, the better to explain as he choked on his drink. The jumpsuit gaped to reveal a thoroughly upholstered, flower-patterned bikini, which somehow reminded him of an apron.

'Oh, for God's sake,' she said, crossly, 'I was only teasing, but I do sometimes think. I miss *religion*, God help me.'

'Buddhists tend not to drink,' he told her, gently. 'And you wouldn't be allowed to swat a fly, let alone kill a bird. Can I bring Anna Calvert to see you?'

She sat bolt upright, startled. 'Why? Why the hell should I see her?'

'Because Sister Jude died. And apart from me and my scanty knowledge, you're the only one left who knew her parents, properly.'

'So that gives me a duty, does it? Bollocks. No, I shan't see her. I've had it up to here with sodding duty. But you can take me to bed if you like.'

He laughed and shook his head. It was an old joke, as old as sin. 'I wished you'd told me as soon as Theodore went and drowned,' he said. 'I could have helped.'

She shuddered, violently. 'No,' she said, 'you couldn't. I wouldn't want anyone else to see that poor, bloated body on the beach. So near home, too. It was horrible. And besides, he would turn in his grave if he thought you were standing over his corpse, saying prayers.'

Two in the morning, and Anna was walking home. No drinking, no shagging, just shift work at the taxi place. Therese would

46

have been right not to fear for her soul tonight since all she had done was listen to voices.

It was wrong to be so fearless of the dark, but it was a fear she had never learned and the lack of it made her indifferent to being followed at night. Girls being followed was a fact of life. She could run far faster than any thief and, besides, had nothing to steal in her shoulder pack, except, tonight, the missal she had placed in there without being quite aware she had done so. Placed it on the table at work alongside the sandwich and put it back in the bag to go home, unopened.

The footsteps tailed away as she neared her own flat. Probably the one who followed tonight was one of the homeless who parked themselves at the back door of the convent, encouraged by the rumour of Christian charity. They had banged on the door last winter in the middle of the night, persisting until the ivy had grown down to shield the exit and announce its permanent disuse. The garden door was a false signal to the one or two who gathered in the hope that it would open and benefits would arrive.

She was ashamed of herself because she should have told Sister Barbara about the pistol shot breaking the window, but she had run away instead. When the footsteps behind her trailed away into silence, long before she drew level to the back door on the way to her own, she saw that the ivy had been clipped, neatly trimmed to frame the wood. She stopped and looked.

Once inside, she went upstairs and on to the roof to gaze down into the garden where there was nothing to see. Looking up she could see the stars, imagine the souls in the firmament. Sister Jude and her darling mother. Her father would surely be in hell.

Tucked in bed, she took the elastic band from the missal and let it fall open. It was stuffed with holy pictures, memoriam cards, decorative bookmarks with saintly depictions and messages scrawled on the back. Not so much a book of prayer, but one of memorabilia. Anna stuffed back the notes, letters, cards, pictures, as alienated by the sentimental reproductions as she was by the texture of the old leather and the tissue-thin pages, which stuck to her fingers. Still, it looked like a holy book rather than anything else, and that would do. Maybe it would provoke Ravi to talk to her, since he always had one himself. It would be a strange way to attract attention.

Still sleepless, warm with the indigestible anger that had hounded the day, she picked up the notebook which always remained by her bed and, propped by pillows, wrote in it, in pursuit of an old habit started by her father and encouraged by her mother, when she and Therese were confined to bed and told to record their symptoms, the better to diagnose the strange sickness afflicting them. Sometimes the notebook filled those distressing minutes when sleep was as vital as it was impossible and there was nothing else to do. When TV bored her, music failed to console and the radio was just another voice.

My name is Anna Calvert. (She always began this way.)

A benefactor pays my rent. I am a lucky girl.

I want anything but guidance.

I have read lots of books.

I would like not to be a freak. I miss Aunt Jude.

I wish I had never been baptised; it leaves a big black hole in my brain.

My father was a giant.

I am not fully formed.

Her eyelids began to feel heavy and the pen faltered.

There are four whole years of my life missing.

Four whole years, and I can never get them back.

Then she scribbled, *Therese is safe! Ravi smiled at me! The old man phoned again! Can't be bad!*

And everyone else is DEAD.

Then she slept.

CHAPTER THREE

I am the Lord thy God

Therese saw that they were lined up by the refectory door, like a waiting tribe, with Sister Joseph at the head of the queue. Today was the feast day of St Joseph, not the more famous St Joseph of Nazareth, husband of Mary and father to Jesus, but another Joseph altogether, an obscure man of Aragon, who founded a religious congregation for the education of the poor. Sister Joseph had taken the name when she entered the Order and although it was better than her own, it could never be as good as a martyr, like Agnes. The taste in her mouth was sour.

Her feast day was going to be, if not ignored, at least diminished by more important events, such as the breaking of the chapel window, discovered last evening by Barbara on her last round of the building, the funeral of Sister Jude the day before and the consequent emptying of the larder. Her own grief and her participation in the singing did not count. She looked at the others with irritation. Helpless ninnies. Sister Bernadette had twisted her ankle and moved with a crutch and obvious heroism. Matilda, the dearest, kindest friend she had rebuffed, was waiting to eat everything available. Joseph tried to despise her. Margaret was sniffing with her usual incessancy, while Sister Joan, named for a warrior and really a mouse, sparkled with anticipation of her pathetic weekly excursion to the market. Therese, the postulant, finished off the laying out of breakfast with her usual serene efficiency, smiling as if they were all new-found friends. Silly creature. Joseph's own room was draughty from the broken window catch; the door to this room would not shut from warping; the place was falling apart. Joseph's feast day would be forgotten. She eyed the array of sensible cereals, already cold toast, jams and milk with the contempt she might otherwise have shown to humanity. The one thing she wanted was a drink.

She was going to be ignored, when she was surely now the highest in the pecking order when it came to deserving respect for her achievements. She had followed the example of her saint, had worked in the missions, knew about the world, heat, dust, starvation and the devil of alcoholic addiction. Dear God, she wanted a drink. Plus a touch of respect for her age and someone to notice it was *her* day. And an end to the guilt she felt about hurting Matilda.

'Happy feast day, Sister,' Therese murmured, helping Joseph with the milk jug. Trust that bright-eyed girl to notice that her hands were shaking. Joseph grunted a non-committal response and went to her usual seat at the table. A single rose, glistening with dew from the garden, lay across her place and she had the grace to feel momentarily ashamed. Matilda would have done that. Matilda never forgot. The coffee looked weak. There was the usual twittering of conversation. Barbara tapped a spoon against her cup and stood at the head of the table. The murmuring ceased.

Not a pretty bunch, Barbara was thinking as she waited for silence. A community of thirty, once, shrunk to fifteen, with the inevitable prospect of further wastage through old age and death, although they were not dying off fast enough by certain standards. Clingers to the wreckage. Only the Irish had existing relatives, excluding Agnes, although Agnes waited at the door every day in the hope that one would arrive. The family of Christ and the Blessed Virgin were not a substitute for the ties of blood, whatever vows they had taken, and as for what they actually, individually believed, Barbara neither knew nor minded. It was bad enough keeping them fed and the fabric of their shelter from further decay.

'Sisters,' she began, knowing the need to be brief. Food was of paramount importance. 'Sisters, a word, please. I think you all know there was an unfortunate accident with the chapel window being blown in by the wind last night, so there may be an extra bit of activity around the place while we work out how to get it fixed. There'll be a team of useless, expensive men, I daresay,' she added bitterly. 'That's all. For what we are about to receive, may the Lord make us truly thankful, Amen.'

'Amen.'

Each made the sign of the cross with different degrees of absent-mindedness. Conversation began again, interspersed with the noise of cutlery. Therese took her place at the foot of the table and ate her chewy toast. From where Barbara sat at the opposite end, she looked like a little princess, small and golden and pink, doing nothing to make herself shine the way she did. It was simply youth, with nothing bleached out of her strong hair or the healthy, luminous complexion with which no other skin compared. Eight of the Sisters still wore the veil, the oldest ones who would have felt indecently undressed without the uniform they had worn for a lifetime and thus wore it still. Among the others, dressed either in the charcoal calf-length tunic or ordinary clothes of their own choice, style was difficult to detect, although here and there, there was a hint of vanity. A bright blue hairslide for Sister Joan, bought from her beloved market, and a blouse with a bow for Monica, who was given her clothes by a niece.

Otherwise, they seemed to exist in various shades of grey. Barbara looked down at her plate, thought of the budget and how, if selling a soul to the devil was worth hard cash, she might do it. She was slow to notice that silence had fallen, a silence of curious wonder.

At the door of the refectory stood the boy, Francis. He was standing awkwardly, like an old-fashioned servant anxious not to command attention, but needing it, and like Therese, he did nothing to attract the eye, although all eyes strayed towards him until eating stopped and the silence was total. He was not a complete stranger; the minority who ever went more than one or two steps into the garden knew who he was, just as they all knew Edmund, but it took a year for a face to be familiar. The decision to take him on had been hers alone, because he was free, and even she scarcely knew him. That was just after the last monthly meeting where her decisions could be discussed democratically if ever a quorum bothered to attend. Really, both she and they preferred dictatorship. The boy had simply arrived at least a couple of weeks before and, up until now, he had never come indoors. He was a creature of the garden and the garden had a life of its own. Agnes, for one, found the sheer size of it frightening and sat now, halfway up the table, with her mouth open in a smile of recognition. Matilda, always hungry, chewed methodically and thought he looked like St Michael today, clad for fighting. Joseph, with her wider education, thought he looked like the God Pan.

There was nothing pagan about bare arms and bare knees on a boy wearing shorts and a vest on a humid morning. Loose working clothes suited his slender physique, which was in itself a lesson in anatomy. His broad shoulders and sculpted arms looked as if they had been carved out of oak to illustrate the perfect function of interconnecting sinew. Long, baggy shorts, so large they might have belonged to another man entirely, revealed brown, grubby knees and athletic calves. He stood, shyly, flexing his hands by his sides, nodding awkwardly towards the head of the table, and his knuckles, like his knees, were convincingly dirty. He looked fit to run away; a boy with work-stained knees, inhabiting the body of a man, held together with a belt round his middle, his head crowned by golden curls as if he had stepped from a medieval painting. When Barbara got up and hustled him out into the kitchen, conversation resumed behind them. The tips of his ears grew red, as if he knew he was being discussed.

'You're welcome, Francis,' Barbara said tartly, unfazed by his beauty, but rattled by the sudden silence it had caused. 'But we like to take our breakfast in private. What is it?'

'Oh, sorry. I didn't know what else to do but try to find you, soonest. Edmund tells me you're going to call in the glaziers and all to do the window. It'll cost a bomb, Sister, really it will, and . . .'

He stuck his hands in his pockets and bowed his head. The golden curls danced. There was a single gold ring in one ear, and she noticed, with relief, a small crucifix suspended from a gold chain round his neck.

'And?'

'I could do it, Sister. I promise I could, only he won't believe me. It's only the one pane, God love us. For the price of hiring a ladder and buying the glass, I could do it, easy. To be honest, I was desperate to stop you before you spent the money. If they charge you fifty, they charge you a hundred.'

She did a mental review of the quotations she had solicited in the last hour, from any emergency firm who happened to be awake. He was right, if inaccurate on the downside of what they quoted to do any job involving ladders and height. Nothing was done for charity, not any more.

'Are you sure?'

'Sure I'm sure. I'm older than I look, Sister, worked all my life. I can do anything.'

53

He nodded vigorously. When he raised his head, she caught the full blast of brilliant, turquoise eyes, before he lowered them again, to stare at his own feet, clad in boots, without socks. The calves were marked with scratches. He looked competent, from this close distance, definitely more of a man than a boy and quite outstandingly endearing.

'What else can you do?'

'Oh, for sure, Sister, anything. Basic plumbing, electrics, washing machines, woodwork, changing plugs, mending fuses, painting, filling holes, changing carpets, shifting things, dealing with damp . . . all that. No good with cars or gas cookers, but most things else. I want to be a gardener, though, but isn't that a waste if there's nothing to do in a garden and you have a window to mend? If you see what I mean.'

It was a rushed and breathless delivery, a race to provide information and, to her ears, oddly touching in its eager boastfulness. It had ever been the dream of her life to find an able-bodied man desperate to work.

'You really can do all those things?'

He nodded.

'Why didn't Edmund tell us?'

He shook his head and scuffed his feet. 'I don't know. He thinks he needs me more. But I don't think he does. It's coming on colder, Sister, the garden can wait.'

Barbara felt as if a cloud had been lifted as she marched him back into the refectory, guided him back to her place at the head of the table and banged again with her spoon against her cup. Undrunk tea slopped on the table and the prospect of money saved made her clumsily cheerful.

'Sisters! A word, please. Francis here is going to fix the window, OK? And if there's any one of you needs something else fixing in their own room, or knows of something needing fixing anywhere else, will you please raise your hand?'

54

There was a pause, before arms were raised in an almost universal salute. White hands, pink hands, one gnarled brown hand with a missing finger.

'I also do errands,' Francis whispered to Barbara, audibly.

Sister Joseph raised her hand, last. Agnes gazed at him, mesmerised. Therese kept her eyes fixed on the surface of the table and her hands in her lap. She did not want to look at the boy she had glimpsed before. Instead she looked at Kim, staring at him from the door of the kitchen. Kim would like that.

Later, to the sound of distant hammering, she and Kim stacked the dishwasher, which was a vintage model with settings of sheer simplicity and so far indestructible. There was a butler sink for the equally indestructible pans and a gas cooking range of industrial size, installed in the days when there had been more to feed and more money to go round, a sound investment. The kitchen surfaces were chipped, but that was merely cosmetic. Nothing prevented Therese from preparing the delicate food for invalids which was her speciality. One day, God willing, said Barbara, she would turn those skills into qualifications and make herself employable. She had no ambition to do anything else. Kim was the dogsbody who came in daily for the morning, Monday to Friday, foraging for cash to feed two children. Kim liked it here because it was so quiet, but for the exclusive benefit of Therese, her language was deliberately and provocatively filthy.

'By yie! He's shaggable, in't he?'

'Who?'

'That lad, Francis, isn't it? Shaggable, I said. Phaw! I'd like to gerra hold of him! Have you been hiding him, or what?'

'No. He's never come in before. Edmund comes for tea.'

'Yeah, I bet. Well, you better get that Francis to come for tea when I'm around. I could teach him a thing or two. My old man's not bad in the sack, mind, but it does a girl good to have a change. Someone who'd take it a bit slower, for a start, though if I'm in the mood for a shag, I don't care how long. Usually takes him the same time it takes to boil a kettle.'

'Does it?' Therese asked. 'Why does it take so long?'

'Shagging?' Kim asked incredulously.

'No, boiling a bloody kettle.'

Kim cackled. This kid was smart, for a virgin. Dead easy to shock and dead good at fighting back.

'So, what do you know about shagging, then?' Kim said.

'You could put it on the back of a postage stamp.'

She was busying herself about the sink and Kim, looking at the deftness of her movements as well as the pink blush of her face, wondered how the two personalities she had could be reconciled to one another. Therese was sexy and impossible to understand.

'How fucking old are you, Therese? Don't you think you should have given it a try before saying you'd never do it?'

'Twenty-one.'

'Twenty-one, never been shagged, and a bloody nun. You're every bloke's wet dream, you are. Bloody disgrace.'

'So you tell me. Can't say I miss it. Look where it's got you. Two kids and no money.'

'Yeah, right. Funny, you're not like your sister, then. She gets around, I reckon. Shaggable, both of you.'

'I know. I worry about her, and she worries about me. Daft, isn't it?'

Kim crashed the last plate into place. 'I should like someone to explain to me,' she said, 'well, I'd like *you* to explain to me, why someone like you who's got looks and brains *and* tits should want to keep it all under wraps. You could get rich and lucky with looks like yours. You wouldn't even need to shag for it. Beats me. Oh, *Treesa*, lay off, will you?'

Therese was doing her catwalk, parading past the cooker with the exaggerated pelvic thrust of a model, hands on undulating hips, head thrown back and her wide mouth pursed in a kiss. She flung herself into a chair, lounged against the back, ran her hands through her hair, crossed her legs, ran her hands down the sides of her body, hitched up her skirt to show her knees and then lowered one eyelid in a vampish wink. Kim screamed with laughter.

'Yeah, just like that. Oh, you slay me, you do. Christ, I'd kill for legs like yours.'

The distant hammering resumed. The dishwasher rumbled.

'But you aren't going to get away with it, *Sister*. You never answer a question, you. Come on, you've been a holy nun for a year, you've got a bloody lifetime of answering questions, so you might as well start with me. Why the fuck are you doing it? *Why?*'

Therese sat up straight, adjusted her skirt and straightened her face. An expressive face, designed for laughter, although at other times, as blank as an empty page.

'Oh, Kim, you're as bad as Anna. I never thought it would be so difficult to understand or, at least, respect. There isn't a choice, not for me. I dreamed of a life like this, I dreamed of it, when other girls would dream of men and money and Lord knows what. I'm not giving anything up. Nothing I want, anyway.' She drummed her fingers on the table, seeking the right words and knowing that none would do. 'Don't you see? If you dedicate your life to God, then it means that every single thing you do has value.'

'Yeah, right.'

'It means every single thing has a purpose. I might hate scrubbing pans, but if I offer it to God, it has a purpose. It has a value. And I myself have a purpose. I have a straight line to follow. Everything I do is for the greater glory of God, and that makes me joyful. It's so simple, Kim. It means I can endure

57

anything and I don't need approval from anyone, even though I'm only human and I want to be liked. It means I don't need to be loved . . .'

'Approval? Where do you get all your long words? And don't tell me you don't need to be loved. Everyone does. Except your bloody sister.'

'I *am* loved, Kim. I'm loved by a father and a brother, whose guidance I can trust with absolute conviction, which is more than most people could ever say. And I got my faith and my vocation from my mother.'

The fridge door slammed. 'Blimey, I got two beltings a week from mine. Did she also teach you to cook?'

'Nutrition and contemplation. Also singing.'

'But nothing about shagging?'

'Come on, Kim, what mother ever teaches her daughter that? She got us books, she made us read, she made us learn and she taught us to pray . . . Even Anna can't shake that.'

'I can't get my kids to sit still.'

Therese laughed, scratched her head. Three golden hairs fell on to the table and she brushed them away. However she got her hair to gleam like that with that rotten, cheap shampoo they all used in their crappy bathrooms, Kim never knew. It was a greater mystery than the whole of religious life.

'I don't know how she managed. But we were very ill, you know, Anna and I. We didn't leave the house for four years. That's when we learned to pray.'

She jumped up from the table with the spring of a dancer, flourished a duster from out of her pocket and flicked it round Kim's head. Kim giggled and wrenched it away.

'Go and find Mr Shaggable, Kim,' Therese said. 'Stop him tempting Sister Agnes into mortal sin, and be nice to Joseph. It's her feast day and she's feeling her age.'

'She's a miserable old cow.'

'No, she's not. She's seventy-five, forgotten more than she remembers and I think she has a drink problem. Don't you women of the world notice anything?'

It was a big, overbright world that morning. On balance, when it came to the shift work she did (Anna called it shifty work), she preferred to work at night. Up on the rooftop at eight o'clock in the morning, the view into the convent garden was as misty as if someone had lit a fire. There was a fog about the place, an early, misplaced, rogue sense of autumn, as if the mist, which belonged in a field, had been dumped in the wrong place in the middle of the wrong town and lingered there, looking uncomfortable. It was as if it knew it did not belong, but could not find another place to go. Edmund was visible in the unravelling threads of fog, unconscious of it, although from the height of her roof, Anna could see his confusion as he moved away from his over-large shed, which also seemed out of place. He was looking for something he could not find. His bumbling progress was mesmerising to her tired eyes; he looked like a lazy bumblebee. The sun promised to shine and she did not want to move. She watched him get down on to his knees to retrieve something from under a bush, and watched him again while he picked himself up without damage. Maybe he was praying. He carried something cupped in his palms towards the statue of St Michael, where Matilda so often sat in summer, but never this early in the morning. Edmund's bent posture foretold the imminence of autumn. In May, she had seen him out there at dawn, standing as still and upright as a soldier, mesmerised by the music of the dawn chorus, and she knew his secret; he had never queried her presence and she loved him for that. Anna looked out for the Golden Boy and could not see him at all. It was time to go to work.

Compucab's office was a mile away. A brisk walk, a bus ride, a run, sometimes a combination. She worked five shifts a week,

59

three nights, two days, eight hours a time among the employees, who were all treated with suspicion until they had turned up regularly for months on end and worked their unsociable hours. Payment was per shift and there was no payment for absentees. Each of them was a mouthpiece at the end of a phone, connecting someone who wanted a taxi to someone who was driving it. That simple. Anna entered a big, open-plan office with fifty people clamped like cars into their tiny, individual stations, each with a headphone, mouthpiece and screen. The seat at her station was still warm from the last incumbent and the phone rang immediately. Somehow the missal had crept back into her knapsack. She put it on the desk, hoping someone would notice, unable to get over her unreasonable expectation that the first call of each shift would be personal. Someone out of the blue would know she was there and would call to say hello.

'Hello, Compucab, how can I help you?'

Which was, she thought, a foolish greeting. There was only one form of help they could offer and it came in the form of a taxi. They were either phoning to ask for one, or phoning to complain that the one they had ordered had failed to arrive, and it was only in the latter kind of conversation that she had to employ charm. Otherwise tact was sufficient, even in emergencies.

'Can I have your account number, please? And the account name? Same name for the passenger? Do you want him to come to the door?'

Anna liked the fact that it was all so repetitive. She was hired for being a voice, which spoke first to a customer, then to a driver, while her fingers typed the details on to the screen, flying across the keyboard, faster than she could read.

'Paddington Station, you said? Shall I give you the job number?'

Conversations with the drivers were equally brief and she had trained herself out of any show of annoyance to become a valued

60

veteran after eighteen months. There was nothing else she felt fit to do. Few lasted as long, although some seemed to have been there for ever. Stop-gap job, well-paid, no questions asked. Inside this room, with its buzz of repetitive words, she felt she had gained approval, and that however simple the routine was, she had mastered it entirely and won respect. The whole place reminded her of a well-disciplined school classroom where no child teased another.

They were friends. They chatted in a scruffy, smoke-filled restroom at the back during teabreaks, where the opaque fog of nicotine was sometimes undercut by the smell of dope when Jon was there and he thought no one would notice, although they all noticed and no one cared. You could be a serial killer, a tur-banned sheikh, an ancient tart or a shepherd from Outer Mongolia and no one would care. Ravi read his battered scrip-ture book and drank nothing but water, saying little, other than into his mouthpiece, but he smiled at her, exclusively. Anna always wanted to talk to Ravi and sensed that he might have liked to talk to her, from the way he eyed her from beneath his fierce black eyebrows, but so far it was confined to pleasantries and a shy, mutual awareness. Instead she talked to Jon the smoker, and Sylla, the Chinese girl, who always brought some knitting, fash-ioning in between calls a succession of tiny white garments for babies that she was always willing to describe and Anna to admire. She and Ravi were the only ones who always carried a book. Perhaps that gave them something in common. Maybe Sister Jude's missal, another book of prayer, would finally break the ice. Amid the frenetic activity in the open-plan room with the muted buzz of voices, it was a peaceful, intimate place without scope for rivalry or rows. They could only be as good as one another, they were all paid exactly the same and there was a sense of camaraderie at night.

Which was one of the reasons why she preferred the night

61

shift, especially in summer when it left the day free to sleep in the sun on the roof. She found it easier to sleep in the day; the night was crowded with images, while afternoon siestas were sound, sound sleep. Anna did not relish sleep and the dreadful waste of time it was, did not even like her own bed and knew it was because Therese and she had spent so much time lying down a whole, separate lifetime ago: a great, yawning hole, which left them incomplete, gullible, untouchable, out of sync with the rest of the world, alien to their contemporaries and only at home with strangers. Warped, somehow. At least, she was.

The day slid by quickly.

'Good afternoon, Compucab, how can I help you?'

'I want a taxi.' It was him, again.

She smiled. 'Well, you've come to the right place, sir. What was the account number?'

'Haven't got one.'

'Might take a little longer in that case. Have you ever thought of opening an account with us, sir?'

Account holders had priority. They had to pay for the journey as soon as it was booked, even if they changed their minds. Drivers preferred them: payment was guaranteed; less chance of a drunk en route to an unpleasant destination at the far end of a back alley.

'I don't want an account, I want a taxi. I *think* I want a taxi.'

'Right you are. From where?'

She knew from the voices when the use of 'sir' or 'madam' was going to soothe. She could pick up the nuances of anxiety, inebriation, arrogance, loneliness. She knew that a twenty-four-hour number prominently displayed in the London telephone directory attracted the lonely and the cranks, and there was training on the subject too, drummed into them from day one. Get rid of them, quick; the lonely were losers, they did not have cash. Get them off the line; time is money. But Anna could not resist the voices. She was a sucker for voices.

'Do I need a taxi?' the voice asked. An old voice, full of tiredness and indecision. A voice as old as Sister Jude's and so reminiscent of it, she was suddenly moved. Probably an old man, staring at a page in the directory, wondering why he had picked up the phone at all. Nothing like the brash, confident voices, bellowing into mobiles, wanting transport now, now, now.

'Are you going somewhere nice?' Anna asked pleasantly. 'Only you might be a bit late for lunch.'

It was the slow time of the day, one forty-five, when half of the population were either eating or thinking of it. She had a sudden yearning to be one of those people, sitting in a restaurant, eating whatever she liked and the only person in the group who could translate the menu. The telephone line crackled with silence. A sigh.

'I never go anywhere.'

'Why not? It's a lovely day out there. At least it was. Is it raining yet? The forecast was for rain, wasn't it?'

'No, it isn't raining yet. Yes, I'll do that. Yes, I'll go out.'

'Will you be wanting a taxi, then, sir?'

'Whatever for? I'll walk.'

'Have a very nice day. 'Bye.'

A variation on his last conversation, poor old thing. Anna had taken calls from people who dreamed of getting out of the house, and used the calling of a taxi to fulfil an unfulfillable wish. Called it then cancelled it, because they knew they could not move. Businessmen called taxis in the middle of meetings as a way of encouraging the meeting to end, dreaming of getting away. This old gent, whom she visualised with grey hair to go with his somehow artificially refined voice, was merely muddled and she hoped he lived in comfort with someone to tie his shoelaces before he went out. The spookiest callers were in the middle of the night shift, one, two or three in the morning, lonely or drunk or drugged, forgetful of where they were and unable to quote either a meeting place or a destination, and even when they irritated her, she could sometimes smell their fear, prised information out of them with infinite patience and hated it when she had to leave them on the side of the road. They haunted the rest of the shift. At least the lonely callers, who simply wanted to talk, phoned from indoors.

Ravi passed by her station on his way and placed a paper cup of water in front of her, pausing only to smile. So much went into a smile. It occurred to her to wonder if they were the only two in the room who ever thought about God and she had worked out that he must think about God, for him to carry his prayerbook with him, refusing to part with it except when he went to the lavatory and left it by his phone. Maybe she should look at his prayerbook, find a clue in it as to how to conduct daily life better than she did. Maybe other people's scriptures were better than the ones she abhorred. She knew when people were sad, or tired or hungry, but she was otherwise ignorant. The sense of it overwhelmed her. She was twenty-two and she felt like a stupid baby.

In the slack hours, right up to a fortnight before, Anna would phone Sister Jude. Sister Jude had the dispensation of a phone by her bed, purely for receiving calls, never for the expense of making them. Anna would phone and tell her jokes, infantile communications to punctuate Jude's insomnia, instead of the urgent requests for information she had wanted to make. Instead of asking, *What was my mother really like? Do you know where my money comes from? Why, if you believe in God, are you so frightened to die?* she would say, Hi, Jude, it's me. Have you heard the one about the Catholic priest on the aeroplane just about to make a forced landing? Well, anyway, the stewardess asks him to do something religious to comfort the passengers. So he says, yes, I'll just organise a collection . . . And they had never had the final conversation. And Anna was suddenly, unspeakably angry with her for dying, severing that last link with what she was and what she was to become. And setting the hound of heaven upon her. She pushed back the wheeled chair and left the big room.

Outside, the rain fell in a soft drizzle. She stood in the shelter of the porch and smoked a cigarette. Now what had brought that on? A lonely old voice on a phone? The memory of the day before? The pistol shot through the chapel window? She wiped her nose on her sleeve, remembering being told, *Don't do that.* Once she was in the open air, the need to weep had turned itself into a runny nose. There were dripping trees in this quiet street. No one would have guessed the function of the building, which looked like a meeting hall without windows, dwarfed by larger buildings, not ugly but nondescript.

Ten minutes max, that was all that was allowed before the reprimand followed, in accordance with the strict regime in there, although not slavery and all the restrictions seemed perfectly fair in Anna's inexperienced estimation. Work and you were paid; don't work and you got the sack. There was nothing complicated about that. She had only had one other job with which to compare it and that had been in a shop. They had liked her there, too, because she could pick up the complications of the till quicker than anyone else, but when it came to customer relations, she was less successful. Telling someone that if they didn't like the goods they didn't have to buy them and why didn't they just fuck off was not what you did. It was the faces frightened her, not the voices. With voices she was fine: she could afford patience. Five minutes gone. Anna sighed. Time to go back.

And then Ravi was standing beside her in the rain, his battered copy of whatever it was stuffed into the top pocket of his shirt and his brown eyes squinting at her with concern. He seemed breathless, as if he had been running, and stood with his hands on his hips as if that would help to get the breath back.

'Wassa matter? You all right?' He sounded gruff and aggressive, more challenging than comforting. From this close, she could smell what she thought might have been cloves. There was oil in his hair, which made it shine. His sudden appearance and the abruptness of his surprisingly deep voice made her defensive.

'Course I'm all right, you made me jump. Go away.'

He did not move, stared at her so intently she could not meet his eyes. She never met anyone's eyes, except, in these last weeks, the washed-out eyes of Sister Jude and now and then, those pale green eyes of Father Goodwin, yearning to explain. Clove oil: she remembered it was an inefficient antidote for toothache, a sharp and pleasant smell when removed from those associations.

'You aren't all right.'

There are very few people who deserve for you to be rude to them, a sentence flashing through her mind like a neon sign from the many sayings of Sister Jude, delivered in one of her memorably mild, generalised remonstrances, such as, *Treat people as you would like to be treated*. Strange how the epithets of an old woman had come to predominate, even to be ignored. Anna smiled apologetically, thought of a shortcut to an explanation in a form anyone might understand.

'Nah, sorry. Only my aunt died, you see. Bit upset, that's all.'

He nodded gravely, sat on the step beside her. 'Walk you home later?' he asked.

Again, the voice startled her with its depth, while the words sounded like the sort of invitation a ten-year-old might risk at school before they knew the tyranny of teasing, and that was what they would look like too if he did walk her home, two little kids walking home hand in hand down a tree-lined avenue, like something from a dimly remembered advert for Start Rite shoes. And then, a more uncomfortable thought: how did he know that she walked home, or that home was within walking distance? Was he psychic, was he guessing, or was he the one who followed her? She decided, in a fraction of a second, that it did not matter if he was, might even be nice, but she still spoke sharply.

66

'No, thanks.' The thanks sounded lame, the rejection immediate. He shrugged, in that 'No offence taken' kind of way a teenager might think they had perfected to hide wounded pride, but that was only a guess. He was almost as small as she was, at least when they were sitting down.

'Can I tell you something?' he said, ignoring the knock-back. 'There is always something you can do when you're sad. You can always pray. I find it works best. For me.'

This advice suddenly seemed hysterically funny. Anna threw back her head and laughed loudly.

'Does it work?'

'What do you mean, work? You have brought your book of prayer with you yesterday and today. I noticed.'

She took a deep breath. 'I meant does it *work*? As in getting you what you want. Do you get what you ask for after you've prayed for it?'

He shook his head, puzzled. 'We do not pray to ask for *things*. We pray for guidance.'

'Yeah, right,' she said sharply. 'Like those Muslims bombing New York. Guide this plane for me, God. Let's take out a few thousand. Must have been one helluva powerful prayer.'

She heard his sharp intake of breath, listened to it exhale in a patient sigh.

'Why should a Muslim understand a terrorist murderer any more than a Christian understands an IRA bomber? I am Hindu, by the way. You and I are the freaks who carry prayer books. And I was worried about you.'

It was a surreal conversation to be having on the steps of Compucabs telephone exchange.

'Yeah, well. Right. We'd better get back to work.'

'Walk you home?' he repeated.

'All right,' she said. 'That'd be nice.'

CHAPTER FOUR

This wasn't nice. It wasn't nice at all.

'Father! It's you! I'm sent to collect you for the meeting. So you wouldn't be late. I'm to give you a lift.'

On that evening, Christopher Goodwin would rather have walked through the valley of death. His heart sank as he stood at the door, looking down at the squashed face of Sister Margaret, who wore her veil halfway down her forehead like a helmet, forcing her eyebrows into a frown which was at odds with her smile. Her control of the red Volkswagen made it a death trap. His TV muttered in the background with the soothing noises of a cricket commentary. He was refreshed, if troubled, by his day away and Barbara was perfectly right, he *had* forgotten the nuns' meeting and his tedious role of de facto chairman. All he could remember was that he could no more refuse the lift for the mere half mile than he could otherwise have turned off the television when Beckham was about to score a goal, and wasn't it marvellous, the way that the obligation of manners and the desire not to cause even minor offence could make a man risk his own life without a word of protest. Such was the priesthood.

She winked at him. 'C'mon, now, Father. It's your last chance in this veh-icle. Barbara says we have to sell the car and that's a topic for this evening as well. What a shame.'

He got into the passenger seat and fumbled for the belt with a fixed smile on his face. Sister Margaret never bothered with hers, or with locking the car doors when she left it parked, so that it was a doubtful act of mercy that the beast had never been stolen. She made the sign of the cross, sang out a prayer as she gunned the engine and the car lurched off the kerb with a screaming clutch. At the first junction, he closed his eyes, waiting for her to slow down and indicate, listening to her loud humming, which was the only sound above the protests of the wrong gears. She consigned each journey to Jesus and relied entirely on His protection, a faith so far rewarded, apart from the time she had taken Edmund to hospital with his stroke scare and he had fainted in the back. Sister Margaret knew that Jesus and Mary would see her through traffic lights of any colour and five-point turns on any highway, as long as she began with a prayer and did not stop. They arrived within five terrible minutes. He opened his eyes as the car hit the kerb and he was hauling himself out like an animal escaping captivity before he remembered the seat belt. So much for dignity. He could have murdered them both. The relentless good nature and blithe optimism worn on the sleeves of the likes of Margaret this afternoon was so intensely irritating that he wanted to scream, or bark, while on another day it might infect him with a broad smile and an awful tendency towards platitudes, such as, *Have a nice day, It'll be all right on the night, Don't worry about anything*, phrases that were no use to any troubled mind. He hardly noticed the black and white tiles of the passageway as Margaret spirited him through, only hoped that someone would come along and crush the damn car before there was any chance that he would be prevailed upon to get in it again, especially after dark. And it was that time of the year when darkness began to make itself felt earlier and earlier and the idle, polite talk would be of an Indian summer to compensate for the disappointments of the real summer passing and the sky broody with rain.

He could imagine who would be at the meeting, and hoped it included Anna, to add some substance and enliven the usual dull proceedings. They were pseudo democratic, these ill-attended meetings, invented by Barbara and frequented only by those who either were too humble to make suggestions or might otherwise be asleep. He did not know why Barbara convened them or why he, as Chaplain, should have to attend with the usual smattering of volunteers not clever enough to find alternative duties. Damn, damn, damn.

When he entered the parlour, he was late and cross, and found, dear God and all the saints, it was full to bursting. Anna sat at a table in the corner, looking suspiciously demure and tiny, facing a laptop, ready to take official minutes. She really did look useful like that and he was touched that Barbara had found her something to do.

'Ah, here you are, Father,' Barbara said, beaming. 'And here we all are,' she added irrelevantly. 'Including Anna, who *insists* upon being helpful. She can work that machine that Monica's niece gave us, which is more than I can. Now we're hoping to keep this brief and be finished in time for supper. I've two motions to put before the meeting. The first is that we sell the car—'

'But we need the car, Sister.' The voice of Agnes rose, quavering. 'Shopping and emergencies and—'

'It costs about three thousand a year to keep the car,' Barbara said firmly. 'More, if you take into account all the repairs.' She looked at Margaret, kindly. Divine protection had saved lives inside that car, but had not preserved the bodywork from her driving or the wing mirrors and windows from the attention of vandals. 'Margaret is our only driver until Therese has a chance to learn, and even that'll cost money.'

'If I could make a suggestion,' Anna said, raising her hand. They looked at her in alarm, ready to tolerate until she opened her mouth. Today, the laptop gave her a role and the proceedings a more official status. For once, Barbara was pleased with her, although she never liked to admit they needed help.

'Yes?'

'You could do the bulk shopping on-line,' she tapped the screen of the computer, 'and have it delivered, all the heavy goods anyway. That would save leg-work. And you could get a taxi account, so that whenever you needed one, you just phone. You'd have to go mad on taxis to spend anything like three thousand a year, even if you all use them.'

'Excellent idea,' Father Goodwin said. 'A money saver *and* you'd have the money from the car itself to play with.'

'That's not the way it works,' Barbara said. 'There's no money to *play* with.'

He rebuked himself.

'And who would do the ordering of the stuff off the computer, which I suppose is what you mean by *on-line*,' Barbara went on. 'It was good to be given that thing, but nobody knows how to use it.'

'I do,' Anna said mildly. 'Therese does and somebody else could learn.'

'I bet you Francis knows how,' said a voice from the side. Father Goodwin turned to look at poor Sister Joseph. She was always 'poor' Sister Joseph in his mind because of all them, she was the only one who struck him as profoundly unhappy, on a different scale to the others with their various moods disciplined into an even state, while her misery was permanent and unconsolable, although he had tried more than once to define it and been turned away. In Joseph, he sensed a person who was not a natural celibate or even a believer; like himself, someone who had to fight for her state of grace.

'Francis could do it,' she repeated. 'Francis can do everything.'

He realised, with a shock of surprise, that she was drunk. Badly inebriated rather than falling-off-the-chair drunk, her voice slurred and her face mottled. No one else appeared to notice and, as he watched, Joseph clamped her mouth shut, crossed her arms and sat straighter, aware of the danger of saying anything more. The hubbub that followed her contribution deflected attention and brought them round nicely to what they were all desperately anxious to discuss. Francis. Father Goodwin was puzzled, a frequent state and not always alarming. Francis, ah yes, the garden boy.

'Can we sell the car and everything else, but keep Francis?' Agnes asked, breathlessly. 'That boy is a marvel. He's mended my curtain rail and the hinge on the door . . .'

'He mended the chapel window . . . no time at all . . .'

'He changed the washer and stopped the tap leaking . . .'

'He changed the sash cord . . .'

'He put those shelves straight . . .'

'And he *sings*, Father, he sings. Like an angel.'

'What does he sing?' Father Goodwin asked, still seeking clues, bewildered by the chorus. It seemed that he and Anna were the only ones in the room who needed them. The others were vying in the giving of praise.

'He sings hymns, Father. Beautifully. "Praise to the Lord, the Almighty, the King of all nations" and "I know this my Redeemer lives" . . .'

'And how he works. Like a wee slave.'

He scanned the faces, alive with enthusiasm, and succumbed to the slow realisation that in the course of a day, this boy Francis had been elevated to the level of a saint, into that dizzy realm of sanctified indispensability, which he himself had never occupied.

72

A talented lad with a screwdriver and a bag of nails. It annoyed him. Only Matilda sat silent, counting the beads of her rosary, slower to believe in miracles.

'Sisters,' Barbara said, 'Francis is a temporary worker, brought in by Edmund. We cannot possibly afford to keep them both. And we cannot let Edmund go.'

She looked at the priest for confirmation. He nodded.

'Besides,' she added, 'he's a young man and he wouldn't stay for long. They never do.'

'He said he would stay as long as we needed,' Agnes said.

There was a silence, in which the priest detected disappointment rather than mutiny and wished that excitement came to them more naturally than resignation. He glanced at Joseph and wondered how the hell she had got hold of the drink or who had given it to her. Matilda gazed sadly in the same direction. Joseph kept her eyes on the ground.

'But he'll be here for a few days?' someone asked, hopefully.

'Yes. Not tomorrow. He's away to see his mother. A good boy.'

Again, that chorus of approval.

'You should get about five thousand for the car,' Anna said, flatly. 'I looked up the prices and Father Goodwin could announce it in church. It'll go by the end of the day, for cash.'

Something had been accomplished. The buzz was satisfying.

Over the heads, Anna looked at Father Goodwin and smiled. A real smile, not the usual perfunctory thing, warm enough to have a temporary effect on the acute feeling of unease that had suddenly engulfed him even as he tried to fathom the source of it in the bustle of departures. It was his own, self-taught custom, which owed less to religious discipline than to necessity, that he should control the uncertainties of his temper by asking himself why, at any given time, should he feel as he did. Am I hurt to have another man praised to the skies and my presence ignored? Am I upset by that dreadful car journey? Is my blood sugar low?

Am I an old man who hates change, even for the better, or am I worried by the fact that I must soon have this serious conversation with Anna and I dread it? Or has it occurred to me that the only person who could have fed poor Joseph with her own poison would be this gardening boy, because Barbara scarcely lets her out?

The meeting broke, as inconclusively as always. There was a drift towards supper. He was invited and refused; they had no time for him really. He walked through and into the garden, looking for Anna, hoping she had gone. Or maybe to find some trace of the miracle worker, Francis. The garden soothed him. It was exactly as a garden should be, with a small area of scarcely tamed ground leading on to a labyrinth, a total contrast to Kay's garden. It was, he thought, a garden to the greater glory of God, because, like the Garden of Eden, it might well contain a serpent or two and of itself it revealed to man his own inadequacy in the face of nature. At least it did if the man in control was Edmund.

> The kiss of the sun for pardon
> The song of the birds for mirth,
> One is nearer God's heart in a garden
> Than anywhere else on earth.

Surely there was a tune to go with that? He began to hum. Halfway between the beginning and the end of this garden, from the point when he met that hideous statue of St Michael, only dignified in his own eyes by the amount of lichen obscuring the details of the figure, he realised that a person in search of hygienised nature in the middle of a city might be better off in the park. Indeed, that was where most of the Sisters tended to go, and with the park so near, perhaps the garden really was a waste. There was always the suspicion that Edmund let it run riot in order to deter intruders, to make life uncomfortable, since he was an awkward bugger, who might also be a breeder of rare spiders for all he knew. There was a sort of nurture going on here, which was difficult to detect. The path was swept, the bindweed under control and the shrubs were healthy. There was an interesting variety of plants of what Father Goodwin would have called the jungle variety, based only on his reading of the style sections of magazines where he so often looked and admired, the better to be able to hold informed conversations with the increasingly rich end of his parish when he visited their houses. He sighed as he pushed aside the fronds of a fern, disliking the feel of it while acknowledging that it was handsome in a savage kind of way. Whatever had happened to lawns and roses? The sigh was on account of his inability to stop his thoughts hopping about like so many baby frogs – or more like errant toads, he told himself, because down near the bottom of this garden, he was remembering that it had shocked him to realise he preferred to visit the houses and apartments of the rich, not only for the many pleasures of looking at their arrangements, but because it was usually easier on the spirit. If the rich were in spiritual need, he was rarely the only source to which they looked. They looked also towards doctors and psychiatrists and new age gurus, or they cured themselves, while the poor of the parish sometimes reached towards him like drowning men and he the only one to save them from hell. The only one who could fill in a form, contact a relative, claim housing benefit and tell them how to get legal aid and avoid deportation, or evict a violent husband, while he, so often, would have to shake his head and say, I cannot do all that. I cannot keep you alive. It is the lot of a priest in a secular society to have responsibility without the power to influence events, let alone pull strings down at the Department of Health and Social Security. Or the Inland Revenue or the Police or the Bailiff. He paused and fished in his pockets.

75

Difficult to explain to a mother that he could not get her child off the street and into school and that all he could do was invite her to pray, be optimistic and resign herself to fate, because fate was the will of God, and belief would help, it would, honestly. He could only put her in touch with others in the same boat and mitigate the isolation. Nor could he tell the man that he was not going to die in hospital without his children around him although he had been called purely for the purpose of denial. He did not want the communicants who believed his every platitude, and on balance, was it so bad to prefer the rich? He had been a priest for a long time, become afraid of being considered indispensable, nervous of his inabilities in the face of raw need. It was simply that it was refreshing to be asked his advice by those who had other options, rather than being the one who was asked to throw the rope to the drowning man, while knowing that not only was the rope frayed, but it would not reach. Fewer and fewer of them called for a priest and he was ashamed of himself for being grateful.

He stopped by the fern, beyond what he called the St Michael Bend, and lit a cigarette. Five a day only, usually reserved for that blissful time when he sat in front of the television and listened to the roar of a crowd. If football had replaced religion as the opiate of the masses, he could not criticise since it certainly worked with him. God forgave everything, surely, even a priest who liked looking at the decor of handsome houses and gossiping about them more than he liked the insides of impoverished flats, and enjoyed spectator sports better than anything. At least he had no envy in him. He just liked the looking, was all, just as he enjoyed the sight of a beautiful woman. He was, he supposed, running out of emotional steam, wanted to be useful, but no longer wanted to be furious with pity. Compassion ate you alive. Someone was calling his name.

'Is that you, Father?'

Even being called Father irritated him. He had a *name*, for

God's sake. He was nobody's *father*, more was the pity, and he particularly disliked being called Father by men older than himself. Like Edmund, who had the same shape and reminded him of his own wrong turnings. But it wasn't so bad to be hailed by Edmund, who had never, so far, demanded spiritual solace, thank God, and seemed devoid of day-to-day problems, apart from his health. Edmund would want one of his cigarettes and was welcome, even though he should not, since the man had had one stroke at least. Not a big one, but a warning and not bad enough to prevent him from racing back to his garden, Christopher remembered, although, looking at it now, it was difficult to see quite what it was that made him feel so necessary. Edmund was wonderfully slow moving. Whatever had provoked the stroke was not his excitable temperament, but probably an unfortunate genetic disposition together with an acquired addiction for booze and fags and a tendency towards tears, as well as all those wrong choices a single life makes.

He was crying now. A big, sad, clumsy man, sitting on the dirty bench, which would always be in the shade on the brightest day, and after a summer of plentiful, if inconsistent good weather, he was still pale, with the sagging abdomen Father Goodwin somehow associated with the celibate and hated to see in himself. Approaching, he disposed himself towards sympathy and fumbled again in his trouser pocket for the cigarettes. He should carry more than his own ration: they were far more effective consolation for those so inclined than anything else, and he could hardly refuse to offer one when he had one lit himself. Without the cigarette, Edmund might not have known he was there. Oh, dear, how tiresome it was to have to manufacture sympathy instead of having it available in an endless, free supply. And to have those hopping thoughts interfere to remind him that while Edmund was a good soul, he was also a very plain man for whom washing was not a priority. It was easier to help clean, healthy people. A true saint would not notice the difference, but Christopher was not a saint, and he did.

'What ails you, Edmund?' he asked, heartily, sitting beside him and patting his thigh with his left hand, determined not to relinquish the cigarette. Then he looked down at Edmund's big feet, preparing himself to meet his eyes, and he could see exactly what was making the man cry. Within a yard were four bird corpses, blackbirds, he guessed without knowing one from another, although a closer glance showed them to be different sizes, and, it followed, different breeds. The cigarette dropped from his fingers and he brushed it away.

'Will you bless them, Father?' Edmund asked, calmly. 'Before I bury them?'

'They can have the full rites.'

He improvised. 'In your mercy, Lord, dispel the darkness of their night. Let their household so sleep in peace, that at the dawn of a new day, they may, with joy, awaken in your name. Through Christ our Lord, Amen.' This did not seem adequate. The priest moved to the corpses, made the sign of the Cross over each in turn, intoning softly, 'Upon you no evil shall fall, no plague approach where you dwell. For you He has commanded his angels, to keep you in all His ways. Amen.'

Edmund blew his nose. 'Thank you, Father.'

Christopher Goodwin sat down again and produced the cigarettes. Maybe it was disrespectful to smoke in the presence of death but Edmund would be the judge of that. He took a cigarette from the miserable packet of ten and Father Goodwin had an irrelevant memory of a grieving son who, when it came to the time to toss the clod of earth on to the coffin, had absent-mindedly thrown in a fag end instead. It was still grief.

'Were they killed by a cat?' he asked. Edmund began to shake. It looked as if he might weep again. He looked at the cigarette burning in his fingers and took a shuddering draw on it instead.

78

'They were . . . they were . . . murdered.'

'Surely not.'

'She was right,' he murmured. 'Matilda was right . . . She told me this morning he was a wicked boy and he shot the magpie and he poisoned these. What am I to think, Father? I loved him.'

'Loved who, Edmund?'

The cigarette was finished during this halting speech, which contained more pauses than words. They were as many words as Edmund could manage. He seemed, finally, to sense Father's inadequacy and pity him for it.

'Never mind, Father. The wicked get punished, don't they?'

'Not always in this life, Edmund, but often enough. Are you all right now? Shall I help you with the burial?'

'He's careful. He killed the females so the big boys won't come back to nest,' Edmund said.

'Who did?'

'Never mind,' Edmund repeated. 'I'd better get on. And so'd you, I expect.'

'Can I send someone to you?'

'No, thank you. Matilda will be out after supper. She says her prayers out here, you know.'

'Does she?'

'Thanks for the cigarette, Father. I owe you.'

The sense of unease had come back in full force, along with that familiar sense of being redundant. Feeling insensitive and unkind, Christopher Goodwin left.

It was half past six, the ridiculously early hour at which the Sisters sat down to a meal which he would have called tea and they, in their wisdom, called supper. Cold meats and salads at this time of year, augmented by soups and things on toast when the weather grew brisk. Some ate like troopers, others like sparrows, and the virtually bed-ridden group, which had included

Sister Jude, ate nursery food in solitude. These he was supposed to visit on a weekly basis at least, depending on their state of health, which meant that up until now, he had stayed five minutes with Pauline and Dympna (who, as befitted one with the name of the patron saint of mental illness, was away with the fairies), and as many hours as he could spare with Sister Jude, who was never asleep and always lucid. He missed her and it reminded him that he was too frail for further effort this evening, too much on his mind even before Edmund and his dead birds. He detoured to the chapel. Snatched items from the meeting had lodged in his memory, something about the window being broken and mended in a miraculous way, leaving a residue of curiosity which, when he was as tired as he felt today, remained the only emotion he could sustain.

It looked the same as ever, the same as it had been when he said Mass here the Sunday before and less adorned than it had been when he had seen it with Jude's body lying in state amid the floral tributes she would have enjoyed better if she had received them when she was alive. There was no sign that any window had been broken: the room remained quiet and serene, mercifully free from the excessive and lurid statuary that marred so many a Holy Roman Church. Really, he was becoming so intolerant, reaching a state in life when mere opinion became so callused it turned into a prejudice. Maybe that joyful anarchist Kay was right and it was time to look for another religion. One without recrimination, prospects of hell and promises of heaven; one entirely without decorative gold leaf. One actually shared by the majority of the population. A life without duty and the burden of secrets.

Ahead of him, nearest the altar, was Anna, sitting, not kneeling mind, but still in an attitude of thought. The sight of her was obscurely disappointing. It should have gladdened his heart but had the reverse effect. He slunk down the black and white corridor, feeling like a criminal for the second time in ten minutes, past the refectory and the sound of talking, out of the front door, which was for once unguarded by Agnes. He felt like Judas.

Christopher: named for a famous saint and yet there was no benevolence about him today, no blessing from that saint as he strode down the road, so relieved not to be in the car that he walked like an athlete in training, thinking of the legend of his name and how he would tell it. That saint was a big man, a giant who wished to serve only the strongest and most magnificent of kings. Now, one great king and the promises of the devil had tempted him into service, but their demands were so puerile they disappointed him, and he defected into the life of a hermit, settled by the side of a dangerous river, where his self-appointed task was to carry travellers across, in a humble but useful employment for his physique, until one dark and stormy night, while he was carrying a mere baby across the torrent, the child became heavier and heavier, until he stumbled and sweated and almost fell, in despair of his own strength. Ah, said the child, I am Jesus, the king you have always been seeking, you are carrying the weight of the whole world.

My dear Anna, Father Goodwin, née Christopher, told her in mental communication, which lasted him until he turned into the park, that is what it is to have this belief. It is a tyranny as well as a blessing. Please do not succumb, or at least, not yet. Let the hound of heaven bite at your heels for a long time before you turn and feed it.

It was a park of peculiar beauty, his frequent solace. As an added incentive for him to walk further, it surrounded a football ground for children to practise and he loved to watch them. Tiny schoolboys, kicking the shit out of the thing, sometimes indistinguishable in mud, playing in all weathers with no audience, no cries from a crowd, only exhortations from coaches and parents, and a burning desire to win in an orchestrated riot of energy. He never watched for long, in case anyone should assume that a dog-collared, cheap-suited man must be either a halfwit or a paedophile, although no one had ever thought so, as far as he knew. Paedophiles didn't chat to parents and yell themselves hoarse as he was inclined to do, but still, he left before the end. There was always a point in a game where he knew who would win, but it was a shame to miss the individual act of courage, the verve of the one who could play in the team and play without it.

He could write her a letter, rehearsed it in his head. *Dear Anna, Please continue being a pagan. Do not assume the mantle of a creed. Make your own rules. You have had the most appalling examples to follow, although you don't know it yet. Your mother, the saint . . . Ah well. Leave us, make a life without rules. Just make one. Do not kneel to anyone or anything. Never, ever kneel.*

And then he thought, what about all the other letters Anna must have received and Sister Jude alluded to? Letters regarding deaths, her mother's and her father's. What would she want with an old fool adding his own?

Inside the chapel, she did not kneel. She never knelt, she simply conversed, in the manner Sister Jude had suggested, without the suggestion ever becoming an order. The window was mended without a trace of the destruction she had seen, as if it had never happened, truly a miracle.

'He walked me home, Lord, but I left him on the corner for the last bit. I don't want him to know where I live, although he might know already. Christ almighty, is he serious or is he *serious*? Anyway, I might have been late for the meeting if I hadn't run. I'm sure you approve.'

She eased her shoes off her feet. They were all still at supper and much more animated than usual, so that would last longer and leave her in peace. Her feet smelled slightly from a long day in trainers, but the Lord would have to put up with that. This wasn't the climate for going about barefoot. or wearing a long cotton robe like a disciple.

'Trust me to find another God freak,' she continued, twiddling her toes. 'With a hole in the brain, but maybe that's what you intended. Anyway, I'm sure you'll be delighted to know I've signed all these silly billies up for a taxi account. Told bloody Barbara I could get her a discount, and as you know that's always a draw. 'S'what Catholics have in common, always after a discount. Poor cow. I can't get her a discount, of course, but that isn't the point. How do you feel about lies?'

Black and white tiles in the corridor. Black lies are bad, white lies are fair.

'You know the trouble with you?' Anna said. 'You're looking such a pillock. Time to change the garments and upgrade. Get yourself an image. Make them speak Latin or something, get back a bit of that old mystique that everyone can sing along with. *Credo in Unum Deum*, get it chanted on a single note by absolute wallies in pink cassocks, that'll get them in. Evening classes. You'll get all the anoraks who can't otherwise string a tune. Plenty of those.'

She rested her bare feet on the chairback in front, tilting it towards her, the better to examine her toes. Fine little feet, which did not, at the moment, seem admirable. Too small for further use and uselessly perfect, apart from the grime between the toes.

'I tell you what, Lord. You were my best fucking mate when I was a kid, and then you buggered off and left me. And I could quite see why, because you were never there at all. Big-time illusion. Why didn't you make us well? Why have I got that priest on my back trying to tell me why we were cooped up for so long and my father left? Does he think I don't know? Well, I do know. Simple. He was too bad and she was too good.'

She put her feet back into shoes. It was getting cold and she did not want to lose her sense of jubilation. She leant towards the window, stared at the mended pane, willing it to do it again, wanting the sound of the smash, sitting back with her feet warm, wanting to be home and knowing it was near.

'You know what he said, Lordy? He said, aren't you small, and why are you so small? I said, you aren't so tall, either, you're half the size of my father and what's it got to do with you if I never grew? He's called Ravi. He's a Hindu. And do you know what he said to me? He said that all Gods are good Gods and all religions teach harmony. Why didn't anyone tell me that when I was ten? Anyway, I kidded him about it. Aren't we a sad pair? I told him. Two people of our age, walking down roads on a nice afternoon, talking about God. I mean, how sad can you get?'

She considered her feet and turned her face to the window.

'Anyway, I thought I'd let you know that for all the bad stuff Allah's supposed to have inspired, I think I like the sound of him better than you. And if I took up with Mohammed, I could still have Jesus and the Archangel Michael. But it looks like I'd better look at the Hindu first.'

She bent down and retied her shoelaces.

'Speaking of which,' she addressed the window behind the crucifix, 'I don't know what you did with that guardian angel of mine. Aren't we all supposed to have one? Muslims have two, you know. I'd be no good to a Hindu. No point thinking about it, I'm too impure. And I haven't got the option of honouring my father and my mother, have I? He left us and she's dead. That shocked Ravi. He said Hindus wouldn't do that. Do what, I said, die? Completely fucking pathetic, he is, when he should have been saying your place or mine if he knew what he was dealing with, just so I could say I never fuck in my place.'

Silence.

She yawned and rose.

'Night-night, Lord. Take care of Therese, even if you do a lousy job.' Then she sat down again. 'Look, OK. I'm beginning to see something about my sister. If this is where she thinks she belongs, she'd better stay. If this is where she gets happiness, she's got to have it. And that means I do anything, I mean anything, to keep this place afloat. Understood?'

She went slowly down the black and white corridor. Agnes was by the door. Agnes loved to be touched and hugged, so on an impulse, remembering with gratitude her voice, singing so unaffectedly by Sister Jude's grave, Anna patted her on her plump shoulder and found her own hand gripped and squeezed hard.

'Night, Aggie. You should do some more singing.'

'Goodnight, dear. I'm a very happy woman today. Do you know why?' She pulled Anna down to whisper in her ear. 'My son came to find me.'

Ah well, they all talked in code, sometimes. God made everyone batty, not necessarily bad.

Back inside her own flat, Anna went up to the roof. The sky was clear in one of those perfect evenings that made her feel cheated of the day until she remembered the rain, and Ravi. The trees by the chapel window shimmered as the shadows deepened. At the rear of the garden, she could make out the figure of Edmund, sitting. Too cold for an old man to sit out as if he had no home; it was late for him to be there, but that was his choice and Matilda would be somewhere around until darkness fell completely. How well she knew their routines in the garden, although not what any one of them really thought, believed, needed, and she was suddenly humbled. If Ravi the Hindu paid respect to other, alien creeds, then so should she.

Down below, among the silent shrubs, she thought she saw a flash of gold. A moving head, standing by Edmund's side and just as suddenly obscured. There would be a full moon tonight and Anna was too tired to watch for it; she would wait for the new moon and wish on that. Her whole small body vibrated with a massive, satisfying yawn. It was so peaceful out there and she had made her mark today, spoken out and someone had listened. She knew, for once, what it was like not to be angry. Maybe God lived on the moon and that was his face.

'Matilda? Are you there? Help me, please . . .'

'It isn't Matilda.'

'In the name of God, help me. Oh, you bastard boy. You killed them.'

'And I shall kill all the others. The thrush and the sparrow. Destroy all the nests. You can die as soon as you like, old man.'

'Help me . . .'

Darkness fell early.

Autumn began with a scowl on the face of the moon.

CHAPTER FIVE

Thou shalt not steal

It might be the last hot morning of the year.

Dear Mrs McQuaid

Re: The estate of Theodore Calvert

Thank you for yours of the 8th Inst.
    This is to confirm that your tenure of the house remains
secure for at least the next six months, from today's date. As
I know you will understand, Mr Calvert's investments were
of the global variety and it will take some considerable time
to convert the same into cash and assess the tax situation . . .
Please apply to the signatory should you require funds for
the maintenance of the house . . .

So that was all right then.

It was only in the unholy light of a milky morning that Kay
liked the sea with the kind of emotion that was anywhere near
genuine affection. She was fond of it when it was calm enough to
look like something out of a travel brochure advertising long days

in the sun somewhere else entirely, where the language, the food and the climate were so different it was surprising that the humans beings had the same shape. The house was one road back from the front itself, sheltered from storms. She could hear the sea from there without being able to see it.

Today, it was warm, inviting and friendly, without much of a hint of the mysterious, which she did not like, and even less of a hint of power, which she liked even less. On a morning like this, it looked like a great big bath, with some strange jacuzzi effect going on underneath the surface. Clad in her ankle-length dressing gown of pale lilac towelling, shower cap and plastic shoes, Kay walked gingerly across the shallow incline of the shingle, shed the robe and waded into the water. Up to the chest in three steps, four strokes left and four right without ever taking her sunglasses off, that was enough, and emerged triumphant. The days when she might have stayed in longer and offered up the pain as a penance for her sins were long gone. The water was pleasantly bracing rather than cold, but there was no point getting chilly. Chilliness was uncomfortable.

Theodore Calvert, her employer, went swimming until well into winter, but then he always had something to prove. Either he was proving his virility, or he must have been a closet Catholic. What was it the Jesuits said? Give me a boy before he is eight and he is mine for ever? Even if he railed against that religion for as long as she knew him, Kay theorised that he might have been got at as a boy and that was what had given him that awful mindset, which she was still doing her best to eradicate in herself, namely the strange belief that discomfort equalled virtue and, by the same token, luxury bordered on sinfulness.

The problem about the open sky, mirrored in the endless stretch of invigorating water, was that it drew her towards it and made her think, even when breakfast was more what she had in mind. The lulling noise of the quiet waves, so welcoming to her feet, was the voice of conscience. The sea was calm enough for a prophet to walk upon it. She looked at her toes through the opaque material of the plastic shoes and tried to concentrate on the fact that it was time for a pedicure, let the towelling robe soak the salty moisture from her skin as she sat comfortably on the warm shingle, telling herself she would be better off in the garden with a less awe-inspiring view, but she could not move. Theo Calvert had loved the sea and regarded it as a kind of playground, while, most of the time, she thought of it as cold, wet and inconvenient. After he had left his wife, he had moved to the coast because that was where he had always wanted to live. He had bought a house big enough for his daughters, but of course they had never arrived, not even for a visit. Theo had been a fool to expect any such thing. Also a fool to battle for custody of children who were not only ill but easily old enough to make up their own minds. His lawyers had told him he was mad. He was the one who had left the matrimonial home, was more of the grandfatherly age and bellowed that all his daughters needed was plenty of fresh air and an introduction to sex. His daughters had told a judge that they hated him and Theo had cursed and invoked the devil and thrown himself into the sea for early morning swims in the bitter cold. If she had told him then that he was mortifying his flesh to distract his thoughts, he would not have believed her.

Theodore Calvert claimed that he did not understand any of that. The religion of his wife, which informed her motherly self-sacrifice, was anathema to him, and the sea would be his undoing. It made him brood. Kay dragged herself back into the present world by fishing in her pocket for cigarettes. Too much oxygen was bad for the body. She must look a rare sight, walking from the big house up the side road and sitting on the beach dressed like this, but who cared? The place had its fair share of eccentrics, of which she was among the youngest. It was a seaside resort that had always attracted the elderly, close enough to London for an easy train ride, far enough away to be remote. Why the hell he had chosen it, God knows. He said he wanted a big sky, room to breathe. She lay back on the shingle so that she did not have to look at the sea. Definitely the voice of conscience.

Why the hell had she accompanied him all those years ago? She could have stayed in London and got another job, although not on those wages. Calvert was ludicrously generous, one of the reasons why she had stayed with the damn family as long as she had. Stayed, and been indispensable long after she had sussed what Mrs Calvert was like. It took one Roman Catholic, however lapsed, to recognise the symptoms of a terrible holiness in another. A tiny creature, Mrs Calvert, with huge eyes and an elegant gentleness in everything she did. Beautiful manners, soft, solicitous voice, the quiet movements of a convent-educated girl who had never kicked over the traces, although her dress sense was not anything she could have learned in a nunnery. She made you feel like a carthorse, but she was a lady, and it would have been a lady Theodore had wanted. Kay stuffed the cigarettes back into her pocket, suddenly sick at the thought of one, pushed her sunglasses up on her forehead and down again. The sunlight on the water was so bright it was an accusation to her eyes.

Look, she told herself, it's easy. She had followed Theodore to his rich retreat by the sea because she would never repeat such wages for the relatively easy work, and because of her son. Also, to be fair, because she could not bear to see those girls so sick or watch what Mrs Calvert was doing or be anywhere near it, but mostly because of Jack, or was it? A better life for rebellious Jack. That was it. Bring Jack with you, Theodore had said, he'll only get into trouble if you don't. Kay got to her feet and turned her back on the water. No, she had done it to spite that dreadful woman who had begged her to stay, she had done it

90

out of solidarity with him and to please herself, the way she usually did. Oh, for God's sake, woman, you did what you thought was best and you still do.

Only, for someone raised as a Catholic, 'best' was never enough. What was it with them, she raged at herself, walking faster and faster on the way home, suddenly self-conscious about the shower cap, that made them such miseries? Not *them*, YOU. Hadn't she dumped the whole Catholic, nun-ridden Irish girlhood before she'd so much as looked at a boy? Didn't she poke fun at it? Didn't she take the fear of hell and drown it good and proper? She was thrown out and threw it out, been throwing it out ever since. What Christopher Goodwin had disturbed in his visit the day before last was an entirely irreligious, natural conscience, the sort that lived in the sea and shone light in her eyes like a torch, with a delayed effect, along with his plea that she should meet Anna Calvert and tell her what her father had been like, so that the child had a chance to form an honest picture of her past. In order to construct a future, Christopher had said. Excuse me, I'm on holiday, she said. I don't owe anything, I just do as I'm told.

She squelched to the back door without seeing a soul. A quiet place, sometimes too quiet. What had she ever done that was so wrong? She had not really encouraged old Theodore to give up fighting for his daughters and love her own Jack instead. No, that was *not* the way it was. That was not what she had intended, but that was what had happened. She had wanted so much better for sulky Jack. She had never meant Theo to treat him as a son. She was breathing heavily, the shoes rubbed. Definitely the last swim of the year. Her body tingled and her head felt light. She touched the key to the house, held round her neck on a piece of string.

Nor had she meant it to filter back to Isabel Calvert that Theodore lived with his housekeeper as a convenient tart and preferred her boy to his own flesh and blood. Now that would have added to Mrs Calvert's saintly martyrdom no end. And it was not true. Theo adored his daughters. He had their movements monitored, although there was little enough to report when they never left the house. He also had his wife hounded by every official agency under the sun and Kay supposed that, in the end, he won. Mrs Calvert was forced to relinquish her hold on her invalids. The children were, in a manner of speaking, freed, with liberty to hate him even more for what he had done, but it was certainly true that he had been fond of Jack.

Kay unlocked the back door and padded upstairs to the master bedroom, which faced the main road. Theo's room, which she used as a dressing room, sitting on the balcony to get the late afternoon sun and watch the world go by, such as there was. It was the main thoroughfare into the town and nicely removed from it. She remembered that the regatta would be passing in the early evening and the thought cheered her. As soon as the bath was so full that the foam began to creep over the rim, she wallowed into it with a grateful sigh, a brown face emerging from white bubbles. Once she was immobilised, she began to think that the bath was a bad idea. It was not the sea that played havoc with conscience; it was the act of immersion in any old water. Some horrible throwback to baptism. She sank beneath the foam. The fact that she was a natural born liar was not a new realisation, or even a shameful one. It came from a lifetime's practice of telling people what they wanted to hear.

Anna Calvert had been a kid who loved sunshine. When Kay had been deputed to take that ten-year-old to the park, they both ignored the command to have a nice, healthy walk and sat on the grass instead, with their tops off and their skirts tucked into their knickers. Therese would have been younger, giggling like mad at the mention of a word like knickers, hopping around them like a plump pigeon. Nice, easy girls, then. The scene played before

92

her eyes. Then she remembered the day when she had tried to introduce them to her son by bringing him along to say hello. Eighteen months older than Anna, he might have seemed glamorous to them, but there were not to be any dirty little boys in Mrs Calvert's house. Kay blew water out of her nose and reached for the bath plug. Surely they all could have played together? Maybe those girls would have civilised him. Crap. Nothing could have done that. Jack was streets ahead. He was eleven going on fifty and he never saw them again, except in photos, which Theo had in every room of this house. Kay finished the towelling dry (big, fluffy, indestructible towels she had persuaded Theo to buy), and felt conscience recede. It was soluble in soapy water, wiped away by moisturiser. Funny, the way she bothered about her skin and her appearance when her life was so isolated. Self-love was what it was, in deference to those advertisements that said, pamper yourself because you're worth it, and it was more to do with the sheer joy of idleness than attracting men, although there were always a few fellows hopping round like seagulls, making equally silly noises. Sod that. She did not really want the mess or the sheer effort of a man, and however much she might tease poor Christopher on his monthly visits, she only did it because he was a priest. If she was ever offered a night of passion, or a tumbler of Drambuie, she knew which she would choose. OK, she was a liar and she was lazy and she was sometimes a flirt, and that was fine. The only real question was what to wear.

A door downstairs slammed. Kay heard it, even with her head muffled in a towel, and she froze. Had she left the back door open, the fool that she was, while she was lying in her bath waiting to be drowned? She ran into the bedroom, naked as a beast, clung to the doorframe for comfort. The wind must have taken the patio door and slammed it shut, that would be what it was. She was not a housekeeper for nothing; she was paranoid about security. She knew she had left no doors open, and there was not the slightest breeze. Kay listened, waiting for the sound of footsteps, of breathing, a cough. Waited two whole minutes, getting cold. Nothing, until she heard the reassuring sound of a car passing in the road. Pulling on her gown, she tiptoed to the top of the stairs and sniffed the air. All she could smell was the familiar emptiness of the house, free from anything but the lingering scent of bubble bath. She must stop behaving like this, reacting so dramatically to sudden sounds. It was an old house; it had a language of its own. Let other silly women become neurotic about living alone; she loved it and she was not going to be one of them. Kay thumped down the corridor to her own room at the back, reminding herself it was the regatta today, so she would enter into the spirit of the town's annual celebration and wear something just a bit festive. Sex was too much trouble for words, but she did like to be admired, and the balcony of Theo's room was a ringside seat for the carnival parade.

She had made her own room pretty as a picture. Pastel wallpaper with a flowered border, toning colours on the deep flounce of her bed, frilled net curtains of snowy white beneath the pale velvet of the heavier drapes, which she pulled at night. A series of flower prints on the walls and a dressing table with the legs hidden by lace. She made her bed and realigned the decorative cushions as soon as she got out of it in the morning, so that whenever she came back into the room, it would look as she liked to see it, as sweet as it was orderly. Not now.

The differences were small, but significant. One of the pictures was crooked, as if someone had brushed by. There was a bottom-shaped indentation on the bed. The top drawer of the chest was half-open. She felt sick, made herself breathe slowly. Someone had been here and she thought she knew who it was. He had been, he was gone and he would be back.

Just a kid looking for money.

For letters, for papers, for something.

For her.

Like before.

Today was the afternoon shift. Anna could have slept far longer if the blind in her attic room blocked out the light. She lay where she was, torn between curling herself back into sleep and the compulsion to find the source of the light and bask in it. Summer was ending, the heat of the sun was rationed, wasting it was tantamount to a sin and getting up, putting on shorts and T-shirt to climb on to the roof, was almost a duty. She hauled up a sleeping bag and a cup of coffee. Sleep could be resumed in the sun. It was a grumpy pleasure. First, she examined the view. A ritualistic prowl around the small space of the roof, as if she were a sentry patrolling the ramparts of a castle.

The road at the front was fully awake. The newsagent was open, water was being sloshed over the pavement in front of the bar, two people waited at the bus stop. The sound of cars was pleasant from this distance. Leaning over, she could see a figure emerge from the main entrance of the block and walk away purposefully. What other people did all day was a subject of intense curiosity. They were all trained for life in ways she was not and it was better not to make comparisons, but few of them were as free as she was. Looking down at the bustle of the street below, she wondered how she would ever explain to Ravi how or why it was her rent was paid until the end of the year by some blood money arrangement set up by her father before he drowned and how she had no choice but to accept it because she could not possibly live anywhere else. She had to be close to Therese. It was a lovely day, and that, for the moment, was all that mattered. Anna yawned, clasped her hands above her head, and stretched as far as she could, rotating her hips, unknotting sleepy joints and enjoying the sensation. She would do the exercises later. The bathroom towel rail served as a barre and the bedroom as a gymnasium. All she needed was a floor. She had to be strong for the day when Therese would need her again.

With looser limbs, she moved round to the other side of the roof and looked down into the convent garden. The trees were turning autumn coloured; soon there would be bare branches rattling against the chapel windows with their own music and there would be the carpet of leaves, which she had seen the year before and which Edmund would be slow to clear. When it was done, and the leaves were dry, he would pick a grey day and take the risk of lighting a delicious fire, forbidden in a smoke-free zone, and all the more exciting. She recalled from last year, in her first autumn here, her delight in the pure smoke, which rose and drifted away across her roof. What harm in burning leaves, instead of piling them into bags for someone else to do? She would offer to help this year, unless this Francis, whom she had nicknamed the Golden Boy, was all he needed. She must meet this boy, whom the nuns had so taken to heart. They could make money out of their garden; there were innumerable things they must do if they were going to survive. Edmund would have to help. She peered over the wall. Why there he was, sitting on his bench, looking comfortable and remote from this height. She was tempted to call out to him, but he would never hear, and besides, no one inside the convent walls knew that she watched and no one must know. They tolerated her, but she was always on probation. Barbara was beginning to find her useful, but if anyone knew she watched like an amateur spy, she would be banished, with Therese's blessing, and that would be unbearable. Anna ducked back in case Edmund looked up, as if he ever would, he who never seemed to lift his eyes higher than the walls. Then she looked again.

He was sitting so still, in the same place he sat in the spring of the year to listen to the dawn chorus of his birds. He sat in the same immobile way she had seen the night before, with a slight difference in attitude, so his body twisted sideways, uncomfortably, the way a person might sit in order to have a conversation with someone who stood behind them. One hand appeared to grip the back of the bench. It was not natural to sit like that when alone, especially not for a weighty man like himself, who always adjusted his stance to accommodate his bulk. It came to her, in a slow, dark realisation, that he had sat there all night. Entirely against the rules. Everyone other than the Sisters went home before supper, via the front door.

She scrambled down the ladder, paused only for shoes, raced down the stairs, out of the block and round to the convent door. Left, left and left again, bumping into two pedestrians without having enough breath to say sorry. She stabbed at the bell at the side of the door, waited and stabbed at it again. She looked at her watch. Christ, it was scarcely breakfast time in there, they might all be in chapel or asleep. It occurred to her, even in the rising panic, which made her heart race, that she did not *know* what they did in there in the majority of time when she was absent; she did not even know what her beloved sister did with each of her waking hours, only that she disapproved of it with all the fury of a rabid dog. Where was Agnes? Where was anyone? What was the fucking point of being at fucking prayer when you should be answering the door? Who do you think you are?

The door was flung open, with none of Agnes's creeping, smiling reticence, which always gave the impression she had slid three or four bolts and removed a chain to get that far and, however welcoming, would replace all the armoury as soon as you left. To Anna's discomfiture, it was Barbara, all bossy briskness and twinkling, interrogative eyes behind her glasses, looking as if she had slept well enough to slap down the nonsense of the day with a firm hand. The likes of Anna could be consumed before breakfast. To Anna's further alarm, she smiled. Perhaps this was her best time of day.

'Ah, Anna, my dear. How nice to know you young things are up and about at a decent hour. Although scarcely dressed, I see. I wanted to have a chat, as it happened. Come in.'

She followed, meekly. Another time, the tart reference to shorts and T-shirt would have made her furious, but she was suddenly aware of the quandary she was in. She wanted to shout, *There is something the matter with Edmund,* but yelling any such thing would be too much of a revelation to Sister gimlet eyes, who would be sure to say, *How do you know?* And then she would have to say, *I can see him from my rooftop,* and Barbara would say, *You what?* She was dumbstruck, followed in the draught of Sister Barbara's voluminous tunic, which hung from her big bosom as if supported on balloons, until they were both in the passage with the black and white tiles.

'Come into the parlour, dear. We've things to discuss. I've decided I haven't been entirely fair to you and you had such *good* ideas at the meeting yesterday, entirely in accord with my own. Of course we have to get rid of the car. The idea of a taxi account is brilliant. Are you sure about the discount? But what I chiefly wanted to explain to you, dear, is what Therese does here, because I've got an awful feeling you might not know.

'For a start, this is a liberal, secular order. She does not have to wear a hairshirt, she does not have to sing Matins, Lauds, Prime, Sext or even Vespers, although she is exhorted to pray, in a formal fashion, and we do still have the Angelus, because we like it. A lovely prayer, I think. I just wanted to reassure you, as her nearest and dearest, that she isn't in for a life of flogging and she can go whenever she wants, but I'm sure dear Sister Jude reassured you of that. Things have changed since your mother was a child. Not always for the better, but there it is. I still prefer the Latin, myself. So much more poetic.'

It was a virtual torrent of words from someone who was indeed at their best first thing in the morning, after her restless nights had digested facts and advice and spat them out as priorities. Anna found herself thinking, She's a kind old tart, telling me useful information, and dear Lord why didn't I realise that before instead of being so frightened of her, while still mightily frightened.

'Father Goodwin told me you were awfully sensible, and I must admit, I was slow to comprehend. But you are, my dear, you are admirable. Full of good *initiatives*. Was there something you wanted? Breakfast will be in a minute. You're welcome.'

Just in time, she remembered the vernacular of their relentless courtesy, which, in the past, made her itch.

'You're kind, Sister. It was just that . . . just that . . . I heard on the news about a bomb, oh not real, just one of those scares. Wanted to check you knew about it. I don't know what you know, if you see what I mean. It's very warm, Sister. Do you think we could go into the garden?'

'Jolly good idea. Don't use it enough.'

There were French doors from the parlour out on to the terrace part of the garden. Barbara flung them open with the same potentially destructive aplomb she used on the front door, impatient but efficient with all the clumsy locks that surrounded them.

'Such a nuisance,' she announced as she struggled with the grille. 'But we have to keep people out, you know, especially these days. As soon as anyone knows the existence of a convent, they're outside the doors wanting food and everything. Which we want to give as far as we can, but not if they abuse us. There's beggars and beggars.'

The door was open. That was what a convent was like, Anna thought, door upon door, upon door. The garden was like an escape to another planet. Barbara went on talking.

'We've got to make use of space. My dear, that's a buzz word, or do I mean *phrase*, years old. Now, if you have any ideas of what to do about this, I'd be grateful to hear, in fact I'm all ears.'

She had big ears, Anna noticed, clamped to the side of her thick, close-cropped grey hair like a pair of horns. They went with her bosom.

'Perhaps we could walk down to the end,' Anna suggested. 'Get the measure of it.'

'Good idea. Brave the bugs and walk the estate, such as it is? Yes!'

They found Edmund on his bench, by his shed, a short walk only impeded by the brushing away of branches.

Barbara saw him first and called out merrily, 'Edmund, dear, so soon? What a fine day it is!'

Anna wanted to catch hold of her sleeve and hold her back, but Barbara ploughed forward, delighted at the thought of lazy old Edmund being so soon for work, not wondering yet about who had let him in. A fly crawled on his forehead; another hovered around his open mouth, from which a line of dried saliva crept down to his chin. It was his tolerance of the flies that signified his death. Barbara waved them away, touched his cold hand without saying a word. She withdrew her own, quickly, as if she had been stung, then, shielding the body from Anna's gaze, she deftly closed Edmund's ghastly eyes and made the sign of the Cross. She was perfectly calm; she had closed the eyes of the dead more often than she could count, but never in these circumstances and she did not know quite what to do.

'I'm afraid he's dead. Must have been a stroke.' It was an inadequate remark, but that was all she could say, although she wanted to bite back the words as soon as they were spoken. She was expecting screams, but Anna was not to be protected. She had moved behind the bench and looked down at him. This was an obscenity, Barbara thought, suddenly angrier with Edmund than she had ever been. No girl of her age should witness death. Anna surprised her.

'You'll be needing to phone for the doctor and Father Goodwin. I'll stay with him, shall I?'

'Are you sure?'

'Yes. We can't just leave him, can we?'

'No. I'll send Therese.'

'Don't—'

'She'll be the only one dressed.'

She was gone, running up the garden with enough noise to make the birds rise from the trees. Anna registered the sound of their tuneless alarm as she sat on the bench beside Edmund's body. She could not touch him, confined herself to waving the flies away from his face and standing guard against the nameless enemy, which had already struck. And praying. *Kyrie eleison*, Lord, have mercy. In the silence that followed the chatter of the birds, she wished she had told Barbara to fetch Matilda, because Matilda was Edmund's friend, but that, too, would have begged an awkward question, even if it was one delayed until Barbara had time to reflect. The guilt was as acute as pain; she had seen Edmund sitting here yesterday; she could have intervened, knocked on the door. She tried to concentrate on Edmund himself, maybe speed his soul to a painless heaven and deny her own revulsion at this defunct bundle of oddly sweet-smelling flesh. She had not seen the corpse of her mother, nor had she seen Sister Jude; she had reeled from the impact of death, but of bodies, she knew nothing. The curiosity about it was greater than the shock.

On the bench, beside Edmund's clenched fist, was a small, gold crucifix on a broken chain. She picked it up and examined it. Cheap, but durable, easy to mend. She supposed it was his in the same moment she hid it inside her shoe. Thinking that if there was any memento of Edmund, it should go to Matilda and Barbara could not be trusted to do that.

There were light footsteps coming back down the garden. Therese appeared, carrying a blanket.

'Go away!' Anna yelled.

Therese paused, came forward with the blanket. 'Don't be silly.'

With soothing sounds, she tucked it round Edmund's form. Anna stood up to make room. They hugged, fiercely.

'Come away, Anna, do. You're cold. He was a good man, gone to a better life.'

The pious platitude made her blood boil.

'Oh, for *Chrissakes* . . . Can't you do better than that?'

'Be quiet, Anna.'

They stood with their arms around each other, Therese tugging her hair as if that would keep her warm, making Anna wonder, with the unexpected objectivity that follows shock, which of them was designed to protect the other and wondering all the more, because she had always thought the role was hers.

Kay felt protective about this house. Nothing else had been disturbed, not Theo's desk, nothing. Kay was sure she would notice and knew at the same time that maybe she would not. It was vanity on the part of a zealous housekeeper to think she would detect any other fingerprint than her own, when in reality, a burglar could cover his tracks if he was careful and refrained from the obvious such as eating the food. No marks on the clean bottles of the drinks trolley, but then, not even burglars fancied liqueurs before breakfast.

By late morning, after another bath, she was trying to make herself laugh, as well as tell herself that the burglar, with his minimal interference, was a complete stranger. A big old house with no man in it was bound to be a draw. Envy was what it was. There were several possible culprits, but none with a key. Crap. She knew the neighbours in a polite and cooperative way, which had been forged when Theo had been carried home drunk by the man of the house on the left. There existed between herself and the house on the right an adequate relationship founded by her never refusing to return a football or complaining about children's noise, even if she did try to clip their tree. They kept her house keys in case of emergencies and she kept theirs. Kids . . . that explained it all. Like the very first time she had an illicit visitor, soon after Theo departed life.

She was reluctant to change the keys. They had been the same keys ever since she came here. By mid-afternoon, she told herself it was not serious and all would be well. Little, bitty, pathetic attempts at theft were not important, a fact confirmed when she went back to her bedroom and had a sudden vision of little Anna Calvert, caught in the act of stealing. Frozen, she had been, that titchy ten-year-old, about to filch her mother's earrings as Kay barged in with the Hoover, the little mite so mesmerised by making her selection, trying them on and stuffing the favourite bits in her pockets, that she would not have heard an elephant, let alone the anonymous cleaning lady lugging a machine and wondering how soon she could get this done and have a smoke. Bashing the Hoover against the door and catching Anna, facing the mirror, her small face as pale as a ghost, the mouth a gash of her mother's lipstick and guilt oozing out of every pore, as if, at that age, she was even capable of sweat. The conscience of a child was so variable and so brave. It had the same capability of an adult in lust, with self-delusion to the fore, suppressing the native knowledge of what was wrong and what was going to be a heap of trouble, until the two came together in a moment of shameful truth. Kay had caught Anna at just such a moment and knew when she did so that the actions of the child would be treated as if they were serious sins. So, aware of Mrs Calvert in the kitchen, she had simply gone into the bathroom and handed Anna a sheet of loo paper to wipe her lips and then, over the sound of the Hoover, mouthed, *Put them back*. The child had emptied her pockets, stuffed jewellery back where it belonged, cast Kay a beseeching glance and run from the room after interpreting Kay's *and wash your face* with a desperate nod. This little vignette of memory cheered Kay no end. If she had found the little shit who had got into Theo's house this morning, she knew she would have done something along the same lines. Attempted theft was not the worst of crimes. Besides, the sun was out, and she could lie in the sheltered patio for an hour, and that made everything bearable and believable, all by itself. The day passed.

No, she owed that child nothing.

The light would be going by half past seven. The carnival parade was due about seven. Funny old town, this, she thought with affection. Everyone else has their sodding parades earlier. She got a drink, turned on every light in the house in case she had to come back indoors into darkness, stuck her amazingly sensible casserole, which had displaced another hour of the day in the making, into the oven, and settled herself on the balcony in Theo's star-gazing chair. It was rusted from the salt, but the cover was as clean as her hair and the air was warm. There was a thumping of drums in the distance. The carnival parade would be unsophisticated, amateur, a bit trashy, a dying but lively tradition, but it would be fine. On the second gin and tonic, sipped to forestall the inevitable delay, Kay reflected to herself that she was easy to please. You could take the girl out of her small town, but you could never take the small town out of the girl.

And yet, when the parade began, rumbling into view from the distance on its final leg of the loop around the town, where it had begun and got stalled an hour before it reached her, she felt as lonely as all hell. So what, it was simply one of those days when cheerful things were depressing and somebody's story about having breast cancer would be positively cheering. She lived here, without belonging, without certainty, with a past she chose to

104

ignore, obligations, loyalties and a future that depended on promises. The first float came level with the window and the mood passed.

Such an effort they made, such things they revealed. The parade was headed by a Scottish band, swinging along as if they meant it. A man with a leopardskin cloak to cushion the strap of the enormous drum strapped over his belly, with legs like tree trunks, socks like a footballer and a hat down over his brow. Another man, equally large, with a wailing bagpipe and a red face, the last of his lament drowned by the stereo sound of the float behind, booming out *Yeah, yeah!* something to herald the arrival of three carnival queens dressed like bridesmaids with the maquillage of forty-year-olds plastered on teenage faces above corseted, bosom-uplifting frocks with nothing to uplift. Kay frowned in disapproval. They waved in a sketchy fashion to the hangers-on walking alongside; they were tired. Not as fatigued as the boys on the Boy Scouts' float that followed theirs. Five cub scouts huddled around a large leader, recognisable as Mrs Smith, an enormous woman dressed in feathers who otherwise worked in the fish shop. Another band, girls this time and far more alert, followed by the Kitty's Tea Room float, featuring jolly women sitting around a huge papier mâché teapot, sipping wine from china teacups and pretending to eat cake. No one could eat cake for an hour. They were nicely merry and Kay raised her glass to them. More carnival queens, poor little ducks in their gooseflesh-revealing evening gowns. There was a loud float for a disco, a small float for Julian's Kidney Appeal towards which she threw money, a nice float for a dancing school, which included sweet little tots with plenty of energy left to boogie to the music, followed by the rugby club float, with a whole lot of men dressed like apes, benignly drunk, firing water pistols at the accompanying crowd, who fired back, followed by another set of those wretched carnival queens. A crowd of camp followers followed either side of each performance. A tired wee show, with too much booming for her taste. Singing was always better. The last three floats belonged to the churches.

The town had three at the last count. Episcopalian, Methodist and Catholic, where she had, contrary to every other instinct, made Jack go, with his talisman of a necklace, and it was as if, in their annual advertisement, they competed in a vain attempt to draw followers. The first two had the best hymns, belting out 'When the Saints Come Marching In' and promising real joy in the delivery, even though their voices were hoarse. The flatbed lorry on which they travelled had no followers and nobody collecting money in buckets, the way the others did. The third float, for St Augustine's Holy Romans, singing 'Abide With Me' faster than usual, almost in ragtime, also had the figure of the devil dancing like a dervish, whirling and writhing in his lizard-like costume of scales and tail, his headdress of horns already gone with the effort of lying down every few minutes in a mimic of surrender, while one of the hymn singers, dressed as an angel, poked him with a long-handled, obviously plastic fork as he lay down, before springing up and doing the whole business all over again. As they passed her balcony, the devil got up and bowed. And then he spat. A magnificent spitting unnoticed in the split second it took for the spittle to land at the edge of the balcony, on her feet. A posse of three fat policemen followed behind, encouraging the tail end of the parade to turn the corner.

That was Jack.

Her bastard, Jack, whatever he called himself now.

A policeman on a motorbike looked up at her and smiled in admiration.

She smiled back, frozen with terror.

Wishing she could pray.

CHAPTER SIX

Honour the Sabbath Day

It was at the next Sunday Mass, six days later, when the convent chapel was open to the public, that Anna first saw the Golden Boy at close quarters. There was something peculiarly striking about him, quite apart from the obvious fact of good looks. What it was did not strike her immediately, but somewhere near the end of the recitation of the Creed, when the rest of the congregation were mumbling in unison . . . *we acknowledge one baptism for the remission of sins. We look for the resurrection of the dead and the life of the world to come* . . . while she was keeping her own mouth firmly shut, sneaking a glimpse at the crucifix and the trees beyond the windows so that she could keep herself from fidgeting and try not to show how much she was there on sufferance. For the reasons that it would please Therese, make a gesture of respect for Edmund, who would be the subject of prayers, maybe afford an opportunity not available in the last few days to give his crucifix to Matilda and because it was convenient for her meeting Father Goodwin immediately afterwards. An appointment for counselling, no doubt, heavily and clumsily described as an invitation to lunch. He had been hovering ever since the death of Sister Jude.

The priest was resplendent in a chasuble of peculiar beauty, which did not suit an old boy who would look better in jeans, as he led the congregation in the undramatic translation of the Creed, which he probably thought was infinitely better in Latin. She concentrated on the back of the head of the Golden Boy and worked out what it was about him that struck such a chord.

He could have been the model for a painting of St Sebastian, the soldier martyr, pinned against a tree and shot to death with arrows, only Sebastian had dark hair. He could have been a saint or an angel, that was it, Michael the Archangel, with an expression of suffering. It meant that he simply looked as if he belonged, he could almost have stepped down from the walls of a church in Florence, straight out of a fresco. Even in a shabby suit too large for him, he could equally have been one of the figures from the Stations of the Cross, which mimicked the same style of haughty faces and plentiful hair. Anna looked at the ground. She had made a concession to the occasion, as well as to the rest of the day. Proper shoes, little red pumps, and a long skirt, which almost reached her ankles. Father Goodwin turned to face them all. Cynically, she considered that full attendance at this particular Sunday Mass might be explained by the extreme brevity of his sermons.

Which would consist of kind words for Edmund, plus a homily on the nature of impermanence for a man buried two days before and not, it had to be said, extravagantly mourned. Anna felt she was the only one to notice, not because she had really known him, but because she had seen him and it came on top of another death. For the community as a whole, it seemed to be a bit of a relief, but then if death was merely a rite of passage to heaven, they could take it as a mere blip in infinity. She tried to imagine Edmund's lumbering form suddenly transformed into a lithe body fluttering about with wings, like the birds in the garden, and stifled a smile. It was funny and it helped to suppress the notion that Edmund's dying was a blessing to the dear Sisters, because now they could have Francis, instead. She hoped in his early morning Mass at the parish church, Father Goodwin had remembered to mention that the convent car was for sale.

In the early stage of the Mass, there was the rite of penance. *I confess to Almighty God, to you, my brothers and sisters, that I have sinned through my own fault, my own fault, my most grievous fault . . .* She could no more say that aloud either, than she could fly over the moon. Sin was an inexplicable concept in her interpretation of the catechism, because it seemed to have so little to do with the causing of harm, and surely a sin demanding penance and forgiveness should at least have done that. When she, as a newly emancipated twenty-year-old, had hunted down a couple of men a week until she had systematically rid herself of her virginity, simply to find out what it was like and prove that she could, there didn't seem to be any harm to anyone. It had been a curiously impersonal exercise and she could not see how it qualified as sin. All she had done was read a couple of books about it, then went out and did it, because that's what everyone did and it was easy if you weren't fussy and got drunk first. Lord, she addressed the window, You're a repressive old git. Let me know what sin is before I do worse to find out. That was the difference between her and Therese. Same upbringing, same shackles of love and faith, but in her case it was like an inoculation that did not take, leaving this incomplete, contemptuous disbelief. Perhaps it was simply the difference between good and bad.

Her gaze drifted back to the Golden Boy, examining his profile during the moment in the service when they all turned round and shook each other's hands in one of those poxy little rituals she particularly disliked. A saintly face, rather mournfully handsome and sensual, making her shiver as she remembered the couplings of her experimental months without shame, but a sense of wasted time. None of them had looked like him. He was entirely at home in here, but still exotic.

109

Ite missa est . . . The Mass is ended. The insoluble mystery of the Son of God becoming man, dying horribly, rising nobly and making his flesh available with each consecration of the host. Bloody barbaric. How could Therese believe it? She lingered at the end, hoping for a word, but the chapel was slow to empty and the Lord was never available in a crowd. Sister Barbara was standing by the exit, defying anyone to ignore the wooden collection box fixed to the wall. There were no children today.

She met Father Goodwin by the front door, flanked by Agnes, who looked radiantly happy and ready for the lunch that would follow and was better than average on Sundays in case there were guests. Anna hated the way they kept the best for everyone else and the worst for themselves. Christopher Goodwin, freed from vestments, looked like a tired horse at the starting gate, wanting to run but fatigued at the thought of the effort. It had taken her a long time to realise that she frightened him and now she realised he wanted to get away from all this smiling goodness as much as she did. She crooked her arm through his, and led him out. In accord, they scuttled down the street, liberated, almost at ease.

'I got paid, yesterday,' she said. 'So I'm buying, OK?'

'Oh no, you mustn't . . . I thought . . . McDonald's,' he said, delighting in the contact, pressing her arm against his side, embarrassed about his budget for this, or any occasion.

'Is that as far as your pocket money stretches?' she asked. 'I thought we might go for curry and beer.'

The mention of pocket money riled him for a second, but that passed before they turned the corner. It was one of his embarrassments, to live on an allowance that never quite stretched and made him more than slightly dependent on the charity of others, not for dull necessities, but certainly for luxuries. He would never, ever be able to reciprocate the hospitality he received, and that irked him, particularly in the company of a young woman who needed a father figure in his estimation, preferably one who could say that the price of a meal was not a problem, unless it was inside his own, self-catering kitchen, where he produced for himself an endless succession of things on toast. Tasty things on toast, to be fair, and infinitely better than the ruthless convent meals to which he was so automatically invited. Toast and butter never failed. He could compromise on things on top in order to buy a beer to go with an important match on the telly. Two cans for a Cup Final, although that was always tempting fate. Someone was bound to interrupt. The thought of curry and beer made him weak with pleasure he did not want to reveal. This was a serious occasion, although she was so skittish, she seemed to have no comprehension.

'Lead on!' he commanded, feeling a berk. He was desperately hungry: Sundays always did that.

'I forget how young you are,' he said, relinquishing her arm because she was going faster. 'You won't have had the regime I was born to. If you went to Mass on Sunday, you had to fast from midnight on Saturday, which was all well and fine if you took your Communion early in the day, not otherwise. A good rule, I think. I've always kept it. I could eat a horse.'

'So could I,' she said fervently. 'We'll ask for it.'

Thanks be to God, he told himself. So far so good. Let her take charge.

'So how much do you earn at the taxi place, that you're taking an old man out for his food when it should be the other way round?'

'Enough,' she said.

The Standard Tandoori was everything it should have been, dark, dismal and almost deserted, with tables in booths that reminded him of an old confessional. She lit up a cigarette, offering one, too, which he thought it prudent to refuse and then changed his mind, to hell with it. Who was trying to make an impression on whom? He had known this child, spoken to her on and off, for over a dozen years, yet he did not know her at all. It was difficult to know how to get on with her, especially when he knew so much about her from other sources, Sister Jude and Kay, to be precise, their information overlaid with his memory of what Anna had been like as a young teenager, which was pretty, pugnacious and sweet.

'I'll order for us, shall I?' she asked.

He was touched to see that there was enough of that child left in her to enjoy her current superiority. He did not know where to start with this menu and it gave her an advantage. She was on familiar territory; he was not.

'Of course,' he said humbly. 'Unless you're meaning to poison me.'

She laughed at that, and reeled off a list of orders to a hovering waiter, who wrote nothing down and went away.

'So how are you keeping?'

'I'm fine. I thought this curry was a good idea though. Indian food might get me in the mood. I'm off to visit a temple this afternoon.'

'A temple?'

'As in a Hindu temple,' she said, watching the waiter pouring the beer into his glass.

'Ah yes,' he said, recognising this as some sort of challenge. 'Would that be the one in Neasden, or the one in Watford? They vary a great deal, you know. Each has a different character. I find the Hindu tolerance of diversity quite amazing. I wish we had it.'

He did not know if she expected him to question her about why the hell she might be venturing into the buildings of some pagan faith and pour scorn on the idea, but she simply nodded, satisfied with the response. The food arrived with indecent speed and they began to eat, with quiet and intense enjoyment. Looking at her eat was a pleasure. She was like a delicate little cat, making sure not to miss a morsel.

'Lord, I don't know where you put it,' he said, confidence restored along with his blood sugar. 'And now will you tell me how you really are? Just humour an old friend, will you? I want nothing, but I need to know. And if you're telling me that you're about to embrace another faith and run off with a Hindu, let me be the first to congratulate you. I've scarcely had the chance to tell you how sorry I am about Sister Jude.'

She sat back, relaxed, no aggression at all. How hard it was to cross the age gap, and convince someone almost three decades younger than yourself that you actually had something in common, such as normal human emotions. Then he remembered Anna was different, had always been at home with her elders, entirely undeterred from argument by the age factor, and had as Sister Jude had told him, an extraordinary range of sympathy for someone of her age. Don't condescend to her.

'Yes,' she said, slowly. 'I'm sorry for the conversations we might have had, and all the things she might have told me. Selfish. We had excellent conversations, but a lot of the time I raged at her about Therese. Blamed her for influencing Therese into the Order. She told me she had tried to stop her and I told her she was a liar. I should have known better. Therese is as stubborn as a mule and does what she wants, always has, and Jude couldn't lie. She was bloody economical with the truth, though. She held out on me, she always did. We could joke with each other, but she still held out on me. So now I have to think about what she said. Examine the innuendoes.' She laughed. 'I think most of this happens in my sleep. The thinking, I mean. I can't do it consciously, it has to happen when I'm not aware. Isn't that a contradiction in terms?'

'Like children, growing in their sleep.'

'Not that much in my case.' She leaned forward, eyes on the last piece of thick naan bread, tearing a piece off the corner.

He hesitated. 'You know, I'm a bit puzzled about basic information when it comes to you and Therese,' he said. 'Slightly at sea on some of the details. I was parish priest when you lived in the big house on Somertown Road, when you got ill the first time. Lord, it's less than a mile from here, but it seems so far. Your mother was devout, very helpful in the parish, but I was not, er, *encouraged*, to visit.'

'That would be my father. The sod.'

He did not correct her. 'I don't think I was paying sufficient attention. It's easy to assume, you see, that a family as well off as yours can take care of its own needs, spiritual and otherwise. Then I was away for almost two years. I had . . . a nervous breakdown.'

'Did you? I never knew.'

'Well, we Catholics don't talk about embarrassing things like that. Especially mental affliction, it's a terrible sign of weakness.'

'Why did you have the breakdown?'

Don't condescend to her. 'Ah well, that's difficult to explain, but I think it was because of a slow-burning realisation that I shouldn't be a priest, that I should be something else, and I got better when I realised that I had no choice, because it was what I was fit for and even if I was a square peg in a round hole, there was no better way for me to serve God. But we aren't talking about myself.'

'I'd rather you did.'

'Another time I should like to as well. Very much, but not now. When did you and Therese become ill? You were only a nipper.'

'I'm still a nipper,' she said, bitterly. 'But I was too old to count as one.'

Apparently unbidden, two large glasses of sweet lassi arrived. He eyed his with suspicion, drank cautiously and was surprised to find how much he liked it, despite a general aversion to things that tasted as if they were good for him. He was staggered with relief that she was in the mood for talking. Something nice must have happened to her.

114

'It started with me. I got some bad viral infection, might have been pneumonia. Thought it was the wrath of God for experimenting with drink and getting sick as a dog at the age of fourteen, or whenever it was. I just didn't get better, for months. It was like having flu all the time. Then Therese succumbed and I suppose, basically, we took to our beds. ME was the diagnosis, after lots of proddings and tests. We both stopped school, of course. Mum waited on us hand and foot, like a slave, bought us books so we could understand our own symptoms, chivied us along and it just went on like that. We were ferried off to hospital several times, but Mum got us out. She was wonderful.'

She swallowed, not liking this recall, wanting to hurry it up. Someone cleared the plates. Christopher could feel the spicy food, eaten too fast, percolating in his stomach.

'Friends from school used to come for the first year, but that stopped. We must have been incredibly boring, even on the good days when Therese could manage cooking lessons and I could read, which was all I could do, all I did do, most of the time. We were terrified of germs. Mum had the theory that if we lived in a germ-free zone, our own natural resources would make us better, only they didn't. Only prayers could do it. One year went into two, three . . . four. That's it, really.'

'And your father?'

'He was a bastard. Didn't believe in this ME mumbo-jumbo. Ranted and raved and kept on trying to put us in a car and take us to the seaside, which he thought was the cure for all ills, even when I could scarcely get down the stairs. Shelled out a fortune for doctors without ideas, had rows. In between work, of course. He was a workaholic to save himself being an alcoholic. Bastard. Then, about two years into it, he went, just like that.'

'Well, he had to work to earn the money,' Christopher said, choosing his words carefully. 'Did he just *go*, or could it have been, do you think, that your mother *locked* him out?'

She looked at him with cold fury. Such amazing eyes, she had. He almost winced.

'Forgive me,' he went on. 'Simply an idea, something she might have done if she thought he was interfering with your treatment. Preventing your development by his attitude. That was the time when I was off the planet myself, so to speak.'

'Climbing walls,' she said, smiling. 'I know that one. You might have been like us, wishing the illness was because of some big, dramatic car smash with plenty of wounds and broken bones to show. A noble sort of illness. Something to boast about, instead of mere paralysis.'

'Yes,' he said, delighted by her understanding. '*Yes*, yes. I wished I'd been mugged.'

She signalled for coffee by sticking one finger up in the air in a gesture that looked rude, but had the desired effect, without offence. Meals in restaurants involved a different language.

'And I don't see how he could be locked out when it was his house. He just went with Kay, the cleaning lady. We stayed where we were, only more peacefully, just drifting in and out of one long doze. Then someone came and took Mum away. We were dumped in a nursing home and we got stronger. My mother, well . . . my mother died. I think my father and the effort of looking after us must have driven her mad. It can't have been suicide, she was a Catholic, she would never have done that. Pneumonia, like us. Then we went into that hostel, you know, the one near the station, which was . . . terrible. We were middle-class freaks. I spent my whole time stopping us getting beaten up. Then the flat I have now. Some arrangement through Sister Jude, she would never explain that, either. My father wanted to see us then. It was too late and we said no. He might as well have killed her. We came back into the real world, clinging to each other. Then we were told he had drowned. Therese joined the Order. My mother had always wanted that. Are you thoroughly up to date?'

Five years, he calculated, of abnormal life. Of missed education, of bonding with peers, of everything crucial to development. He felt unspeakably angry. She continued, airily, as if it were not painful.

'At least my father paid for things, even if he never came near, and he pays my rent. If he's going to leave us any money, I don't want mine. That's quite enough of that.'

She folded her arms and leant across the table. 'Now tell me, Father, what do you think of the Golden Boy?'

He shook himself back into the present, stirred his coffee, the colour of treacle and almost as thick, laced with a small carton of cream, which splashed on his cassock as he struggled to undo it. He crushed the carton in his fist and accepted the change of subject. It was her party.

'Francis? That's a good description for him. I don't know. He's charming in speech and wonderful with the old ladies. Perhaps a bit too good to be true.'

'You don't like him.'

'On brief acquaintance, no. But I mustn't say so, because my feelings are probably inspired by an overpowering envy of his good looks, his physique and the fact he could get any woman he wanted. He's all I could be if I shed twenty kilos, rather more years, and won the lottery. Of course I don't like him.'

Her laughter made him feel part of the human race, glad to be in it. She was still laughing when she paid the bill and they were outside the darkness of the place, where the sun hit like a hammer blow. Christopher knew he was being dismissed and did not mind. They had made a racing start. It had been far more productive than he could have dreamed.

'Well, maybe next week, if you're free, I can do the buying.' Yes, for sure, for the sake of his male pride, even if he had to starve all week and raid the poor box.

'Great, you're on.'

117

'And do me a favour, will you? Once you've been to this temple, go back to the chapel. There's nothing wrong with making comparisons.'

She planted a swift kiss on his cheek and ran off up the road. He stood in the sunshine, touching the spot and feeling blessed.

Until he remembered the four years and regretted the little lies he had told, such as not knowing the bulk of what she had told him, although his knowledge was second-hand. He had known the history, only wanted to hear it from her. And he was wondering if it could ever be the duty of a priest to tell a woman that her mother, the saint, had been a warped power freak and that Anna bore a greater resemblance to her dead father.

There was nothing cathartic about confession. In Catholic terms, it was a Sacrament. At least once a year, the sinner, and they were all sinners, must go to the priest and confess his sins, honestly, omitting none of them and begging for forgiveness. In return for this humiliating exercise, he would receive a penance, a blessing and official, divine absolution, which was the same thing, in Anna's opinion, as a licence to go out and do it all again, confident of another reprieve. To whom did a priest confess? she wondered as she made her way to Compucabs to meet Ravi. She supposed he must confess to another priest, which would be terrible. Another priest would know exactly the shorthand most penitents used to skate over the description of their sins to minimise the shame of them, like a patient going to a doctor and lying about his symptoms in order to receive a more positive diagnosis. She only thought of this as she wondered what Christopher Goodwin did with the burdens of his soul, because she could recognise him as a man who carried a whole sackful of them, and the knowledge of that was oddly comforting. He was *nice* in his old way, even though, like all the others of that generation, he told such dreadful lies. It seemed, in the space of a week, as if she was being offered *friendship* wherever she turned and it was a novelty.

Ravi was standing outside the nondescript building, standing by a black cab, and her heart lifted. She had an absurd desire to thank him for being alive and having this ridiculous effect on her of making her feel giddy, like a vodka on an empty stomach, and all he had ever done was chat and walk her halfway home. *Is he courting you?* Sister Jude would have asked, and she would have laughed at the expression and denied it. *Don't be silly*, she would have said. *He's just someone who has helped me through a very bad week, and yeah, I like him so much, it hurts.*

'Hello,' he said, with a strange little bow to hide a very wide smile. 'I've got us a taxi.'

She noticed he was wearing a suit of dark blue and a white shirt, which made his brown skin glow like velvet, and she was pleased she had made an effort with her own appearance, so that the pair of them were distinguishable from the two workaday people who sat and manned telephones. And a taxi, my word. It was one thing to order them up for other people to take, another thing to ride in one. He ushered her inside. The suit was just right on him. If he had put a tie on as well, he would have looked a prat. They set off like royalty.

'So, how are you?' he asked, rather formally. 'Did you enjoy your lunch?'

She had told him about that. She had told him a lot of things in the last few days, although one of the things that distinguished their early relationship as far as she was concerned was that they so often talked about things outside themselves. Walking around and in the park was all they had ever done, but he was the only person she had ever known who could comment on the beauty of the trees or the sky or the shape of a house without any hint of self-consciousness. And of course, they talked about God – she jeeringly, he patiently – and they talked about food. What an odd way to carry on, but infinitely preferable to any other company. She was not much good with her contemporaries, never knew what to say.

'Did you have a good shift?'

He was conscientious, she knew that, so a difficult shift would affect his mood. Ravi wanted to do whatever he did perfectly. It was only a temporary job before he went back to college, but it still mattered.

'Ah, yes. Before I forget, a man phoned for you.'

'A man?'

'Yes, an old man. Wasn't sure whether he wanted a taxi or not. He said he wanted to speak to the girl with the nice voice who knew what he wanted, so I knew that must be you.'

'Ah, that one. I wonder if he ever goes anywhere. One of these days, I'm going to get his number and find out where he lives. Probably Outer Mongolia.'

'I hope you won't find this strange,' Ravi said, changing tack. 'Going to a temple. Perhaps there is something else you would rather do.'

'No,' she said, 'absolutely nothing.'

This was not strictly true; his suggestion that this would be the way to spend what was their first formal outing together had come as a bit of a surprise, but why not? She was odd, she knew that, so she may as well be odder with another eccentric who looked like he did and was the same height as herself. And then there was this taxi. If the expense of the taxi and the quality of the suit were all for the sake of arriving at his bally temple in style, rather than for her benefit, that didn't matter much either. She loved taxis. Old boxy London cabs, new rounded ones with wheelchair ramps, yellow ones plastered with advertisements; they would always be associated in her mind with childhood treats. They were the first things she had noticed when she swam back into the world, taxis, a slightly different shape from the ones she remembered. Speeding along in spacious comfort, without ever having to think of directions, with all the time to watch, that was luxury. If only everyone of her small acquaintance knew how easy she was to please.

The temple rose from the depth of indifferent streets, which were dwarfed not so much by the height of it, but by the style. It reminded her of a huge white wedding cake, topped with flags and viewed today with the perfect backdrop of a vivid blue sky. On the first glance, it looked as if designed for celebrations, wild parties, raves and spectacular firework displays. A millionaire's folly, devoted to decadence. Ravi was telling her all about the vast quantities of marble involved, the tons of Burmese teak, the years of workmanship, but she was not listening. The taxi dropped them near a vast, low entrance, which seemed humble by comparison. He led her in, holding her arm solicitously, as if she were his grandmother, his anxiety surprising her into the realisation that above everything else, he desperately wanted her to like this place. He was ushering her forward as if showing her his own home. It was warm inside, with the kind of warmth that would tolerate the wearing of either a coat, or the silk garments of the women in the foyer, like so many butterflies. He showed her where to leave shoes and they proceeded through the hall. The floor, even where wood gave way to carpet and then to stone, was pleasantly warm on her bare feet.

There was no problem about liking or respecting. The problem was not to be overwhelmed by the colours of the carpet design and the massive doors into the vaulted hall of the shrines, where the marble ceiling was sectioned into individual areas, each different from the others. She listened, without comprehension, to Ravi's low-voiced explanations. The room of the shrines has three doors, he was explaining; you have seen only the one. They stood in front of the statue of Ganesh, the Elephant God, sitting behind glass, brilliantly illuminated to show his crown, his small, wise

121

eyes, his decorated trunk curled down over his rounded stomach, one of his two sets of hands raised, the other resting on his robed thighs. The one visible foot was plump, with painted nails and bracelets. He looked like a God who lived well and bore the complexities of his appearance with cheerful dignity.

'We begin with Ganaparti when we come to pray,' Ravi said. 'He is the god who preserves health and prosperity. And next to him is Hanuman, the Monkey God, the warrior, who will protect the individual and his possessions from all evil. Here we pray about our daily concerns, pay our respects and make our requests. It frees us up to consider our souls when we pray to the other Gods.'

The Monkey God was as endearing as Ganesh, equally ornamental, but more aggressive and the brilliance of his apparel almost blinding. They moved into the main area of shrines, which smelled uncloyingly sweet, the floor still mysteriously and pleasantly warm. A variety of people in uniformly clean clothes moved around and either bowed to the deities, prostrated themselves, knelt or stood with a complete lack of self-consciousness in a private, public worship which seemed as natural as breathing. There was nothing furtive about this piety. He was explaining the Gods, Krishna and Radha, but they resembled, to her, nothing more than highly dressed dolls. They were brought food, washed and dressed daily, he told her, which, hiding her own reaction to the worshipping of graven images, she found endearing. Even more endearing was Ravi, standing before an image of Swaminarayan and telling her it was his favourite.

'Are you allowed favourites?' she asked.

'Of course. You respect all the Gods and there may come new Gods, but you will always prefer the one who suits you best.'

'Ah.' That was a revelation. 'I think my favourite is Ganesh.'

He smiled at her, bursting with pride. 'The choice of many,' he said. 'Come, I shall show you what might be more familiar.'

He was sensitive to her bewilderment and she was grateful for it. The more familiar aspect of the place came back into view as they went down the stairs away from the shrines. By the entrance was an open shop, selling pictures, books, music tapes and trinkets, which looked for all the world like rosary beads. Throughout the whole building, not at all discordant with anything else, there were collection boxes inviting donations. She turned to him, grinning mischievously, only now aware that this was a place of sublime happiness and she was allowed to tease him. She pointed at the largest collection box of all.

'This is familiar,' she said. 'This makes me feel at home. This tells me I'm in church.'

'The Gods and money,' Ravi said, gravely, 'have always gone hand in hand. Poverty is bad for everything.'

Poverty, chastity and obedience. With every will in the world and with all due deference to the will higher and greater than her own, Therese could not love Sundays. It was not that the world outside beckoned, but that the world inside was so still. For all the fuss of the preparation for Mass, the additional morning prayer, it was still a designated day of rest, where the afternoon and evening were an anticlimax. A day for meditation, but she found that meditation was better when interspersed with work. No one knew better how the devil breeds mischief for idle hands. She had not joined the Order lightly, or because it was already familiar; she had joined it to *work*, for the greater glory of God. The vows she would make at the end of her probation did not frighten her. *Poverty* did not mean starvation: it meant owning nothing of her own, and she rejoiced in the freedom of that. As for *chastity*, she could see nothing negative about it. A free body, divorced from its own urges and restraints, had more to offer the pure service of God and humanity, and if she was honest, it was humanity she wished to serve. She wanted people to be happy, fulfilled, cured, imbued with love and well-fed, and she did not see how she could ever do that under the yoke of some man like her father, and how could she ever fall for a man, when God had called first? Others could serve both God and man; she could not see it as an option, and besides, she had no real curiosity about the longings of the flesh. It was enough to be strong and healthy, to feel energy and sound bones. *Obedience* made sense. She knew so little, she must wait to be guided, how could she do otherwise? She would have to be guided until she could form her own judgements and she did not believe that this prevented her from asking questions, but she was coming to understand, all the same, it was obedience that was the problem.

Not obedience to discipline, adherence to the strict routine of the days, but to the dictates of others, whatever the impulse in the other direction. Following rules that did not seem necessary. She must look for guidance, and the guidance for this lonely afternoon was to read the words of St Therese of Lisieux and her contemplations of the God of love, which ranged from the obtuse to simple tips for coping with the vicissitudes of religious life. Therese turned the page. St Therese had been a contemplative of remarkable youth and holiness, who advocated the turning of daily irritations into acts of patience and forbearance which, if offered to God, would aid the world and bring Him closer. She described in the *Little Way*, from which her namesake read, how, when she was engaged in the laundry of her convent, she was always stood alongside another, clumsy nun, who constantly splashed her with dirty water. Rather than draw back and express annoyance, this Therese learned to welcome the irritation, suffered it and offered it in expiation for the sins of the world. Which might be easier if the water was warm, and the irritation unintentional. There was an apposite proverb lingering somewhere. *The patient man is better than the valiant, and he who rules his own spirit is better than he who takes cities.* None of it was making sense.

124

Therese decided it would be better to go to the chapel. God and his guidance were everywhere: she had plenty of experience of being confined to a room, but to go to read in a room entirely dedicated to worship must be an improvement. She had so much to learn. She had no belief in an entitlement to happiness every moment of the day; she had known this would be hard, but no one could quite know when and where it would be most difficult.

Therese wished she had been as dedicated a reader as her sister. It was Anna who should be in here in these idle hours, with her thumb stuck in her mouth, content to read and digest like a cat who slept on its food. In this institution, where the elderly were prevalent, the rule of Sunday afternoon was slumber. There was no Kim, no noise. There was simply Barbara's instruction to watch over them all and report anything untoward. This was the test of obedience.

She reached the chapel and found it chilly and empty. The glory of the place at this time of year was early evening when the sun hit, while her kitchen, at the other end, was favoured in the morning. There was nobody there, apart from Joseph, slumped in a chair. Therese was on the one hand pleased to see her, and on the other dismayed. It was not company she wanted, but another form of solitude. If she were to follow the lessons of St Therese of Lisieux, she would sit beside Joseph, listen to her breathing and let it interfere with her already muddled thinking, which was telling her that she really did not like her chosen saint at all and found the self-sacrifice that had once inspired her puzzling and repugnant. She sat apart, and after one, pregnant minute, realised that Joseph was snoring rather than slumbering, maintaining her balance on the rush-seated chair as a result of a miraculous accident. She had heard this stertorous breathing when her father had drunk too much and lain down in uncomfortable places, such as kitchen, landing, study, although her memories of that were confused. It had been a phase of his, not permanent, but etched on memory.

She had never known, for as long as it had lasted, when he was sick or merely pretending, only that when he was like that, he was unreliable, not available for questions or games, and Anna was the only one who could chivy him out of it and make him move. Joseph turned in her sleep and collapsed to the floor, noisily. She lay awkwardly, with her left arm doubled beneath her, her bare head with her scratchy hair hitting the floor with a mild thud.

Therese knelt beside her and tapped her shoulder. Then she shook it, so that the head remained still and the torso moved, slightly, as if she were pushing a dummy. Then the eyes opened and the mouth moved. She thought she heard the words 'You silly little cow,' before the eyes closed again and she made an automatic movement to cross her arms across her chest for warmth. The skin of her wrist, mottled with liver spots, felt cold to the touch. Therese shook her again.

This time she came wide awake and ready to fight. She levered herself off the floor and spat words and fury – 'Leave me alone, bugger, bugger, bugger . . .' – levered herself half upright and began to cry. Sitting there, sluggishly gathering her old limbs until she sat cross-legged with one hand supporting her and the other over her face with the tears coursing between her fingers. She stank. Of disinfectant and white spirit, like new paint, overlaid with bile and despair. The prevalent smell was soap. The smell of Therese's father had been whisky, with the same overtones of desperation. At a point in her life, it had filled her dreams, and become part of his monstrous identity. How often had it happened? Once? Twice?

'Who got you the drink, Sister?'

Therese found herself sounding like Barbara.

'The devil.'

'And what form did he take, Sister?'

She was becoming an inquisitor, sharper with every note, more furious as the weeping went on. *Poverty* meant no money for indulgences, *chastity* meant freedom from cravings, *obedience* meant adherence to a rule of conduct. Joseph was an appalling example, a disgrace; she was too disgusting to touch. And yet, she was also a crying, mortified woman, stinking with shame on a Sunday afternoon, pitiful and frightened in the place she had come either to be forgiven, or to hide.

'Who got it for you, Sister?'

'Francis.'

She thought of obedience and the way Sister Barbara would be angry. The anger of that woman was excoriating. Barbara would make Joseph squirm, but the rule of obedience demanded Barbara be told everything. Therese glanced around, expecting her any minute, then tugged Joseph to her feet. Humiliation was best not shared.

'Better get to bed, then, hadn't we?' C'mon, c'mon, quick as you can. It's all right, it's all right, come on, this way.'

Joseph was thin, but heavy. Her arm laid across Therese's shoulders was the weight of lead and the route to her room was long. The smell of her, particularly in her tiny, enclosed room, was nauseating. She lay on her bed with her arms crossed again while Therese made sure the water was in reach. With gritted teeth, she removed her shoes, brushed her hair and forced the window open. Joseph gripped her wrist so hard, she was sure it would leave a bruise. Patience: slowly the bony hand released its hold and Joseph fell asleep. Therese turned her head on one side. It all seemed to take a long time.

There were three empty cans of Diamond White in a polythene bag. She padded them out with a newspaper she found under the bed and took them away. The Angelus bell went at six o'clock. Halfway down the black and white corridor, Therese met Sister Barbara, cannoning in the other direction. They both paused, briefly.

'*Bendicamus Domino*,' Barbara said, distractedly.

127

'*Deo Gratias.*'

'You look pale, child. Go and rest.'

'I'm fine, Sister.'

'Have you seen Joseph? I couldn't find her anywhere.'

'She was praying in the chapel, Sister, just now, and then she went to rest. You must have missed her.'

'Now why didn't I think of that?'

She sped on, humming. Therese watched her go, half tempted to go after her. Whatever she had just done, it was not obedience. The walls of the black and white corridor seemed to close in on her. Disobedient. Could actions that were entirely instinctive also be disobedient? She fled through the parlour and out into the garden, relieved to find the door unbarred. It was a purposeless flight. The still warm air of early evening cured nothing. She wanted to find Francis and throttle him. How dare he? He could come and go as he pleased, he could work through the heart of the place, whistling and everyone smiling on him, but what he had done was treachery. Restlessly, she moved down the path, reluctantly and only because there was nowhere else to go. The garden was not a place she had ever enjoyed, not even as an aid to meditation, and after seeing Edmund dead in it, she liked it less. She only liked Edmund's shed at the very end, because it reminded her of one they had in the garden at home. His bench had become identified with a corpse, and Francis would not be here on a Sunday. Sunday was the day of rest. Rounding the bend in the path, she almost stumbled across Matilda, sitting at the feet of the statue of St Michael, arms resting on her knees, staring at the ground. Sitting in the middle of the pathway, enjoying a patch of sun and busy in the act of washing, was a large ginger cat. It was a handsome beast, with an undomesticated air, apparently immune from the desire for human contact, indifferent to Matilda and unmoved by the sound of Therese's soft footsteps. There was a chorus of alarm from the birds in the trees, strident and unmusical. There were no animals in this institution. For a moment, the cat distracted her and Therese regarded it with delight. It was such a pretty, powerful and graceful thing, she wanted to pick it up and hold it, stroke that fine fur. The cat finished its self-ministration, stretched and walked away without a backward glance. Oh, for such confidence. It made her want to laugh in admiration. Look at the thing, a trespasser and bold as brass. Then Matilda was by her side, clutching at her arm, in the same spot, with the same insistence as Joseph.

'Therese, oh Therese . . . a cat! How could he?'

'It's a lovely cat, Sister. What's wrong with it?'

Her arm was sore. She did not want to be touched and pulled and could not resist the urge to shake Matilda off, pull herself free of another old hand of surprising strength. She did not want the breath of another old body, standing too close and looking crestfallen and beseeching, staring at her, wanting something she could not give or understand. St Therese of Lisieux would have embraced her. Matilda stepped back and felt for her rosary.

'Yes,' she said, 'it's a pretty cat. Edmund would have hated it, but I can't expect you to understand, you're too young. Therese, my dear, when your sister comes next, will you ask her to come and see me? It's very important.'

'Yes, of course, Sister. Does it matter what time?' She was trying to overcome the effects of her own rudeness by putting warmth into her voice.

'Thank you and no, it doesn't matter what time.' She shivered. 'And now I think we had better go in.'

She spoke it like an order. This time, Therese was obedient.

CHAPTER SEVEN

Thou shalt not covet thy neighbour's goods

Sunday: the day of rest, without there ever being any rest for the wicked. Kay had so few yearnings of the flesh she should have been a nun, provided she could have been an unusually pampered kind, with access to long immersions in water, facials, sunbathing, pedicures and the general stroking of self, none of which was any substitute for her present, intense desire to be hugged. Embraced into oblivion. Kidnapped, taken away into a deep warm forest and hidden in a cave. She had been sitting in Theo's study during the day and wishing he was there. There had been something of the grizzly bear about Theo. He could snarl, he could prowl, he could hug and he could fight. Sitting at the back of the church and hating herself for being there, Kay wished he was alongside, threatening to bomb the priest and whispering heretical remarks in her ear. Theo would have observed the congregation and told her how that woman over there needed a hairdresser more than she needed God. If he were here, where he would not be seen dead, he would mock her for this blatant backsliding, this superstitious slinking into church in the silly hope it might do something for her.

Kay argued with Theo in her mind, telling him she was here for a purpose and the reason behind the purpose was all his fault. She was not here for forgiveness or enlightenment, and it had taken her five days to find the strength. A little Dutch courage helped, as well as the pall of boredom that hung over Sundays. She entered a bland church, brick-built Edwardian in a side street, surrounded by suburban houses in a similar style, east facing on the dark side of the road, so that it was never light or warm. It had been stripped of idolatrous ornamentation in the happy clappy days of the seventies, when a few tambourines and guitars had been the essential ingredients of feelgood services. The original personality of the place had never recovered. The wooden pews had made way for a shrinking number of seats, drawn close to the altar in an attempt at cosiness. The priest did his best, but he was a dual-purpose priest, who also taught at the school on the edge of town and campaigned for converts to his community with a zeal not quite marked by results, but characterised by hope and a distant memory of the Ireland of his birth. He still thought that a club serving lemonade and playing music until the ungodly hour of nine at night would keep the youth of the town from drugs, and believed that a float in the carnival parade would have them flocking to the doors.

In that sense, he was right. Kay was here because of the parade after all, although she was clearly in advance of a flock. She sat dumbly through an amorphous service she did not recognise; an amalgam of a Church of England evensong without singing and the Catholic service of benediction without pomp. Things had changed since she had last attended, apart from the predictable sprinkling of old devotees, chatting in the backlog of departure, waiting to say hello and goodbye to the priest who would be wanting to lock the door and go home.

Kay did not want to speak to the wretched priest; well, yes, she did and no, she didn't, because it was information from the

131

likes of him she both needed and dreaded. He was youngish, prematurely old, held together with a thin, vibrating enthusiasm, a stud in one ear and fashionable glasses on the end of his nose. A little oik from Connemara. Someone pulled at the sleeve of her coat.

It was her second-best mackintosh with a silvery sheen and she resented it being touched by any sticky fingers not her own. Facing her was Mrs Boyle, teacher from the school where Kay had forced Jack to go and where, against all the odds, he had done surprisingly well.

Probably, this was because of the likes of Mrs Boyle, a slab of no-nonsense woman who looked like a dour Presbyterian, but taught English and drama and knew that negotiating with teenagers was a waste of time. She ruled by terror, slaps on the legs and threats of exclusion from the school play. Kay remembered Jack coming home, surprisingly upset about such severities, and her own response, which was to say, *It must have been your fault. You're a bad boy, always were.*

'Ah, Mrs McQuaid.'

She was one of those women who never, ever forgot how to put a name to a face, and when she did, you would know the world was about to end. A classroom voice, which, even reduced to the respectful levels of church, still resonated like a stage whisper. 'I'm so pleased to see you. And wasn't it nice to see young Jack in the week?'

Kay thought she might faint. She felt her face was suffused with the single gin consumed before she set out. Nodded.

'Such a happy chance. Called in to see us, sweet boy, just as we were getting the carnival thing ready, and one of our stars went down with the flu. Wasn't it good of your boy, stepping into the breach like a good 'un? Played the devil to perfection! You must have been so pleased to see him.'

'Yes.'

She was not about to confess to Mrs Boyle that her son could travel the distance to what had once been his home town from the age of fifteen to eighteen, without coming to see her at all. And a complete stranger for the four years since, to her own, enormous relief.

'Doing so well, isn't he, but fancy changing his name. Says he never liked being called Jack. Too much like Jack the Lad, ha ha! He said he'd gone for being called Francis, on account of the fact that there wasn't a St Jack, and Francis suited a gardener. Bless.'

'Francis,' Kay echoed. A *gardener*? Him? She rallied and put on her chattering face.

'Well, Francis was always his second name. I think he sort of grew into it. I expect kids do that all the time, now. I mean, change their names if they don't like what they've been given.'

'They do what they want.' The queue for departure shuffled forward, impeded by an earnest man who was bending the ear of the priest in urgent tones. 'And he's far from a child now. That hair! I ask you! How old will he be?'

A note of cunning, in that bossy, Scottish voice, sensing her hesitation, waiting to pounce and exploit her ignorance of her own son.

Kay knew the game, tapped Mrs Boyle's handbag, confidentially. 'You should have seen the colour it was before. Terrible.'

'Well, I thought it suited him. Whoever would have thought he'd knuckle down to be training for a gardener, with a job in a convent, of all places, with looks like that? But he is in London, I suppose. That makes it different.'

'A *convent*?'

She recovered herself quickly, before her voice rose to a squeak. The thin priest had got rid of the fat man and the desultory queue shuffled forward. Kay pretended to search her pockets for coins, acknowledging the presence of the inevitable collection box. Things did not change that much. You had to pay to come in from the cold, even if it was colder within. She made herself smile widely at Mrs Boyle.

'He must always have liked you, Mrs Boyle, to tell you that. A secret, I thought. A boy like that, working in a convent, it's hardly *cool*, is it?'

'Well, I suppose it's all comparative. Better than staying in this backwater. Half his old girlfriends have babies already.'

Mrs Boyle smiled, knowingly. She was so sharp, she could cut herself. Kay was remembering everything she hated about church services, which included all those bitches, lurking with their poisonous information network. She was the next in line for that runt of a priest, knew his handshake would be as wet as fresh cod, took it, dropped it and ran. Mrs Boyle was one of those who could distinguish gin on the breath from the night before, let alone the hour, and she herself was in desperate need of sea air. She had got exactly the confirmation she had been dreading. It seemed a long way home, and although she was wearing the right shoes for the short taxi drive it had taken her to get there, they were wrong for the way back. Silly shoes, with kitten heels, under her bright red trousers. No wonder Mrs Boyle had stared at her feet. Kay tottered through the back streets, into the main street and on to the front. At the very end of a humid day, with darkness threatening, a mist had formed, blurring the horizon. It gave her the privacy to scream. Standing there, like a lunatic, making animal sounds. *Aaarrgh*, beating her chest with her fists, like some mad penitent, the *aaarrgh* turning to *shiit*, *bugger*, *dammmn*, without providing either satisfaction or relief. A man walking a dog stopped to stare at her. She found to her horror that she crossed herself automatically before she hurried on. *Francis? A gardener in a convent?* There was more than one convent in London, there were probably dozens, but she only knew of the one and was willing to bet that he did too. Big, bold Jack, who thought everything should be his for the taking, still never departed far from the places he knew best. He would stick to where he knew, that parish of his wretched, screaming babyhood where she had no idea what to do with him. A place of terrible loneliness for her, until things had improved, and there were moments, if only moments, when she stopped wishing he had never been born. Jack would have gone back to home territories when he was cast out of Theo's house, and that is where he would have remained. She had written to him, at a Post Office address, the last letter telling him of Theo's demise, but there had never been replies. Jack always had friends and places to stay. Strange, older friends, shifty men with whom he took refuge when he was still a child, acquaintances from whom she had dragged him away when they moved with Theo. He had seemed to blossom in this new, smaller school, his city streetwise aura making him king of the class. And what had her illogical insistence on a Catholic school done for him? Only given him enough religious knowledge to be able to fool anyone naive that he was a Roman Catholic Christian, if that would help him get a job. He liked the hymns. *A gardener?* A quick learner, with enough knowledge of pruning and such in this back yard to pass muster, but a proper gardener? Maybe a leopard can change spots, and Jack, *she must remember to call him Francis*, had found a vocation. A helluva strange one for a boy who only seemed to like nasty films, power tools and sex. The sky grew darker; she looked at her watch and could scarcely see the dial. It always seemed to get darker sooner on Sundays and probably that was her fault, too. She had hated the Church and all it stood for, added her voice to Theo's chorus of derision, but she used it whenever she needed it for herself or her son and that might be why a Sunday would always seem like a day without joy.

She determined not to break into a run along the quiet seashore. It would ruin her shoes and add to the fear, so she walked smartly until the road bent away from the sea and turned

135

into her own with the good houses and the street lights respond-
ing to the premature darkness by casting little pools of light every
fifteen yards. There were cars in driveways, life conducted
indoors, a child's tricycle of the kind she could never have
afforded for Jack lying abandoned on a doorstep. In his youth
Jack, no, *Francis*, would have pinched that and sold it. Theo's
house stood solid and comfortable.

She always had to remind herself that it was Theo's house, not
hers. Ignoring the fine front door as usual, she went round the
back. If *Francis* had found his way in again, she would have to
face him, but *Francis* was a long way away, being a *gardener*. In
the same convent as that little Calvert girl. Before she put the key
in the lock, Kay screamed again, *Shiit!* and then entered, calmly.

The golden Buddha glowed in the living room, providing no
more comfort than church, but the donkey drinks cart was reassuringly full. She patted the Buddha, which was really there
because it felt so nice to touch and she liked to talk to it sometimes and ask it what it would like to drink. The habit of talking
to statues was probably ingrained from infancy. Gin in hand,
feeling mightily better after the second scream, she went to
Theo's study.

All his assorted, unsent letters and the several drafts of that
wretched will. Letters to his daughters, returned to sender,
unopened, until he had stopped writing to them, preserving the
returned letters and their envelopes in date order. A few letters to
Francis (she was learning to think of him as that) also returned,
but not unread. She wondered if it was more insulting to have a
letter read, spat upon and returned than it was to have it sent
back without even the effort of opening it, decided the former
was worse. *My dear boy*, Theo had written to Jack, *I wish you all
the luck in the world, but it's better you don't come back. I don't want
what you have to offer . . . Cheque enclosed, which I hope you will find
useful. Please write to your mother.* The cheques were kept, only

the letters themselves derisorily returned. Talk about biting the hand that fed.

She sat back in Theo's chair, the gin refusing to remove the gnarled knot of worry, which settled in her gut like an ulcer and made everything taste foul. Admitting to herself that darling Francis could have got into this house with his old keys any time he wanted, time after time, months ago even, and she would not have noticed, or at least not after the drink or two she invariably needed before she could bring herself to look at this stuff. She was trying to concentrate. If Francis was gardening in the convent of the old parish, he wouldn't be let near the nuns, and dear old Father Goodwin, who said he was there more often than he liked, would have rumbled him by now. Relief coursed through her veins, and the gin tasted better, until she thought, would he, though? How long since Christopher had seen her boy in the flesh? Years, and my, how they grew and disguised themselves. The blond hair on the devil in the parade had even fooled her, for a second. She choked on the drink, sat back in the chair, with watering eyes. Francis, a gardener? What a joke. Why, everyone knew what Francis was going to be. A tart. 'A *tart*,' she yelled at the wall. 'A tart.'

She thought of him let loose in a convent and screamed with shrill laughter. A piece of corruption among the lily-white nuns, serve them right. Then she stopped laughing and began to shake. Stuffed her fingers into her mouth and continued shaking, swallowing flakes of her own rose-pink nail varnish as she chewed and considered the phenomenon of her own creation. Francis, Jack, a creature of the devil and his own illusions, the product of a rape.

She leant over Theo's desk and stuffed the documents back into their neat folders. He who sups with the devil requires a long spoon, Theo said, or was that Christopher? Her hand hovered over the phone. She withdrew it quickly, slapped her own wrist.

137

She would do what she had always done. Tell lies by silence. Do nothing, look capable. Now, which of the drafts of Theo's will had her bastard read?

Sundays had a blight. It was too late to gain entry to the convent by the time Anna got back. Not late by the standards of the outside world, only late because it was dark and they had been walking in the park for far too long. At least, she had. Ravi had suddenly turned into a Dracula, needing to be home as soon as it was dark, just at the point when she would have preferred him to kiss her, and then it all turned on its head, just like a Sunday.

'I have to go home. My parents expect me and they worry.'

She was suddenly, excruciatingly, breathtakingly furious.

'How old are you, Ravi? Twenty-two? Do you still get pocket money?'

She had thought the afternoon would extend into evening, that they had all the time in the world, and the disappointment was bitter, but she was beginning to understand that every hour of his day was accounted for in work and duty, with so few gaps it was a miracle he had ever had the time to walk her home. He could add an hour or two to each of his shifts, and get away with it, but no more. He did not say as much, but she sort of guessed, and although she did not realise it, envied him the omnipresence of demanding parents. She tried to swallow both her pride and her curiosity and failed.

'Do your mother and father get on?'

'Yes, of course. They irritate each other, sometimes, but they talk, and they love us. Fed us, taught us, tolerated us, were there when we breathed our first, so we must be there for them.'

'Whenever they want?'

'Yes.'

'And they come before everyone else?'

'Yes. Here,' he said, handing her a tiny statue of Ganesh. 'You said you liked him. I bought it for you.'

It was no compensation. It came from his pocket and was stuffed into hers, a small, plaster statue of a sturdy elephant man with too many limbs, a gift of kindness and one that failed to placate, although there was nothing to be angry about, no promise made, or broken. That bit was by the duck pond, where the birds muttered and nestled down with families, chirping and burping as the last of the year's fledglings tried to stay close while Mummy and Daddy drove them away into independence. Her envy was so acute, she was glad when he had to go. Even though she said, *Fine, go then, just fucking well bugger off. I've gone to your temple and then you've got no more time. Just bugger off, you wanker.* All of it rage and frustration in the dying embers of a lovely day. Because she was being left. Rootless, parentless, without direction, fucking deserted, everything else forgotten. She sat by the pond in the growing dark, traversed the football ground at a fast, furious pace, wished she was going to work, wished every living, chirping thing would belt up and when she got to the gates of the fucking park, found them shut. Measured them with her eye, ran at them from ten yards away, clambered over the top. Easy. Pain in her chest, easy; running home easier still. Wanker. She stopped in a pub and had two double vodkas, quickly, left when someone tried to talk.

On the way home, still cantering, she ran past the convent door and knew it was too late to go in. Agnes might still be sitting in her porch, but after the dot of nine o'clock she was under orders not to answer until she had fetched Barbara to see whoever it was. Barbara might have mellowed towards her, but she was still not going to let Anna inside so late, even if Anna said she wanted to pray. Nor would she be allowed entry to say goodnight to Therese.

There was an overpowering desire to see Therese. Her sister

was a physical presence she missed all the time. She skittered past, left and left again, unready to go home, passing the door at the back, and pausing beside it to draw breath. Stuck with the unpleasant realisation that she had probably shouted at Ravi only because he had better things to do with his evening than spend it with her, and he had left her with all this energy and nowhere to go. That was a lie; there were plenty of places to go and drink away the energy, let everyone know that she knew how to have a good time. Bars and clubs by the dozen, just beginning to warm up for the night, and none of them places where she wanted to be. If she could not have the chapel, she wanted the forbidden territory of the park or the silence of that garden for a quiet shouting match with God. She was shut out from everywhere. Knowing she was behaving like a spoiled child, she kicked the door. Winced and then looked at it more closely.

It still looked peculiarly naked without the curtain of ivy, which had almost covered it and was now shaggily trimmed so that a couple of branches hung like tendrils around the frame, escaping from the dense foliage that covered the whole wall. The handle was still so rusted, it looked as if it had not been used in several lifetimes, but there were marks in the woodwork on the door, as if someone with heavy boots had kicked, hard and repeatedly. They were futile dents in an obdurately solid door, but they were ugly, angry marks. Anna stared at them in the street light. A car passed, booming with music; on the other side of the road, the houses were softly lit. No one would notice. She thought of Edmund, dying in the garden while she had slept, and the desire to get inside became overpowering. It was simply not enough to spy from the rooftop.

She went to the middle of the road, zipped her purse into the pocket of her jacket and measured the distance. Ran and leapt for the ivy. Found herself spreadeagled against the wall with her feet scrabbling for hold and her hands seizing fistfuls of branches.

The sinews of the ivy held her up. She was a lightweight. Her small feet slithered among the leaves and found purchase. In the distance she could hear another car and the sound of it had the effect of adrenaline. After that it was easy. In another second, before the car headlights passed, she was astride the top of the wall, looking down into the other side, feeling exhilarated but foolish. What the hell did she think she was doing? Below her was a further mass of ivy; getting down the other side and up again was well within her powers. Anna enjoyed sitting on top of the wall; it crossed her mind to stay there, triumphantly, and wave. Not such a high wall after all, a mere fifteen feet, strange that no one had tried this route before, but why should anyone bother? A small amount of street light penetrated far enough into the garden to show the contours of Edmund's shed and his bench. Otherwise the darkness was intense. The door of the shed was open and the bench was unoccupied. That was a relief. She had been afraid she would find someone sitting there, listening for the quiet birds. Looking up, she could see the outlines of her block with the small back windows of the apartments. She was, after all, very close to home and slithered down the other side, noisily.

The walls of the garden blocked sound from the road and created the effect of a tunnel. The shrubbery was less dense than it appeared from her high view, when the foliage seemed to cover most of the garden in a carpet of various greens with scarcely a hint of the walkways. On ground level, the grey stone of the path was almost luminous. Anna had scarcely ever been in the garden, except the other day, when the dead presence of Edmund on the bench had blinded her to anything else. Her sense of its geography was skewed by her own perspective: down here, in the dark to which her eyes were slowly adjusting, it seemed bigger and easier to penetrate, although the distance between where she stood and the high window of the chapel seemed further than she could have imagined. The top end of the garden and this were separate worlds, and the world on the outside different again. Without any particular purpose, but drawn as always to the chapel, she began to walk up the winding path, arms outstretched to feel her way, as if she was playing Blindman's Buff, trying to define the different scents she could smell. Something like juniper, walnut, the mossy smell of soil, a whiff of lavender, the oily scent of evergreens and the sharp, ammonia smell of urine. Something brushed against her legs, slinking into the bushes to the left, emerging again, spitting with a guttural hiss, which sounded as loud as a shout. A cat without colour; she could only guess at the size. Its eyes glared like beacons before it disappeared with an angry flourish. Anna's heartbeat slowed back down to almost normal. Her foot encountered something slimy on the path. Up until then, she had been feeling apologetic to the cat, until she scraped the slime from the bottom of her shoe with the realisation that whatever it was was bloody and fleshy and as likely as not the indigestible portion of a feral meal. She could visualise, without seeing, the uneaten gizzard of a blackbird, shook herself and stepped forward, gingerly, angry with the cat, knowing it should not be here. It was the trespasser, not herself. It should be trapped and taken away from a place that was a sanctuary for birds. At a bend in the path, she could smell blackcurrant, something with the scent of pepper, gooseberry and rust. Her outstretched hand encountered mossy stone. She touched it, felt the damp hem of the robe of St Michael, with big, cold feet, and with that came the realisation that this was all stupid and infantile, because she had no more place here and even less purpose than the cat. Anna turned to retrace her steps, walking away from the light of the windows and back towards the wall. There was a sudden change in the smells, a sensation of warmth.

There were no footsteps, there was simply a presence, cannoning into her from behind, sending her stumbling to the ground.

She broke the fall with her hands, felt the bones in her wrists jarring against stone. He had hit her with the full force of his body, launching out of space, like a heat-seeking missile, *wham* into her shoulders. She twisted as she fell, resisting some of the force, and was slithering out of his grasp in a frantic crawling away towards the bushes, like the cat. Slower than the cat, easier to pursue, clumsy as a cripple. There were big paws, grasping at her ankles, then her thighs as she crawled ineffectually until he pressed her into the ground of the grey path, and she felt he would bite her in the neck. Her feet drummed against the ground; she lay, pinned beneath him, his torso coming to rest against her back like a dead man, while her legs thrashed and his hand circled her throat and as they lay, breathless, groin to buttock, she could feel his prick against the curve of her buttocks, rigid as a stick. She struggled with every ounce of strength and as he began to release her, screamed every obscenity she knew, so loud that the birds flew out of the trees with a *caw! caw! caw!* of outrage and the ground-floor lights of the building flickered awake. *You fucking cunt bastard shitface leggo of me bastard.*

'Scream away,' he whispered into her ear. 'Love it. That'll get them running.'

He pulled her up against himself, raising them both so that he seemed to have her in his lap in a willing embrace. As the lights from inside grew visible, they were suddenly partially outlined, her silhouette drawn against his, extremities entwined, legs and bodies fixed in an unholy glow. He lifted her to her feet, held her in his arms briefly and dropped her unceremoniously on to the path. Then he placed his foot on her waist, so great a foot, bigger than St Michael's, it could have crushed her spleen unless he held it there, neatly balanced, like some big game hunter posing for a photo with the newly killed prey he did not want to damage. Leaning over her gently with the lights coming closer, he took hold of her right, curled fist and held it against his face.

'Go on, my lovely, Go on.'

She clawed at him, vainly, scratching him harmlessly down the left cheek. He took her open hand, fastened his own around her knuckles and dragged the imprisoned fingers with their long nails down the other side of his face.

'Good girl,' he murmured, hauling her to her feet, pinning her arms behind her, linking his own through her crooked elbows, bending her forward. Her shoulder blades seemed to scrape together and she began to cough with a ghastly, chest-clearing throttle, like an old man fetching up phlegm. He yanked her upright with the same deceptive gentility, hair hanging over her face, until she found herself staring through it at the waist of Sister Barbara's dressing gown, and saw her large feet lit by a torch. She could see the glimpses of another uniform, up to the neck and down to the ankles, with cloth slippers resembling boots, on which Anna kept her eyes fastened, listening to the angry voice of fear.

'Francis, what is this?'

Barbara was trying to exert control, but the voice, even with the muted resonance of plainchant attached, sounded shrill in the silence, descending to a *tut, tut, tut* as she squinted at the tableau they made. There was large, manly Francis, pillar of the Establishment, with blood beginning to seep from the scratches on his face, holding a captive as sweetly as a trainer might hold a potentially fierce dog, with one hand on her bent neck, the other pinning her arms.

'Are you all right?' Francis addressed the back of Anna's neck. 'I'll let you go if you behave.' He was speaking unnecessarily loudly.

'What's going on?' Barbara yelled.

'Shhh. Wait a minute, Sister. I'll just get her to sit.'

Propelled by sheer weight, Anna sat at the feet of Michael, Archangel, where the stray light from the parlour, augmented by

144

Barbara's torch, almost penetrated. The voices of Francis and Barbara seemed to come from another planet. Hers was sharp.

'What are you doing here, Francis? We don't pay you for Sundays.'

He took a deep breath and stood calmly in the light of her torch, which wavered at the end of her wrist. Someone hovered behind him. Anna raised her head and gazed into the limpid eyes of Sister Matilda, who was standing to one side gazing at her, with one finger pressed against her own lips, the instruction for silence. Anna scarcely needed any such advice; she could hardly speak, but she refrained from trying. Of all of them, Matilda was a favourite, the one she trusted simply because she was the most visible, the one who came into the garden most often as a gentle and undemanding presence, just visible from the roof and therefore the most familiar, and she had forgotten to give her Edmund's crucifix. It lay in her pocket, ready for morning Mass, with Ganesh alongside. Matilda was fully dressed, as if the veil was something she never shed, even in sleep.

'Oh, do get out of the way, Matilda.' The light from Barbara's torch swung into Anna's face and down over her body. Her dress was filthy. Barbara gasped, swung the beam back towards Francis, where it lingered on the scratches, oozing blood. He reached his hand towards Anna, then let it drop to his side.

'Are you all right?' he asked softly. 'I didn't mean to hurt you.'

The torchlight wavered back to her face. Matilda had disappeared into the background. In a gesture of extraordinary childishness, which she would remember afterwards with greater embarrassment than anything else, Anna stuck her tongue out and pulled a face. It was a stupid, unsympathetic thing to do, acting as an admission of guilt, and if there was any chance that Barbara was going to side with her, she lost it in that moment of puerile rebellion. The voice of Francis continued.

'I know I shouldn't be here, Sister,' he was saying to Barbara, apologetically. 'But I was passing on my way home and I saw someone climbing over the wall. There was no time to phone you, which would have been the most sensible thing. So I came in after her. I thought it was a kid. I didn't realise it was someone you knew. Someone I saw in chapel this morning.'

Apology and certainty oozed from him and Anna was suddenly furious all over again, for being so small. His voice was so quiet and confident and masculine, it could cut a swathe through all their female voices and command instant attention. If she spoke now, she would sound as silly as a parrot. A man could always do that, with the same ease he had knocked her over. The grit on the dress felt like ash as she clutched at the fabric to cover her knees, automatically trying to hide the grazes. She could almost have believed his voice herself, apart from knowing what a noise it made to scramble down the ivy and knowing that she would have heard him long before he could ever have surprised her. He had been there, waiting. She opened her mouth to protest, closed it again. Nausea threatened. Barbara's sympathy, if it had ever been there for the taking, was waning so fast words would not help, although when Anna thought about it later, she would wonder what she could have said. *I had two vodkas and fancied climbing a wall for a chat to God. Wanted to tell him he would look better if he grew a long nose.* Yeah, great. There was nothing to say. The last realisation before he overpowered her had been the right one. She had no business here. She began to shiver. Barbara was listening to him.

'I thought it was a kid,' he was repeating. 'And . . .' He hesitated. 'I thought it was the same kid I saw last week, hanging round on the day the chapel window was broken. I thought it was the same kid, with a catapult, maybe even an air gun. I couldn't take the risk of it happening again.'

'You bastard,' she hissed. 'You bloody liar.'

'Be *quiet!*'

He turned to Barbara beseechingly. 'On that evening, Sister, I walked on by, because it was still light and I didn't want to interfere. I was always sorry about that, which is why I didn't tonight. I didn't think, I just reacted. I haven't hurt her, have I? I'm so sorry. I only asked her who she was and she leapt at me like a cat. Is she a friend of yours?'

The torchlight wavered between them with increasing agitation, finally focusing on Francis's ravaged and beautiful features. Not so much ravaged as scratched, the marks enhancing the planes of his cheekbones and making him look like . . . a martyr. That instant familiarity of the holy picture face, glimpsed in the chapel that morning, as if it had been transferred from the sanitised but tortured face of an apostle on the Stations of the Cross.

'No,' she shouted. 'I didn't break the fucking window. I came in the front door that night, you great turd, I was *in* the sodding chapel . . .'

She was twisting the skirt of her dress in her fist. The statue of Ganesh that Ravi had given her fell out of the pocket with a suspicious clunk; she scooped it up and pushed it back, feeling and looking like a burglar caught in the act. Sneaking in some subversive idol, hiding an implement of harm. No one investigated it, but the noise and the flurry of movement was incriminating. The gold crucifix on the broken chain remained glowing on the ground. She watched, disbelieving her own eyes, as Francis scooped it up in one smooth, surreptitious movement.

'That's mine,' he said. 'You poor little girl, was that all you wanted?'

Barbara sighed. 'Oh Anna, how could you? I thought you had stopped hating us.'

'I don't . . . I didn't . . .'

'What is it you want?'

Barbara's voice was low. In the torchlight, she looked like an elderly lioness leaning over prey, still willing to explain why she was about to eat it. Anna lost the last of her dignity and credibility by being sick. It took her entirely by surprise. Vomit splashed over Barbara's sensible slippers and she could not hide a *yeugh* of disgust. It could have been deliberate, like the silly, insulting face with the tongue out.

'Perhaps we should call the police,' Francis murmured. Looking at her own feet in the torchlight made Barbara suddenly decisive. Decision making was her strong point.

'No, Francis dear. That is simply not appropriate. We'll all go inside.' She was directing her decisions and the explanations for them entirely towards him, as if no one else was present, relying on him to carry Anna with them as she used one foot to wipe the muck on the other. Rancid smells, far removed from those of the garden, assailed their nostrils. Anna felt entirely despicable.

'Anna here has a relative in the community,' Barbara was saying to Francis. 'It would not be kind to her sister to involve anyone else. Besides, she's a little touched in the head. Come along.'

Silent Matilda led the way up the path, through the open door of the parlour and into the bright light of the room. Prodded by Francis, Anna followed. On the far side of the parlour, Matilda disappeared into the other regions of the building, melting away like a ghost. Barbara had no intention of lingering either. They did not pause among the ugly chairs, but followed her down the black and white corridor to the front door, watched her struggle with the bolts and keys until the door was open. She made an expansive, sweeping motion with one hand, as if brushing rubbish out into the street.

'Off you go, Anna. And I don't think you'd better come back. Now, Francis, I'm sure I can trust you to see this child to her door. The morning is soon enough for a discussion.'

She stood back to let them through, commanding obedience in the very rigidity of her posture, so that without a word of the furious protest that fizzed in her throat, Anna passed by and began to walk away. *Don't come back.* The words ringing in her ears blotting out pain, eradicating anything else, including fear of the man who fell into step behind her and Barbara's casual cruelty in sending her away *with him.* The enormity of that struck her after fifteen steps. Barbara had thrown her out into the city night with an enemy for company. A lying, creeping, dangerous *bastard.* She began to run, only to find her legs were made of jelly. He caught her at the corner, grabbed her elbow.

'I'm to see you home,' he said, mildly. 'Pretty little things shouldn't be out after dark, all on their own.'

'You sod.'

Traffic passed in the road. A couple walked on the opposite pavement, reassuringly normal, a reminder that it was not even near the middle of the night, scarcely bedtime for those who lived normally. He put his arm through hers, holding her close to his side, mimicking the couple in their affectionate stroll. They walked stiffly for a few more steps. She had the sensation that he knew exactly where she was going; just as he had known her identity long before the bizarre introduction of Sister Barbara. *Anna here has a relative in the community.* The things Anna holds most dear are inside those walls. She pulled herself free of him.

'I'm the king of the castle, you're the dirty rascal,' he taunted. 'But you're even prettier than your sister. I wouldn't know which to have first.'

He pulled her towards him by the hair and ignoring the sour taste of her mouth, kissed her. Then pushed her away from him, so that she nearly stumbled again. She heard him laugh as he turned and left.

'You heard what she said,' he shouted after her. 'Don't come back. No one will let you in.'

And those were the only words that echoed.

149

Chapter Eight

Therese was wide awake.

She had sensed the disturbances of the early part of the night, rather than heard. She kept to her room in obedience to the general rule made for the good and the peace of them all.

Hers was on the first floor, at an angle of the building facing the roof of the opposite house, with a limited view of the road. The other Sisters on this floor included the habit-wearing seniors of the sorority, which long ago she and Anna described as penguins. Most had a TV or radio, and although the rule of respecting personal privacy was not written in stone, it was followed out of preference. Each room was sparse without being spartan, equipped with a washbasin; there was an amicable sharing of one bathroom and two lavatories and an unspoken agreement of silence at night. None of the rooms had a mirror.

Therese had heard the swish of Matilda's robes down the linoleum corridor as she began to contemplate sleep, guessed who it was by the footsteps, which she knew by heart. Matilda stayed awake late and when Agnes sometimes wept at night, it was Matilda who went to her. There would be brief, soft murmurings, followed by silence, occasions when Therese realised that she could never quite share their thoughts or their preoccupations, because she did not know what they were. They might share a set of circumstances and a code of behaviour, but they were old and she was young.

Sister Joseph's room was immediately above Therese's on the next floor, with an empty room on either side, an unplanned isolation occurring by accident after one Sister had moved to another convent and Sister Jude had died, leaving Joseph almost exclusive use of the bathroom on that floor, which suited such an assiduous washer who insisted upon doing her own laundry instead of putting it in a laundry bag for Sunday night collection like all the others. The old partition walls were solid enough to deaden most sound, except cries, the loudest of snores and the most persistent of coughs, which Therese could hear now as a long night moved towards dawn.

The sound of it vexed her beyond endurance and she blamed it for her inability to pray. By the weak light of her reading lamp, she had read again the advice of St Therese of Lisieux on how to turn an irritating noise into a sacrifice. *I set myself to listen attentively as though it were delightful music, and my meditation was passed in offering this music to Our Lord.*

Therese found this exercise impossible and so she tried the comforting, formulaic prayer of the rosary, skipping the beginning, going on to the Lord's Prayer, followed by ten, whispered Hail Marys, while she tried to keep her mind fixed on the Joyful Mysteries of the Annunciation of the Conception of Jesus and His Nativity, her mind slipping constantly into the present. There were spells of blissful silence between the distant coughing; in each pause, she would hold her breath and pray it had finished. Then it started again.

Therese gritted her teeth and thought about faces instead, which put the origin of the cough into perspective. Poor Joseph.

151

Surely, when you were as *old* as Joseph, you had got life sorted. She lay back in her bed and stared at the ceiling, seeing, in colour, Joseph's mottled face in the stark white of the paint, finding that her contemplation of that face lessened her irritation with the owner of it, realising, not for the first time, that she was merely a practical person without the makings of a mystic. She was better at doing than thinking: she would never be able to make her mind transcend the interruption of sound, or the memory of a face.

It had never really occurred to her before seeing Joseph in the chapel that a person with their profound and all-encompassing belief in God could be *lonely*. They could be unhappy, from time to time, yes; troubled by events, and personal inadequacies, beset by challenges, often ashamed, but never *lonely*. It was impossible to comprehend, because it was the very essence of her belief that God and his saints never slept, that they never failed to listen and always forgave. God was a father, tied by an umbilical cord to all his children. Forgiveness was natural; His face was never turned away from an apology. Saints did not sulk and take umbrage like parents even if you disappointed them; they were constant companions, friends and family for life and beyond. So how could anyone be lonely, even if they were sad? Repentance for failures always equalled forgiveness.

And yet that was what Joseph had been; gut-churningly, utterly lonely, beyond the reach of any intercession, beyond asking. The thought of that frightened Therese because she could not see how it could happen. The coughing resumed. This time it was more pitiful than irritating. If Joseph did not seek help, it was not for her to interfere, other than to tell her superiors and let them, in their wisdom, find solutions. To act otherwise was to compound yesterday's disobedience.

And then, other favourite words swam into mind. *Love is patient; love is kind and envies no one. Love is never boastful or conceited, nor rude, never selfish, not quick to take offence. Love keeps no score of*

wrongs . . . I may speak in tongues of men or angels, but if I am
without love, I am a sounding gong or a clanging cymbal . . .

Therese buttoned her heavy nightgown up to the neck, slipped out of her room, down the corridor towards the stairs. Light framed Matilda's door, but if she was awake, she would not hear. Therese had not needed to learn the art of quiet movement; she had seemed to know it in advance of living here, could not remember ever making a noise. The door of Joseph's room was also framed in light. She was relieved about that; at least she was not saving electricity by sharing her misery with the dark. Therese knocked softly and entered without invitation. There was a fusty smell to the room, although the small window was open wide, and Joseph was hunched over the washbasin. She turned a baleful glare on her visitor and began to splash water on her face. The front of her white nightgown was splattered with blood.

Therese swallowed. The splatters of blood were brilliantly red against the white of the old gown, which Joseph would have cleaned herself. She finished washing her face. The vomiting spasm had passed and her skin was as pale as plaster. Therese stood awkwardly, staring at her as she wiped her face dry. Joseph smiled. There was always something sardonic about Joseph's smile, as if she had to force it into operation.

'Hello, little Therese. Come to help again? Could you reach me my other nightgown – from the cupboard, there. If I don't soak this one, it'll stain.'

Therese did as she was told. There was a folded nightgown, identical to the one Joseph wore, on the top shelf of the tiny wardrobe, which was otherwise occupied by nothing but a coat, a blouse and a pair of shoes. She reached down the gown and stood holding it until Joseph snatched it from her hands.

'Turn round, child.'

Therese turned her face to the door, heard the rustle of cotton as Joseph pulled the soiled dress over her head, and replaced it

153

with the clean one. Only in the event of illness were the Sisters ever on such intimate terms as this. Therese knew she could cope with a dead body, but she had a horror of seeing Joseph naked.

'There, that's better. You can turn round now.'

Therese turned. Joseph bent to collect the nightdress crumpled at her feet, groaning as she did so.

'Here, let me—'

'*No!*'

She watched as Joseph began to rinse the bodice of the gown in the washbasin, which was too small to accommodate it. Everything in the room was small. Therese felt she fitted into her own, identical space as neatly as if it had been made for her, but could imagine that Joseph, tall, gaunt, clumsy and twice her weight, would bruise herself in the restricted space as she prepared for bed. She watched, mesmerised by the pink water, as Joseph rinsed. Cleanliness is next to godliness, but it seemed strange in someone who was content to poison her own body, to say nothing of her own mind. Perhaps the washing was a secret penance; maybe it had a purpose. Joseph began to shiver.

'Get into bed, Sister. I'll finish that.'

Joseph lurched the two steps to the bed, which also seemed too small for her. The window was alongside, curtains drawn back, showing a shiny new catch, which kept it propped open. For Therese, obedience from someone so much older was a disturbing novelty. She wrung moisture from the nightgown and spread it over the basin. Then she took the cushion from the single chair and placed it behind Joseph's head to supplement the single pillow.

'Thank you, child. You're very kind. May your reward be on earth, rather than in heaven.'

Therese sat on the edge of the bed, gingerly. 'What's the matter with you?' she asked bluntly. She had been considering the wisdom of asking, Do you want me to call Barbara, the doctor, anyone? but she knew the answer would be no.

154

'Cirrhosis, dear. Acquired in the service of Jesus, in foreign parts.'

Therese understood. The medical dictionary had once been a Bible for herself and Anna as they looked up their own symptoms without ever finding any real answers. They began with A and went on to Z. Mother had encouraged it.

'So drink could kill you.'

'*Will* kill me, with a bit of luck.'

'Is that why you want it?'

Joseph fiddled with the neck of the gown. The brown liver spots on her hands were like extra large, misshapen freckles.

'Possibly. Mostly I want it because I want it, and life is completely meaningless, dull and futile without it. Not worth having. Don't worry your head, child. You couldn't possibly understand.'

'No, Sister, I don't understand. I can't—'

'Sister Jude understood,' Joseph went on. 'But then Jude understood everything, that old fraud.'

'Fraud?'

'Such a liar, that woman. I never knew one half as good at keeping opinions to herself, which is the same as lying. No one's interested in my opinions, she would say. I write them on the back of holy pictures to keep them short and stuff them in my missal, she said.'

'And what do you do with yours, Sister?' Therese asked, trying to lighten the tone.

'Swallow them whole and cough them up.' She laughed drily. She was beginning to become sleepy; it softened the lines of her face.

'You seem to have forgotten to ask God to help you.'

Joseph's eyes shot wide open. She was terrifyingly amused. 'Oh, Him? My dear, we parted company a long time ago. No more transmissions. Over and out. Neither giving or receiving. The radio bust. Knock, knock, nobody home. I told him, God, you're so *boring*. He left.'

If Joseph had spat or peed, Therese could not have been more shocked. She struggled with the very idea of believing that God the Father would simply go away, like her own parent had done, leaving behind a great big space. She knew such a prospect would make sense to Anna, or someone like Kim, who had never crossed that barrier or felt that *presence*, like a pair of enfolding arms, but for an old woman who was a lifetime servant of the Lord, it seemed an obscene admission of negligence. One who knew God could never send Him away; He would not allow it. It was impossible to lose something that was essentially yours and as much a part of you as the blood in your veins. The martyrs had preferred to die rather than take that risk; so, she thought, would she.

'Inconceivable, you think? Faith might be a gift, Therese, but don't bank on it being permanent. It can leave you just like that, or you leave it. And once it's gone, you can't nurture it back into life, whatever St bloody Therese says. Once you start to realise the possibility that man made God for his own convenience, rather than the other way round, you've got Him on the run. Let in the light of logic and He goes to ground. As unreliable as anything else synthetic and man-made.'

She laughed again, humourlessly. Therese kept her gaze fixed on the bedspread, to avoid scrutiny and the pounding of her own heart.

'How many of us have real belief, Therese? How many of us *here*? We, the quintessential believers? What do you imagine we think about? Agnes dreams of the bastard son who was taken from her. She sees him in every young man she encounters, although he'd be old himself, now. Barbara thinks of the Lord as an occupational hazard. Poor Father Goodwin continues with what tattered remnants of faith he has left. My dear Matilda, to whom I dare not speak in case I spread corruption . . . Matilda spends all day chatting to St Michael, who probably resembles someone she once saw in a film. He is, after all, the patron saint of

156

policemen and other fascists. It isn't worship, it's idolatrous hero worship. Everyone has their own God. We make the one that suits us.'

Therese wanted to scream at her to stop. It wasn't true, any of it. It was the drink talking, even if Joseph was sickly sober. Drink made people mad: it made Anna nasty, her father pathetic, it was the stuff of devilment. Tomorrow, she was going to get Francis, tell him what he had done . . . For the moment, she was angrily calm.

'If you don't believe, Sister, and you feel God has deserted you, why do you stay?'

'Don't be naive, child. Where would I go? With *what* would I go? No, the Church has had the best of me, it can have the worst.'

She pulled the blankets up over her chin, so that all Anna could see was her haunting, blazing eyes.

'I'm sorry, child. I'm being grotesquely unkind. Loneliness should not be contagious. You'd better go for your beauty sleep. I'd rather you didn't tell Barbara about the coughing. She has enough to do. It wouldn't be *charitable* to either of us.'

Therese nodded, aware that it was a promise. Joseph closed her eyes. On the other side of the door, with the first hint of daylight beginning to creep along the floor from the long window at the end, Therese paused. Instead of going straight back to her room, she went to the one next to Joseph's which Sister Jude had occupied. It was clean, but not entirely cleared. Each of the Order and Jude's relatives had taken from her shelves whatever they had wished, either to remember her by, or because they liked it. The selection had been small. Poetry, prose, a minimum of religion, the maximum of music for her walkman, which had gone, the radio, which was gone, leaving a few literary souvenirs. Therese found herself searching for the spot where the missal had been, remembered how she had taken it for Anna, because it was Anna Jude loved. Anna who did what Jude liked best, argued, raised the devil, asked questions and demanded answers, making Jude test herself, age against youth, so that they lost their tempers with one another. Therese would never have dared to do that, any more than she would have wanted to do it. She hated confrontation. She had thought obedience was natural. Jude had never respected her for that. Her sainted aunt had a preference for sinners, did not believe what her own mother had taught her by example, *Be good, sweet maid. And let who will be clever.*

It was Jude who advised her against following her vocation; Jude who said no child should ever do a thing because her mother wished it. But that was not why she had done it. Nor had she entered the Order because she thought it would be easy. She had done it because it felt entirely natural and she had been confident it would always feel like that. On her way back to her own room, grateful for the dawn, she found herself feeling envious of Anna. Wanted a touch of that anger, as well as a touch of the street wisdom, which would teach her what to do with Francis, who by the simple act of supplying Joseph with her own poison had made her imagine that she had lost her faith. Faith could be spat upon and scorned, but never lost. What rubbish. She would find Francis and tell him not to do this and then everything would be all right. She would appeal to the better nature every soul had. Stripping off her own nightgown, pulling on her day clothes and washing her own face before she clipped back her hair, she encountered the sneaky, unknown thought that she would prefer a better, less scratchy nightdress than this, and if she were ever to die, which seemed a remote possibility, she would also prefer to have more than a single pair of shoes.

Kim came in early. 'Only thing that bastard ever does,' she grumbled, 'is give the little sods breakfast and take them to school. Bastard. I'd rather be here than round our place. It's a madhouse. Hey, Treesa, are you awake? How long have you been sitting there? You gonna talk to me or what? Otherwise, I might as well stay home.'

The kitchen was beautifully empty; a place waiting to spring into life. Being in it cheered Therese immeasurably. It was her favourite place; there was nothing wrong with being Mary rather than Martha and she desperately needed to laugh. So, sighing dramatically, she launched into the familiar Monday morning routine she and Kim had perfected.

'I'm a bit weary, to be honest. Shagged out, as a matter of fact, Kim. Weekends in here get so *wild*. Clubbing Saturday night. Vodka and ketchup, ever tried it? Lethal. Sunday morning, ended up God knows where with the Sisters, sobering up and hanging out with the priests. Back up here for a line of coke and bacon sandwiches. You know how it is. Tiring.'

'That's better! Thought you were dead. So who got luvverly Francis, then? No luck?'

'No, we took a vote. We decided he preferred blokes.'

'You don't say! Makes sense, though, doesn't it? Such a pretty boy.'

'What makes sense? Nuns on coke, or what?'

'Francis, being gay. Name like that, hair like that, you know. Shame, innit? What a bloody waste. Oh, forget it. He's still shaggable.'

Overwhelmed by a sudden sense of her own ignorance, Therese sat down. She could never play this game for very long.

'How do you know if a man's gay?'

Kim was decanting milk into a jug. The kettle was coming to the boil. Everything was cheerful and soon there would be food on the table. Therese was ravenously hungry.

'Gay men? You don't know. Only they're often too good-looking for their own good and they sometimes wear their willies on the outside. They like perfume, wash more than ordinary. That's

159

one sign, anyway. Oh, and they know how to be nice to women. Come to think of it, that would suit Francis down to a T. Gay chaps know how to get on with girls. I mean they talk to us, which is more than the other buggers do.'

'Ah.'

'Shame none of you scored. Do you want coffee for your hangover?'

'Yes, please.'

'I think you ought to stay indoors more, Treesa. Have an early night for a change. Get Francis to tuck you in. If he's gay, he'll be safe as houses, even if you throw your knickers at him. Which reminds me. We've got to do the laundry today. Get it started before breakfast.'

The laundry bags, collected from the Sisters' rooms each week, stood in the scullery off the kitchen, which housed the boiler, a hanging rail and a large, noisy washing machine.

'I think we ought to get Francis in to look at that washer, Treesa. Give you a chance to get to know him, like everyone else. You just smile at him and scuttle away. You haven't talked to him yet, have you?'

'No, but I want to.'

'Get you, you cheeky sod! Why's that then?'

'I want to ask him not to run errands for Sister Joseph.'

'Oh, he does, does he? Well, I can hardly blame him for that. She's very persuasive. She was always asking me and it was hard to say no. Sweet youth like Francis hasn't got a chance. She'll tell him he was doing her a kindness.'

Therese sat, rooted to the chair. How very, very little she knew. As little about their bodies as their souls. How much they conspired to protect her.

'I don't understand where she gets the money.'

'She's got some of her own. And I can tell it isn't you polishes the collection box by the chapel. Someone gets the bottom off and robs a bit every week before anyone counts. Easy. Are you all right, Treesa?'

She was not all right; she was reeling with shock all over again. Poor Joseph really was a soul damned to eternity, or at least in the eyes of Sister Barbara. She sipped the coffee and wished it had more taste.

'Laundry,' she said.

Dealing with the personal laundry of a dozen women bore no resemblance to the tasks described by St Therese of Lisieux in her cold convent cellar, battling with dirty water and filthy suds. It was merely a simple job of sorting the contents of the laundry bags into two piles with the rough division of delicate and hardy. Most of it was hardy, but the process of sorting always felt like prying to Therese. Each Sister placed her underwear into the bag in which she would receive it back. There were a vast number of handkerchiefs, which seemed to be essential. Therese hated the handkerchiefs, while Kim always either laughed or tut tutted over the rest. There were Agnes's flannelette bloomers, worn winter and summer, Barbara's monstrous, indestructible bras, the sometimes more holey than godly vests preferred by the others, the schoolgirl sensible stuff used by the youngest, including Therese, and not a trace of lace anywhere. Except on the handkerchiefs, those items most often given to the Sisters by relatives for lack of anything else appropriate. Embroidered hankies, colourful hankies, linen and silk hankies. Matilda went through a dozen a week. They formed the bulk of her laundry. Nestled down among them at the bottom of her bag was a knife.

Not a particularly sinister-looking knife, but lethal all the same. A fruit knife with a rope-strapped handle and a short blade which looked as if it had been honed to dangerous, surgical sharpness on a stone. If Therese had not been so timid in extracting the handkerchiefs, the pointed blade would have nicked her fingers. She put it on top of the washing machine and both of them looked at

161

it. A laundry bag was a good hiding place, but why was she keeping a knife? Such a sharp knife.

Barbara's voice rang out from the kitchen. '*Bendicamus Domino!*'

'*Deo Gratias,*' Therese murmured, slipping the knife into the pocket of her tunic while Kim carried on as if nothing had happened. Secrecy was becoming second nature.

Kim grabbed the last garment, which she had been waving round her head like a flag, stuffed it inside and slammed the door of the washing machine. Barbara hove into view, filling the door of the utility room with her feet, as if she was about to flow inside and all around them, like lava. Her normal demeanour was one of relentless cheerfulness, overseen by those scrutinising eyes, which seemed to take in every detail, while smiling throughout. The smile was missing today. She looked indefatigable, but tired. It was Kim's daily complaint that she hated the woman, which Therese had long since translated as a benign kind of fear and a hearty dislike of being bossed about. For Therese, Barbara was in another sphere. She was the first adult human being she could remember as having taken her seriously and she was afraid of her in an awesome way. Barbara was the embodiment of all higher authority, the representative of the Order she obeyed and the person who knew the answers to everything. But in that one moment, with Barbara's feet and Barbara's bosom swelling into the small space, she could only think of the bosom and the monstrous brassiere Kim had just stuffed into the circular mouth of the washing machine.

The item, lying within sight in the machine, resembled part of a comical suit of armour. Therese looked at it as if she had never seen it before. Barbara's posture was part of her authority. She wore her bosom high, so that it preceded her, like a woman carrying a box, and only the two of them here knew the superstructure that lay behind.

'Good, good. You're at work.'

She was a trifle agitated, but the solid bosom trembled not a bit. Two white bras she had, wire and cotton, grey straps and six hooks and eyes. When she was agitated, she forgot to keep her voice down and she had not remembered to brush her hair.

'Always, Sister,' Kim said demurely.

'Terrific,' Barbara said. 'Keep it up. Keep your pecker up! Therese, a word with you after breakfast, please.'

She swept away, and as soon as her squeaky shoes were out of hearing they both began to giggle, nervously.

'What does she know about peckers?' Kim said.

'Probably more than me,' Therese said, unsure of what she meant. In Kim's laughter, somehow the knife was forgotten. Being late with the breakfast had all the makings of a sin. Despite her hunger she would not eat the breakfast, in reparation for the laughter, which felt, if not sinful, something close to it.

There was a hierarchy of sins. There were the sins committed on a daily basis – evasions, dishonesties, the failures to remember holy things. Therese had learned her catechism the way other children learned to count, but the definitions of what made a sin mortal and what made it venial were more difficult. There was no straight line between the two. The venial was the daily sin, easily expunged; the mortal was the sin that divorced the soul from God. If a person died with such an unrepented sin scarring their soul, they would never be reunited in the next life with the God who had made them. The thought was enough to strike terror: it was the threat of permanent expulsion from everything that could provide happiness or safety, but all the same, she was never sure what kind of a sin it could be. A sin that slaps God in the face, Jude had defined it. A really serious sin. Your conscience will tell you when it is yours, even if the reactions of others do not make it clear, because you will despise yourself and know that your Father waits for you to acknowledge what you have done and make amends. You will feel it in your bones. But what kind of sin is it? she had asked. Is there a list? No, no list, apart from the ten commandments and the catechism.

All that Therese knew as she moved round the dining room table, delivering milk and juice, finally standing with her head bowed during the prayer, was that she felt in a state of sin, unable to join in with the words, *For what we are about to receive, may the Lord make us truly thankful.* The hunger had gone and she formed her bread into small pellets to avoid eating it, knowing that here, wasting food was regarded as far worse than eating too much of it. She should have sat next to Matilda, who would have eaten it for her. But what is my sin? she was asking herself, furiously, as the pellets of bread stuck in her throat. I have listened to Joseph's heresy and slander, and I have helped her to hide her own sins. I have laughed at Barbara and disobeyed her, in spirit at least. Is that enough to make me feel so bad that my sin is mortal? Forgive me, Lord. She looked at the face of Matilda watching her anxiously from halfway down the table and found herself suspicious of the glance. Matilda's knife was in her pocket; Matilda wanted to see Anna; they were keeping secrets. Agnes, supposedly the mother of a child, sat staring towards the door, as if expecting a vision. Joseph was serene. She waited until the last as Therese was stacking plates and the others had filed away, came up behind her and touched her on the shoulder.

'Therese, my dear, I must apologise for troubling you. It was selfish of me.' She hesitated, but it was not the hesitation of conscience. She looked surprisingly decisive and fresh, a woman capable of self-reinvention, looking at Therese closely but kindly, as if trying to ascertain if Therese could remember a fraction of what she had said. That was how Therese's newly suspicious mind interpreted it.

'It was no trouble, Sister. The less said, the soonest mended.'

She was becoming like the rest of them, resorting to well-worn clichés.

Joseph nodded. 'But there is one thing I wanted to say, child. I mentioned Sister Jude's missal. Don't look at it. She put her opinions of your mother in there.'

She departed as Matilda sidled back, smiling, dipping her head in greeting to Joseph's departing back and resting her hand on Therese's shoulder. In her heightened state of nervous awareness, Therese had the unbidden impression that the two women wanted to behave differently.

'Therese, lovey, you won't forget to tell Anna to come and see me, will you? As soon as Barbara has the sense to let her back.'

Therese was confused. 'Of course, Sister, but I never know when she's going to appear.'

'No, but if she ever does . . . She will, soon, won't she? It's very important that I see her.'

It could not be soon enough. Therese was swept away by a longing to see her flesh-and-blood sister. Hear her voice, even if it mocked. Confess her miseries to someone who did not rely on God for an answer, and for once, be touched by the flesh of someone who was not old. Old flesh, old smells, old, old . . . old sins.

Barbara's office, with her bedroom behind it, was next to the parlour, off the black and white corridor. Agnes had already taken up residence by the front door. The day and the week was beginning like every other week for the last year, but without the same optimism that buoyed her being and without the comforting sense of it being *right*. The three younger Sisters, who never spoke to her, like new postgraduates to a student in her first term, had departed in their usual quiet flurry of activity to their teaching jobs. Without quite realising it, Therese had formed a settled dislike of them, because they were so importantly useful. They were allowed to be exhausted in the evening and they had more to say to their elders, who had followed similar careers, than they ever would have to say to her. It was Martha and Mary all over again. As she stood back, dutifully, to let them pass, she saw Agnes open the door to the outside world, chirruping farewells like a squirrel. The door was halfway closed, Agnes being as efficient at closing as she was at opening, leaving Therese with the sour thought that she should have been a lift attendant, *oh, what was the matter with her today?* when Agnes leapt forward to open it wide. Seen in profile, her smile was one of sheer adoration, the sort reserved for spiritual ecstasy, as she opened her arms. Francis stepped into the hall, picked her up in a hug and swung her round as if she were weightless. Agnes had lost the knack of screaming, but she made, instead, small squealing noises of protesting pleasure. He was so strong, he could measure the swing he made with her bulky body held at her belted waist, so that her feet only left the ground by a couple of inches and she had no cause for alarm before she found herself back with both shoes on the floor, guided towards her accustomed seat with a deft kiss planted on her left cheek.

'How's my boy?' she crooned.

'Never better, Mother. Gotta go, work to do.'

'Of course, son, of course.'

The light was bad in the vicinity of the front door once it was closed, and Agnes's eyesight was even worse. She was content with her embrace, patted him on the arm and shooed him on, not noticing the details of his face. The black and white corridor was the route to the garden as well as everything else. He turned into it and collided with Therese, lightly, she moving and he moving faster, a glancing contact between her shoulder and his elbow, enough to stop him and make him recoil.

'I'm so sorry, I beg your pardon,' both of them speaking in chorus, before she stood back, yet again, to let him pass. She was sick of standing back; soon she would fall over herself. She knew who he was and that she disapproved of him, and kept her eyes to the black and white floor. Strange, that in so small a place, she had been able to avoid the conversation with him that everyone else had so enthusiastically enjoyed in the last ten days, to find she

166

needed it now. Everyone else had come to know and love him. There was no mistaking Francis. He was a foot taller than anyone else and smelled of man.

'Francis? I'm Therese. We haven't met. Can I talk to you later?'

It came out in a stutter. She had no social graces appropriate to men: she could only be silly, or silent, or gruff. She did not quite know what to do when he offered his hand, except take it, shake it and feel the fact that it was twice the size of her own and like dry sandpaper encircling her own, callused palm. He shook her hand vigorously, holding her arm by the elbow with his other hand as he did so, steadying her.

'Very pleased to meet you, Therese. Sure, I'm in the garden today. Or somewhere. Wherever Barbara lets me go.'

Which was everywhere, she thought, remembering the new window catch in Joseph's room as he relinquished the hand and the arm. She had the sensation of the grin and the eyes without really seeing either, rubbed her hand down the side of her tunic and heard him stride away, as softly as the rest of them, in indefinable shoes, which made no sound. She touched her right palm with her left and relived the feeling of his handshake. It had been so spontaneous and undemanding, not like the grasp of the old. There was no time for thinking about it. Their dual motion, the moving handshake, had brought her to Barbara's door. She would tell Barbara everything. She would confess.

You are even prettier than your sister. Anna clambered up to the roof and gazed down into the convent garden, seeking him out. It was a cold morning: summer had ceased the rearguard action against autumn and it seemed as if, overnight, the last of the leaves had gone from the deciduous trees, leaving them stripped bare. If she knew how, she could shoot him dead from here and she wished she did know how. She tried to imagine what it was like not to feel in disgrace. It felt like a state of sin, and she wished

167

she could not recall the stupid act of putting out her tongue. She tried to be nonchalant about being dismissed from the Garden of Eden and told herself there were others.

Facile. The garden was empty and her mouth was dry with a sense of dread, the half-formed knowledge of something she had to do. So much confusing rubbish floating round in her sore head, the prospect of going to work and immersing herself in that other world beckoned attractively. She wanted to forget the place she watched, and everyone in it, as well as her own wretched stupidity. What was the worst thing she had done? Put out her tongue? Scratched his face? Encountered evil and run away? Torn herself from its grasp.

The breeze was strong, gusting in the night and tearing at the leaves. She settled herself down in the gully behind the parapet out of the wind. If she could not berate Therese's God in the chapel ever again, she would have to do it here. She took the little statue of Ganesh out of her pocket and put it down beside her, trying to find defiance, but it was difficult.

'Well, a fat lot of good you were,' she said, clutching her knees to her chest. 'I know you didn't have the power, but I still say you should have stopped me climbing over the wall, but there you go. If I hadn't climbed over the wall, I wouldn't know what was going on.'

She could feel the grazes on her knees through the stiff fabric of her jeans. Punishment.

'I'm sorry, Elephant God, but I really can't talk to you. Nothing personal. You're just far too nice. I want an ugly, vengeful sort of God. A brute. I want someone to shout at.'

She adjusted herself for comfort, looked at her feet. Boot weather today, all the better for kicking shit. Shit, shit, shit. She stood up stiffly, and with folded arms regarded the sky. There were scudding clouds, grey and greyer, no inspiration. Down in the garden, she could see the stripped trees and the figure of

Matilda, aimlessly waving. Without Edmund, it seemed as if she was calling down the birds to eat. Anna ducked back behind the wall.

'Look here, Lord, I don't know what it is, but you seem hell bent on destruction.'

She closed her eyes and imagined the chapel crucifix, with its weary face and artistic blood. The image was fuzzy and pale. Anna rubbed her eyes, furiously. All she could feel was the repellent sensation of Golden Boy's kiss, the confirmation of utter humiliation. Tried to remember when she had ever felt so claustrophobically powerless inside the embrace of someone who wished her harm. Without any prompting, she remembered struggling in the arms of her mother.

There were two hours before the start of her shift. Just enough time to find Father Goodwin, if she ran on her jelly legs. She wanted to ask him something in particular – *did Edmund wear a little crucifix, I can't remember* – but when she arrived at his door, there was no reply. God and his officials were always out.

Therese came back to the kitchen about eleven. She had detoured via the chapel, stayed there a long time. Kim had unloaded the laundry into the dryer and was bagging rubbish for the Tuesday collection. Somewhere in her sorting, she had found six cans of Diamond White and an empty vodka bottle.

'Bugger me, Treesa. No wonder you're so pale. You weren't fucking joking, were you?'

CHAPTER NINE

'Weren't you a little harsh?' Father Goodwin asked.

He remembered that St Barbara was the patron saint of gunners: a virtuous virgin imprisoned sometime in the third century AD and then executed by her father in some bloody fashion for espousing the Christian faith. But as soon as he murdered her, he was himself struck by lightning and reduced to ashes, leaving his daughter's legend to be symbolised as a tower of strength. All that fitted the current image, although he was finding it hard to reconcile this bosomy Barbara with the beautiful girl of the story, as well as finding it easy to imagine why the parent of the original saint had wanted to kill her.

They had removed themselves from the office to which he had been summoned peremptorily for the interview with Therese, and into the parlour with the view of the first part of the garden. The paved area he could see through the French windows was cleaner and tidier than he recalled, so much so that it was faintly reminiscent of the immaculately manicured patio where Kay McQuaid lived. This time last year, he was sure that all he could see was a mess of dead leaves and leggy plants long past their best. Now he could see black bin-liner bags ready for removal, a colourful array of busy lizzies in the pot nearest the window, and Francis, stage left, tidying an already clean and empty border. In less than a fortnight, he had made a revolution. The dead and the dying souvenirs of summer had been ruthlessly removed.

'We've loads of bulbs for a good show in the spring,' Barbara said, chattily, evading the issue.

'Isn't it a little early yet to plant bulbs?' Father Goodwin asked.

'Francis says not. Bulbs are so cheap. We shall have three dozen daffodils for a matter of pennies.'

'But no birds.'

'Why not?'

'No Edmund to encourage them. And there's a cat.'

'Has Francis provided a cat? How clever of him. We had mice in the place last winter. I never thought of a cat. You were saying, Father?'

'I was saying, weren't you a little harsh on Therese?'

She reached for the coffee pot and filled his cup. He was unsure if the taste was blander than the tea and decided he would not take bets on it. Later, in the afternoon, he would be visiting the sick, namely a virtually speechless old man equipped with a huge television. They would join in pastoral care by the silent watching of old football replays. The prospect beckoned sweetly.

'I didn't mean to sound harsh, Father. Should I apologise?'

He remembered, reluctantly, Barbara's good points, including her occasional bouts of humility.

'What you told her will have made her very unhappy.'

'Oh, come now, Father, I only told her that her sister was a disgrace and we didn't want her coming in here ever again.'

'You told her Anna was a thieving little savage with aspirations to burglary and assault, and also the person who broke the window. You told her all that on what seemed to me to be the scantiest of evidence—'

'But Frances told me. He was *hurt*.'

'*Yes*, Francis *said* and has the wounds to prove it, but tell me, Sister, does any of this accord with the Anna Calvert you know? The one who makes helpful suggestions, supplies useful outside knowledge, and was so kind when Edmund died? An orphan of considerable bravery. A young woman with no elders of her own. Dead mother, dead father, and then Sister Jude? Surely she's allowed to be a little unhinged.'

Barbara was breathing like a horse at the end of a race.

'Not on our premises, she isn't. I can't take responsibility for her, I simply can't. We're stretched to the limit as it is. We haven't either the financial or spiritual resources to deal with a window-breaking heathen who wants to undermine us. Of course, it's terrible she's had to face so much death, but I can't shoulder that, either. She *hurt* Francis, how could she? Poor, dear Francis, so good to us. And we all lose people sooner or later and their father was no loss at all.'

He spluttered over the coffee, temper rising, thought of a perfect goal, soaring high and down into the net and the elated roar of a crowd.

'How do you know? They hadn't seen him for years, but it doesn't mean it didn't matter. The point is that *there is no one left*, for either of them. You can't ban Anna from Therese, because Anna's all she's got.'

'Anna annoys her and Therese has *us*,' Barbara said, defensively.

It seemed imprudent to say, *It isn't enough.*

'Well, you can't forbid Anna from Sunday Mass. It's open to the public and if you do, I can't possibly say it for you.'

'There are other priests,' she said, loftily.

He found he was biting his tongue to the point of pain.

172

'I believe,' he said, 'that the business of Theodore Calvert's estate remains unsettled . . .'

She shifted uncomfortably.

'Well, yes and no. I've meant to discuss it with you ever since Sister Jude died, but it's been so *busy*. I get regular letters from a dry lawyer who speaks gobbledygook. He tells me that there is an ongoing argument about something or other. At first he wrote that the will was complex, and then he says there must be investigation into blood relatives, in case the will is invalid, which won't make any difference, because under the rules of intestacy, his daughters inherited anyway, but he has to look for forebears, or something. Only a matter of time, he keeps saying.'

'You get the letters?'

'Yes. I don't censor incoming mail for everyone, if that's what you think. Therese asked me to do it for her, and some of the others do as well. They want bad news to be filtered and they want complicated news to be decoded. What I mean is that they'd rather hear about illness in the family from me than read it before breakfast.'

'But you never hide anything from them?'

She cleared her throat and considered the question. She *wants* to be truthful, Christopher realised with a start of surprise. She just can't quite do it.

'No, of course not. But I do ration, we all have to do that. If Matilda was stricken with pneumonia, I might decide that the time was not right to tell her that her brother had died. And if ever it happened that Agnes's so-called son demanded to see her again, I might not tell her at all.'

'Ah.'

'I can't discuss it with her because I'm not supposed to know. There's a lot of it about, Father,' she said kindly, in deference to his ignorance of things sexual, 'just as there was forty years ago.'

He was silent, thinking of Agnes waiting at the door, day in, day out. Of the cruelties of youth and how Barbara's decision might endorse them: of a disgraced girl from rural Ireland being taken in by a convent, to sit by the door ever since. Of Barbara as the buffer zone between herself and her Sisters, and how she did, at least, take decisions and stick to them, rather than use his own evasive techniques, and he humbly supposed there was a degree of moral courage in that. He held his hands steady in his lap, almost sorry that his temper was under control.

'Did Therese ever get a copy of her father's will?'

'She handed it to me, unread. A will and a draft will, which seems to be there by mistake. I'm afraid I kept it from her. It was obscene. I shall let the lawyer sort it out.'

'You kept it from her?' He found his voice was rising again.

'As I was *asked* to do.'

She sat, elbows on the knees spread beneath her long tunic, leaning forward for emphasis. She was plain and wholesome, he thought dispassionately, the most unfeminine creature he had ever known. Was it wrong to prefer a woman who smelled of perfume and cared for her skin?

'Where Therese entered the Order, eighteen months ago, it was just before they'd been told, by Calvert's fancy woman, I believe, that he had drowned. Therese was no stranger to us, as you recall, she brought with her all her worldly goods. Including a pile of correspondence addressed to Anna and herself. They were all with the same lawyer's frank and none of them were opened. I don't know if that was a joint decision, or if Therese kept them from Anna when they shared that flat. They are ridiculously protective of each other. I've no doubt Therese kept house . . . she's the responsible one. She told me that neither of them had any interest in their father . . . why should they respond to letters from the grave when he had never responded

174

to the letters they wrote to him when they were ill? So the lawyer writes to me. Oh, come, Father, you know very well that I didn't just sit on them when Sister Jude was alive. She agreed with me that the will was obscure but obscene. She saw all the correspondence and very likely showed it to you.'

There was a hint of something, a kind of jealousy. Barbara was suspicious of clever people conversing with one another. It was bound to be subversive.

'No. She discussed the situation with me in broad terms, not the letters or the will itself.'

'Oh Lord, the pedantry of priests. Isn't it better for them not to know that their father was as mad as a snake?'

'And their mother . . .'

'Died of a broken heart when she was parted from them. A saint.'

'Oh yes, I'd forgotten.'

He rose, stiff in the limbs and suddenly cold. The parlour was never really warm, not even in summer. He tried to imagine the empty fireplace full of logs and cheerful flames, and found it a leap of imagination too far. Perhaps the wonderful Francis could sweep the chimney and provide cheap fuel: all he would have to do was cut down the trees in the garden. Father Goodwin moved to the windows and looked out over the clean patio towards the forest of shrubs beyond the bend in the path. Francis had disappeared. Christopher had a vision of a golden serpent slinking back into obscurity and the clarity of the image shocked him.

'Shall I apologise to Therese?' Barbara asked, humbly.

'I can't advise you on that, Sister. You are the one in loco parentis. But I do think you should reconsider about Anna.'

'No.'

'In which case, I think you should give me copies of the letters and that wretched will. You might have the right to withhold such things from your postulant, but not from her sister, who is not, as you say, your responsibility.'

She nodded, patently relieved. 'I'll get the copies for you.'

And that, he thought to himself, as she fetched a bulky envelope of papers, was what you call an Own Goal. The final confirmation of an uncomfortable commitment to interfere in other lives. As he took the parcel and turned to leave, he saw Francis entering through the French windows and heard Barbara greet him with anxious affection.

'Ah, you poor *pet* . . .'

The boy was welcome to the remainder of the coffee and the sympathy of his adoring employer. He had more power here than Father Goodwin had ever had and the priest was ashamed of his own petulance.

The nondescript premises of Compucabs looked as safe as any prison. All Anna wanted was a longer shift than six hours, ten until four with no time to think. From her knapsack, she took the little statue of Ganesh and put it next to the paper cup of coffee she had brought in with her. It would have been kind to bring one for Ravi, but, as she remembered, he drank neither tea nor coffee, only water. The presence of Ganesh by the telephone would be her conciliatory gesture for all that infantile, childish footstamping of the distant afternoon before, which sneaked in around the edges of bigger anxieties and made her blush.

She had distracted herself on the way here, pushing back the essential, indigestible weight of panicky worry, by trying to think up an alternative place to pray. Not praying as in pathetic rosary bead praying, or kissing the ground, but praying as in thinking and arguing with a logical force, and that, she had realised on the rooftop this morning, definitely required a designated place. That was what places of worship were *for*. She wanted a place where she could shout inside her own head and ask, *What are*

176

you going to do about my sister? She wanted a place where she could hear some reassuring voice come back and say, *It is all your imagination that she is locked inside strong walls with a virus that has already affected all her brethren. She is not in danger. She is really stronger than you and all the more strong with a barrage of saints and angels to protect her.* Of course.

As she walked, not jogging today in her autumn jeans, because her legs were wooden, she was remembering the grander churches they had frequented as children on the high days of her mother's religion. Wherever they went, they had found a church, entered it and exited quickly if the church was not one of Rome. It was as if her mother was drawn to them all, regardless of denomination, purely for the purposes of comparison, so that she could say, see? Ours are so much better. Cathedrals in Coventry, Ely and Canterbury had all been spurned. She had promised them Chartres and Palma, although it had never happened. She mourned the fact that they lived in the wrong country for the best examples of Roman Catholic cathedrals and they had to make do with Westminster, where they had gone sometimes, like tourists to a palace. There had been an Easter service there where Therese had sneezed at the incense and Anna, prodded by her father, had giggled.

The other item in the rucksack was the missal, carried around for no good reason but the comfort granted by its weight. Anna surveyed the room, looking for Ravi's sleek black head and listening to the buzz of conversation. He looked up and smiled at her, stuck up his thumb in a brief salute and carried on talking into his mouthpiece. The smile was like a blessing. Everyone knew that Ravi was incapable of smiling to order. She was forgiven. He found it impossible to pretend. Unlike herself, who made an effort to smile, because she knew a smile helped to offset the sullen and ferocious impression she so often created. The smile of a person so insecure, she had practised it earnestly

177

and used it not necessarily to express pleasure but to please. Somewhere in the sick years, she had lost the art of smiling and had made an effort to reacquire it, in shops, the hall, the bedroom or bathroom, wherever there was a mirror. She could be a smile counsellor now, with all that practice, and smiled at the thought, for a brief moment, laughing at herself for no longer ever knowing when she smiled or scowled. Maybe concentrate on being ridiculous; she could turn it into a whole way of life, wear scarlet and feathers and furs and hats, or nothing at all . . . She waved at Ravi and the room, wiggled her hips in the way she and Therese had done as they aped magazine models in the invalid years and sat down to imagined applause. Her phone buzzed as she donned the headpiece.

'Good morning, Compucabs.'

There was a whole second of hesitation, then a deep voice.

'I asked for you yesterday and you weren't there. I was so worried, I nearly, oh never mind what I nearly did, dear, dear, dear . . .'

'Account number, sir?'

'I'm not sure, must be about here somewhere . . .'

She recognised the voice of her caller and knew, for once, she was smiling for real. He was a waste of space, but he made her smile.

'Bit early for worrying about where to go for lunch, sir. No need to book early, it isn't Christmas yet.'

'No, it isn't. Are you all right?'

'Never finer, how about you?'

'I was worried about you. Tried you yesterday.'

'I have days off, Sundays, you know how it is.'

Another sigh. 'Bloody Sundays. Why are they always awful? They just go on so long . . .'

'You're so right,' she said ruefully. They go on long enough for unsmiling people to commit acts of inexplicable folly.

'You know what Sundays are?' He was shouting into the phone. 'The dog days of the year. Did you go to church?'

She thought of the temple, touched the little statue of Ganesh with her spare hand. Ganesh did not mind looking silly; perhaps he was one of her Gods, after all.

'Yes, I did, in a manner of speaking. Now what about that taxi?'

'I wanted to ask you to come to lunch.'

'I'm working today, sir, another time, perhaps.'

He hesitated again. 'What church did you go to?'

'Well, I tried the Catholics first and then the Hindus. They're a lot more fun, but they still have collection boxes.'

There was a soft chuckle and the line went dead. He did that sometimes, her elderly gentleman caller with the strained voice and the manners of confusion. Anna waited for the phone to ring again. Today of all days, it failed her. The silence of it was reproachful. Half an hour passed. Ravi might have smiled but he did not come close. In the surrounding buzz, it was as if she were contagious. It was warm and she was overpoweringly tired. To pass the time, she began reading the messages scrawled on the backs of the holy pictures in the missal. Then she closed the book, folded her hands over the soft leather of the volume and used them to cushion her head. There was no alternative to thinking, after all.

Someone was shaking her awake, supervisors standing over her, jiggling her left shoulder, making her yelp. She was in the middle of a dream where she was being touched and kissed. Hugged by Therese, who had grown a whole foot taller.

'Steady on, girl. What do you think you're doing, coming here to kip? You've got your set turned off. What do you think we pay you for?'

It was more puzzled than censorious: concern for a good worker.

179

'Sorry.'

'Wouldn't have noticed, only everyone else is busy. And this parcel came for you. Your birthday or something? Or was that yesterday and you're sleeping it off? You look bloody rough. Go home, why don't you?'

'I don't want—'

'You don't want to let us down, right?'

She did not want to go home. She saw Ravi, standing by the supervisor, and loathed the way he looked at her, with all that genuine concern, making her feel like a sick cat.

'Just come back tomorrow, love, when you feel better. Do you need a taxi?'

The irony of that almost made her laugh, but not quite. Ravi put the missal and the statue of Ganesh inside her knapsack. The supervisor looked at her through glasses which made her eyes seem enormous. They had seen the scratches on the backs of her hands: sleep made her face pink and flushed. They were being kind, but she was profoundly suspicious of any sort of kindness and simply felt a sickening sense of repetition. First they were kind, then they sent you away.

'Sorry,' she repeated, scrabbling for dignity.

'No worries, love. Get your head down. Don't forget your parcel.' Ravi went back to his desk. The supervisor took her to the door. She carried a gift-wrapped package under her arm and felt as if she were running the gauntlet of eyes, although nobody here took any notice of anyone else: that was the whole point of it. Outside, she stood alone, waiting for the taxi, absent-mindedly ripping at the parcel. Two layers of brightly coloured, much-sellotaped paper encased a polythene envelope, which had a slight, indefinable smell. With nothing to do but wait, she persisted. Inside the polythene, inside two layers of white tissue, was a dead bird with a red bow round the neck. A very small bird, long dead, desiccated rather than putrefying.

180

The note, folded alongside, was on dry paper, cool to the touch.

Are not sparrows five for tuppence? And yet not one of them is overlooked by God. More than that, even the hairs of your head have all been counted. Have no fear: you are worth more than any number of sparrows. Luke 11.

She was stuffing it back inside the paper when the taxi arrived. Put the thing in the haversack, wiped her hands on her jeans before opening the door.

'Where to, sweetheart?'

'Westminster.'

'Going up in the world, are you?'

She was shaking and looking for the wisecrack when Ravi opened the door and jumped in beside her.

'Walk you home?' he said.

Barbara did not apologise. Kim went home as soon as the midday meal was cleared away and Therese watched her go with regret, waving from the kitchen door as if she would never see her again. Barbara, the indefatigable chairwoman of three local charities and also due a meeting with the Bishop's bursar, nodded curtly to Agnes on the door and strode away for the bus with noticeable relief. The convent car, with its respectable pedigree and low mileage, had sold with such ridiculous speed, she wondered if they had asked enough. The light in the kitchen was grey. The sisters dispersed to their various pursuits: a posse of three went into the parlour and knitted for a cause. Matilda came into the kitchen to find Therese setting up the ironing board.

'Has Anna been?'

'No, Sister. Not yet. She has a job. She comes in when she can.' Her throat felt tight and the words emerged tersely.

'Will she come in today, I wonder?'

'I don't know, Sister, I never know.'

'But she'll be in soon? Surely she'll be allowed . . . we need her . . .'

'Sometime soon, I expect. Oh, Sister, will you wait a minute?' She fished into the pocket of her tunic and brought out the knife she had rescued from the laundry bag, wrapped in a bag and not immediately obvious for what it was, except to someone who already knew. Matilda's eyes opened wide: she grabbed the knife furtively and transferred it to the depths of her gown with a mumble of thanks.

'Might I ask why you keep it, Sister?'

Matilda hesitated, studying Therese's pale face anxiously and then shaking her head.

'It's all to do with what I need to discuss with your sister, child.'

'Perhaps I could help.'

Matilda shook her head. 'No, dear. I need to talk to Anna . . . because she is not one of us.'

'She certainly isn't one of us,' Therese said bitterly, continuing in a rush of words she could not control. 'She broke the chapel window.'

'Who told you that?'

'Sister Barbara.'

Matilda felt for her beads, fingered them nervously, struggling with the uncritical, ingrained behaviour of fifty-five years.

'I can assure you, child, Barbara was . . . misinformed. Anna did no such thing.' She reached out and stroked Therese's hot cheek with a bent finger. Therese tried not to flinch. She was so often petted and stroked like a furry mascot and today she hated it in particular. Matilda smiled her beatific smile and continued the futile fingering of her rosary. The click, click, click of the beads made Therese twitch.

'And as for the knife, my dear. Let's say I use it for fruit in my room. Edmund used to sharpen it for me. You know what a greedy old thing I am.'

The afternoon yawned. Therese finished the ironing. Sick of the smell of it, she moved to the chapel for a prescribed hour of reading. Scripture of her own choice, so she always went back to favourite passages, or let the New Testament fall open wherever it would. Luke 12,22:

> I bid you put away anxious thoughts about food to keep you alive and clothes to cover your body. Life is worth more than food, the body more than clothes. Think of the ravens: they neither sow nor reap: they have no storehouse or barn; yet God feeds them. You are worth far more than the birds. Is there a man among you who by anxious thought can add a foot to his height? If then, you cannot do even a very little thing, why are you anxious about the rest?

The last two lines were the perfect tract for her sister, who had always tried to grow, and after that, Therese could read no more. Silly Anna, who practised smiling in front of the mirror and always wanted to be taller. She could think of nothing else but Anna and what Barbara had said. Not only what Barbara had said, but her own, complete silence in the face of that barrage, a silence provoked by shock, but disloyally maintained. It was one thing to be angry with her own sister, but another to have someone else insult her, and when she had first come in here to pray to God and the departed soul of her mother, there had been the ominous silence of disapproval. Therese went up to her room to fetch her coat.

There was no rule forbidding her to go out: she was not encouraged to hide away from the world beyond the walls; she was not incarcerated. She could walk in the park and gaze into shop windows like any other free agent. She had been told in no uncertain terms that the Order did not want someone who was a refugee from an ordinary, secular life purely because they were afraid of it. At the point when she would be sent out to learn to pay her way, she was not to be frightened of crossing the road, but it had not happened yet and she had become not only indispensable indoors, but increasingly reluctant to go out. It was a progression no one had forced. Her tasks complete, she was unfettered, free as a bird, with nothing to stop her going and finding Anna, or anyone else. She came back down the stairs. Agnes opened the door without comment or enthusiasm and Therese stood in the street for the first time in weeks. Free as a bird with a broken wing. Freedom required practice and equipment. She had no handbag, no money, none of the armoury of the urban foot soldier. It took so short a time to forget what it was like, the noise, the petrol smell, the slight dampness of the pavement and the light. The light, blinding even on a grey day, a whole expanse of it, weighing her down, making her lose direction. Left and left again, hugging the perimeter of the garden wall until she reached the junction, where the noise was greater. She passed the naked door in the back wall, looked at it longingly, went on to the block of flats where Anna lived and rang the bell, buoying herself up with what she would say, trying to control it, plan it, make it a strategy of calm questions. There was a niggling thought in the back of her mind that she also wanted Jude's missal. Barbara had hinted that Anna must have stolen it, and still, she had not said a word.

Standing by the panel of names on the door, each with its own buzzer, she felt conspicuous and alien, and then when there was no reply, no crackling voice from the old entryphone system, she felt entirely bereft. Therese leant towards the panel in case she had missed the response. The lack of it was total rejection.

Instead of making the logical assumption that Anna was out, all Therese could imagine was Anna upstairs, listening to the sound of her breath through the machine and laughing at her. Anna had never laughed at her, but the image of Anna grinning and jeering remained. Therese turned and walked briskly back. Agnes took a long time to open the door and by the time she did, Therese had begun to chew her nails. The day was greyer than ever: the sound of the door closing behind her was a leaden relief.

She was tired, that was all. Tired and overwrought and hungry, as her mother used to say. *There will be tears before bedtime if we don't pull ourselves together and realise what's good for us.* She would have liked to have been scolded: she would like to be given a set of rules far more rigid than those that bound her. She wanted order, predictability and work, and as soon as the door was closed, she missed the sky.

In a little while, the lull of the afternoon would be over. Still with her coat on, Therese slipped past the three dozing sisters in the parlour, asleep over their knitting, and went into the garden to find Francis. Fail in one task, find another. He was nowhere to be seen. Halfway down the path, level with the statue of St Michael, she saw the ginger cat, sitting where Matilda normally sat, washing itself. She reached out a hand to touch it. It sprang away and slunk down the path with an indignant backwards glance. Feeling like Alice in Wonderland, she followed.

This church was a million miles from the chapel, nearer in spirit and magnificence to the Hindu temple Ravi had shown her with such pride and although he had scarcely spoken a word, apart from agreeing to be taken wherever she went, she was glad he was there. Strange, to feel ever so slightly competitive about the artefacts and decorations displayed by the religion into which she had been born and did not believe, as if it was part of a birthright, to be shown off in all its splendid glory, like the kind of rich and famous celebrity relative who gave a girl status and credibility at school, even if she hardly knew him. Really, she thought, nothing beat the church of Rome for showing off. This temple glittered with gold. She liked best the smaller chapels to the sides and the soft light of the iron candle stalls, ten pence each, minimum, small night lights, aching to be lit, irresistible whatever the price, as if the small act of lighting one from another were all that illuminated the darkness. It felt as if ten pence would save a soul. The side chapel she liked the most was St Paul's, with a small, domed ceiling of brilliant blue, lit with golden stars, flanked in front by a ceiling of green mosaic, inset with three stern heads of haloed saints, more symbolic than human, looking for all the world like three gentlemen suffering from dyspepsia. It seemed from all the other evidence that it was impossible to create a smiling face from small pieces of stone. Anna said to Ravi that the cathedral, with its huge collection of recumbent cardinals, laid on top of stone coffins in vast dark corners, was made not to the greater glory of God, whose depiction was rare, but to the greater glory of men, especially those who worked in marble, because there was every shade and variety of this cold stone. He nodded. The pulpit for the high priest of the day was like a huge, white version of one of the coffins, standing on eight pillars beribboned with twists of contrasting colours, the body of it heavily inlaid with mosaic and big enough to hold thirty. A single cardinal, even with a hat, would be dwarfed in there.

Halfway down the nave, a huge crucifix hung from the ceiling. Far beyond, in the fraction of the vast space used for services, a crowd, three hundred strong, sat facing the newly gathered choristers as they filed into their designated rows flanking the altar. Anna sat, too, Ravi beside her, nearer the door for a quick escape, watching the long black robes and broad red sashes of the clergy, deftly dividing the wandering tourists from the devotional seeking entry to the service. She wondered what kind of feast day this was. The devotional would know; the tourist neither knew nor cared. Anna found it a foreign place, made smaller by memory, and peculiarly unholy by the riotous lack of harmony of the interior. Ravi's temple did it better, she decided. In a whisper, she told him so and he nodded again.

She fixed her eyes on the huge crucifix suspended on chains. Perhaps it was freakish to be so consistently drawn to so cruel an image and she wondered when it had started. Ten years old or something like that when Daddy had pointed out how comfortable a particular Jesus had looked on a particular cross. Seeing Jesus as an object was probably the death to faith. Father had always been subversive and she had never missed him more. She pointed out the crucifix to Ravi. He did not like it.

This was not a comfortable crucifix, but it had the familiar effect of concentrating her mind, and it was, in its own way, as hideous as any she had ever seen. The cadaverous figure, with a long-haired, haloed head and a crown of thorns well off the forehead, was looking to the left, supported on emaciated arms extended at rigid right angles. The long, bloodless torso of a starved man twisted into a knee-length wrap, from which slender legs led down to feet which looked as if they were agonised by shyness. The wood against which he rested was brilliant red, edged with green and gold decoration and finished above his head and at each end of his extended limbs with symbolic pictures she could not discern from her distance, also edged in gold. All the same, this was a Jesus who inspired the reverse version of wonder and the scorn she needed. There were things to ask, scolding to be done. Ravi sensed her preoccupation, moved away to the side chapel of St Paul with a signal that he would be back. She sat, refusing to kneel, began, silently, another version of a conversation.

'You know what you are, Lord, you're a little bleeder. Spoiled rotten. It's no good for people like you to be adored. You were too young.'

The organ music began, rolling down the nave. The three hundred devotees gathered for the service sat unfussily, waiting for a command. Anna ignored them and continued her own address.

'Too much attention too young, maybe that's why your judgements aren't always sound. And Dad's theory was probably right. Your old man sent you on a mission to the men of the world, and look what they did to you. Reviled, tortured and humiliated you, and then made you look as undressed as this. So what does Papa God do? Spends the next few centuries taking revenge on the world. That's what a normal father would do. Stuff forgiveness.'

The choir began to sing, an exultant blast of sound.

'Is that why you treat your devoted servants so badly? You've got a bunch of impoverished old women, headed up by Attila the Nun, threatened by hobos at the back door and the Bishop at the front, and what do you do for fun? You send them someone who looks like a saint and put him in control. What are you trying to do? Oh, for God's sake, *why*?'

In a single movement, the crowd in front of her stood. The noise of their movement had a greater resonance than the music or the singing. It was wave upon wave of shuffling vibration, the movement of coats, the clearing of throats, the motion of the bodies creating a living sound and sensation like the beating of wings, sending a draught rolling down the aisle and fluttering echoes into the rafters. It struck her that the movement of people was the most powerful of sounds. Then she heard it, back inside the frontal lobes of her brain, Sister Jude's favourite poem:

> Still with unhurried chase,
> And unperturbed pace,
> Deliberate speed, majestic instancy,
> Came on the following feet.
> And a Voice above their beat –
> 'Naught shelters thee who will not shelter Me.'

'What do you want me to do?' she whispered.

Honour thy Father. Seek the truth.

She was as cold as ice when Ravi came back. He put his arm round her shoulders, the first time he had touched her. Warmth flooded into her veins; she could smell cloves.

'It's a beautiful place,' he whispered in her ear. 'As good as ours, I think. And now I know why you are so sad.'

'Because my mother tried to kill me,' she said evenly.

He laid his head against hers. 'Because you never knew your father and you speak to him all the time. And most of all, because your Gods are so unhappy.'

The crowd in front of them sat with the same great wave of quiet sound.

Chapter Ten

Think of the lilies: they neither spin nor weave

Gardens had always been mysterious places to Therese and although they too were built to the greater glory of God, buildings always seemed a better reflection of his ingenuity. Anna and herself had been turned out into this garden when they had visited the convent the very first time as children. It was Anna who had climbed the trees and come back inside dirty. She could have sworn Edmund's old shed was there, even then. The dim memory of that had nothing to do with the fact that Therese had rarely ventured this far into the depths of it, and she felt ashamed of the fact that although it was an exceptionally long garden, it was only a matter of yards rather than miles, but it had never presented itself to her as a peaceful wilderness. In the spring, she had been dive-bombed by tiny fledglings, deafened by the sound of them and always shy of the presence of slow-moving Edmund with his tacitly discouraging manners. Besides, there was nowhere to sit or even to lean except for his bench, which was so clearly shared with the birds, festooned with the droppings that clung to his clothes. It was a litter-filled, unsavoury place, made more so by his dying in it. Coming round the last bend in the path, aware of the shushing sounds of the trees behind, she half expected to see him there on the dirty bench, outside his malodorous shed with the broken door, as dead as he was when she had covered him with a blanket only two weeks ago.

Instead, the area was swept clean, old paving stones emerging as if by magic from the beaten earth that had been there before. The bench had been scrubbed, revealing a seat of graceful proportions in pale wood with black, wrought iron legs. As she drew closer, there was a smell of creosote, which she was slow to recognise as anything other than a smell both faint and cloying. To the left of the shed, there was a small bundle of rubbish and a selection of tools, and from the side of it, the sound of singing.

> Praise Father, Son and Holy Ghost
> Whose gift is faith that never dies:
> A light in darkness now, until
> The day star in our heart arise.

A hymn for the morning, rather than the afternoon, but still a hymn, sung in a robust, unselfconscious baritone. Therese called out, hesitantly. The singing stopped abruptly. Francis emerged with a paint pot in one hand and a brush in the other, perfectly unsurprised to see her. She noticed that the door of the shed no longer hung askew, but stood open, revealing a clean, white-washed interior. He was indeed a miracle worker. He had even silenced the raucous birds of spring and his grin was infectious.

'Sister Therese!' He flourished a bow and she could only laugh, nervously, remembering what Kim had said: *Gay men know how to be nice to women.*

'Try the spring-cleaned bench,' he said. 'And be the first to admire my work. Even Barbara doesn't know. Sit, please, it's perfectly dry.'

She sat, tentatively. The wood felt warm against her back. He sat at the other end of the bench, a body's width away, and placed the paint pot at his feet. Then he leaned forward. The movement startled her, but he kept the distance between them.

'Don't tell anyone.'

'There are no secrets here, Francis,' she said severely, and even in saying it realised how far from the truth she was. 'What exactly is it you're doing?'

'I'm making an *arbour*.' He swept his arm expansively. 'Well, an *arbour* might be a bit of an exaggeration. What I'm doing is *creating a space*, like they do in those gardening programmes on the TV. Do you ever watch them?'

'I'm afraid not.'

'I didn't think you would.' He grinned at her. The day was suddenly less grey.

'Although I'm not actually creating anything,' he went on. 'We never do, do we? That's God's privilege. I'm just digging out what there was before. A clean place to sit and think, for a start. Then I can cut back the ivy, plant things round the edges, and lo and behold, it will be an area for use rather than disuse. And I don't want you to tell, because I would like it to be a treat in store.'

He had a slight accent; London, overlaid with somewhere else.

'How kind,' she murmured, meaning it. For a moment, she had quite forgotten the purpose of her expedition. His enthusiasm was as warming as the wooden seat on which she sat.

'And I'm afraid Matilda disapproves. She thinks it should stay the way it was, but old people don't like change, do they? Would you like tea, Sister?'

The invitation surprised her. How would even someone as innovative as Francis create tea at the bottom of the garden? Without waiting for a reply, he leapt from the bench and into the shed, where she could see the flame of a camping gas stove and hear the rattle of spoons. There was a rough-built bunk bed against the far wall. He poked his golden head out and seemed to bring the sun with him, reminding her of a small boy she had once met, displaying a new conjuring trick with all the aplomb of a performer anxious to impress. The shed had taken on the appearance of a summer house, bigger than she remembered, large enough for a person to sleep and quaintly romantic.

'We have water, and I provide the rest.' He arrived back with a mug of strong, orange brew. 'When I can get some lights down here, it'll be a fine place for a summer evening.'

'Yes.'

'So, you won't tell yet?'

'No.'

He placed the mug into her hands and pressed his own around hers so briefly, she would scarcely have noticed, except that she did not flinch from such a careful gesture, so far removed from the grasping demands of elderly, quavering hands. She was half aware that she was committed to yet another secret, but it did not seem to matter much. The tea was strong, the way she liked it, unlike the pallid brew dictated by convent economy, and it was too comfortable for words. The cat sprang on to the bench between them and settled itself close to Francis, startling her, until she thought, Why should it? St Francis was the saint of animals and birds; it was natural this creature would go to his namesake and the intrusion reminded her of some of the things she had come to say.

'Francis, were you the one who found my sister in the garden last night?'

There was no evasion.

'Yes, I'm sorry. I was.'

'Barbara just told me *someone* apprehended her. What on earth was she doing?'

'I wish I could tell you. Something about *praying*. I don't know.

I just followed her over the wall, thinking she was a burglar . . . I'm sorry, but she was drunk and foul-mouthed. And she has long nails.'

He turned his perfect profile to exhibit the worst of the linear scratches and then bowed his head. Dear God. Anna had always cherished her nails, an odd vanity for a tomboy.

'Did you hurt her?'

'No, *no*, I promise you, no. She's so small, there was no need to hurt her. Spitting angry at first, that was all, but harmless and calm by the time I saw her home safely.'

She was suddenly, enormously grateful to him for that, because Barbara's assurance that Anna had been unscathed was no longer reliable and it mattered.

'I was sorry for her,' Francis said, softly. 'And I rather admired her. She fought like a cat and I like cats. There's a way of handling them, you see.'

Therese did not want to discuss it further. She could feel nothing but Anna's humiliation and an angry helplessness, and if anyone was protecting Anna, she would rather it was either the Lord or herself.

'And were you sorry for Sister Joseph, too?' she demanded. 'That you take her money and buy her drink when she asks you?'

He hung his head, the golden curls falling over his face as he sighed, and she thought, irrelevantly, how odd that such hair should look effeminate on one man, yet not on another.

'Joseph was desperate, Sister. I thought it would do more harm than good, she twisted my arm and I was wrong, I suppose. I shan't do it again, but I'm new to all this, Therese, I have to learn. I didn't know the effect of the stuff, and I thought it would make her happy. She's a powerful woman. How are we going to make Joseph happy?'

The use of her name without the prefix of 'Sister', the use of 'we', as if they were allies, made Therese feel warmer, a pleasant feeling of a burden shared and thus lifted, and a mission partly achieved. Pleasant feelings were to be resisted. She finished the tea, put the mug carefully on the bench and rose to go. Francis rose too, with the alacrity of an old-fashioned gentleman.

'You must be the first to discover the *arbour*,' he said, with another of his bows. 'And come here whenever you need.'

She turned back as she reached the first bend in the path. Her last sight of Francis, just as it began to spit with rain, was that of a golden-haired, bare-armed man, cradling an orange cat.

She knew she would come back. She would come back before anyone else discovered it, at a time when Francis, with his disturbing, charming presence, had gone home, because although the convent was really too big for them all, there was absolutely nowhere else where she could be sure of being alone and she thought she had better get used to it. And the shed reminded her of another place, another garden in her first home.

It was an almost soundless rain, a damp, persistent drizzle.

'You mean,' Anna said slowly to Ravi, 'that all the time I argue with God, I'm really talking to my own father?'

'It's an idea.'

'Which could be psychobabble bullshit.'

'That could be true, also. It would be natural. If your father is in heaven, why not?'

'I think he's more likely in hell.'

They were sitting in the wooden shelter near the gates to the park, the last customers of the ice cream van, which had done a bad day's business, and although it seemed less than appropriate to talk of God and the tricks of the soul while eating ice cream sprinkled with chocolate, Ravi had no problem with that. In my religion, he told her, food is a source of joy. We offer it to the Gods and then we eat it in celebration. Food is often sacred and never profane.

'Do you think if we fed our saints they would be less miserable?' she asked.

He nodded agreement, unwilling to speak as he ate. There was such delicacy in him, she wanted to study the way he made each movement of hand to mouth and resisted the temptation to stare at him rudely.

'Perhaps. But I do not think food would appease them. They are all so thin. They all look hungry and they would still be unhappy. These saints, these Gods of yours . . . such unfulfilled lives, it seems. Such agonies, and it is the agonies they show on their faces. Never the joy of the holy state. Always they show the punishment, never the reward.'

She thought of the doll-like Gods in the temple, beautifully dressed, bedecked with jewels, missions accomplished and tranquil in their prosperity.

'And do yours have rivalries?' she asked politely, as if they were discussing relatives.

'No.'

'How do you know?'

'They would tell me, and anyway, why should they? They have given their examples and now they live in peace. They look after us and we look after them. They are not there to punish; we do that to ourselves, by not listening. Did you ever listen to your real father?'

She thought about that. 'Oh yes. He made me laugh.'

'Ganesh makes you laugh, too, but he does not mind.'

'Ravi, do you have holy pictures like these?'

She flicked open Jude's tired old missal. The spine of it was cracked with the weight of the picture cards inserted between the wafer-thin pages. Single card pictures of saints, Matthew, Mark, Ignatius, Bernadette, the Sacred Heart, but mostly of Mary, the virgin mother. Little pictures, sold by the gross, used as birthday cards, message cards, note cards, one side blank for messages and the other printed with pictures or prayers, symbols or faces, variously decorative or garish, sentimental or simple, part of the currency of Catholic devotion. Each of these had notes scrawled on the back, in Jude's spidery hand.

Take care of my niece's soul, Lord. I know what evil she does in your name. She has made those children invalids, brainwashed and poisoned them because she cannot bear the thought that they will grow and leave her. Help them, Lord. I am powerless in their service.

'We have the holy pictures, yes,' Ravi said. 'But I don't understand this prayer.'

'It's difficult.'

He looked at his watch, apologetically, glanced at her out of the corner of his eye, checking. 'I'm sorry, I have to go home now. My parents . . .'

'I know you must,' she said, gently. 'Thank you for this. It's going to rain in a minute. You'd better run, or you'll get wet.'

And then there was nothing to do but go home herself and let the anxieties rumble quietly on the bus, watching the faces and comparing them all to theirs. Two masculine faces, Ravi's and her father's, wildly different but strangely interchangeable. Ravi, dark and inscrutable, her father, weathered and pugnacious, both of them blurring into the post-rush-hour faces of the top deck. Tired faces, lively faces, a preponderance of middle-aged faces going home before the other generation came out to play. A pretty face on the other side of the aisle, reminiscent of her mother, but the reminder was as vague and distorted as her mother's face. She must remember not to stare, and if caught in the act of staring, smile to show no offence was intended.

It was pointless to stare as hungrily as she did. There were few enough clues to the universe to be found in faces. An artist could paint the devil as handsome as a Jesus; a mad mullah could look like an angel and Golden Boy could look like a saint, and he was wicked. She transferred her gaze out of the window and imagined she could see him, walking in the street, waiting to cross the road, and all the tenuous calm of the park and Ravi fled as soon as she was in the vicinity of her home. She ran for her own front door although there was as yet scarcely a hint of dusk, and as she flung herself inside, she thought, that's what he has done: he had made her afraid of the dark and she had never been afraid of it before. And then she thought it was not he who made her afraid. *The Gods do not punish us, we punish ourselves.* She scrambled up the ladder on to the roof before the light should begin its slow, autumn eclipse.

An ungenerous light, because of the now persistent drizzle, which slicked the dry roads and made them slippier than a cloud-burst. She thought of the damp paths leading beyond St Michael in the convent garden, moss covered even in summer, thought of the damp foliage around Edmund's bench, and thought finally of Golden Boy, and what the hell it was he wanted. Perhaps, like the devil, he demanded a sacrifice. The rain made the lead-covered valleys of the roof slippery too, but it was a warm wet on her bare feet. She brought the knapsack with her, and in the remaining light detached the dead bird from its wrapping, stuffed the note in her pocket, and threw the corpse into the garden, aiming left for the trees and away from the bench with a good strong over-arm throw, watching where it went until she saw it land in a bush. That was where it belonged and where it might continue to decay in peace because that was where it had died. No one else but Francis could have sent it. Unless, in some perverted attempt to give a message, Therese had done so, and that was the worst thought, which persisted eerily.

The rain brought mist in the wake of itself, but she could still see through the trees, towards the new semi-circle created out of chaos around Edmund's bench. Golden Boy Francis should have gone home by now, via the front door, like everyone else. She looked at her watch: supper-time in there; still warm, if damp, outside. She could see the clean bench, the painted shed, the decimated shrubs, the fresh-swept ground and a light from inside the shed.

You are even prettier than your sister.

He is making a trap for her. He was inside the garden last night. He does not go home.

Oh, nonsense.

She chewed a fingernail, tried to scold herself for being so dramatic. *Nothing* happens in that convent, that was the point of it. Who needs *you*, Anna, and what was poxy little Francis anyway? Some supped-up, odd-job man, their self-appointed, self-important guardian, the wanker: a boy with nowhere else to go for all his looks and an itty bitty morsel of power gone to his silly little golden head. She looked at her watch again. Definitely eating time in there. She could taste the remnants of chocolate and ice cream, like a moustache around her lips. By the whitish stone of St Michael, she could see the black-clad figure of Matilda, invisible to anyone else, vainly waving. She blinked and the figure was gone. Anna scrambled down the steps and shoved the ladder back. Searched her mind for the convent number, dialled it. Agnes would have instructions not to let her in through the door, but they could not stop her dialling. The phone rang and rang and rang, the way it did during meals. She paced the floor. Redialled. Same response.

Drizzly rain soaking the cassock he wore for visiting the sick, as if this uniform gave him credibility, and as if it had been worth it, Father Goodwin hung on the doorbell, muttering beneath his breath, 'Bugger, bugger, bugger.' His shoes did not keep out the damp, the sick had been comatose and all that was left was the urgency of duty. He rang again, before consulting the time on the watch he could scarcely see without the spectacles he could never find. Damn, damn, damn and buggery. The convent door opened to Barbara. She was still chewing and it did not add to her attraction. She would have shut the door if he had not barged past, straight down the black and white corridor, into the parlour. Barbara followed in the high temper which had been so much a feature of the day that interrupted food could only make it worse. The room was chillingly cold. She put on a single light and sat a long distance away from him.

'This *will*, Sister. Didn't you see it for what it was? It's a dangerous document, it surely is . . . It's a time bomb . . . it's *blackmail*. Did you not understand what he was trying to do?'

She sat, as frozen as a statue, looking like a basilisk on an Egyptian temple.

'He's wishing his children to the devil, Sister. Can't you read?'

She got up and turned the key in the central door that led from the parlour to the garden. The bolt at each side of the window, a grille pulled across, a padlock to secure the grille would be the final precaution for the night, as early as she chose. Then she skirted around the back of his chair, as if reluctant to come closer, sat in her own, a dozen feet away. She may as well have addressed him through a megaphone. Noise passed softly here. There was no hint of the presence of a chapel where people sang on Sundays, even less of a crowd of old women eating at the other end of the corridor.

'You think yourself so very clever, Christopher Goodwin, but why should I pay any attention to a nervous breakdown priest?'

'I beg your pardon?'

'You went mad, didn't you, Father?'

He laughed, uncertainly. Who had been talking to whom? He remembered that Barbara had only been here four years, long enough surely.

'Unfortunately not. I had a nervous breakdown, yes, which was common knowledge. Before your time here, Sister, and a matter for sympathy rather than concern, especially since you seem to be heading for one yourself.'

'Well, whatever, but I won't be breaking down on account of sexual interference with little boys, shall I? Not like you. Not like you at all.'

He gasped as if she had struck him, and then started to smile, because of all the things of which he had been accused, including the things of which he accused himself, this was so far from truth, it was risible. Wee football-playing boys? That really was rich. He thought of Kay McQuaid and the agony of her proximity, of his necessarily understated and nevertheless passionate love of women and the hell it had given him, and laughed and laughed, even while knowing that laughing was the worst thing to do, and only when she did not laugh with him, stopped.

'Jesus, woman, there's a lot more reasons for a nervous breakdown than that. Have you no imagination at all? It was faith and failure that bothered me, not little boys.'

'That's not what Francis says,' she intoned, stubbornly. 'Not what he told me this morning after you'd gone.'

Francis, Francis, Francis. What was this boy? The new Messiah? His temper rose and exploded.

'And how the hell would Francis know? The vain little beast. Is a priest supposed to have fallen upon him, like all you stupid women? Has he been reading to your from a newspaper? Is he better than the official record? For God's sake, you treat him as if you fuck him. How the hell could he know anything about me?'

He was advancing towards her, wagging his finger, eyes blazing, a picture of unbalanced craziness. She stood her ground.

'He knows because he's afraid of you. He knows because he was a tiny little boy in this parish when his mother used to clean for you. He was a teenager when you were removed and he knows exactly why.'

201

He had raised an arm, almost ready to hit her. Instead, a shock of realisation hit him like a tidal wave. He put both his hands over his face and groaned, the very picture of shame. Yes, he remembered the boy.

'Was he one of the victims, Father? Don't say there were so many of them you can't count. A nervous breakdown, was it? What rubbish. I know how the Bishop deals with these things. The way bishops do. The way *men* do. They hide it.'

The clock ticked in the silence.

He was about to say that she had an accurate understanding of the higher clergy, but that even the most recalcitrant bishop from the bogs of somewhere would not send a paedophile back to the parish of his sins within a mere two years of their commission, would at least send him somewhere else. But he knew if he spoke at all he would scream and spit and whatever he said would be futile. The rage had subsided to a furious indigestion, and still it choked him.

'You will regret this, you dumb bitch.'

'Don't threaten me.'

'Where is this bastard Francis?'

'Don't you *dare* call him that, you pervert.'

'At home, I presume.'

'You don't even *know*, do you?'

There was a look of uncertainty, and if he stayed for a moment longer, he really would hit her. He left her standing in the middle of the parlour and slammed the door shut behind him, hoping she would have followed and got it full in that plain face. The noise of the slamming door reverberated in a building where doors were never slammed and his own footsteps sounded angry. And then ahead of him in the poor lighting of the black and white corridor, he saw the unmistakable figure of Therese, hurrying away, back towards the refectory. He roared after her, 'Therese!' but she broke into a run and disappeared.

He could see her, standing on the other side of the half-open parlour door, a minute ago, waiting to knock and ask if the visitor required coffee or tea, listening to it all, and saw, again and again, the death of trust.

The rain settled around him like a cloak as he stood with his back to the door, breathing heavily. The lintel above sent drips on to his thinning hair, shockingly cold. The mist of the drizzle blurred the street lights, so that they looked as if they were wearing haloes. Bring Barbara, or dear old Agnes out here, and they might well fall down in worship. He crossed to the other side of the road and looked at the building, handsome from the outside with its mellow red brick and mullioned windows, giving that oh-so-deceptive impression of calm solidity, a haven of peace in an urban landscape, isolated by that very impression and the height of the walls, and yet they were besieged, from within and without, poor devils. If he left them now and refused to come back, he would be their last link. He counted on his trembling fingers. They had lost the reasoning voice of Sister Jude, who, from her sickbed, had been a surreptitious influence, a quiet counsellor to all of them, the keeper of secrets and reason. And then there was Edmund, with his obdurate independence, the man who listened to no one. And then there was Anna, with her far-seeing eyes and uncanny intelligence, a vital link between their world and her own. And now himself, not banned as yet, but his role made untenable by rumour. He would miss the chapel. Compared to the modern box church where he otherwise officiated, it had a magic charm, and it was the only place he knew where God was not silent.

As He was now, even in the holy glow of the street lights. Easy enough to defect, go home, turn on the television, tuck himself up with his spartan comforts and hope no one would call, but the anger had done him good. He wanted to throttle someone and was briefly, ironically aware that all the targets he would like to murder were of his favourite sex. Kay McQuaid, Sister Barbara, his own dead mother and even silly Therese for running away. And if he stood here any longer in his cassock, with his fists clenching and unclenching and the rain on the back of his neck, looking ready to howl at a non-existent moon, someone would arrest him. Christ, it would almost be a relief. Urgency made his throat dry. There was nowhere to go, except to another person in disgrace. If Anna would not let him in, he would sit on the doorstep and wait.

'Calvert' on the bell, he knew exactly where, although he had never been inside, only glancing up sometimes, as he passed unnecessarily often. He should have visited and told what he knew of the truth, a long time ago. Should have, should have, should have.

'Recrimination,' he said loudly into the entryphone, 'is the death to all endeavour.'

'What's that, Father?' she said, her voice so disembodied it made him leap with shock. There was jarring background noise.

'Can I come up?'

'Of course.'

Even a man could hear the disappointment in that voice. He began the long march up the interminable flights of ill-lit stairs and thought, At least she is safe here.

Music, of a kind, poured from the top flat as he panted up the last flight of stairs. The wailing of sitars and beating of drums almost stopped him. He had forgotten how young she was: with music like that, they had not a cat in hell's chance of understanding one another, but then again, maybe it was not understanding they needed.

The scale of the place was almost that of a dolls' house, to his mind, bigger when he looked from the small living room to the

204

kitchenette beyond, but still too small for all the sound. By now he was so hot inside the damp cassock and anorak, he could not imagine breathing in such a place, even while he noticed it was not as he imagined. It was not strewn with clothes and youthful detritus, but merely functional, two chairs, two pictures, the stereo on the bookshelf, and that was all, as if the space was always needed for something else. Anna turned off the music, for which God be praised, but in the sudden silence, he did not know what to say.

'Have you come to tell me off?'

'No. I've come to build a wax model of Barbara and that bastard boy Francis, and stick pins in them.'

'In which case, you're welcome.'

He sat, presuming he was asked.

'Did the old bitch throw you out?'

'In a manner of speaking, yes. I'd like to think I left.'

'Did you climb over the wall, or something?'

'No, she thinks I'm a paedophile.'

'Bless her,' said Anna, smiling, and then it was all right. 'Would you like a drink?'

'Water,' he said. 'Whiskey by the pint would be better, but I've somewhere else to go.'

A long journey to the sea. He thought of it as she brought the water, with dread, running the train timetable through his mind. Every hour on the hour. Yes, he would get there before midnight. The dark was deceiving; it was early yet. If any parishioner died tonight, they would have to die alone. She was watching him drink the water with a motherly concern at odds with her tiny size.

'A man who interferes with children? I can't see it, myself.'

'A similar accusation to the one applied to your father, as I recall. His own children. At least I'm supposed to have gone for other people's.'

205

She stood completely still. 'That is utterly and completely untrue,' she said, slowly. Then she shook herself. 'Can you manage a few more steps, Father?'

Without waiting for a reply, she pulled the ladder from the wall from behind its curtain, climbed up and pushed the trapdoor at the top. A draught of delicious air descended. He followed her, awkwardly. She pulled him on to the parapet with a grip of surprising strength and before he could begin to wonder how on earth he would get down, he was seeing the stars and realising exactly why she would live in a flat as claustrophobically small as this. He found his footing on the slippery lead, followed her a couple of steps, leant as she leant, with arms folded on the stone wall, safe as houses and quite at home. He had always liked heights. The difference was that even leaning like this, his torso protruded over the parapet a whole foot more than hers. He stood and leant back for balance, a giant next to a midget.

'So what did you come to say, Father?'

'I quite forget. Only that God really will forgive you, whatever you do.'

'I don't care about that. I care about Therese.'

'All right, I came because I felt the corrosive effect of disgrace, which I thought you would understand. And because I feel a great sense of danger hanging over you and Therese. Nothing can begin to cure it other than the brutal truth. Your father's will—'

'Never mind that. Therese hid it from me, I knew she did and I didn't care. What was he like, my father? I mean as man to man. You knew him, a little.'

He fished for the cigarettes. None.

'Knew him a little and liked him a lot. He had great love in him and he adored you both. But love made him naive and he was no match for your mother.'

'No sane person can be a match for somebody *insane*,' she said, slowly. 'No one can match that kind of will power. Especially not when it wears the armour of angels and the great shield of righteousness.'

Father Goodwin caught his breath and found himself suddenly close to tears. It was the lack of bitterness in her voice that moved him more, the dry absence of reproach, and the release of tension in himself which made him stagger and grasp the parapet firmly with both hands, noticing even then how she had flung out her arm to stop him falling. A child with a protective instinct stronger than anything else, which may have come, in a purer form, from her mother.

'When did you realise this?' he whispered.

'I don't know. I don't *know*. Not in the beginning, not for the first year when we were ill. I think that might have been real and he was wrong. There was shouting in the background, all the time. Then my father went; then he tried to kidnap us; then I tried to run away, and oh so many things, all blurred. No strength, you see; no strength to do anything at all, or think a single thought. I could read, but I couldn't think, or rather I couldn't think and carry anything through to a conclusion, and we were *accomplices*, you see. We agreed with her, we had to, there was no one else, but somewhere, sometime, I knew what she did. Munchausen something, isn't it? But she made us believe we were ill and we believed. It became fact. For Therese, it still is fact, but believe me, Father, there was no need for either Sister Jude or your good self to hint to me that those four, dead years were anything other than my mad mother's fixation that she would rather we died than left her to go to the devil. She was terrified for herself and for us. I used to think that it was me who started it, by being naughty. Giving her the hint of how bad it could get.'

'Nonsense.'

She stretched her arms in front of her, palms locked outwards, and he could hear the click of her fingers.

'But it took a long time to *know*, even longer to *admit*. I was a better reader than Therese. I could read the books of symptoms better than her, but it was only later that I queried the drugs. Common stuff. Valium she got for herself, benylin can knock you out, and every variety of mildly poisonous food. She was a dietician and she did the reverse. You can make a person very ill with food combinations and herbal remedies. Especially if you never let them get well. Paint fumes, she was always painting, and joss sticks. I can understand why my father went. I should be grateful he set his lawyers on her. But I wish he had written.'

The anger was coming back; quiet, but useful.

'And how, dear child, would you ever have received his communications? Who opened the door to the postman? Who answered the phone? Was there email?'

'He could have sent someone.'

'He was forbidden by law. He was accused of molesting you, and the law moves slowly. He was arrested six times outside your door. A mother has the real power. He sent me, slender reed that I am; he sent Sister Jude . . . the door was barred, and we, of course, were weak.'

'As frail as all flesh,' she said. 'Never mind. I wish I had known, but there it is. And the irony of it all is that Therese has tried to protect me from any hint of him, while I have tried never to sully her abiding memory of our mother. It would be nice if she could keep that. Even if it did give her the infection of faith and her bloody vocation.'

'Theodore's last will and testament—' he began.

'Not now, Father, it doesn't matter. I can't take it and you have somewhere else to go.'

She stood up straight, grasping the parapet as firmly as he had. In this proximity, her shoulders were the height of his chest and yet he knew which of them was the stronger. The urge to weep remained.

'Tell me what you can see,' she said.

He did not look down, he looked across. 'I think I can see the whole of the park. I can see Knightsbridge. I can see an aeroplane, oh Lord, I can see lights. It's marvellous, I can see—'

'I should have realised before,' she said in that dry, matter-of-fact tone, 'that a tall man sees such very different things.'

She smiled with that dreadful wryness he hoped would never become permanent.

'My father, you see, was a giant. As tall as you. Or at least, that's how I remember him.'

He ran down the stairs feeling the weight of the bundle of documents inside the anorak pocket, cooler now, just as wet, racing for that damn train. There was enough money for a taxi to the station, no cigarettes, no food and just enough of the anger to get him there. Inside the station, the dog collar got him a discount, and as he waited on the platform, a sad old geezer offered him a cigarette. God forgive him, he took one for later as well.

Sister Barbara looked up from the bookwork in the office next to the parlour, disturbed by footsteps. They padded by her door, but the direction they took before beginning to fade was uncertain, backwards or forwards, she did not know: towards the front door, or away, she did not know. Her nerves, as she told herself, were frayed and there was something askew with the conscience she did not want to consider just at the moment and never in the middle of arithmetic at any time. *Pitter, pitter, pitter*, quiet as a cat, skirting round the light of her door on the black and white corridor, and then, she was sure she was right, going back as if nervous to go on. Barbara knocked her heavy ledger on to the floor where it fell with a bang. An indication she had heard and whoever it was risked displeasure.

She waited for a minute. Too late to do anything more useful here, anyway. Young men in offices worked after ten at night, but she was not one of those, and even if sleepless, she was past her best at least three hours earlier. A good thing, too.

Because of conscience, or something related to it, she opened her office door carefully and looked to left and right. Nothing. In her stockinged feet, she walked into the parlour. She pulled the grilles and checked the bolts and put the keys back in her office. Good. Then she went in the other direction to the chapel.

The moon rose behind the huge windows, enhanced by the bare, still branches of the trees. She looked upwards towards it, remembered how long it was since she had last prayed in here, and hurried away. Safe for the night.

CHAPTER ELEVEN

Do not fear those who kill the body and after that, have nothing more they can do

Matilda saw Father Goodwin striding down the black and white corridor after supper and tried to stop him, but he did not notice. Before that unmemorable meal, she had seen Francis leave via the front door, and although she could not quite hear the fond farewells and suggestions he eat something sensible for his own supper which she was sure would come from Agnes, she could imagine the sentiments. It filled her with angry misery. Delusions were the stock in trade of the devil. All that she could remember after a sojourn in the chapel was that the rain had stopped and it would be safe to linger in the garden for more than a few minutes alongside St Michael.

The parlour was deserted as she crept through, turned the key and went out with a feeling of relief, bearing her gifts. For the last days, she had been afraid to spend any time in her favourite place, confining her visits to quick, furtive forays, never staying for long, waving her arms towards the sky, in the hope that the little person who sometimes watched from that roof over there would see her. But Anna had been forbidden: perhaps little Anna would never come, and Matilda, with an endless capacity for forgiveness, could quite understand why she should not. She was a rash, brave child, who might have seen what she herself had seen, since she had tried to wound Francis after all and scratched his face in that futile process, poor child, but no one could be brave all the time. So, there was nothing for it but prayer, and even in the relative cold and dark, which made her mourn the blessed warmth of a kindly spring, she was pleased to see St Michael and sit in a familiar place. The benefit of small mercies was something she had learned in a long life. Each moment of peace counted; regret was as futile as the endless questions, which were a constant source of indigestible pain.

Such as, why did God engineer life in such a way that those whom you loved were always the victims of pride and held their sufferings from you in case you should understand them all too well? Why had Joseph, her closest friend, turned away from her in such bitterness, as if she had not already accepted her frailties entirely? Perhaps because of the deafness, which inhibited their once endless conversations. And why did the God of forgiveness and understanding make those very same virtues so difficult for proud people to accept? Shame was a foreign concept to Matilda. You did what you did, felt sorry and puzzled about it, since to err was human and forgiveness just as natural. Pain was pain, to be offered comfort and the promise it would be better tomorrow, that was all. She sat heavily on the stone bench at Michael's feet with her back to him, hating the need to ask questions at all without relying on plain, simple acceptance, which was the real virtuous state. Doubt was sin and questions were anathema.

Such as, could she have prevented Edmund's death? To that particular question, the answer was no, because death was the will of God and a matter entirely of His timing, and she doubted, in all honesty, if she could have done much about the method. Francis had been the instrument, first by the simple expedient of finding a way to Edmund's heart and then breaking it by killing the birds. Heart first, spirit second, and the fragile body last. On the evening of the decimation of the chapel window, she had heard the *pop* of the air rifle, clear against the blur of other sounds, which her incipient deafness selected with a random choice that still amazed her, and quite apart from that, she had seen the young devil with his weapon and his artfulness, passing her by as she sat as quiet as the statue of St Michael, amused at first by his young man's arrogant assumption that someone as old as herself would be blind as well as hard of hearing, concluding that, in the way of the young, he simply did not *see* her at all. But, then, most people didn't. And she had refrained from insisting to Edmund that it was Francis who killed the birds, because that would have broken his heart sooner, at a time when he wanted love from the boy, and hoped for it. He would not have listened, and no one would listen now.

Except Anna, who must know exactly what he was like, because Anna lived in a world full of evil persons just like that, and Anna watched, from her roof. But Anna was in disgrace, and might not come back, and Joseph, dear Joseph, as well as Barbara, had made herself blind to the boy. Oh dear, oh dear.

Supper had been bad tonight. Cold meats and bread, leaden and inadequate, leaving an unsatisfying lining to the stomach. Therese had eaten nothing and she worried about that, too. Matilda had taken extra fruit from the plate and a lump of cheese in the same way she had when Edmund was alive and they would share her fruit in exchange for his biscuits. Grapes were his favourite, but they rarely had grapes unless they were given. Instead, there were endless apples with slightly wrinkled skin, better eaten peeled with Edmund's fruit knife, which she had taken from where he had left it last, and kept to ward off the devil. Which was Francis, no doubt it was Francis, and she was so afraid of him she kept the knife in her pocket with her handkerchief. Sighing, she took out the lump of cheese from the

213

wrapping of another handkerchief, the best-looking apple from the bowl plus two chocolates, which she really wanted, and laid them on the seat beside her. There were times when nothing else but sacrifice would do.

'Help us, dear Michael, there's a love. I brought them specially for you. If I leave them and don't eat them, will you ask the Lord to take note of my hunger and make something good from it? Such as get rid of that boy, before he murders us all?'

She sat forward, resolutely ignoring the sight of her own, tempting offerings, wanting them to be snatched away, before she could retrieve them. She watched the darkening sky and stood to greet it, moving two steps down the path so that she could see if the back bathroom window of Anna's place was lit at all. The girl was prodigal with electricity, like the young, and she herself was a silly old woman, and it was late to be out, mourning unchangeable things, feeling herself swell with fury when she thought of that boy. Because he *knew* she knew his wickedness: she had seen it in a single, frightened glance of his and in his conspicuous failure to approach her at all, the only one of them who was not eating out of his hand. It took God years to win a heart, but the devil could do it in five minutes.

'Eat it up, Michael dear, or give it away. There's no telling what else you might get in heaven.'

She sat, puzzling it all, elbows on knees, refusing to rest against the stone of the feet, which had once seemed so warm, trying to resist the feeling of great, helpless sadness, which her own blithe optimism kept at bay most of the time, whatever happened, even when Joseph turned her back. Then she stood and wandered the few steps further to the bend in the path, which had always delineated the beginning of Edmund's domain and that of the birds, listening. In the height of spring, she could hear them in the morning; at this time of last year, she could hear only the shrill sounds of alarm and now there was nothing. Another few steps

214

led on to the best view of the back bathroom window of Anna's place. The path was slippery with the rain which still hung in the air with the promise of more. Matilda put out her hand to feel the way she knew better than the way to her own room: always wished her sight had gone sooner than the refinements of her hearing, if there had been any choice about either. Her hand felt the wire across the path. There was a rustling behind her.

In the best of worlds, it would be St Michael, eating his food, but she knew it was the cat. She clutched the waist-height wire, which was thin, cold and moist. Which saint was it, killed by the garotte? St Agnes. She pulled at the wire; it was a further trap for the birds, as if he had not already massacred them all, the bastard. It was a warning, a keep out sign, it was abominable, and held fast. The rustling behind continued. Dear God, the wire should be around the neck of that murderous cat. Matilda yanked the wire. It loosened suddenly, so that she stumbled on her own weight, falling backwards as her feet skidded from beneath her, and stayed half upright by still holding the wire and pulling it free, as if it were bindweed. She was breathless with the effort, shaken with the overbalance.

Thin, harmless wire, which would not have impeded anything other than a midget running at it full pelt. She flung it to one side, aware of her terrible weariness, the darkness, the futility of waving at that distant light, and retraced her steps, unsteadily. The statue of St Michael had its own familiar outline and she felt as if she were wading towards it. Sat, once she was there, and then turned to place her hands on his feet. There were countless times she had done that; her hands on his lichen-covered toes, dozing in good company, peacefully. She rested like that for a minute, trying to recapture the peace of summer. Then she noticed the damp between her fingers, raised her head and examined the strange sensation of soap that oozed between them.

She could just about see that the feet of St Michael were covered in a foamy substance, reaching up to his manly calves. She withdrew her hands with muttered disgust and looked for somewhere to wipe them, finding nothing but the handkerchief she had left with her offerings. She worked with that, until her palms began to tingle, then to burn, and then she began to brush them against her habit frantically, until they stuck to the cloth and still burned as if they were on fire. She wiped them on her breast, spat on them, wiped again, and then, trembling, stumbled towards the patio with its light and promise of water. Fell on the slippery path, found the cool of the stone a benison to the burning skin and after that, crawled. She crawled towards the parlour door, with the cold, damp stone of the patio giving the only relief, and when she reached it, unable to bear the thought of taking her hands off the ground, raised her feet and kicked at the door. There was no response. The security light showed the closed grille and the drawn curtains.

Matilda crawled to the planter at the side, and dug her hands into the damp soil, and even in the extremes of this dull pain cursed at the irony of a regime of obedience and silence, which in making such efforts to keep people out forgot the importance of letting them in. And as she tried to stand, feeling her feet slip from under her and her head hit the side of the pot with a thud, wondered what she had done for St Michael to reject her so much he covered his own feet with acid. Remembering asking Edmund to clean the moss away, wishing against any other wish that she had not done that, calling softly for Joseph to come and help her, hearing nothing.

Anna needed sleep, more than anything else in the world, but pyjama-clad and restless, she climbed back on to the roof. On the busy side of the view, traffic passed and the Oppo Bar thrived, far from closing time, with a few brave customers sitting

216

outside beneath the awning to celebrate the end of the rain and the end of the summer. On the convent side, the garden was black, until she stared down into it, and the familiar shapes began to emerge, clearer through the leafless trees. The contrast between this side of the building and the other was almost bizarre, live music and traffic visible from one angle, and from the other a place disused because everyone went ridiculously early to bed. It was not so much their style of life that isolated the dear Sisters, she thought, but the way they kept to a sleeping and eating timetable suitable for children younger than eight. What did they do with all those wasted hours? Could you dedicate sleep to God?

The peace of the garden and the darkness of the house infuriated her: they did not deserve it.

The new bareness of the trees allowed her to see as far as the patio, faintly illuminated by the security light, which, only a week before, had twinkled with dim insignificance behind leaves. She was too far away to observe detail, wished she had Father Goodwin's height, which would enable her to see more, but she could see enough to notice that the patio had changed, very slightly, from when she had last looked, with him, an hour or so before. No major change, simply the addition of a big black bag in front of the door.

Which meant, in her exhausted estimation, that someone had put it there. That someone had, perhaps, been working in the garden at an hour which was late by their standards of lateness, and the thought induced panic, because the obvious person was Francis, coming and going as he pleased, plotting whatever sabotage he meant for their lives. The panic succeeded the anger at their stupid somnolence and the anger succeeded the panic. Why should Barbara not answer her phone and why should she be allowed to sleep? Anna slithered downstairs, picked up the phone and dialled 999. She remembered to withhold the number and

was the model of succinctness in her speech. She was a neighbour of the Blessed Sacrament Convent in Selwyn Road, she
told the calm voice that asked her which emergency service she
required: she had seen three people climb over the wall at the
back and knew that everyone in the building would be dead to the
world. They were old and vulnerable. Would they send someone
quick? They would need to bang long and hard on the front
door to get a response; the old dears never knew their danger,
and no, she would not give her name.

That done, she put the roof ladder back against the wall and
drew the curtain around it, which made it look like a makeshift
student's wardrobe, and put out the bathroom light. Perhaps this
piece of mischief would allow her to sleep, but oh God, she had
done it again, stupid, so she was not going to watch what happened. It would invite disclosure and compound the childishness,
but she hoped they caught him. Duvet over the head, willing
herself into the cure of sleep, she regretted the 999 call, because
it was what she did all the time, react without thinking and then
regret it. Other people thought before acting, while she lived
with the gaps in her life and fought with the conclusions like a
mud wrestler, making futile gestures as she slithered around, and
she was sick of simply reacting, rather than planning, but she did
not know what else to do, except cry, for her mother, her father
and Therese, not necessarily in that order, and then try to sleep,
because whatever else, there was work the next day and that was
the only certainty. Tomorrow, there would be a metamorphosis.
She would wake up wiser, and begin to plan . . . And in the midst
of this, the entryphone buzzer went on buzzing.

It was like a wasp, trapped in the room, and for all the time she
had lived there, with visitors as scarce as friends, it was still an
unfamiliar sound to be buzzing without the normal backdrop of
the music she turned up loud as soon as she came inside. Against
the silence, it was commanding and offered no alternative. It

went against every instinct she had *not* to respond to the sound and fail to let someone in, because it could always be Therese; it might be Father Goodwin again. But that tiny bit of logic said, shit and damnation, it would be the police, because that was the consequence and she'd better face the music. Wearily, she pressed the button on the console: a simple, automatic reaction, followed by the single thought that maybe this was a foolish thing to do.

Foolish, at eleven o'clock at night, when she was crazy tired, mixed up, bound to make every explanation for every stupid action sound sillier than it was. She had enough time to consider that if it was a copper asking why the hell she had called them out, she would have the option to shrug and say Who? and act like some dumb child they would be reluctant to arrest. She *had* to get to work the next day, *had* to: it was the only fixed thing in her life and she needed it. And then she thought, no, she would not behave like a child, taking advantage of her own size; she had done enough of that. She would behave like a truthful adult, tell it like it was.

Music came from the flat below hers, a comforting reminder of close humanity and another reminder of how she had never attempted to make friends with any of them. She held the door half open, composing herself for the portentous footsteps of a policeman making enquiries. They were swifter steps, coming upwards from the well of stairs, until she saw him bounding up the last flight with his yellow hair and she was suddenly completely paralysed, until Francis was there, with an enormous boot, jamming the door open. Golden Boy, with his shining, saintly eyes.

'I've come to apologise,' he said.

In the distance, she could hear sirens. Nothing was ever going to happen in the right sequence. He was supposed to be in the garden, waiting for them. And now he was here, smiling to the

219

thump, thump, thump of the music downstairs, which would never protect her, from anything.

Christopher Goodwin knew his way from the railway station in Kay's town, the way he told people he knew the inside of his own pocket, a comparison he repeated to himself now while knowing it was daft, because he was always so unsure of exactly what his pockets contained. Items collected in there with the ease of dust but greater bulk, such as biros and pieces of paper, receipts for purchases, an umbrella, the crumbled remnants of cigarettes, unanswered letters and a pair of useless nail scissors, which his fingers clutched in the search for cash. The pocket of a cassock and the capacious pockets of his anorak were probably the equivalent of a handbag for a woman and, getting out at the right station and setting off at a good speed, he had a vision of himself with one of those, instead of the routine, design accessory of an ugly old polythene bag.

He walked by the sea, which was nothing at first but a cold, dark backdrop, calling Kay McQuaid all the names under the moon. If she were not in her house, he would bomb the place, and the very thought of that made him pause with the thought of his own impotence. All right, he would pick up pebbles from the shore where Theodore Calvert had drowned and break all her windows. Oddly enough, the anger had been easy to sustain over an hour and a half's journey in a cold train. All he had to do was to think of that poisonous document of a will and the sad draft that accompanied it, the posse of drunken youths at the far end of the carriage, Sister Barbara and that boy, Francis, to make him hyperventilate to screaming point, cross his arms over his chest and rock back and forth. Understandably, no one bothered him on the train and no one was going to bother him on this road by the sea, a kind of small esplanade where the street lights illuminated the wet concrete and the curl of the waves breaking into foam on the shingle below mocked him with their patient consistency. What's it like to do the same thing every day? he asked the waves, pausing for a moment to watch a piece of flotsam move sluggishly on the current, floating inwards and sideways towards the foam, trying to guess how far it would travel before it hit the shore. In the brief time he watched, considering how his own St Christopher would have waded into the waves and rescued it, it moved far to the right, almost out of sight, edging closer and moving back in a coy dance. Even a broken crate could move with grace, fighting the strength of the current. He shuddered at the thought of Theo Calvert's body, deposited here with far less care. The man Anna referred to as her giant of a father.

Kay McQuaid was not a person who went early to bed, or one to be alarmed in her somnolent, ultra-respectable road, to have someone knock at her door on the right side of midnight. He went to the back of the house, where light shone through the glazed kitchen door, and knocked thunderously. Timid knocking made people ever more nervous. There was a new lock, a big brute of a seven-lever Banham, of the kind favoured by his rich parishioners, although perversely, it was the poor who were burgled most. He could see a bright-coloured dressing gown hovering behind the door.

'Open up!' he roared. 'For God's sake, woman, it's only the priest.'

She opened it slowly, to show a tired face, in which relief was notable for its presence and the lack of cosmetics for their absence. A different gown to any he had seen, with a stain down the front of its satin texture, and not a hint of surprise in her whole bearing, only a degree of resignation. Christopher Goodwin realised that his old friend Kay was moderately drunk. Good.

'Hello, Kay. Surprise, surprise.'

221

'Not really,' she said dully, letting him past her with all the enthusiasm she may have offered someone who had come to read the gas meter, following him through the kitchen into the living room, still fashioned around the donkey cart of drinks and the Buddha squatting in the fireplace, looking ready to burp. He noticed how the doors to her garden were curtained, shutting it out, making an announcement that life had moved indoors and summer was now officially finished until next year. She always had been a bit of a control freak, trying to influence the weather and then shutting it out if she didn't like it, changing her face to overcome her mood, changing her clothes, latterly, to control the time of day. She was a one, that Kay McQuaid, but even in the electric light, he could see that her eyes were pink, her eyebrows unattended, so that they looked fierce, and the room subtly disorganised. It was not the living room of someone at the end of their tether, but the room of someone who had not moved very much or very far for more than a day.

'Help yourself,' she said, sinking back into an armchair, which had obviously borne her weight for several hours without any of the obsessive plumping of cushions that was her custom. He went for the Jameson's, relieved to find it pristine, fussing over it with umming and ahing, going out for a clean glass, to give her time to compose herself, hide the stain on the gown and whatever she needed. He found a piece of stale bread, sitting on a crumb-filled bread board, and ate it. Once settled in the opposite chair, with a glass in hand, he put the damp parcel of documents on to the smeared glass table between them both.

'Don't, she said. 'I've never been much good with the written word.'

'What a liar you are, Kay,' he said, agreeably, easing himself down and wishing he was not so hungry, thinking he might go back into the kitchen to find that open packet of peanuts he had also seen, spilling on to the floor. 'You were always good with a letter. You were granted a primary education, somewhere. Always wrote well. Good signatures.'

She grunted and smiled at him, vacantly, a fatuous smile spreading across her face, and then two parallel sets of tears coursed down her cheeks. Plump cheeks, like the rest of her, hidden bones in a pulpy face he had always found so vivid before. Beauty was ever in the eye of the beholder.

A scar, ticking away beneath the disorganised eyebrow, otherwise disguised.

'I've something to tell you,' he said. 'Your boy Jack is working in the convent garden, the convent itself, more like, and had them all in various states of sublime adoration. Francis, he calls himself now. Blond and beautiful and poisonous. Have you any idea of what it is he might be trying to do?'

She shook her head and moaned.

'Of course you do,' he continued evenly, although it was an effort. 'Theodore's will says that it all goes to his daughters, provided they do not *sin*. Should they be *seduced* away from the paths of virtue he had come to loathe, he would rather leave his inheritance to the devil. Otherwise known as Jack McQuaid, bypassing the middleman, so to speak. Who the hell persuaded him to write such a thing, darling? You?'

She roused herself.

'*No.*'

'But you knew. You signed it.'

'I signed whatever Theo wanted me to sign.'

'Ah, yes. As one does. And you have a copy in the house?'

'Yes.'

'And you have the draft with the notes?'

'No. I never had that.'

He waited. She pulled herself further up the chair and used her index finger to stroke her eyebrows straight. Alas, he thought, drunk, but no drunker. Pity. He preferred confessions from those of the slurred voice, Help me Father for I have sinned, with enough of the drug- or alcohol-induced inebriation aboard to tell some approximation of truth or at least as much as the confessional ever offered. He drummed his heels on the floor. The vibration seemed to echo in her chair. The closed-in room reminded him of the convent parlour and he was, to his own relief, as angry as ever.

'*Francis*,' she pronounced it with the emphatic care of someone unused to the syllables and adding a lisp on the S, 'stayed here for three years. Theodore treated him as a son. But long before that, ever since he was ever so small, he was convinced he was Theo's son. He started to believe it when I left you and went to work for the Calverts. Remains convinced.'

'On what grounds, darling? Why the devil would he think that?'

She squirmed in the armchair, looked at her gin. Empty. He got up, swifter-footed than he would ever have thought, and poured, into a fresh glass. The one from which she drank had done service far too long and there was no shortage of glasses. She gulped at it. Christopher Goodwin felt slightly ashamed of himself.

'I don't know quite why. He'd always asked. I never said. Drove us both mad, those questions. I took him to meet the girls when I worked for the Calverts. They fascinated him, they were so pretty and so small. *Petite*,' she snapped. 'Tiny little over-privileged things, like dolls. With a mother who chucked him out, the bitch. Couldn't stand a raw-blooded male, even one with a crucifix round his neck, even if he was only twelve at the time. Ha, ha, ha.'

'A crucifix?'

'I put one round his neck when he was small. To ward off the evil eye. He always liked it.'

She got up, steadily, and went to the bathroom. He heard her footsteps trailing away and, after an interval, coming back. Bathroom on every floor in this house, all luxurious, equipped with toothbrushes, soap, talcum powder, flowers, in case anyone should ever arrive, the points in the compass of this big house where she still did everything Theo had suggested. Christopher did not prompt her as she sat back in her armchair, where he had rearranged the cushions in her absence, for comfort. It made him feel ever so slightly offended that she did not notice. Women should appreciate such small attentions, even if the intention was subversive. Maybe he was just another unreconstructed male after all.

'And?'

'I suppose I let him think it.'

'Think what?'

'That Theodore was his long-lost father and the girls were his younger sisters. I let him think it by refusing to tell him who his father was. I had always refused to tell him that, *always*. He created the myth of Theo as his daddy out of his own mind. I don't know when it took root. When I sneaked him into the Calverts' house? Later, when I moved here, bringing him with me? It must have looked like Theo coming into his own as a parent at long last. Offering his boy a home and a start in life, to make up for what had gone before. And Theo had this huge, bitter gap in his life. He wanted a young thing to make a fuss of. A substitute daughter. He was *very* kind to Jack. Spoiled him. I never had, never could. It must have been like coming in from the cold.'

The whiskey was warm and acrid. Kay had washed her face in the bathroom, making it pink and herself more fluent. Christopher did not know if this was good or bad. The fluency was an effort. She lapsed into silence.

'Surely you told him it was all nonsense? That he was just a lucky boy, to have found a place like this to live, someone who would take care of him . . .'

225

'Jack, I mean *Francis*,' she spat, 'didn't want *luck*. He wanted a birthright. He wanted the *right* to live in a big house with no worries. Always wanted to go to a posh school when he was a kid and be like the sort who came home in a uniform with a mobile phone in each pocket in case Daddy got worried. *Francis* wanted everything. I told him Theo was not his father. He wouldn't have it. He hated me.'

'But he left. You told me. Ditched the idea of college and went for a job in London. If he liked it so much, why did he go?'

She got up again, sloshed more gin into her glass, added tonic, spilling some. She produced her cigarettes from the pocket of the gown, lit one and threw the packet towards him. Old friendships die hard.

'Whatever gave you the idea he simply went? Oh, I see, *I* did. Well, he was bound to be the one who bit the hand that fed him. Jack was corrupt from the moment he was born. By that time, I couldn't have shifted him from the notion that Theodore was his father even if I'd tried, but Jack would always want an insurance policy. And he could see Theo going demented, trying to get his daughters away from their mother. Distancing himself from everything else . . . killing himself with love and anxiety, although, God help him, he never went for the drink again. Saving himself to be a father.'

'Oh, for heaven's sake, woman. Didn't Francis ever demand proof that Theo was his father? Something simple? One of those DNA tests? People in the parish do it all the time. Or at least, I don't know if they do it, but they ask me how it's done.'

Kay gazed at him with disdain. He was being slow. 'You don't ask for proof if you have no doubt. Would you ask for proof of your own paternity?'

He thought of his mild father, and his quiet mother, who had always wanted more children and brought up their own with a rod of iron, their vocations all decided for them.

'No, I wouldn't have dreamed of it.'

'No more did he. But in case his father should reject him first, he thought of another angle to keep him loyal. Sex. I told you he was corrupt. Lost his cherry to some old man when he was about ten, I think. He traded in sex before we left London. He could see poor Theo was starved of it, even at his age, so he tried to seduce him.'

The spiral of smoke from the cigarette in Christopher's hand shook. He took a long drag on it, trying to suppress shock. Get a grip, man: you've heard worse, and she may be lying again, but he did not think she was.

'It's an odd thing to try with your daddy,' he said, conversationally.

'Not at all,' she said in the same tone. 'Daddies do it with babies all the time, so what's the difference the other way round? So Theo's unhappy and half asleep, Francis crawls in beside him and gets to work. Mistake. Didn't get far. He was gone next day, with a bit of money, to be sure, but gone.'

Father Goodwin stubbed out the cigarette, somewhat at a loss for words. Then he sighed.

'Well, at least the boy knows which sex he likes. He has an orientation—'

'Oh, is that what you call it? Don't kid yourself. Francis would have fucked his own mother if he thought it would help. Anything goes with Francis. Women, men, dogs for all I know. You must have known boys like that.'

He did, feral creatures, from an early parish somewhere else: orphan predators.

'Would it not have helped if you had told him who his father was? Would it not have given him some pride?'

She laughed. Laughed until she choked and he moved to her side to pat her on the back. It did him good to slap her between the shoulder blades, belting out some of his own tension and bugger the bruises. Tears seeped down her face. He could see, with the ice chip in his soul, the wisdom of not wearing face powder to be streaked and ruined by such tears, tried not to let them distract him as he sat back in his own chair, away from her. They had some distance to go yet.

'You don't tell a child that he's the product of a gang rape in an Irish garage shed. That you don't know who his father is, except that he might come from a mixture of all the bad blood in a small place. That he would have been aborted if his mother's parents hadn't listened to the priest. He was born with me screaming hatred, Father. What else is there to tell? Do you wonder I never loved him?'

He was determined to avoid pity. There was no time for it. It was late, he had got her on the run and there was no telling what she would be like in the morning. Pity was for another time. A good priest, even an indifferent priest, learns to ration compassion. He made coffee in the kitchen, leaving her to stare blankly towards the pattern of the curtains, which shut out the night, brought it back, pulled his chair closer and spread a copy of the Calvert will on the table between them.

'I take it you knew that *Francis* was working for the convent?'

'I didn't know, I promise you. But I do now.'

'And he's seen this will of Theodore's?'

'He could have done. I wrote to him after Theo . . . died. Told him to expect nothing. He wouldn't have believed me.'

'But he's seen *this*.' He stabbed his finger at the official-looking will, rather than the other document festooned with notes.

'Yes. He's probably been back here . . . many times.'

'Which means he has.'

He took another of her cigarettes. Lit it on the third attempt with trembling fingers. She was shrinking back into her chair.

'So he knows that if he manages to make Theo's daughters stray from the path of virtue, if he makes them *sin*, in a very obvious way, he stands to inherit.'

228

'Yes.'

'What better *sin* could the boy imagine than, say, to make a girl commit incest? He believes these girls are his blood sisters. Surely it would be a *sin* to be seduced by a *brother*? To be tempted into wickedness by him? What worse *sin* could he imagine? Or does he imagine that he could drive them to sin another way? Drive them into some outer darkness, like his own?'

She shrank back further, muttering under her breath.

'What?'

'I said, Francis would do it just because he hated them. That would be reason enough. They had everything he thought should be his.'

Christopher Goodwin leaned forward, picked up the copy of the will and tore it in half. The sound of tearing paper seemed abnormally loud.

'This thing is a piece of useless rubbish. It might be signed, but it's only a draft. It's no more valid than a piece of toilet paper. You can't put conditions like this in a will. You signed it as a witness, too. A beneficiary can't be a witness. The whole thing's crap.'

'And Jack's belief that Theo was his father is also *CRAP!*' she shouted. 'But the point is, he *believes*.'

Christopher imagined someone looking at this will and finding its legal verbiage entirely convincing. The mention of trustees thereof and devising and bequeathing would lend credibility at first and even second sight. It would be easy to credit.

She let her cigarette fall and ground it into the carpet with a slippered foot.

'So what's so odd about him believing all that? For Chrissakes, *Father*, you should know all about that. You're an expert in believing the unbelievable. The more incredible it is, the more you believe. The Resurrection? The Virgin Mary. Belief without doubt? Hope? It's what you bastards call having *FAITH*. Francis has his own version.'

CHAPTER TWELVE

Thou shalt not bear false witness

She knew that she was mortally afraid of him, more afraid than she had ever been. The top of her head was somewhere level with his chest and looking up at him, she fixed her eyes on the golden crucifix round his neck. Edmund's crucifix with a mended chain. A crucifix rather than a simple cross, because of the tiny figure resting on it. The cross was too small to be ornamental and the chain too fine for the breadth of Francis's neck, and yet they belonged as if he had always worn them. It transfixed her as he came into the room diffidently and sat in one of her two, facing chairs. She fell into the one opposite. When he leaned forward with his elbows on his knees, their eyes were almost level, but she kept hers fixed on that miniature figure visible in the gap at the neck of his shirt.

'Do you remember me?' he asked, earnestly, somehow taking command, but anxious to appease. She was forced to look at him, one brief look into his eyes, and then back to the golden cross. The symbol of sacrifice.

'Remember me, I mean, from a long time ago?'

'No.'

'No? But we look like one another. The same hair. Surely you noticed that?'

'No.'

'Perhaps it's my imagination then. We are all brothers and sisters in Christ.'

'Yuk.'

He sat back. She looked at his feet, ankles, knees, waist. Good shoes, soft chinos, clothes that made him all the more intimidating, although it was the ease with which he sat that was worse; the way he made no effort to keep her in place, because there was no need. She tried to remember if the door behind was shut, if he had kicked it closed, glanced sideways. The last time she had hated him rather than been afraid of him. Now, he seemed able to read her mind.

'Please don't think of running away. I don't want you running away from me. It wouldn't be right. It's your own home. And I thought you invited me in.'

'No, I didn't.'

'You didn't? Oh, I'm sorry. Did someone else open the door and wait for me? I'll go, if you like. It's a pretty place you have here, you've made it nice. I'm always looking for a place. What's it like to have a place of your own? Is it expensive? Please don't look at me all frightened like that. I think I like it better when you pull faces.'

She could feel the blush rise. To her dying day, she would regret that puerile gesture to Barbara, and yet had the absurd desire to repeat it now and the desire loosened her tongue. She held the fabric of her pyjama jacket with both hands and spoke clearly. She was vulnerable to anyone who admired her room: it flattered her. She focused on his neck. An elegant neck, the only vulnerable thing about him.

'Where did you get that crucifix?'

'This?' he said, surprised, touching it. 'My mother gave it to me. Why do you ask?'

His mother gave it to him.

'What do you want?'

'I want to be friends.'

The *thump, thump, thump* of the music downstairs ceased abruptly, making his voice sound louder, so that the words echoed like an announcement.

'You *what?*'

'I want to be friends.'

'Oh, very funny.'

She did up the button of her pyjamas for something to do, glad that her bedtime clothes were the same as they had always been. Modest and unsexy, little-boy striped pyjamas to which she had always been devoted. She was suddenly cold and her teeth chattered. It was a different crucifix he wore. His mother gave it to him. He had grown into it and it was still too small.

'Friends? Don't be bloody silly. You beat me up, you *lie* about me . . . Go and stuff yourself.'

'I didn't lie,' he said with soft indignation. 'I did think you were a burglar and I had to say it was you who broke the window. And when I said it, I thought it was true. I'd seen you before, but I didn't know who it was in the dark and I'd no idea how small you were. And if I've done you wrong, I want to put it right, I really do.'

Looking up at him, meeting the eyes, she noticed the brilliant blue and, to her amazement, the sheen of unshed tears. Again, she fixed her own eyes on the cross around his neck. The tears were embarrassing: she never knew what to do, except pity them, and the memory of him throwing her to the floor with that mixture of casual strength and the careful reining back of it, which saved her from serious harm, suddenly became confused, the details blurred as if it were all in her imagination. He could have broken her neck, but he had not. The omission seemed kind. She put her hands on her knees, felt the grazes beneath the cloth of her pyjamas to remind herself, refusing to look at the scratches on his face.

'I suppose,' Francis said, hurrying as if he wanted to get a shameful confession out of the way, 'that I wanted to impress Sister Barbara. I can't tell you how much I *need* this job. It's my lifeline and she could fire me any time. I wanted to look like a hero. I really need this job. I don't know if you can understand that. It's the first time I've ever felt safe.'

She watched him lace his fingers together, head bowed, so that she could see the curly thatch of his blond hair, smelling clean and fresh, like the rest of him, and making her feel faintly dirty.

'It makes me feel wanted, and I'm not used to that. They're good to me. It went to my head a bit, if you see what I mean. I really wanted to protect them. I want them to admire me. I went overboard.'

She looked at the cross, glinting round his neck. The presence of it teased at the back of her brain; it puzzled her and yet helped her focus. She looked steadily at the symbol of sacrifice, the aid to contemplation, the tiny figure of the crucified Christ. She looked at it and willed the chain to swell in size and choke him, watched it intently, imagining in miniature the ornate crucifix of Westminster Abbey and that brilliant shushing sound of hundreds of people moving to kneel and then to stand, feeling in the air, the breath of their movement, making her calm.

'Yes,' she said, reluctantly. 'I can understand that.'

He was nodding eagerly, boyish, foolish, apologetic.

'Look, I know you don't want the story of my life, but it hasn't been lucky. I was brought up to think I was bad all the way through. Then I met Edmund and knew I wasn't. And then I meet a whole lot of other people who don't think so either. It takes some getting used to.'

'Who broke the window?' she interrupted.

233

He hung his head further, so that she could scarcely hear the mumble.

'It was Edmund. He was shooting at a magpie, but I couldn't tell anyone that, could I? It's not fair now he's dead. I don't think he really knew he'd done it. I only just found the air rifle in his shed, yesterday. I'm spring cleaning for the autumn, you see.'

She thought again of the cathedral sounds, and heard in her mind the smashing of the glass in the window, finding it easier to listen to him if she kept removing herself. He was pulling at her heartstrings and she wanted it to stop, because in this humble state, she could feel the lure of his beauty and see why the dear Sisters would eat out of his hand, like the garden birds with Edmund. There was something else, too: a slippage of facts, an incomplete equation, an unfinished crossword puzzle, which his sheer presence made her unable to complete. She was listening, yes, but there was something she could not hear. She always wanted forgiveness to be freely given and received; she wanted it now.

'And I came tonight,' he said, 'because Therese told me I must. She could see I was worried, and so was she. She sent me to the place where you work with that present for you.'

Her head spun. There was a flash of uncontrollable jealousy, a spurt of protective fury. The juxtaposition of this man, this *boy*, alongside her sister was intolerable, and yet at the mention of Therese, all her defences slid and her heart began to beat with slow anxiety, so loud she was sure he could hear it. *Therese* sent her the dead bird? Or Therese sent her the scripture? That was the worst fear; Therese unbalanced by something fearful, like her mother. Therese was losing her mind. Or she was losing hers. She *must* see Therese, before it was too late. His voice reached her from a distance.

'She and I talk, you see, we always did from the first day I got there. I suppose because we're the only young ones, apart from the girl in the kitchen.' He took a deep breath. 'Therese wants to see you, but she says the only way that can happen is if Barbara allows it. She asks that you understand the rules of obedience. And look, I know this seems arrogant, but I reckon I can bring Barbara round to that, if anyone can, if I say that you and I are friends, now. Therese sends you her love, by the way. She's a lovely girl, isn't she? She knows you miss the chapel. Sweetest person I ever met. I wish she was my sister. She's teaching me not to tell lies.'

Anna was speechless.

'So I told her that I'd kissed you on the way home. Which was a bad thing to do, but I couldn't help it, because you're so pretty. I'd noticed you before, you know, sooner than you did me, and then at Mass, even if I wouldn't have known you in the dark.'

'And what did Therese say about that?'

'She said it was insulting and I needed my head straightening out.' He paused. 'But she also said it was time you found a nice Catholic boy. And that please, could you and I forgive and forget and be *amiable* for her sake?'

It sounded so like Therese, she could only laugh, and as if to copy Francis, felt tears pricking at her eyelids. She rubbed her nose on her pyjama sleeve.

'We've got a lot in common, you and I,' he said. 'All the Sisters, and what to do for the best for them all. We could do so much, you know. They won't survive without people like us. They have no mirrors. They cannot see themselves. Anyway, Therese says, will you try?'

She sat, silently, resenting *people like us* and yet suddenly buoyed up with hope. Therese thought of her. Therese spoke of her. Therese might go mad without her. Therese needed her.

He rose, awkward and concerned. 'I'm sorry. It's late and I've stayed too long. I'd have phoned . . . she gave me the number, but I thought you'd put the phone down. So I took the risk. Thanks for listening.'

'Wait.' He waited.

'What sort of friends do you want us to be?'

He had a complicated smile. He could have sold it for a million. A devastating mix of the smile of a saint, the grin of an innocent boy looking for trust, and a hopeful suitor with the lips and teeth of a pop star sportsman.

'Any kind you like. How about doing something tomorrow night? Seven? After work. I could bring you flowers, start over, properly.'

'That kind of friend?'

His eyes swept down the length of her body, back again to her face. They were knowing eyes.

'Oh yes, that kind. I'll see Therese in the morning. If two people meet in the wrong way and then get it right, I think that's romantic, don't you?'

She cringed and then tried to smile. He couldn't help being clumsy, could he? He liked Therese, he wanted to like her, he was only another lost soul who made mistakes. If only he didn't wear that crucifix.

'Yes. All right, whatever you like. Give her my love.'

His footsteps echoed away down the stairs. The sound of his whistling lingered behind him. Something about the whistling disturbed her. It had a note of triumph. Anna brushed her teeth, and after half an hour of frantic activity wrote a few words in the notebook and then, in a fury of confusion, cried herself to sleep. He made her feel, above all, ungrateful.

Christopher Goodwin made Kay McQuaid brush her teeth before he tucked her up in her own bed and told her everything was going to be all right, knowing that a statement as optimistic as that made him as much a liar as she was herself. Because, even as unstrung as she was, Kay could still hide, by which he meant she would answer the questions he uttered, but not the ones he did not know to ask. He ignored the small spare room where he was normally placed on the rare occasions he missed the last train and went and lay down in Theodore's room because he liked the sight of the moon through the balconied window. It was a restful moon and he needed something to stare at while he willed his eyes to close.

Composing himself for sleep was difficult enough and harder still in a room devoted to the use of another. It was a strange sensation and made him feel as if he were not alone. He opened the door of a handsome wardrobe to hang his jacket and found it was still full of Theodore's clothes, old-fashioned tweed jackets, well-worn, neatly pressed shirts and a heavy winter coat. No need for any of these in the other world and he wondered briefly which way Theodore had travelled after death, heaven, hell, or purgatory? One thing was certain and that was that he would not have asked for forgiveness for his sins, not even at the end. There were blankets but no sheets on the bed. Christopher crawled beneath them in his underwear, wishing he could remember the man better, or that he had known him well enough to read the complications of his mind. A man who played with power and loved games, but unlike himself, who only enjoyed them as a spectator.

It was a good bed. Everything in this house, apart from Kay's additions, reeked of solid quality. Good, soft, clean-smelling blankets, too. She was an excellent housekeeper, whatever else she was. Judge not that you may not be judged. It was always assumed, he was telling himself, that a celibate cleric like himself could have little understanding of that peculiar love of parent towards child, which could turn a quiet woman into a virago and a father into a murderous protector, the love that made every other commandment and consideration entirely irrelevant. He could hear the common cry from a desperate mother in his parish, shouting at him that he did not understand, but he thought he did, however incompletely. The accusation always felt like an insult to his imagination, which could *feel* the sensation of a child in his arms and know, like his own St Christopher, that he would carry it until he dropped or drowned rather than let it go. Oh Lord, I would have loved a child, he thought, and on that anguished note, he slept.

And woke, disorientated by the strangeness of the cool room, with dawn pressing against the windows and prodding him awake through the half-closed curtains. He washed in the bathroom, fretted about the problem of being without a razor or tooth-brush, until he saw everything he needed on the shelf above the basin, which he used in a guilty fashion, feeling as if he were, in a strange way, standing in another man's shadow, benefiting from the failure of that man's housekeeper to clear away the effects of the deceased. Either she was not equal to the task or disqualified herself from it and his only complaint about the arrangement was the mirror being set too low, so that he had to stoop to see his own chin, all of which distracted him sufficiently to allow him to complete his ablutions without cutting himself. The anger lay curled in his abdomen, like indigestion waiting to strike as soon as he was fully free of the drug of sleep. He would walk for the early train and clear his head by the sea. In the living room, he collected the documents he had brought with him, wondered how many more of them Kay had and where she had put them, decided not to wake her and ask. He had more than he needed. Instead, he left her a note, it was kinder to let her sleep, and let himself out through the back door.

He could see Theodore Calvert's point in living so near the sea on a morning like this, when it moved and heaved with a cheerful sluggishness and almost invited the full baptism John the Evangelist gave to the new followers of the Messiah in the River Jordan. This sea looked more like a river, easily crossed. It was water to walk upon, glinting with light and disappearing into a misty horizon. Father Goodwin stood and watched, praying that it would calm his soul and inspire a course of action, because in between sleeping and waking, he knew no better what he should do, or what he *could* do on his return to his neglected parish, other than commit murder. He was unsure of the preferred order of the homicides, Barbara or Francis first. He could discuss things with the Bishop's emissary, insist on an interview with Therese, if he could insist, but the rights and duties of a priest were ever vague. He may have been an accidental parental substitute for two orphans, with enough love for the task, an appalling responsibility, but no rights whatsoever. It was perplexing, to say the least, even without consideration of the unpredictability of Satan. In the name of God, what had Theodore Calvert thought he was doing, making a pact with the devil, or had he been drunk when he drafted that will, the last delirium of a man who wanted to die, with no idea of the effect? Christopher Goodwin watched the sea, imagined it parting into two towering walls to let through the tribes of Israel, led by Moses. It was the most convincing image he had ever retained from the Old Testament and the only one to impress him as a boy. The single scene that convinced him of the power of the good God, together with the rendering of the next scene by Cecil B. De Mille, where the waters fell back and killed the army of Egyptians. Why did he wait to do it until they were in the middle? Why not hold them back on the other bank? The God of the Israelites was a murderer, after all, simply selective in genocide. And that was the trouble with religious knowledge. It created a superstructure of images, which got in the way of every view and prevented one from looking simply at what there was.

As he looked, trying to concentrate on what there was, noticing the dark gathering of clouds and delighting in the sharp light on the water, Christopher noticed another piece of flotsam, at first sight similar to the one he had seen dancing on the waves in almost the same place the night before. On second sight, squinting at it and wishing he possessed such a thing as a pair of sunglasses, he could see it was different, a green barrel, or something of the kind, rounded and heavier looking, bobbing along sweetly and moving fast. He walked along level with it, feeling like a dog playing a game and about to bark at a stick, trying to match the casual speed of his steps with its floating pace and finding he had to move faster to keep up. Despite his foul mood and the underlying indigestible distress that weighed him down, he enjoyed the game until the road turned towards the station away from the sea and he had to leave it. Regret made him pause, then he stopped altogether.

Such strong currents on this stretch of coast. If Theodore Calvert had gone swimming on the piece of shore nearest his home and drowned, he would never in a million years have come floating back to the same place. And if Theodore Calvert had left a bogus decoy of a will, where was the real one?

The green barrel passed out of sight. He watched it until it disappeared, the light blinding his eyes. He hesitated, blinking furiously. Then he turned round and went back towards the house. He would wake her and shake her until she rattled. He would not be welcome. He slunk past the kitchen window, angry and uncertain, ready to hammer on the door, saw her inside in another dressing gown, talking on the phone.

Dawn yelled like a curse and she was naked in her own bed, light and floating on a tide of sleeplessness. *My name is Anna Calvert,* she had written in the notebook, *I am an orphan and I must go to work.* The eight in the morning through until two in the afternoon shift, and that was all that counted. Cling to certainties. *I need this job.* She crawled down to the bottom of the bed and held on to her own feet, hoping that the light of dawn would make sense. The scribbling in the notebook, learned from her father, to make the words clear. *Do you hate that boy at school?* her father would say. *If you do, write down, I hate him, and see what happens. You might not hate him quite so much. You write to clarify your emotions.*

240

The room was tidy and cold. A chair was jammed beneath the door knob, a futile precaution against trespass. A breeze rattled the window left open wide to dispel the smell. The other chair on which he had sat was pushed into a corner out of sight with the cushion from the seat removed, cut in half and stuffed into the kitchen bin along with the torn pyjamas. There was damp on the carpet where she had scrubbed the area he had trodden. She looked at the room, sanitized by her own mysterious hyper-activity in the middle of the night, and was struck by the awful thought that when he came back, Francis would think she had done all this for him. He was going to come back and she was going to let him in. Probably. Almost certainly. She had gone over in her mind everything he had said and revisited the scenes in which he had so completely and effortlessly overwhelmed her, not once, but twice. Made her stand in her shower after the first time, scrubbing away the touch of him, cutting her long nails in case they should hide traces of his skin. And then, this second time, when she had been disarmed by him equally effec-tively and then gone on to such frantic lengths in a haze of exhaustion to fumigate the room as if he carried an infectious disease.

Francis, the Golden Boy, knew everything that went on in the convent. He was the only acceptable outsider, now the only link between herself and Therese, which gave him power. He was the key to the garden, and in some strange way, he wanted her, because that was the message in his eyes. Well, if he was the link, so be it. And if it was her useless, undersized body he wanted, well, he could have that, too. Listen to yourself, she told herself, someone offers you *friendship* and all you can do is suspect. But most of all, she wanted to stop fighting. She was sick of it. But she did not want to stop fighting when she felt so powerless, as if there was no single other card in her hand, at a time when her brain felt as if it had turned to sludge.

At six-thirty in the morning, she pulled out the ladder and went up. If she were to look up from the convent garden, all that she or anyone else would see of her apartment block was the blank back wall of it, punctuated with the small, opaque bathroom windows, which were oblongs of light after dark. The most one could ever see from below was a silhouette through frosted glass. Francis did not know what she could see from here and the thought gave her a kind of comfort. It balanced out the power a little, this extra, useless eye. The uneven parapet was her own chest height at this vantage point. Francis would not need to lean forward in order to admire the view. Like Father Goodwin, the parapet, which guarded her completely, would provide less protection for a man of his height. She could see him toppling over, turning in mid-air without a sound, before he disappeared. *What was wrong with her?* He wanted to be friends, and she was continuing in the same old way, looking for enemies.

Still looking down, she remembered Matilda, and the way she no longer sat outside since Edmund's death. Matilda with her finger on her lips, the other watcher. She scrambled back down the ladder, put it away, turned on the music for one long blast before she ran downstairs and slammed the door. She would have one more try at the convent door, borrowing his phrase, *I've come to apologise.* A bright, rational smile, a request to come back later and make her peace, that should work fine. The sunshine really did make all the difference. Monsters were fostered by the dark: they only grew in the culture of night-time dreams. Early in the morning, they shrank. Until she banged on the convent door, checking the time, almost breakfast, make this quick, can't be late for work, compose the smile, checking the clothes while she waited, jeans and clean training shoes, polo neck because it was not warm, hair fresh with shampoo, who could resist her? Agnes, standing behind the door like a concrete post, opened it partially and then, immediately, tried to close it until Anna pitched her whole weight against it, only succeeding in delaying the momentum and keeping the heavy thing open only by a big enough crack for Agnes to shout through, '*Go away.*'

'Could I come in, Sister? I want to see Matilda . . .'

'Oh, in God's name, *go away.*' And the door pushed shut.

She stood away from it, imagining all the other doors inside, the black and white corridor, the chapel, the smell of food, and as she stood, the ambulance arrived.

Anna moved further down the quiet street and watched from the recessed door of the next house. They were quick; someone inside was ready. She saw the wheelchair, which went in folded and came out, rapidly, fully burdened. There were sounds of argument, a discussion on the appropriateness of a stretcher, Barbara's voice saying, fine, fine, fine, yes, yes, no, no, no, and a man pushing Matilda in the chair up the ramp, making soothing sounds into her ear. She was recognisably Matilda, with large, red-raw hands twitching in her lap, her eyes closed, her face as slack as her body, dressed in her habit, but without the veil, which was, instead of its natural decorum, wrapped round her head like a towel over wet hair. The sounds of argument increased. Barbara was on the step. The chair went into the ambulance. Sister Joseph, fully dressed, knocked everyone aside and followed, her face purple with rage and wet with tears.

Matilda, kind Matilda. The only other one who watched over the garden. Anna's feet were rooted to the spot. Until she uprooted them and ran to work. Mind still like sludge, optimism fading and the sunlight with it. Inside Compucabs, there was the same buzz of noise, which stabilised her again, but once she was in the safest of places, it was as if the delayed intellect started to kick against her skull, making the inside of her head thump. Matilda with her blistered hands dominated her vision, and Ravi, over there, with a face like the moon and a smile as wide as the sea, fading slowly when she made a grimace and put on the headphones, ignoring him.

'Compucabs, how can I help you? Account number? Thanks. Your job number is . . .'

'Feeling better, are we?' The supervisor, standing by the desk.

'Great. Thanks, I'm fine.'

'Great.'

The phones did not stop for three whole hours. There was always a busiest day of the week and on balance, she would rather tap out the keys and repeat the same words again and again than do anything else. It was as calming in its own fashion as the telling of rosary beads to others. Ravi hovered by the desk, raising his eyebrows in an invitation to adjourn somewhere else, either outside for the air or for tea or water and the desultory chat of the back room. She followed him outside. Somewhere in the course of the last three hours, looking at his serene face from time to time between the screens and headphones, she had come to realise that she could not tell him anything about Golden Boy. It would somehow wreck whatever it was they had; some precious little thing, like a fragile gemstone, easily lost. They sat on the step and she sipped at the tea he had made for her in the kitchen, the way he imagined she would like it, laced with sugar, which she did not like, but drank gratefully, keeping her distance.

'Walk you home?' he asked.

'Not today, Ravi, I've got to go somewhere else. Can I ask you something?'

'Of course.'

'Something I asked you before, only I can't remember what you said. I know. Praying. What exactly do you do it for?'

'And I told you I don't pray to get things.'

'Why ever not? What's wrong with asking?'

'Nothing is *wrong*, but you can't demand. You can't make bargains. You can't say, look, if you do this for me, I'll do that for you.

244

What have you got to offer that the Gods don't already have? Nothing.' He hesitated. 'You pray to give honour and praise. You pray for guidance. You don't say, give me that thing, God. You say, please give me the wisdom to see if this is the thing I should find for myself. You pray for the wisdom and strength to do it. You pray to give praise and all you can ask is the ability to *see*, for yourself.'

'Ah,' she said, 'that's where I'm going wrong.'

'What are you staring at me for?'

'Because I like to. I like looking at you.'

He smiled and cuffed her arm, and that was the point when a whole number of impressions began to slip into place, and all because of Ravi's peculiar, lopsided, spontaneous smile, which felt like a benediction, a ray of sunshine through the chapel window, and made her think how she was in the presence of someone who was, for want of a better description, *good*. Which did not mean flawless, but possessed of a kind of purity, which was not the same as innocence. She looked at him and, without intending to, made a comparison between him and Golden Boy, which went far deeper than their colouring and disparate size. If Ravi were put into a fighting ring with Francis, Ravi would not stand a chance. He would have all the inhibitions of decency while Francis would have none. In Ravi's kind, inquisitive face there was a spirit entirely absent from that of Francis.

The contrast shocked her. She smiled at him.

'I like looking at you,' she repeated. 'So just let me, OK?'

There, she was being stupid again, seeing phantoms. They returned to work.

Back at her desk, the phone rang.

'Good afternoon, Compucabs.'

'Ah, *there* you are. Thank goodness.'

'Hello, sir. How are you? Are you going out to lunch?'

Despite herself, she was grinning. That old, familiar voice, talking over hers.

'. . . very worried. I keep getting someone else when I wanted to speak to you. Are you all right?'

There was something about that old, tired voice that made it impossible to lie.

'No. Not firing on all cylinders today. Confused and worried.'

'You can come to me. Drop everything and come here. At once.'

'I can't do that.'

'I wish you would. Here's the address. Write it down.'

She wrote it down in a meaningless scrawl.

'But you won't, will you? I know you won't. Listen, I phoned to warn you. I had a premonition. Don't believe anything that boy says. You can't trade with the wicked. When did the devil ever honour a bargain? Evil has no inhibitions and always the advantage of surprise because the good don't know what it is and don't see it coming. The uncunning cannot see the cunning. You know where I am.'

The phone went dead. She dialled 1471. She looked at her writing on the scribble pad and found she could not read it. The phone rang again. The screen blinked the time, three in the afternoon.

'Compusoddingcabs.'

'No need to swear, love. It's cab number 110. Got a call from one of you lot to pick up a Sister Joseph from Paddington Community Hospital, only I can't find her.'

'Sorry, you're on the wrong line for queries. I just do bookings, try 291.'

Shaking slightly, wanting to scream. The phone rang again. Somebody wanted to go to an airport. It seemed like the most desirable place on earth.

A jet plane sped through the sky, way above her gaze, crossing the blue and passing into the clouds like a distant exotic bird leaving

246

a trail of plumage. Therese rose from the pristine white feet of St Michael and stood idly, watching the sky in the middle of the afternoon. What a terrible day, beginning with the evening before, when Barbara had been so peculiarly watchful. Watchful and guilty, dismissively kind in her approach and her words – *you're tired, child, and we all need an early night, off to bed with you, plenty to do tomorrow* – almost as if it were an apology and a promise of more, or was it just wanting everyone out of the way and the place secure. Therese did not know, only aware she was watched as she passed the phone by the door, in case she should try to use it; watched until she was up the stairs and probably checked for the sound of her washing. Watched, not trusted, as if her unintentional eavesdropping had been noticed; as if she was like her sister. Which she wanted to be, but the proof she was not must lie in her own actions of quiet obedience. Agnes cried in her sleep, the way she did, and Matilda did not respond, until there were anxious sounds along the corridor and Agnes left her room. Therese waited to be called, but no one did. And then, in the morning, when she went downstairs, earlier than ever, yearning for something to do and long past the point of even attempting to pray, there was a secretive bustle around the parlour, as if everyone but herself was there.

She could not work it out. Someone had knocked at the door in the night and said Matilda was in the garden. Someone had brought her in and made her comfortable in the night down there, because that was what she wanted and it was important not to disturb anyone else, and even that Therese only knew later from the conversation at breakfast, which was not directed at her, and where someone had suggested that, knowing Matilda, it was because of something she ate and surely she would be fine. But she had not been fine when Therese had seen her being wheeled down the black and white corridor. Whatever it was that had blistered and purpled her hands seemed to have also been smeared on her face. Her eyes stared wide, seeing nothing, not even Joseph battling for possession of the chair; she was not hearing the tide of argument that followed her. It was an awful, suffering face, etched on her memory now, so that she preferred to look at the sky whilst trying to make her makeshift prayers in what had been Matilda's favourite place in the hope that the very action of sitting here would bring her back, with the hopeless conviction that it would not, wanting to apologise to her for her own resentment of that patting and clutching. There seemed little purpose in prayer; it was achieving nothing.

No one knew what had happened, and if Barbara knew, she was not about to explain. Looking at the smooth feet of St Michael, completely free of lichens so that the stone was unnaturally white, she touched them gingerly. However infrequently she passed anywhere, she always noticed change. What would it take to remove moss? Some form of caustic, like oven cleaner, and that was perhaps what Matilda was doing. An act of devotion to her saint, like Mary Magdalene washing the feet of Christ with her tears and drying them with her hair. Clumsy, undomesticated Matilda who dropped things and hid them, expressing her devotion. Suddenly all such acts of piety seemed revolting.

It had been a day of fitful weather, bursts of sunshine drying out the lethal slipperiness of the ground, temporary dark clouds, which threatened rain and then desisted, mirroring the fractious mood indoors. Even Kim was surly, pleading a sick child to leave early, allowed by Barbara with her strange watchfulness, looking at them all, Therese in particular, as if to see which of them was the interloper who had brought them misfortune, and daring anyone to criticise. Even Kim had been hurtfully shrill, when Therese had tried to sympathise about the child. *Oh, shuttit, you wouldn't understand*, she said. *You don't know what it's like.*

A dull luncheon, with stilted conversation, punctuated by Joan and Agnes discussing among themselves how Joseph and Matilda had been inseparable once and whatever had happened. Was it the fact that Matilda had gone so deaf and Joseph so lacking in patience and wasn't it grand they were together now? The empty places left by them both looked like the spaces of missing teeth in a mouth. They talked about Matilda as if she had already died, and it was all the will of God, no less, a mere rite of passage. It made Therese sick and took away any hint of appetite. It made her sick with the knowledge that she did not want the kind of faith that made them accept the unacceptable.

The aeroplane passed out of sight, and the prospect of going back indoors to the uneasy somnolence of a typical late afternoon inside was . . . bad. How long was it since she had eaten anything of substance? Not today, nor yesterday either. Bread pellets, an apple. She was queasy with the lack of food and repelled by the thought of it. She could have stepped outside and run to Anna, but she knew she was afraid to do that after the last time and equally afraid that if she did, there would be another rejection. She had, after all, taken sides by silence. She patted the clean white foot of St Michael and asked him if men in brotherhood were different. Do brothers have this problem? Because sister-hood, whether of blood or affinity of purpose, like Joseph and Matilda, or the sisterhood of Anna and herself, posed huge prob-lems. It was as if she and Anna had a hypodermic syringe permanently parked in the vein of the other, ready to trigger into the opposite bloodstream a fine cocktail of uncomfortable mutual knowledge, love, anxiety, DNA and need, with a percentage of irritation. There was no antidote, no pill to take to offset the effect of that sometimes destructive bond. Absence, in times of distress, did not make the heart grow fonder; it broke it into little bits, sharp crystals of loneliness. Everybody said that she and Anna had been too close. At breakfast and lunch, the same thing had been said about Joseph and Matilda.

Sunlight again, the traitor, while perversely, she wanted the flavour of the dark and the aspect of her own, prayerless room, rather than the dread of Joseph's return from a long vigil at hospital with news she could foretell even now. Anything rather than her own conclusion that Sister Barbara should have called the ambulance far, far sooner, instead of trying to keep what was laughingly known as 'the peace'. Oh, Lord, who was there to trust?

It was chilly in the shade. Therese hesitated – forward or back? – and then went further down the garden, pretending to herself she was only looking for the lonely cat and knowing it was a pretence, because she was really looking for sanctuary, and there it was.

The clean oak bench, utterly devoid of Edmund's ghost, the area around it wonderfully silent and colourful. A riot of busy lizzies in pink and white framed the semi-circle, which widened inside the compass to the new table in front of the bench, so scrubbed it was fit to eat food straight from the surface, standing on ground swept to reveal the contours of the paving stones. Off to the side was the shed, which now looked like a tiny house, fit for a small, not very useful person, with no other purpose in life, to look inside. There was a small bed against the back wall, covered with chintz. Warmth seemed to waft from the doorway. A gingerbread house, with a kettle on a camping stove, a smell. A person could pray in here. She had been looking for a place to pray.

In the background, Francis was singing.

He came round from behind the structure, still humming, the most cheerful sound of the day, stopped and smiled, the only smile of the day. He was so wholesome, so very far away from death. Even the scratches on his face had faded to nothing and there was a smudge of dirt on his nose.

'Hello, I was just making tea. Do you want some?'

Tea, the palliative for all ills. Good tea, she remembered, outdoor tea, but she shook her head.

'No, thank you.'

'Are you all right? You look tired. Not much fun indoors today, I suppose. Any news of Sister Matilda?'

There was a colossal lump in her throat, announcing the imminence of tears. It was always thus. She could hold them back, repress any display of emotion, until something insignificant triggered it, such as a kind inquiry, or the sight of something that appealed to her, like the cat, slinking away into the undergrowth, or the sight of the chintz on the little bed. The cat was probably on some murderous mission, but that did not matter, it was a beautiful creature governed entirely by its own rules.

'No news,' she said.

'I'm keeping out of the way, too,' he said, softly. 'It was me made Barbara call the ambulance, you know. She should have done it sooner. She hasn't needed me since.'

'Nor me. They don't need me, either. I wonder if anyone does.'

And then she was inside the circle of his arms and he was hugging her gently. Her head was pressed into his chest and his body shielded hers. She stood, unable to move, arms at her sides, unresisting, unshocked, but warmed by the feeling of him and provoked into intense curiosity by the smell of him, which was earthy and sweet, and she only knew that when he withdrew, with a brief, friendly pat on her shoulder, she did not want him to leave her and it was a touching she could not resent. The embrace had brought them closer to the door of the gingerbread shed. They had moved a couple of paces and she had not noticed. The desire to weep had gone; she felt oddly relieved and shakily tired.

'You must always remember you have a brother in me,' Francis said. 'And do you like what I've done with this rotten old shed?'

251

She peered inside. The warmth of the interior seemed to spill outside and surround her. Therese wrinkled her nose at the smell of burning joss sticks.

'For the bugs,' he said.

It was a smell reminiscent of the room she had shared with Anna in the days when they were ill, scented sometimes with joss sticks to mask medicinal smells, a heavy scent, which had come to be associated in her mind with safety, lassitude and a pleasant sleepiness.

'I had a little room like this once,' she said. 'I used to want to live in a cupboard under the stairs.'

He laughed, standing away from her, just when she preferred his closeness.

'Your size rather than mine. Why don't you stay here and rest? Get away from it all?' He looked at his watch. 'No one'll know and I'm going home in a minute. You can have some peace, away from the kitchen.'

Therese stepped inside, drawn to it, and sat on the chintz-covered bed, which looked and felt like a hard bed for a child. There was little else in the interior, apart from the large paint can, which formed the table for the camping stove, and a set of shelves on the wall to the left, containing smaller, jaunty paint cans, matches and a box of candles. Francis plucked his coat from the back of the door.

'All right?' he asked.

'Yes.'

'I'll leave you to it, then.'

She heard his footsteps go away. It began to patter with rain, an almost comic, whispering sound at first, becoming soporific as the drops hit the roof of the shed with a quiet, musical tempo. Therese closed her eyes. The wooden wall of the shed seemed to hold the warmth of summer and refused to let it go. The rain grew louder. So peaceful, sitting still in a small space of warmth

252

with an open door, and the dizzying smell of man, and joss sticks stuck in a paint can, adding to the heat.

Then she opened her eyes to a different sound. The door, swinging shut, quietly.

Francis met Barbara standing in front of the parlour door, looking for him, scanning the garden anxiously.

'Are you away home, dear?'

'Yes, unless there's anything I can do?'

'Do? There's nothing anyone can do.' The voice was tinged with hysteria, muffled by sadness. 'Matilda was getting better, chatting away, and then she had a heart attack this afternoon at the hospital, so there's another one gone, and we seem to have lost Joseph. No, there's nothing anyone can do. Have you seen Therese?'

'I'm so sorry, Sister. I'll pray for Matilda. Therese? The little one? I thought I heard Agnes say that she'd gone out to help Kim with a sick child or something. An errand of mercy.'

'Well, mercy be damned. We'll need her here. She's no right to run off.'

She was tapping her foot in agitation, then braced herself.

'Off you go, Francis, dear. There'll be plenty to do tomorrow when they bring back the body. I don't suppose there's anyone lingering out there in the rain?'

He shook his head.

'Bless you, what would we do without you?'

The phone rang and she shot back into her office. Francis proceeded over the tiles to the front door, where Agnes sat, red-eyed and waiting for him. He embraced her and detached her with an audible kiss and the whispered words, *Goodnight, Mother*, and closed the door behind him.

CHAPTER THIRTEEN

Thou shalt not kill

There was no doubt about the door being jammed shut and about it being darker inside here. The small window in the door was the only source of light, a square of grey on which Therese kept her eyes fixed when she returned to the chintz couch after feeling for the presence of a handle in the rough wood of the door and finding there was none. Therese could visualise the shiny new latch on the outside of the door. If that was all keeping her inside, she was quite sure she could press it open with her own strength, and one thing she had learned after more than a year in the convent was how to deal with doors and windows warped and stuck by damp. She would be strong enough to get out, but there seemed little point in trying, right this minute, when she was more puzzled than anxious and still suffused with that pleasant laziness. What did it matter if she stayed for a while? Feeling around on the wood of the door had only resulted in a sharp splinter in her palm.

She sat on the bed and looked up at the square of light which was the window in the door, realising as she looked that the relative absence of light changed the contours of her abode. She could see all she needed to see, the outlines of the paint cans on the shelves with their colours more vivid in the half-light, and found herself wondering about the contents. Then she dozed a little. She was simply fulfilling the purpose of a garden, even a small, locked-in corner of a garden like the one she inhabited, and turning it into a place of peace. The long-lasting joss sticks still burned; she stared at the stems of them, sticking out of a paint can on the shelf, rose and took two steps to the door. The window was high and only by standing on tiptoe could she see outside, where the busy lizzies glowed in the grey light and the rain fell.

She went back and sat with her back to the wall, grasping her knees. The wall was warm and seemed to become warmer as the square of light began to fade and the rain made its music on the roof.

There was a nun she had read about who lived in a caravan in the grounds of her own convent, along with volumes of books illustrating the medieval painting which was her passion and her aid to prayer. This sister had featured in a television programme years before and evoked a whole way of life. Therese realised that she had never really had any passions at all, other than the desire not to be touched, prodded, pulled at, and the thought of going on living just like this, on the fringes of sisterhood rather than within it, seemed the best of all options, if she could deal with hunger, thirst and hygiene. Small spaces, spartan surroundings, had their own appeal. They encouraged a degree of acceptance. They were consistent with small ambitions.

A clever person, with different ambitions, like Anna, would have made a greater effort and worked out how to get out by now, Therese thought, but for herself, she would simply wait for whoever had made the mistake of locking her in to rectify it and come along to let her out, and in the meantime, consider the fate of poor Matilda. The Sisters could get their own supper. There was a satisfaction in that.

No need to bother about hygiene, yet. Her bladder seemed to

have shrivelled over the last days, and while hunger had begun to gnaw, it did so with small, soft teeth. It was not unpleasant to be timeless and beyond the call of regime, almost weightless and beyond responsibility, lulled into sleep by the warmth and the smells she could now detect. The lingering fumes of paint and creosote, masked by the joss sticks, a hint of cat and, in her nostrils from that brief contact, the smell of Francis himself, making her wonder briefly what it was that made a man smell like that, what her own smell was like, what material covered the roof to make the rain echo the way it did, and then she noticed the small mirror propped on the shelves next to the paint pots, and rose to look at herself. The light was too dim to see anything more than a very pale face, which seemed to consist mainly of eyes, and she was disturbed to see her own reflection, which seemed to have so little to do with herself. The only mirror in the convent was by the front door, where few of them ever looked and only then to check their own dignities before making an exit into the outside world. Otherwise, if the appearance of one of the Sisters was ever defective, a habit hitched up in a belt, a veil not quite straight, another Sister simply adjusted it, discreetly, to murmured thanks. They could all of them dress themselves in the dark and mutely relied on one another to correct the missed details of rudimentary grooming. It reminded her of primates considerately ridding one another of fleas. The mirror reminded her that the light, such as it was, was fading, and she should use it to find the candles she had noticed earlier. Cheap candles, not like the beeswax candles of the chapel, stickier to touch, and when she found one, struck a match and melted the base before sticking it on the shelf, a fresh small entered the chorus of the others. There, now she could pray. The candle flame, slow and steady without any draught to give it flickering life, was the best aid of all to prayer.

Oh, dear Lord, why are you doing this to me?

Lord, have I sinned, and if so, how? How can I know if I've sinned, unless it's perfectly obvious, or you tell me? Be reasonable, I'm only human.

I don't know if this is punishment . . . And then, thumping the bed impatiently, *Why the hell don't you talk to me?* I'm your child.

She tried the rosary, without benefit of rosary beads, because the rosary was such a useful prayer. The one that allowed daydreaming and prayer at the same time, one Our Father, ten Hail Marys, one Glory Be to the Father, and then begin again. She tried not to daydream, but think of the mysteries, which were the prescribed accompaniment to the stanzas, but found she could only think of the sorrowful ones – Jesus in the garden of Gethsemane, the scourging, Calvary, with the niggling background thought, Oh why, sweet Jesus, why did you let yourself in for that? Why did you think we were worth it and why didn't you escape? What difference did it make? She gave up. The rain stopped.

It was only in the following silence, which seemed to mushroom around her, creating a sensation of stuffy fog, that Therese began to feel the rising of panic. There was no air in here. What little there was was subsumed by the still-glowing joss sticks and the candle flame. She was afraid of staying still, got up and pushed at the door, then banged at it with her fists, but it did not yield, only vibrated with sound. She wanted to tear at her own hair and scream, but was controlled enough to realise that that would make everything worse. This was not a sanctuary, it was a prison cell. She tried to think of a saint in captivity, any saint, and what he or she might do if they were her. Contemplate, offer the indignities to God for the benefit of another soul in purgatory, wait in faith to be released, be patient and still? No. *No.*

Moving lengthways, rather than towards the door, there was a maximum of four small steps between one side of the cell and the other. Therese tried to imagine she was either in the kitchen with

Kim, or back inside her bedroom at home, with Anna, long ago, whiling away the hours of illness on a relatively good day. Both of them playing around and teaching themselves the model walk, copying one another in the exaggerated gyration of hips and the silly, one hip forward, head flung back, stroll they had learned from pictures in magazines and a TV programme of ballroom dancing, which they had watched with the sound turned down until they laughed themselves sick and Mother had to take control. The tango-influenced catwalk-model walk looked effortless, but was full of effort. It had exhausted them, and she did it again and again, now. Two steps forward, two back, flung herself on the bed, posed, got up, did it again. In the tenth circuit, dizzy and over-heated, she stripped off her clothes. She would do this until she was beyond doing anything. Something had bitten her: something scratched. Her skin scorched.

It was late afternoon when Christopher Goodwin arrived back in the city. He breathed the air in the underpass which linked the station to the Underground, noting the various flavours of humanity and dirt, artificial light, organised chaos, noticed a couple of homeless boys who had already given up on the day, and wondered if Francis McQuaid had ever been one of those. An unwashed head stuck out of a dirty sleeping bag and he was ashamed of having no money to give, but on balance, he thought he preferred this inhu-man, human bustle to the relentless pull of the tide and all that heartless sky. Kay McQuaid should come back: this was home. Although he knew it was irresponsible and he would pay later in conscience for the further neglect of his parish, he detoured via the park. On this Wednesday afternoon, the feast day of St Matthew, apostle, evangelist, symbolised as a man with wings, but once a tax collector, the boys' football team was finishing a game. He stood and watched the sheer energy and grace of their movements, listening with delight to the innocent savagery of their yelling,

258

until he sensed he was watched himself as he stood apart, wondering again if Francis, born simple Jack bastard McQuaid, had ever been one of these, playing football in the drizzle with the express purpose of learning how to break the rules.

On the last regretful circuit of this end of the park, Christopher saw a nun, sitting on a bench, and had a distinct temptation to change route and avoid her. He resisted and, as he drew level, watched to see if she was familiar, hoping she was a complete stranger until he saw with a shock that she was one of what he had sourly come to consider as Barbara's bunch. He could recognise them individually, but never quite remember all of their names, except for the one or two of whom he was fond and the ones who had taken the masculine names, and he remembered Sister Joseph all the more as the one who was frequently mentioned in Sister Barbara's catalogues of trouble, as well as being the one who was drunk, but admirably controlled, at the last meeting. A similar condition seemed to apply to her now. She was not drunk, but under the influence; on the way to being drunk and weeping copiously to add to the dampness of her habit, which was muddy at the hem. Pedestrians crossed the path to avoid her and as he sat down beside her, with the old, familiar irritation that accompanied so many a Christian act, especially one that interrupted progress to more important things when he was hungry and tired, he could see why she was being shunned. Even without the frightening accoutrements of a nun's soiled habit, Sister Joseph was eminently resistible.

'It's Joseph, isn't it?' he asked, with his practised gentleness, which so often emerged as more bracing than sensitive and did so now. 'What ails you, Sister? Can I help? Can I walk you home?'

'Piss off.'

This startled him, to the point of laughter. He was used to the deferential smile, the oh no, Father, it's nothing at all response, which typified their stoic reactions to their own distress, even on a deathbed. It was a deference that had often annoyed him, but he found he did not want the opposite either.

'What's the matter, Sister?'

An inane question, but he had to persist.

'What's the *matter*, you fool of a *man*? What's the *matter*?' Her voice was only slightly slurred and rising, so that he could not gauge the level of her inebriation, although experience of others made him guess it had some way to go before violence or oblivion, whichever took hold first. She was a strong old woman. He had often thought that the residual physical strength of the old must be as frustrating as their weaknesses, a formless, useless energy, and he did not look forward to it. She looked up at him with bleary eyes, identifying him for the first time.

'Christ, it's the bloody priest. Where are you when you're needed? No one could rouse you this morning. Just think, you could have sat with me and Matilda. Sat and listened to her telling me how the devil himself had murdered Edmund and the birds and put poison on her hands. She was in such pain. The devil himself, she told me. And then . . . she died, Father. She died without you.' The voice moved from a hiss to a mumble.

He crossed himself, depressed with guilt. 'Matilda's dead?'

'Matilda's *killed*,' she spat. 'And I loved her. We were *real* sisters. She's the only one who ever loved me.'

Tears flowed. He hesitated, then touched her sleeve gingerly. It was smeared with mucus and tears. She slapped at the hand.

'You must go back, Sister, you'll make yourself ill.'

'Get your hands off me,' Joseph said with deliberate venom. 'Save your worry. I've got money in my pocket and a will of my own. I don't need your *blessing*, I need my anger, so *piss off*. Is there anything about that phrase you don't understand?'

It was, he admitted, perfectly clear and did not allow alternatives. She was an adult woman of God, not a child.

'What did she mean, the devil himself?'

'Piss *off.*'

'If you're sure?'

She nodded emphatically. There was a clear glass bottle sticking out of a cloth bag, which looked like a laundry bag or the shoe bag he had carried to school, on the bench beside her. The bag was bulky, probably with Matilda's things, he thought sadly, and not proof against the rain. He felt in the left pocket of his anorak for the small umbrella that always lived there and he never remembered to use, handed it to her. Joseph looked at it in disdain, took it all the same and stuffed it in the bag.

'Not much of a weapon, is it, Father? I can do better than that. Piss off.'

He knew he would have to come back later and see if she was still there, as well as digest what she had said, but he hurried home. Oh, good God, not another death or another fantasy. The papers crackled inside his jacket, he was no lighter without the umbrella, and for all the strangeness of the meeting, the ghastliness of the last twenty-four hours, he was nursing a small nugget of exhilaration and he had a sense of resolution and purpose, which did not usually come from having too much to do. There was always either too much or too little, with the whole of life revolving around the juggling of priorities, obligations, duties, so that indoors there were messages from Barbara, the office of the Bishop, and twelve others, including the last from the carer of the old, brave invalid whose company he had so often kept in front of the football replay videos, offering no more than mute admiration for bravery and the consolation of another, like-minded presence. They had the same way of praying. The message was a plea for the administration of Extreme Unction. A man wanted blessing for the last rite of passage and there was no choice. Christopher Goodwin changed his trousers, seized his paraphernalia and set out for the other end of his parish.

★

Ravi was wrong. Anna shunned the park and longed instead for the chapel. Now, look here, Lord. Prayer was an instinctive activity in anyone who had ever become accustomed to it, even if they no longer knew to whom, or what, they prayed. A bad habit, acquired with ease and training, difficult to break, an affliction, a pain-in-the-neck need, which never went away and could never be shared with anyone who had no idea of what you were talking about. Ravi had a religion, so he knew, although he did not know what it was like to pray to Gods who had already abandoned you, and he was wrong about a person being able to do it anywhere. Perhaps he meant anywhere there was a shrine. She meant anywhere it worked well enough to quell the furies, and the places were limited. It had to be a place she loved, the convent chapel, sometimes the park, and otherwise the roof. Other people were probably the same in choosing a place to have an argument. There had to be something to look up at, something to look down on, or something to look across and preserve the idea there was something beyond that and something beyond even that. Anna thought that an aeroplane would be a good place for prayer, provided she could sit near a window.

She was very, very shaken and feeling in a way she could only describe to herself as odd, although that was an understatement, since oddness was her middle name and anyway, there was plenty about which to feel odd and it only created another phrase, *oddgod*, which she was repeating in the same way she once said bother. And then, *How odd of God, To choose Hindus*, a couplet distorted from something else. Oh, oddgod, odgod, doggod, dogged, dogged, dogged. The flat was pristine. She was waiting and knowing in her heart of hearts, as well as in her churning stomach, that Francis, the Golden Boy, was making her wait. He was not late yet, but he would be late soon. The ladder was out, up to the roof. There was time.

She was dressed like a girl, like a miniature tart, in a dress.

Floral thingummy, with little roses printed in the lightweight cloth, buttoning up the front from mid-calf to neck and a touch of lace, for oddgod's sake, at the neck. She hated it all but her bare feet, climbing the ladder stack and getting them dirty in the gunwales of the roof, who cared? The thought of the wine in the fridge made her sick.

Better, up on the parapet, with sultry city air cleansed by the rain, which only threatened to resume, but not yet, please oddgod, not yet. She propped her elbows on the parapet, so that they were level with her shoulders, and put her feet inside the shelf she had created between the lead flashing and the brick, to give her a better view. Saw a clear evening, prematurely dark, and the garden further darkened by the lights from the chapel window, although, as yet, she could see the details. There was a breeze, teasing at her long, clean hair, washed again for the occasion.

'Oh Lord, help me. Am I to be a sacrifice? Am I going to have to let him have me in order to get to Therese? Help me to see in the dark.'

Edmund's bench began to fade. She thought she could hear from the chapel the sounds of the singing of the Misericordia. *O clemens, O pia, O dulcis Virgo Maria,* sung in those voices by Jude's graveside, followed by the voice of the hound of heaven. *I fled Him, down the nights and down the days, I fled Him down the arches of the years; I hid from Him . . .* She yelled into the darkening sky, *Just leave me alone.* Let me see. Make me concentrate and make me see all that my fogged-up mind is missing. I am not old, I'm not wise.

First she looked at the sky, which was a blank, bumpy landscape, turning dark, but not dark enough for stars. There was nothing on which to focus the eyes, no nice arrangement of clouds, no inspirational moon. She watched the branches of the trees, daring them to move, and then she looked at the window of the chapel, so brightly lit that the shape of it, upturned boat or bishop's hat, was appealingly clear and the desire to be on the other side as sharp as homesickness. To the left of this beacon, lower down, there was a visible light from the parlour windows and from the rooms on the floors above. The place seemed lit for a celebration, indicating crisis, visitors, or a death. This was the way it had looked on the night Sister Jude died, as if the death of a Sister created the need to bustle and spring-clean, to fix everything so that the gap was obscured. They were busy.

There was no birdsong, not a single cry of alarm.

Anna concentrated on the smaller details, the shape of the flower tubs, the shiny damp path into the shrubbery, the point where St Michael stood, currently visible, and then let her eyes follow the path to the point further down where the bushes obscured it and where she had been when Francis had intercepted her. She could not pinpoint the exact spot, but focusing on the likely place made her begin to think of everything she knew about the Golden Boy and place it in the context of what he had said. She knew nothing, but looking at the garden, she could see what he had done.

There were no birds any more.

There was Edmund's bench, with the light, scrubbed wood of it still visible in the clear area surrounding it. Francis had obliterated any sign of his predecessor and mentor so that it was difficult to remember that Edmund had ever existed at all. Edmund, whom she had watched neglecting the garden and feeding the birds with whom he shared that filthy bench. Ironic that Edmund was the gardener who should have been called Francis, after the saint who could magic the birds from the skies. Now there were dead birds in the garden, she had trodden on one; dead birds and a killing cat. The wrongly named Francis had lied last night. Edmund would never have shot at a bird, any bird, and he would never have broken the window. Francis would have done that as part of his ruthless cleansing operation and his preliminary step to the gaining of power. She thought of how he would have achieved that power, first by breaking Edmund's hold on the place, then by becoming indispensable and always by being beautiful. His saintly beauty and his sex, powerful passwords. Agnes would let him to and fro whenever he pleased; Barbara adored him. There was no place sacrosanct, nothing he could not contradict. And then, although she had played a part in her own banishment through her stupidity, it was he who had achieved it. She stroked her fingers down the side of her face, remembered his hand holding her claw and raking it down his own face. The scratches had made him even more beautiful. Why, when she had faced him the night before, had that memory faded, melted by that self-same, humble charm? Why had she believed him? She clenched her own hand into a fist and looked at it. A small, puny weapon.

And as for Therese sending the bird . . . Therese would never have touched a dead bird, except, perhaps, to bury it. She would have been afraid; she was fastidious. *Look at what Francis has done to the birds.*

Then she remembered Edmund's fist, his arm outstretched on the bench, with the gold crucifix and broken chain lying next to it, which she had thought was his and preserved for Matilda until Francis had reclaimed it. A thing he had worn since childhood, almost outgrown. Too small by far for Edmund's fleshy neck. A hypocritical adornment, a badge of solidarity, an indication of faith. She thought of it being inside her pocket alongside the statue of Ganesh, and, staring at the bench now, imagined Edmund in the throes of dying, ripping the crucifix from the neck of the man who might have helped him. Or murdered him. The scene enacted itself in front of her eyes with hideous clarity. Matilda was the only one who might have known. Matilda with her bright eyes, and burned hands. He would have seen to that, too.

Craning over the parapet, she could just see the back door to the garden. That was how he came and went. He did not even need the complicity of Agnes. Most of all, she remembered her frantic scouring of the place the night before, the instinct to eradicate traces of him, although as he had sat there, she had believed everything he said and the mist of credulity had descended. She had been sorry for him; she had wanted to be liked. *Oh, Lord,* she said. *We believe what we want to believe.* And disbelieve what does not suit. Was it you who phoned with the warning? *Good people do not see evil. Evil has no inhibitions.*

She looked at the luminous dial on her watch. She could hear the door buzzer from here. Francis had not arrived and what was more, she could see now that he had never intended to arrive on this particular night. That promise was yet another lie. Perhaps he enjoyed the idea of her waiting for him, a piece of control, designed to humble her and make her long for him next time. Or perhaps it was something else. Perhaps he simply needed her to be captive in her own flat, waiting as he could guess she would wait for the very mention of Therese, or out of the pathetic desire for love or friendship; she would wait, poor, lonely, powerless thing. And then she remembered the other words, *You are even prettier than your sister,* and retched over the wall. He had never wanted her. He wanted her out of the way, and with that settled conviction came another, namely that Therese was suffering.

When they had been ill, their symptoms were originally different, but had come to coincide as if they cross-infected one another, and then it was more than that. It had turned into a physical empathy with how the other felt, an instinctive knowledge, which lessened with health and absence, but still persisted. In the friendlier conversations, the normal ones that followed the confrontational ones after Therese joined the convent, they had laughed about it. Thought of you yesterday, Therese would say. Did you have toothache, because I did. And period pain? Yes. Now, on the parapet, her empty stomach was churning. She felt for her sister an almighty fear, as if Therese was up alongside her and about to jump, and she felt for Francis the Golden Boy a hatred so intense it would have poisoned the moon. He was a monstrous corruption. Instinct said it all. Instinct knew best. He killed the birds. He would hurt and corrupt and never know conscience.

She could not bear to look at the bench, which now blurred into nothing as the last light died and she vainly tried to concentrate on what little she could see, willing it to expand into clarity. The outline of the shed was just visible. There was a light inside.

A tiny, flickering light, so small she could have imagined it. A signal, the arc light of the chapel window pointing the way to the tiny light in Edmund's store.

Lamb of God who takest away the sins of the world, have mercy on us . . . Agnes was muttering, grumbling and frantic and confused and hungry and . . . *Agnus Dei, qui tollis peccata mundi.* Joseph had come home and God bless them all. This was no way to respect the dead, no way at all, coming home from the care of dear Matilda, stinking of the drink and shouting like a banshee, all over the black and white corridor, half sick, half demented, the colour of a bruised plum and yelling, *Where is he, where is he?* not even able to remember if it was day or night. *Where's who, Sister? Who do you mean?* and only getting back, *Where is she, where is she, the bitch?* In the name of the blessed virgin, they couldn't call the police to one of their own, and if only Francis would come back, her darling son, and instead of him, there was Anna running down the road in a pretty frock and those ugly training shoes she wore and which she herself privately craved. Agnes was not going to let in anyone else who made trouble and the only person she wanted to gain entry was her own darling boy. Or maybe the priest. Heaven help her, she was sick of the sight of women. After she slammed the door shut, and returned to her cubicle, waiting against hope for either the food to which they had not been called, or the return to order, which Barbara would surely restore, she put the phone under her chair where it had rested all evening with the receiver detached. She had taken the unilateral decision that they had enough to cope with, and from the depths of the black and white corridor, she could hear Joseph, shouting, tried to close her ears to what Joseph said and could not. Joseph had a way with words.

Fuelled by fear, it was even easier for Anna to get up to the top of the wall than it had been the last time. Bugger who watched, let them. She could kick, she could scream, she could yell, and the extra power came from thinking, if they close that door on me one more time . . . Ripping the dress while straddling the wall did not matter either; she tore a strip off the hem when she paused at the top, wrapped the material round her wrist like a bracelet, and then slithered down the other side with sickening speed, because the ivy was wet and slippery as oil, so that she clutched enough to impede freefall and landed with a silent thud that winded her and shook her into where she was. It was the time of the evening when sounds from outside penetrated as far as they ever would in here. The jarring of the final landing made her breathless, squatting where she landed, suddenly as careful as a cat. And there *was* the cat, eyeball to eyeball. She hissed at it, watched it scurry away, scared of her.

You are even prettier than your sister. Stronger, too. Anna tiptoed from the back door towards the area of the bench, looking for the clutter which had been visible from the window only three weeks before and was now startling for its absence. The scent of autumn flowers arrested her, but the flickering light from the shed drew her into the circle outside it. She could hear whimpering from the half-open door, felt the waft of body heat and sweat. Whimpering from the body beneath the other body on the patterned fabric she could see through the door, in tune with the voice of the Golden

268

Boy, who half knelt, glisteningly naked, with his long legs too long for the couch, above the body of her sister, who lay face down with her hands clutched in her hair, saying no, Mother, no, trying to prise together the legs he had forced apart with his knees, so that her forelegs thrashed without purpose, and as she watched, he bent his whole torso towards her and bit her ear. You know you want this. You waited for me, naked. I am your brother. We do it this way so you don't have to watch, trust me.

Anna hesitated. Then she took in the detail of the way he massaged his enormous prick and smeared it with spit while his other, big, brown hand, held down Therese by the neck. Therese might want this, but Therese was held by the neck. Passion did not whimper, did it? And then Therese screamed, bucked, used all her tiny weight to shrug him away. Anna felt around for a stone. His voice reverberated. *Shush, no one'll hear, sister.*

She was going to kill him, smash in his head, now. To the mind's echo, *Thou shalt not kill, or suffer the death of thine own soul.*

Golden Boy had left a pile of jagged lumps of concrete. She found one at her feet. She was going to kill him.

And then she was knocked sideways. A figure in black superseded her, yanked open the door, and punched repeatedly at that naked back as if she was trying to revive it, making repetitive, unrepeatable sounds, *hmuph, hmumph, humph,* then *humph, humph, humph,* as if she was digging into his neck. The screams grew into a symphony, his like an electrified pig, hers the sound of fury, and the body beneath adding a whimpering chorus. Then Sister Joseph of Aragon yanked back Francis's head and plunged her small-bladed knife into his throat. She did it with a degree of determined attachment, seven times, and even in the frenzy of the attack avoided his eyes. The candle fell with the vibration of movement, caught at the damp hem of her gown, flared and went out. After that, it was all darkness and voices.

★

Anna dropped her lethal piece of concrete. She ran to the shed and dragged Therese from beneath a warm and twitching body. She heard only the sound of the incessant sobbing, which came from Joseph. Then there was a flurry of Sisters surrounding Therese, shushing her, covering her, leading her gently back to the house, three of them, masking the bloody nakedness and saying there, there, there. Someone else took Joseph, equally gently. Barbara remained, scuffing the earth with her shoe, addressing the sky with her authoritative voice, shining her torch into the open doorway. The Golden Boy closely resembled Sebastian, with his multiple wounds. She stepped inside and felt for a pulse, stepped back, with blood on her hands.

'Fed Joseph drink, did he? Burned Matilda's hands, did he? Did you think I was a total fool, Francis? Well, so I was, you devil. You try to rape a bride of Christ and you're as dead as I've been blind.'

Her anger was shimmering hot, the voice colder than ice.

Anna stood behind her. Agnes and Margaret stood either side. Anna wanted to go to Therese, soon she would go to Therese, and even now, in the midst of everything else, she felt an over-powering relief that it was not her who had done this. Three reedy voices rose into the air, chanting. *'To you we cry, poor banished children of Eve, to you do we send up our sighs, mourning and weeping in this vale of tears . . . Turn then your eyes of mercy towards us. O clemens, O pia, O dulcis Virgo Maria . . .*

They faltered on the notes. Then there was a long silence. Barbara's torchlight did not waver. Her bosom heaved.

'Right,' she said. 'Do we bury him or burn him?'

She turned to the others.

A small voice, coming from nowhere, said that perhaps they should call for the priest.

CHAPTER FOURTEEN

In the second week of the month, Kay McQuaid busied herself in the middle of a rainy day by dragging the golden Buddha out of the house and down to the back fence, where she could see it from the kitchen window. It tarnished to a fuller sheen almost overnight. For something else to do the next day, she surrounded it with small evergreen shrubs of the kind she had been told would attract the birds. She buried a small gold crucifix on a chain amongst them. Standing with gin in hand and sweat on her brow, she decided she needed more work of the same kind and went back into town for dozens of bulbs to plant for the spring. The statue had already melded into the right place, and sat there, contentedly, surrounded by fertile attention. It was the best she could do to create a shrine and it gave her peace of a kind. Next year, she would really get to work out here, now that she knew she was not going anywhere else. Make something of it. Scrap those neat borders and fill it with shaggy shapes and colours. She muttered a guilty prayer of thanks, for feeling safe. The garden would help her make amends. It would be a labour of love. Someone Up There, whoever it was, would approve.

The third week of October, and by some miracle, there was a fire lit in the parlour.

'I don't have much belief in the existence of the devil, myself,' Father Goodwin was saying to Anna. 'I find him far too convenient a concept. Evil, yes, the devil, no. Not a devil with horns and a tail. Maybe a fallen angel. That's the way Satan started, after all. The angel separated from God in a messy divorce.'

They were sitting in the back of the chapel, talking in normal voices as if the crucifix did not loom over them. The place smelled clean and chilly with the side windows open. Not a trace of incense or added decoration. There had been no recent funerals; those four in the four weeks behind that, Sister Jude, Edmund, Matilda, Jack McQuaid, had all been conducted with the fullest of honours and amounted to a record and now there had been none for a month. It often happened like that, Christopher Goodwin had stated, firmly. A cycle of disasters do not amount to a permanent pattern, like the corridor floor. Nothing is predictable, other than seasons, and now we have the welcome hint of winter, with the promise of dark, protective nights, things on toast and the blessing of sleep. Think of that and other small mercies.

'Thank you for that, Christopher, but I do not think it is an idea I could share with Therese. It is easier for her to believe in simple miracles. Such as the devil in disguise taking on a human form, just as Christ is supposed to have done, although with the opposite purpose. It's more picturesque to believe in two super-human men slugging it out, with the devil as the force for evil, which only God can recognise and destroy. It makes it easier to rely on God.'

He thrust his hands under his armpits in order to warm them.

'Well, then, she is not equipped for the Christian life, or any religious life, for that matter. If she clings to such concepts, particularly if she trusts in the ultimate reliability of God, she denies herself essential knowledge. As soon as a God takes on human form, which all Gods do, they take on frailty, also. And they are frail. They can only work in cooperation with us. Likewise the so-called devil, and Francis was not the devil incarnate, whatever Therese wants to believe. Although he may have evolved into something devilish, with plenty of human help.

'But he was *evil*, wasn't he? Not born, but made, I concede that, but he must have been already fully evolved when he came here. Beyond redemption. Perhaps it's better to say he was cursed . . .'

'I prefer that,' Father Goodwin interrupted, adjusting himself to the uncomfortable rush seat. 'Cursed, rather than innately evil. Cursed in a way to which many other people contributed. Including his abandoned mother, his friends he may not have chosen, and the way he came to look for recognition. A cursed man will take revenge for the absence of an identity.'

'He was a rent boy . . . once?'

Christopher sighed. 'Yes, I'm told so. From time to time. Which is why the police are disposed to believe that he was a sexual deviant, caught in the act and killed in vicarious self-defence, as he richly deserved, by a woman not in command of her right mind.'

'And all that's true, too. In a manner of speaking.'

He thought of Kay McQuaid and the annotated version of events he had tried to give her, until he saw how she preferred the truth.

'In a manner of *convenient* speaking, although I might not take the risk of setting it in stone. I am afflicted by the idea that after he came here, there may have been moments when he could have been redeemed if he had not been so positively misjudged. You cannot know for certain sure if he killed Edmund or merely watched him die. Or if, when he delivered you to Barbara to the tune of lies, he was merely trying to consolidate a position he knew was precarious, because it always was, you know. Nor do we know if he *intended* Matilda's fate, or if his jealous washing of St Michael's feet was intended as a favour to her. Or a favour to the saint, or a response to a request. He was a *tidy* and domesticated man, like his mother. And how strange it was that he *signalled* what he had done, and what he was going to do, at every turn, as if he wanted to be stopped . . . He let his mother know he was there, he wore the crucifix . . . We don't know what moved him. We do not know, either, if he actually locked Therese in her cell, or if the door jammed.'

'It was him who came back, nobody else.'

'And found a naked girl, waiting for him.'

'He came back. He orchestrated it. You can't suggest otherwise.'

'No, I don't suggest otherwise. But the nakedness was a contributory factor, and that *is* my point entirely. Therese had no idea of what she had aroused by being what she was and where she was, but she still contributed, even with innocence, just as she did otherwise. The point, my dear, is that devils, if they exist, thrive on circumstance. They graduate because of ignorance. They are not clever enough to invent the culture that lets them thrive and cannot, should not, be blamed for everything.'

'And you are the devil's advocate.' She sat down in the aisle. 'Making the opposite point that virtue cannot afford to be blind or it isn't real virtue. And also that anyone can do a wicked deed by default, since neither God nor the devil know what the hell they're doing. She won't find that particularly helpful. I don't find it nearly as useful as my own intelligence.'

'Exactly, my dear. You've arrived where we began.'

She stood, physically restless, but otherwise calm. The long hair was cropped: she looked like an adolescent boy with feminine curves. His heart ached for her survival, by which he meant survival with honours, so that she might become the extraordinary woman he knew she could be. Someone who could love and be loved and act on that furious intellect, perhaps with a belief to sustain her, any positive belief. He had hopes for her, such hopes, they made him determined to stay alive and do what he was good at. Nurture. Debate. Talk. They had been debating and discussing every known fact every day. The chapel was the place for it. She paced forward and then back, sat down again.

'You don't think I haven't thought of any of that, or imagined alternative explanations to the poor old devil, do you? I've had no choice about that. After all, I might have killed Francis myself, on no better basis than what I thought I could *see*, and while I believe my impulse was right, and he was cursed, I sincerely wish he was not dead, whatever he was. I can't see the justice in that. It was my family that added a crucial contribution to the evolution of Francis. And it was my father who set the whole thing running by inventing that wretched, meaningless will. That was what started the last chapter, and then there was *us*, continuing it by not reading his letters. We contributed too.'

'You were very young.' *Us*, he noticed. *We*. Not Therese. Anna was still taking responsibility for Therese. She still wanted that burden.

'Let's go out in the garden for a cigarette.'

'No. It's cold. The Lord won't mind if we smoke in here. The Apostles probably smoked dope at the Last Supper, for God's sake. Here, have one of mine. When can I meet Kay McQuaid?'

'When she's ready. Do you know, I think you're perverse enough to actually *like* her.'

'Unless she's changed, I always did. She was kind to me. How else do you judge?'

'Anyway,' Christopher said, looking at his watch, 'you were starting on the last chapter, but the story began with the first. It started with a rape. It started with a child no one wanted, but no one could destroy. It started with Jack McQuaid's isolation. It continued, after a few intervening chapters, with your father's grief and bitterness on a cold wet night when he drafted a will. Probably after a few drinks. You know what an influence that can be.'

She thought of herself pulling faces at Barbara, that abiding shame which somehow persisted.

'Tell me again what Francis said to you when you arrived in time for the last Sacrament. When he wasn't quite dead.'

'He said, *Tell them their father was a good man.*'

'It sounds like an act of contrition. And highly ambiguous. *Which* father? Forgive me, Christopher, I'm not entirely sure I believe you.'

'You know very well that I cannot influence what you believe.'

'I believe that God, some God, some hound of heaven, helped me to see, and helps me still. I no longer have the arrogance to deny the existence of Gods, nor do I want to, but I couldn't just believe in one. Monotheism is what makes for wars. Anyway, not one of them can make me see clearly enough why my father did it. I don't mean write the will, but write it that way and send it.'

This was old ground.

'Pay attention, that's all, and then you can see. Use your intelligence. He wanted to attract your attention. He wanted you to think. He wanted you to know what moved him to write such a document. He wanted you to be curious, at least. He wanted to upset and surprise you into thinking and discovering. He wanted you to know what he was like. He was terrified that you would be perverted by your mother's religious mania, and he was furious with you, and of course, he never intended this result either.

276

Never in a million years. No one could ever have planned this. He merely wanted to provoke.'

She puffed at the cigarette and watched sacrilegious smoke spiral into the air in the direction of the side window. The bare branches of the trees beyond the big, curved window they faced moved gently. It was these they addressed when they avoided the eyes of each other.

'Christopher, I think it's a bit much to expect me to forgive Francis for what he was and did, or my father, for that matter. I loathe that old cliché, to understand all is to forgive all, blah, blah, blah. It denies the right to be angry, which is often more constructive.'

'Oh, blah, blah, blah, it happens to be true, and I expect no such thing, but invite you to consider. The impact of the works of the so-called devil is not always entirely negative, I think. Look at what Francis has done by accident. Made your sister re-evaluate her vocation, sooner rather than later. Made her remember the hand of your mother pressing against her neck? Jolted her into an existence based on truth? Made you and she recognise the murderous potential of love and lies . . .'

'Also of good intentions. And made me grateful for Joseph. For doing what I might have done. From which I would not have recovered my heart, my soul or anything. I owe her my life.'

'That is her sole consolation. Apart from the fact that she killed him in revenge for Matilda and does not really regret it, she is comforted by the fact that she saved another from the same deed. I was merely hoping that you might have been able to forgive your father, in the same, exceptionally generous way you seem to have been able to forgive your mother.'

'Now, wait a minute . . . What is this? This imposition of virtue? Christopher, we've talked so much, I'm beginning to talk like an old cleric like you. Make no mistake, I don't *forgive* her. To use your *vernacular*, I've simply done her the courtesy of

277

trying to understand what dreadful fear she felt for us, what dreadful madness in herself it was that made her imprison us, what fear of abandonment she had, and her only saving grace is the fact I know it was not hatred. I think she was stupid, beyond self-analysis, full of self-loathing. What she did was a perversion of love, but I'm a long way from forgiving, you better believe. I blame *Him*.' She jerked her thumb in the direction of the crucifix. 'Blessing her every action. Good boy, Jesus.'

This moved him to anger, so that he almost shouted. One of the Sisters was at the door and went away, rapidly. What had this child done to him, apart from renew his faith? He could not have Christ impugned and insulted.

'*No*, He did not! She reinvented the God who would do that. People reinvent God all the time. To whom do you think the terrorist prays? The God of his Bible, or the God of his own invention?'

She grinned at him and he groaned. He was always taking the bait.

'I knew that would get you going. Let's go in the garden, after all. It's wrong to smoke in here.'

'Yes, let's.'

He shuffled nervously out of the chapel, through the parlour, looking round as if pursued. How odd of God to make it warmer out here than in that chilly, elegant space. They finished the cigarettes by the statue of St Michael. Christopher seemed anxious and she felt protective about his persistence and what it cost him, but also cautious. She didn't wish anyone else messing with her mind. She had had enough of that. It didn't want messing with, it wanted all the education it had missed, exercise. It wanted to learn.

'What about your father?' he asked, sweeping the ash from St Michael's foot. If she wanted him to go further into this garden, he would not, could not: it haunted him as the place where he

278

would always arrive too late. She took a deep breath. Nothing else in the last month had made her tearful. Not even telling Ravi it was better they did not see each other until she was a little further down some path or other, maybe then, when she was fit.

'What about my father? I wish, wish, wish I had known him. I wish it had been allowed. I wish it wasn't the reason for not being able to forgive my mother, because that was the worst she did. She taught us to hate him, because she did. I suppose we *contributed*. I suppose he did. How lonely he must have been, lonelier than me, and all I can remember is the laughter in church. The questions. He was like me, he's as angry as me. I'd have liked the chance for a row. I've had no one to learn from and only religion to rebel against. I'd have liked the chance to make reparation. The chance to put it right, as far as it could be. To take back misjudgement and all that bloody ignorance.'

Christopher Goodwin felt himself beginning to sweat.

'Even if he was manipulative, a player of games? Occasionally untruthful?'

'So are the best of people, when they need to be. I might be all of those things, you certainly are, so was Sister Jude. It depends on the motive. You can be all of those things in a vain attempt to be good. Or be listened to. Or avoid causing hurt. They're not incompatible.'

She let out a long, regretful sigh.

'So, I've only got one problem, Christopher, and it's the one I can't handle. One great big area of sheer self-pity. And it's all because I'm just too young to be an orphan. I wish I wasn't. It's the gap I can't cure with my mind. It puts me at risk of creating something unreal, to fill the gap. I feel *cheated*. And so was my father.'

He tried to breathe deeply, speak slowly and carefully, and still choked on the words.

279

'I think he should be waiting in the parlour, by now. Twelve o'clock, he said.'

'*What?*'

'Your father. You might recognise his voice. Although he's quite good at disguising it.'

She stood up and wiped a trace of grime from the back of her jeans. Then slapped her own face, lightly, to stop herself trembling. He blanched, as if he could feel the imprint of her hand. Then she laughed uncertainly.

'Is this a miracle? You liar. I thought we agreed you would never lie to me.'

'And I never have,' he said, crossing his fingers behind his back. 'Not about your father's grief or his motives or why he found his life so unbearable he made a will and disappeared. Or about what he hoped to achieve by dying. The attention of his daughters' souls. An elaborate, stupid, selfish, wicked conspiracy, because he did not die. He simply waited. And as we discussed, the devil himself is rarely worse than a man with good intentions.'

'You talk too much. He phoned me. It was *him*. I used to dream it was him. Oh Christ, you bastard. What on earth shall I say? Where did you say he was?'

'You heard me the first time. In the parlour. Why else would Barbara light a fire?'

She ran. Christopher sat by the feet of St Michael and marvelled how clean they were. Then turned his eyes to the sky and the comforting presence of buildings. For a minute or more, before he failed to resist the temptation to spy. They would not notice.

He could see Theodore Calvert. A very small man, the way he had always imagined Christ and St Christopher to be, small and determined, perhaps a touch aggressive. A little like a rude Italian restaurant owner who knew his food was better than anyone else's.

Anna stood a few feet away from her father. They examined each other, warily. She was not going to be fooled by the tears, which almost made her speechless. Almost. He could not speak. She spoke first.

'So where have you been, all this time?'

'Somewhere like hell,' he said.

'And what's that like?'

He sighed, stumbled on words.

'I think you know. I think you've been there. You carry it with you. A crown of thorns.'

She crossed the room to him then, a small, almost ugly man, instantly familiar with his dome of a forehead and a face as creased and vibrant as an old hound and tears on his chin. She grabbed at his jacket and tugged his hair to prove he was real, and then held on, tightly. They swayed in a clumsy embrace, holding each other upright.

'I'm sorry,' he muttered into her shoulder. 'I'm so sorry. I shouldn't have . . . shouldn't . . .'

'Stop saying that. We're neither of us going to say that. Don't, don't, *don't*.'

He had a deep, broken voice.

'Oh, thank God. Thank God.'

They stood in silence. The fire crackled. Barbara had spared no expense.

Her own voice sounded small from the depths of his jacket.

'Did you really say that?'

'What did I say? Oh, thank God you're alive . . . Thank God.'

'Did you hear yourself, Dad? Did you hear yourself say that? Will you listen to yourself? Shame on you. You never thanked God for anything.'

He had a fine-tuned laugh, remarkably like her own. The sound of their gulping laughter reached the roof, until Anna detached herself from him, still holding his hands at arm's length, to look at him again from head to toe, still crying.

'Oh, Dad, what am I going to do with you?' she wailed. 'I've told everyone you were a big man. A giant. How am I going to take you anywhere?'

He had a wide smile, like hers.

'I'll just stay sitting down.'

Christopher Goodwin thought he had never heard anything more beautiful than laughter. Except, perhaps, the roar of a crowd. In a minute, the two of them might be arguing and that would be fine, too, entirely natural, in fact. He had told Theodore Calvert not to have any illusions about reclaiming his daughters' lives. Or imagining he could tell them what to do.

He blew his nose and considered the next problem. It would be a little harder to persuade Kay McQuaid that her boy had done some good. Because, as rumour had it, when you did good, you were supposed to mean it.